Making Her Wait

Brianna Cash

To Our Own Happily Ever Afters!

Bri Cash

Making Her Wait Copyright © 2019 by Brianna Cash. All Rights Reserved.

All rights reserved. No part of this book may be reproduced in any form or by any electronic or mechanical means including information storage and retrieval systems, without permission in writing from the author. The only exception is by a reviewer, who may quote short excerpts in a review.

Cover designed by Cole Gordon

This book is a work of fiction. Names, characters, places, and incidents either are products of the author's imagination or are used fictitiously. Any resemblance to actual persons, living or dead, events, or locales is entirely coincidental.

Brianna Cash
Visit my website at www.BriannaCash.com

Printed in the United States of America

First Printing: April 2019

Making Her Wait

Genny's everything I've ever wanted.

Except she's one of the many girls that frequent my *roommate's* bed on a regular basis.

Also, Genny doesn't date.

And... I don't do hook-ups.

Considering those three major obstacles, Genny and I will never be anything more to each other than two almost strangers, who occasionally pass each other during the night.

Life throws us together one evening in early spring, deciding it has plans of its own. Genny swears our story has a horrible ending, before we even take a single step down the road we find ourselves on. I think she's right, but I still can't stop myself from trying to figure out all Genny's secrets.

I have a feeling our journey is going to be a hell of a lot of fun, no matter how it ends. And until Genny lets down her walls and gives our ill-fated relationship an honest chance, I'm really going to enjoy making her wait...

Genny

Beep beep, beep beep, beep beep...

I roll onto my back with a groan, reaching for my phone so I can shut off the damn alarm. Slamming onto the floor half a second later, I cringe in pain, realizing I wasn't in *my* bed. Or even my house. And I don't have a scrap of clothing on.

Today sucks already...

From my cold, exhausted, *painful* position on the floor in front of someone *else's* bed, I take two seconds to focus on the sound of my alarm. I need to figure out where that obnoxious noise is coming from. It sounds close, so I do a visual search of my surroundings, cracking first one eye open against the sunlight streaming in through the windows, then the other. Last night comes back to me in a flash as I figure out exactly where I am and who was sharing that bed with me.

What were you *thinking*? I chastise myself, repeatedly, until I'm clutching my phone, the alarm finally falling silent under the murderous poking of my fingers against the screen. My exhale becomes a whimper of despair as I discover that I must have slept right through my first alarm; the one I just turned off was my you're-going-to-be-*late* alarm.

My walk of shame doesn't end at my back door today.

Good thing I keep some mouthwash and deodorant at work... And a spare uniform in my car.

Time to take inventory of the clothes I wore into this room last night. Can I manage to reach all of them from my seated position on the floor? And why the hell doesn't this guy have a throw rug on this side of the bed? The floorboards are freezing against my bare ass!

The answer to my first question is no. And in five minutes, I won't care about the second.

I make it into a standing position, yanking my jeans up over my hips and pulling my bra on a second later. Stuffing my underwear into my pocket, I spin in a slow circle, looking for my shirt. I'm doing a second pass when I finally catch sight of it. At the top of the bed. Being used as a pillow.

Instead of risking waking him up, I steal his from the night before, simply because it's within easy reach and Ben *always* smells nice. He puts *effort* into our late-night hook-ups. He asks me questions about my life while we drink a couple glasses of wine on his couch. He kisses me like he actually missed me since the last time we saw each other. He *woos* me, even if it's just for an hour before we make it to his room.

My other boytoys don't woo me.

One of them might ask a question or two once the reason for our visit has been accomplished. The other one doesn't say anything. Except dirty words that never register in my head because I'm too busy feeling the amazing things he's doing to me.

As I sneak out of Ben's room and down to the front door, I tell myself that I will *not* answer any of his (or anyone else's) texts in the middle of the week from here on out. What if Callie needed me last night? What if my boss decides to make an appearance at my booth today? What if I give in and act like a responsible grownup for once, instead of giving in to the promise of an orgasm or two?

That last one's funny... Acting like a grownup is all I ever get to do.

I stop for coffee because *come on*. I can go to work in a dirty uniform without showering or eating breakfast, but facing the world without at least one cup of coffee is something I'm not willing to do. While waiting for my order at the drive-thru window, I check out the damage last night did in the mirror. My plain brown hair is greasy and unruly, but I smooth it out and secure it in a tight ponytail. My face isn't too bad. Thank God I only put on one swipe of mascara last night before I made the trip to Orgasm-ville. It's almost as if I *expected* to fall asleep in that bed, instead of high-tailing it out of there at half-past three in the morning...

I make it to work on time, but only because I cheat. Snapping the flashers on in my car, I waltz into work with thirty seconds to spare, clock in, then disappear for the fifteen minutes it takes to park my car in employee parking. A few nasty looks get thrown my way when I make it to my computer, but *technically*, I was here on time.

I've been late three times in the last two months. One more incident and I get written up. Michelle, my favorite co-worker and good friend, vouches for me, claiming I was trying to find a new ink cartridge for her printer that's spitting out flawlessly printed pages as we speak.

Work is registering patients for radiology studies and labs. I don't like my job, but who does, really? A job is a means to an end. A paycheck that, if you're lucky, covers all your bills until the next one rolls around. With that said, the best part of my job is the patients. I hate the computer stuff, the paperwork, the mundane data entry bullshit we have to do when we're slow. But I love interacting with the people who come through my booth.

Today, on this sucky morning, a patient strolls into my booth and tells me her name. While searching for her on the schedule, I make small talk, asking where she lives, what she's here for today, and who she brought with her. I'm a master multi-tasker, but today, my thoughts falter as she tells me her story.

She lives two hours away and left her house at five-fifteen this morning because she didn't know how traffic or road construction would alter her arrival time. The procedure she's scheduled for is a specialized breast biopsy, that's done while she's in an MRI machine. She'll be in a very uncomfortable position for over an hour. And she's worried sick about the results, because her sister was diagnosed with breast cancer last year. It was very aggressive. Her sister didn't make it.

I suddenly feel like shit for rolling out of someone's bed a mere half hour ago and cursing what I thought was a bad life and a horrible morning. I had no idea what I was talking about. I have it easy. I love life and everything in it. I'm a spoiled person who doesn't know how good I have it.

Not true.

I *do* know how good I have it. Sometimes I just forget.

On my break, I find a text message from Callie asking if I'm still alive, since I wasn't there when she got up this morning. She calls me a hypocrite and informs me that there's a message from the pharmacy, telling me my script is ready to pick up. I also find an email from my ex-boyfriend, Paul. We broke up four years ago, but he still emails, calls, or texts at least once a month, to tell me he thinks we should give our relationship another try.

I delete it without opening it, although I'm considering sending a snarky, sarcastic response.

The lights above me flicker and die a second later.

Maybe I *should've* opened it?

Rolling my eyes at the power outage, I head back to the department, only to hear that we're moving to downtime procedures. Which means the power outage won't be fixed in a timely manner.

Fantastic.

During downtime procedures, we can still function and register patients, but everything is done on paper. We have to write down ten times more information than we usually need, increasing the average registration time from four minutes, to a horrifyingly long seventeen minutes.

The patients are not appreciative. We, the employees, *definitely* aren't.

Michelle finagles her way into a late lunch with me since we're so backed up. She wastes no time, starting her interrogation with, "How was your morning, Genny?"

"Very short," I reply, searching my pockets for my ID badge, which takes money directly out of my check to pay for anything I buy at the cafeteria. "Shit," I mumble, realizing it's probably at home on my dresser since grabbing my work ID before heading to Orgasm-ville isn't something I normally do. My purse is in my car, but if I go get it, I won't have time to eat. "Can I borrow some cash?"

"I don't have any," she tells me. "I packed today."

Double shit.

Michelle leads us to a picnic table outside, continuing her interrogation. "Have any company this morning?"

"Not at my place," I answer, making her level her eyes at me. "Fine," I relent, not wanting to fight with her. I'm hungry, I feel dirty, my uniform smells and I'm fucking tired. "I woke up at Ben's."

"Dang," she sighs, looking dreamily off into space. "I was hoping you'd woken up with Chad. Those are the best stories to hear."

"No way, Chad never lets me stay. I swear he's pushing me out the door before I even catch my breath... *Totally* worth it though."

I fan myself a little just *thinking* about it.

Chad is the guy you hook up with whenever he sends a text your way. You never text him. You wait for him to text you and thank your lucky stars when he does. I swear he has a waiting list. And you can be damn sure I don't miss my turn when it comes around.

"At least it wasn't Matt again," she complains. "If it had been, I would've told you to cut the others loose already."

Matt is my go-to. Matt doesn't need to talk or catch up. If I stay after, he doesn't care. If I leave after, he doesn't care. He's easy, no pun intended, and very convenient. Ben's the guy I text when I need to feel like someone cares. Matt is the guy I text when I just need to get off.

Life can be stressful. Orgasms are the best cure for that. And I usually like them best without any hassle or idle chit-chat that adds up to nothing in the long run except wasted time.

"Matt's really efficient," I reason defensively. "He's good at what he does, and he does it in a timely matter."

"We're talking about sex, honey. Not work."

"Sometimes it's the same thing."

"It *shouldn't* be," she scolds me, mumbling around her sandwich before reaching for a drink. I would give my left foot for half of that sandwich right now. I really should've gotten breakfast when I stopped for my one cup of coffee. "Not to change the subject, but I have a date tomorrow night."

"What?! With who?"

"Sam in admissions. He asked me yesterday."

"Wow," I murmur, happy for her, but confused at the same time. "What's a date exactly? I thought people didn't do that anymore."

She laughs, shaking her head at my ignorance, or maybe our age difference. She's fifteen years older than me, give or take, and the generation gap is startlingly wide at times. "People who are looking for more than casual sex date all the time."

Who are *those* people? I'm definitely not one of them. Not only do I not have time, but I also don't need the headaches, the time wasted on arguments, or the ultimate break up that having a relationship entails. Sleeping with three different guys, keeping stock in condoms, and getting my quarterly STD checks already take up too much of my time.

We're still on downtime after lunch, and the afternoon rush is just starting. With the way things are going, there's not a chance in hell I'm getting out on time. Unless I wanna come in early tomorrow to finish up the data entry from the patients I had today. I'm pretty sure everyone knows by now there's no chance of me getting up any earlier than is absolutely necessary.

By the time I get out of work, I'm ravenous. There's no way I'm cooking anything tonight, so I stop and grab dinner to take home, using the last of my cash until payday tomorrow, and race to the pharmacy. Literally, *race*. Because I'm miserable and my stomach is growling loud enough for me to hear it over the radio.

A few blocks from the pharmacy, pulsing red and blue lights flash in my review mirror and the distinct sound of a siren drowns out my music…

Un-*fucking*-believable!

"License and insurance ma'am." He doesn't look at me, but he doesn't have to. I recognize his voice instantly. It's Paul, the ex.

Doing my best to not growl out my frustrations at the heavens, I empty out my purse and glove-box looking for the information he requested. Karma's trying to get revenge on me for not making it home last night. This morning. Whenever the hell it was. Today's been one thing after another, but she can bring it on. My day's just about over and there's not much else she can throw at me.

"Well, if it isn't the person I wanted to see! I emailed you earlier, Genny. I don't suppose you were going to reply though, were you?"

"I didn't get it yet," I lie through my teeth, flashing him an extra sweet smile. "I had to put in some overtime at work, so I'm just trying to get home. Any chance you could just give me a warning?"

"Like the warning you gave me when you kicked me out of your life? Let me think about that…"

Hearing my stomach do some of my growling for me, I grip the steering wheel tighter and pray for the day to just be over already. I swear to God and every inch of those pearly white gates that I will stop having casual sex if He can get me home in the next fifteen minutes.

As much, I compromise.

I'll stop having *as much* casual sex.

Or maybe I'll just promise to make it home from now on, because after this day, I could really use an extra dose of stress relief. Which is also known as a trip to Orgasm-ville.

8

I wonder what Matt's doing tonight.

"You realize your insurance is expired?"

"The fuck it is! The new insurance card came in the mail months ago!"

"Says right here," he offers, tapping his fingers on my proof of insurance. "Expired two months ago."

Now that I think back, maybe it was the *bill* that came in the mail two months ago. Maybe I put it to the side to pay later because that was a rough month. Maybe it's still on my desk at home, waiting to be paid. Taunting me now, in my moment of need.

"Want me to let all this go, Gen? I'll give you a warning and say goodnight?"

It's a trick. It has to be. He was never that nice. "I'd like that very much, Paul."

"Go out with me this weekend. Give us another chance."

Come on! The one thing I will *never* do!

"Over my dead body," I calmly reply with a brilliant smile.

"I'll be right back with your ticket then, love."

Fucking asshole.

After shoving my ticket and everything else back in my purse, I pull out into traffic and grumble the short drive to the pharmacy.

The one with the long line.

Browsing the latest Women's Health Magazine, I pretend to not eavesdrop as the man at the front of the line tries to pick up his Viagra script. It's non-covered by his insurance. He seems shocked by this, but I'm sure he got a call from the pharmacy or his insurance company to inform him before they filled it. Paling at the cost, he grumbles his way out of the store empty-handed.

The girl directly in front of me picks up an ointment for her itch problem. Her copay is only three dollars and forty-five cents. Nice. She pays in cash and walks off. I wonder if her itch problem is the reason she's walking funny.

"Name?"

I step toward the cashier. "Genevieve Stotler."

"Date of birth?"

After verifying I am who I'm claiming to be, she brings my script to the register. *My* copay is forty dollars. I'd take that three dollars and forty-five cents copay any day of the week. I almost curse as the cashier clears her throat at the sight of my debit card, pointing to a sign taped to the wall.

"The machines are down," she quickly explains. "We have signs all over the store. You have to pay in cash or check."

"Are you *kidding* me?"

"Cash or check only tonight. The power's back up, but it did something to the lines."

Mumbling obscenities under my breath, I search my purse for forty dollars I know I won't find. Feeling as dejected as Viagra man looked, *I* leave empty handed as well.

Stupid fucking power outage. Ruined my entire day. It came back on a half hour before my shift was over, and I *should've* gotten home around five thirty. Instead, it's almost eight, I'm still not home from work, I haven't showered, I'm wearing dirty clothes, my teeth are fuzzy and gross, I haven't eaten a damn thing since yesterday, I had a run in with my ex *and* got a speeding ticket, and now I can't pick up my meds.

Maybe Karma was just flexing her muscles earlier...

At least it can't get much worse now. All I have to do yet is drive home.

Except my car won't start.

The battery has been sporadically dying on me. I meant to get a new one, but who has the time or the money? The closest auto store is a half hour in the other direction, and I've been keeping my fingers crossed that it'll last another three months until I get my yearly raise.

I decide to go back into the stupid store that only accepts cash or checks and ask if anyone can give me a jump. But I laugh out loud when I catch *another* problem out of the corner of my eye. Because I'm so bummed out, I'm looking down at the ground. Because today sucks, and no matter how many times I try to talk myself out of my foul mood, it comes right back to that exact sentiment. I can no longer pretend that everything's ok and hold my head high. It hangs low as I walk around my car, accepting defeat and planning to ask for help, something I loathe to do.

My car has a flat tire.

Fuck my life.

Sinking onto a bench outside the pharmacy (because what's the point of going inside now?), I let my brain rerun all the things that went wrong today. The pile grows as I work through the day, and the loop in my brain refuses to turn off, slow down, pause, or let me change the channel. The pressure builds in my head, behind my eyes, and the familiar sensation means a migraine is going to hit me very soon. And this one's going to hit me *hard*.

This can't happen. Not *here*. Not *now*...

A few slow deep breaths later, I try again to hit pause on the replay of the day's events. I try to find the silver lining, because there *has* to be one, dammit! Even if I can't see it, there has to be one!

I'm not going to find it in time. My vision is already starting to close in on me.

Finally finding a thought unrelated to the long list of things that went wrong in the last thirteen hours, I latch onto it before realizing what it is.

I want a hug from my mom.

Shit.

Fumbling my phone out of my pocket, I type out a panicky text to Callie. My vision is pretty much gone when I hit what I think is the send button. Instead of seeing my phone in my hand, I see a kaleidoscope of colliding colors across my normal plane of vision.

I let my head rest against the building behind me as tears leak out of my eyes against my will, praying for some miracle that will suddenly make everything better.

Walker

"Higher, Uncle Walk! Higher!"

No matter how high I push my nephew on these swings, it's never high enough. He loves hitting the bumps at the top, the ones that only happen because he's so high the slack catches on the way down. My sister, his mom, used to love to go that high as well on the playground at school. Until the day one of those bumps threw her off the fifteen-foot-high swing and she flew through the air without anything to catch her. She passed out when she landed.

One of my teachers ran to check on her, asking me if she was ok. I shrugged my shoulders and hid my fear. She's my little sister. It was *my* job to watch out for her. If something bad happened, Dad would ring my neck and Mom would ground me for life.

"That's high enough, Zeke," I tell him, not wanting a repeat of that terrifying day. He lets out a disappointed grunt, but otherwise doesn't complain.

My sister's doing an amazing job with her two kids, Zeke, and little Finn. I have no idea how she does it, since her husband is on the road half the time, but she's managing somehow. Every Thursday evening, we get together, so I can see the little terrors. Most of the time, it's at the park right across the street from their house.

"Don't you *dare* jump from there, Zeke!" Reese yells, and I pull my attention back to the four-year-old fearless daredevil that was ready to jump off the swing. When he flies back to me, I grab the chains and bring him to a stop. Zeke pouts, kicking at the dirt under his filthy sneakers in protest.

"Come on, kid. Let's try out those monkey bars." My suggestion is rewarded with a race across the playground.

"Lemme try it myself!" he demands. Eyeing my sister to see how closely she's supervising us, I let him go, keeping my hands ready. He makes it three bars before the metal slides free of his grasp. He lets out a startled cry as he starts falling, but I catch him midair.

Reese glares.

I give her a sheepish smile.

I'm the fun uncle who lets Zeke try daring things his mother says are forbidden. He's a little boy. He's going to fall and scrape his knees, ruining his best pants. He's going to get in fights, learning how to give, but also take a punch. He's going to point fake guns at people and pretend to shoot them dead. He's going to be an aggressive, little, smart-ass, stubborn-as-hell kid.

At least he will if he's anything like me.

After a couple hours of chasing Zeke around, Reese and I start packing up all the gear she insists is necessary for a short trip to the park. I steal Finn from her for the short walk back to her house and she asks, "When're you gonna get your own kids and stop borrowing mine?"

"When hell freezes over."

Zeke giggles at my bad language, but I act surprised that he noticed. Normally, I'm pretty good at not swearing in front of the kids, but Reese's bizarre question had me answering without thinking. We've been doing this for years, why am I suddenly *borrowing* her kids instead of just spending time with them?

"Why? You'll be a *great* dad, Walker. You just have to find the right girl."

Hugging my little man, who's not even a year old, I pretend not hear her. If this is another attempt for her to set me up with some girl she thinks is *perfect* for me, I'll disown her. She and my mother have lost all privileges when it comes to who I should date.

"You need to get your own place, too. Chad's a bad influence and you're almost thirty. It's time for you to find a nice girl and settle down."

"I'd love to find my own girl, Reese. But I don't want her to be all that nice."

Reese shakes her head, looking at me with disappointment as she swats at my chest. "I don't need to know about your s-e-x life."

"Then, *please*, stay out of it. It'll happen when it happens. You know what they say, the second you stop looking, that's when you find it."

"You'll never find it then! You still haven't *started* looking!"

She's wrong, but I'm not going to correct her. I like her being in the dark about my sex life *and* my love life.

After getting them situated at their house, I tickle Zeke until he begs for mercy, then head back to my car. I parked across the other street from the park today, since Reese called demanding I pick something up for her before I came over. That happens a lot. I no longer move my car after picking up whatever she urgently needs, just walk the block to my sister's house.

Whistling a happy tune, I toss my keys in the air, letting them drop into my hand a second later. It's almost dark out, and I look for headlights as I cross the street, pausing my tune and my steps when I see someone sitting on a bench outside the pharmacy.

She's looking away, down the street, the opposite direction of me, and I study her, realizing she's crying. And she looks a lot like someone I know. As I get closer, she lets out a heavy sigh, tipping her head back and closing her eyes.

Definitely her.

I cautiously walk toward her. She hasn't seen me yet, so I can bolt if I change my mind. Normally, I wouldn't even consider changing my mind, because this girl is one I would dream about if I could pick the star of my dreams. But she's crying... Crying girls are unpredictable.

Too late to bolt. She just looked my way.

"Genny?"

Her wide eyes look right through me. Wiping her cheeks, she gives a small, embarrassed, "Hi."

"You ok?"

She snorts out a laugh, sounding a big unhinged, making me think I should've bolted when I had the chance. Leaning forward, she closes her eyes, resting her elbows on her knees. "Peachy."

"I think you got some rotten peaches..."

She laughs, a smile taking over her face, and a feeling similar to pride blossoms in my chest. "I think you're right."

Wondering what she's doing crying on a bench outside the pharmacy, I study her a little closer, noticing she doesn't even have a purse. She only has her phone, and she keeps rubbing the screen, like she's hoping a genie will pop out and grant her three wishes.

What would her wishes be if that happened?

Mine would be for a chance with her.

"Anything I can do for you, Genny?"

She sighs dramatically before answering. "Yes, but who are you?"

We've never been formally introduced, although we've run into each other many times over the last year or so. Thinking she wants my name, I hold out my hand, introducing myself. "Walker Kelley, at your service."

She doesn't take my hand.

She doesn't even *look* at it.

"How do I know you?" she asks, and I shake my head at her audacity. She's checked me out multiple times from across my kitchen. I walked in on her once when she was in my bathroom. We searched my living room together for her keys early one morning. We've never had a real conversation, but I'd like to think that I'm somewhat memorable, especially with the way she looked me up and down every time she saw me.

"Really? You're gonna act like you don't recognize me?"

Her voice drops to a whisper. "I can't *see* you."

I arch an eyebrow, doubting her with every fiber of my being. She's looking right at me. Correction, she's still looking *through* me, with wide green eyes.

"I get migraines with auras, which just means I get weird symptoms before my migraine starts. You're a blur of colors right now. If it makes you feel better, you *sound* familiar."

I step closer and wave my hand in front of her face. Nothing. No reaction at all. She's not pretending. She can't see me, and I'm standing right in front of her.

That's kinda fucked-up.

"Is there something you can take?"

"Yeah, but it doesn't really help the weird shit once it's already started. It just helps with the pain that comes after. How do I know you?"

Right. I still haven't told her how we know each other. "You, ah... know my roommate. Chad."

I doubt she knows my roommate at all, but she knows his bed and his body. She's one of his regulars. I pointed her out to him at the bar when he asked me if anyone looked good, thinking he was going to help me out, be my wingman. Instead, *he* brought her home. Time and time again.

I try not to judge Genny. But I wonder if she knows she's one of many, that he doesn't think she's special, that she's listed in his phone by what he considers to be her best talent, her name in parentheses behind it so he knows what to call her when she shows up.

"Oh," she breathes, her face lighting up in a pretty blush.

"What can I do for you?" I ask again, not wanting to talk about how she knows me or my roommate.

She scrunches up her face, trying to figure out if she wants my help now that she knows who I am. She looks around, her wide eyes still unseeing. Now that I know what's going on with her, I can tell she can't see a damn thing. She's obviously uncomfortable, but I love how much of her bright green eyes I can see. Especially with her hair pulled back the way it is, and that blush still lingering on her cheeks. There're black smudges under those gorgeous eyes from her mascara and tears, but it only creates a contrast of all the colors, making her cheeks and eyes look brilliantly colorful in comparison.

Holding her hand out, the one that has her phone, she asks, "Can you make sure my text went through? I texted Callie to come get me, but it hit me so fast, I guessed where the send button was."

"Do you just want me to give you a ride home?"

"No," she answers quickly. *Too* quickly.

I take her phone. "What's your passcode?"

The text to a Callie went through. So did one to a Ben very early this morning, saying she'd be right over... Maybe Chad isn't her only, either.

"It went through. She didn't reply."

"Shit. Can you call her?"

I put it on speaker, so she can hear it ringing. When it goes unanswered and a generic voicemail recording starts, she breathes out, "Double shit."

"What're you gonna do?"

"Sit here until it stops, I guess. I can't drive like this. Oh wait... I can't drive anyway. My car won't start, and it has a flat tire." She laughs in a humorless way, dropping her head into her hands. "Are you gonna tell Chad you saw me?"

The extremely skeptical look I'm giving her is wasted on her unseeing eyes. "Does it matter?"

"Yes. No... I don't know."

She looks in my direction again, her blank stare driving me crazy. "I don't like to get personal with the guys I hook up with. If you can keep it to yourself, I'd love to ask you for a favor."

She doesn't like to get *personal* with the guys she hooks up with? If sex isn't personal, what the hell is? And how much do I need to know about her personal life before she won't have sex with me?

Doesn't matter, I remind myself. She's fucking my roommate and some other guy named Ben. I need to stay far away from her.

But I don't *want* to stay away from her. I never have. And I feel like I *should* promise her I'll keep it to myself. I feel like I *have* to do her this favor, whatever it might be.

Wrong again. I don't feel like I should. I *want* to. Because I want to know her in a way Chad never will.

"What's your favor, Genny?"

Chewing on her bottom lip, she tries to make up her mind as to whether she should trust me this little bit. I watch her teeth, wishing they were mine. *I* want to nibble on that lip. I want to suck that lip into my mouth until she's breathless and her hands are tangled in my hair, silently begging me for more. I want to find out what she tastes like. Will there be salt from her tears, a lingering hint of whatever she had for dinner, or maybe just the sweet taste of Genny herself.

But I don't do casual sex. And I certainly don't do anyone who's one of my roommate's regulars.

"Will you give me a ride home?"

There's no way I could possibly refuse.

After she accepts my hand, I lead her to my car, my fingers finding her low back when she blindly walks beside me. I like having my hands on her, but I don't focus on it. I do my best to totally forget about it. She's not single in the traditional sense and that's the only way anything could happen between us.

She settles into the passenger seat of my car, handing me her keys. "Can you get my purse for me? And a bag from the sub shop? It's in a blue Jetta parked along the street."

16

Now I *know* she can't see. What girl asks an almost stranger to get her purse?

Realizing she can't exactly give me directions, I ask for her address, typing it into my GPS system. She lives about ten miles away in a brick two story house in desperate need of a front porch and some landscaping. When she feels the car turn into her driveway, she asks, "Is there a white minivan here?"

"No. No one but us."

"Fine," she grumbles, tipping her head back onto the headrest. "Help me to the backdoor? I can take it from there."

"How long does the not-being-able-to-see thing last?"

"Twenty to thirty minutes. The numbness will last about the same amount of time. Then I'll have the worst headache in the world, and be so nauseous I won't be able to sit up without vomiting."

"The *numbness*?" I parrot, shaking my head at what she's describing.

"Different parts of my body go numb. My left hand. My ankle. My tongue, my side. It's always random."

"Is this normal? I've never heard of the type of symptoms you're describing."

Rolling her useless eyes, she huffs out a short breath. "Can you please just help me into my house? After that I'll answer all the questions you want."

I didn't really think about how she might feel while going through whatever it is she's going through. I can't imagine not being able to see and sitting there as calmly as she is. At least her vision should start coming back soon. It's been at least fifteen minutes since I first saw her.

Again leading her by the hand, my other on her back because, why the hell not, I get her to the back door where we stop. She feels her way through each of her keys, and I wonder how she can tell the difference between them. But she does, trying repeatedly and failing each time to get it in the keyhole.

"Let me," I finally mumble, taking it from her hands without waiting for her consent.

She moves through her house with ease, heading straight into the kitchen, where she slides her hand carefully across the island counter, grabbing the paper on it and holding it up to me. "What's this say? Read it to me?"

"*Couldn't wait. Going out. Phone's dead.*"

Flopping down onto a stool at the island, she lets out a frustrated cry, dropping her head into her hands and breathing deeply for a few seconds before remembering she has company. Or a driver. Or something.

"I'm sorry," she explains, her voice somewhat muffled since she hasn't raised her head. "I've had a crappy day, so this is like the cherry on top, ya know? That she's not here? I don't know why you're being so nice to me, but thanks."

Looking around the kitchen we're in, the dinning room off to one side, the living room where we came in off to the other, I try to gain some knowledge about her from what I see. There're several paintings on every wall, on every shelf, and some even stacked on a table behind the couch. "Do you paint?"

"That would be Callie."

"And Callie is... your roommate?" I guess, having no idea. She texted this Callie to come get her, but obviously Callie didn't get the message and went somewhere out without her.

"And my sister," she reluctantly admits. I have a feeling she thinks we're getting really personal, although I'm not sure why. What's it matter if I know she lives with her sister?

I walk away from her, into the dining room, letting my finger run over the spine of some textbooks. There's a laptop open on the table, a printer nearby. "Someone taking college classes?

"Callie."

Running my eyes over the wall space again, I finally find what I'm looking for. A framed family photo.

It's an old picture, Genny looks like she's sixteen or seventeen. The middle child, a brother she hasn't mentioned, looks like he's about twelve, and the youngest, who I'm assuming is Callie, is even younger. Both girls favor their mom, with brown hair, green eyes and high cheek bones. Her brother has brown eyes and an angular nose that I really hope he grew into.

After studying the picture for much longer than is necessary, I ask over my shoulder, "Is this your parents' house?"

"My parents are dead."

Her voice is flat and heavy. I hope it wasn't recent, but I don't offer the standard I'm sorry. I didn't ask if her parents were alive, I asked if this was their house. The random information she just gave me doesn't answer my question.

"You can go," she tells me, and I turn around to look at her. Her arms are crossed on the counter in front of her, her head resting on them. She's in the same spot she sank into when she found out her sister went out and didn't take her phone, staring at nothing in particular.

There's no way I can leave her right now and still feel like a decent human being.

Unless she *wants* me to. Then it's the right thing to do, whether I want to leave her or not.

"Do you *want* me to go? I will, but I don't have anywhere I need to be right now."

She chews on her bottom lip, sitting up slowly, those wide, unfocused eyes swinging in my direction. I tear my gaze away, looking anywhere except at those lips I want so badly to taste.

"You can stay, I guess," she finally answers, shrugging her shoulders. "What were you doing at the park?"

I place my hand lightly on her back as I sit in the stool next to her. I tell myself it's so she knows I'm here, but I really just want another excuse to touch her. Watching her face, I tell her about my sister and my nephews, and our weekly dates at the park or, if the weather's uncooperative, at my sister's house. She laughs when I tell her about how Zeke tackled a little girl on the slide. She told him he needed to kiss her if he wanted to use it. Zeke *hates* kisses. The little girl didn't get one, but they both went down the slide, fighting, until they landed on the ground.

Genny's vision is slowly come back to her. I continue telling her stories about Zeke and Finn, but I'm fascinated at the way she's looking around, testing out exactly how much she can see. It's frustrating her to no end that it's not coming back as fast as it left her. She studies my face, the way my mouth is moving, the way my eyes watch her.

It only makes me want to kiss her.

Reaching out, she gently places her hand on the left side of my jaw, explaining, "This is the only place I can't see right now."

My lips tip into a smile under her fingers. "You just want to touch me."

"I *like* to touch."

Her words shock me into remembering that she's one of Chad's girls. Touch is what they do. They touch and feel. They don't get to know each other. There's no connection. Nothing real between them except sweat and skin.

And *hopefully*, a condom.

How could I have forgotten that in the very little time I've spent with her?

After unwrapping her sub and offering me some, she takes the first bite and lets out a heartfelt moan. I wonder if she would ever let Chad see her like this. If, when she said she liked to touch, there was any way she meant *me*, and not just in general.

In between bites, she explains a little bit about her migraines, telling me that stress or her hormones trigger one, and she had a really stressful, crappy day. After calling off work for the next day, she explains that she's out of her pills because the pharmacy was only accepting cash and she doesn't carry any. She tells me about the people that were in line ahead of her, her descriptions making me laugh, which, in turn, makes her eyes light up.

"How was the rest of your day really stressful?" I ask, wanting to hear her describe every other thing she did. She has an interesting way of explaining things, and I want to keep her talking.

I also don't want her to think I'm not interested and kick me out.

Not that I *am* interested... I just like watching her, listening to her, touching her, her touching me. And I *really* want to kiss her.

"It's probably not a great idea for me to tell you about the rest of my day," she tells me, balling up her sub wrapper and tossing it into the garbage. "You seem like a nice guy, Walker Kelley. But you're already judging me because of how I know Chad. I don't need to add any fuel to that fire."

"I'm not judging you."

Although I am wondering, how does telling me about her day add more fuel to that fire?

Flashing me a wide grin that clearly says she knows I'm lying, she informs me, "You're cute, Walker."

I don't want to be *cute*. Not to her.

I look away, so she can't see even more of whatever I'm thinking on my face. "Wanna play Jenga?" I ask, seeing pieces scattered all over her coffee table. "I have a feeling with your numb hands, I might win."

"Also, not a good idea. That's my sister's adult version of truth-or-dare Jenga."

"Can't be that bad, can it?"

Moving to the coffee table, Genny picks up two wooden pieces. "Truth or dare?"

I go for truth, thinking it will keep us talking.

She reads the question, then watches me with an arched eyebrow and a look that dares me to answer. "What's the weirdest thing you've thought about while masturbating?"

There's no way I'm going there with her.

"I've never played," she insists, collecting the pieces and organizing them in their box. "But Callie loves telling me about it. Her least favorite rule is if you knock over the tower without it going around the entire group at least once, you have to lick the left nipple of everyone playing."

I swallow hard at the mental images playing out in my head. "Why haven't you played?"

"I'm a clutz... And if I'm licking nipples, I'd rather it not be another girl's."

"It sounds like it would be damn fun to *watch* you play," I mutter under my breath. I can't remember the last time I played a drinking game, but if I'm playing with Genny, I think I'd really enjoy myself.

"What was that?" She cocks her head to the side, wondering what I said so low there was no way she could hear me.

"Sounds like it would be fun to watch. You should let me know the next time your sister plays."

She gives me a thoughtful expression. "I don't want you watching my little sister play that game. Besides, I would need your number to tell you anything that happens after you leave."

Screw it, I think, knowing there's no backing out now. "I'm offering you my number, Genny. And it has nothing to do with wanting to see your sister."

She thinks it over, narrowing her eyes as she bites that damn lip. I force my eyes away from her mouth, wondering if I have any idea what I'm doing. I'm playing with fire. There's no way I'm not going to get hurt if I keep this up. But there's also no way I could willingly stop right now, either.

"This is gonna end badly. I want that on record now."

Chuckling at her train of thought, which was pretty close to my own, I reason, "According to you, I know too much about your personal life for you to hook up with me. I'm guessing if I ask, you won't date me..."

"I don't date."

As I expected. "The only option we have left is to just be friends. How can it end badly if we're just friends?"

This is going to end *disastrously*.

I'm still pushing forward, and so far, she isn't saying no. I don' t understand why I want her number in my phone, but I do l, without a doubt. And I want my number in hers. I want her to think about me, late at night, while she texts me. Because she *will* text me. And I'll tell her I want to just *hang out* when I ask her to spend some time with me this weekend.

Genny and I will never be just friends.

But if that's what she wants to hear, I'll lie to her.

Sliding her phone out of her pocket, she tosses it at me, watching my every move. She doesn't need to tell me her passcode again, and I quickly enter my info under her contacts, before calling myself, so I have her number as well. I step in close to her, handing it back, enjoying the smirk that's working its way onto her lips.

"How do you spell your name, Genny?"

Those eyes open wide again, but they can see. She stares at me in shock, spelling it out for me.

"Genny with a G?" I confirm quietly from right in front of her, the whisper adding to the tension surrounding us. She swallows as she nods.

"Yeah. How did you know it would be weird?"

I type out my answer, sending it to her, watching her laugh as she reads my name on her phone. "Just Friends Walker Kelley?"

"That's me," I answer, smiling right back at her.

She absentmindedly rubs her calf with the opposite foot, and it makes me remember why we're here. Some really weird shit she goes through before she gets a migraine. What did she call it? Migraine with... *something*. I'm gonna have to look it up later.

"I don't want to kick you out, Just Friend Walker, but my head is starting to hurt. You won't be offended if I ask you to leave, right? Since we're just friends and all..."

"Not at all," I tell her honestly. I'm not offended. But the *just friends* part is bullshit.

"I probably have a date that I'll tell you all about the next time I see you," I offer, wanting to see her reaction. "Since we're just friends."

She laughs, but not like she did before. It's not with her whole body and it doesn't reach her eyes. "You do that, Walker. And I'll tell you all about my bed-hopping adventures the next time I see you."

Fair play, but *come on*! Reminding me that she's casual about sex and relationships is the last thing I want to hear. Knowing she's watching me, I turn around to look at her one last time as I reach her door. Her teeth are on her bottom lip again, and I drag my eyes up to hers, so I don't give in and prove us both wrong already. "If we *weren't* just friends, I'd kiss you right now."

"Trying to prove you're serious about this *just friends* thing?" she asks, narrowing her eyes, even as she leans toward me. Almost like she wants that kiss as badly as I do.

"Yes." Even if we're both deluding ourselves. Staring in her eyes, at the mischief dancing in those green orbs, I add, "Is it working?"

"Not even for a second."

Her eyes dart down to my mouth, then back up to my eyes. We *both* want that kiss. But my standards are higher than hers, so *I'm* going to have to be the one to keep my word. The second I realize that, she reaches out, her hand landing on my jaw once again. Her eyes light up with a fire burning somewhere deep inside her, making it even harder to walk away.

I walk away anyway.

I won't go back on what I said.

At least not yet.

Not until she begs me for it.

Genny

It's Friday evening when I come back to the land of normally functioning human beings.

Callie pieced everything together at some point, went to pick up my pills, and delivered them to the darkness of my room as I attempted to sleep away my migraine. I remember her shaking me awake and handing me a pill and a water bottle, but that's all.

Waking up on my own a couple hours later, I stand under the hot spray of a much-needed shower, thinking about everything that led up to this moment. I'll have to talk to my boss about missing work today. I'll have to thank Callie. I'll have to figure out my bills and find out if I can pay any of that ticket after getting a new battery for my car and getting caught up on my insurance at the very least. I'll also have to find someone to help me get my car, change the battery, and switch out my flat for the spare.

Which leads my mind directly to Walker Kelley...

Overall, I had a very interesting experience with him.

I'd really prefer to experience him without an oncoming migraine next time.

My head is screaming that that's a very bad idea.

We're going to ruin each other. I can feel it. We can say just friends all we want. We can *try* to be just friends all we want. In the end, it won't matter. He'll be a *very* good friend. Right up until the moment when he breaks my heart and makes me hate him.

I don't need another break up like I had with Paul.

My mind stills tries to come up with a way to make it work. The experiencing him part, not the just friends part. If I spend time with Walker, I'll try to have sex with him. He's hot, sweet, kind. He's not at all my normal type, but there's something about him that makes me want him all the same.

Speaking of friends, or sex, or whatever you want to call it, Walker knows why I see Chad. Walker isn't the type of guy to do casual sex, though I'll do my best to wear him down given the chance. Since he was so determined to give me his number, why didn't he try to get me to stop seeing his roommate?

Maybe he really *does* want to be just friends?

I switch gears, pushing the very attractive Walker Kelly from my mind to focus on my best friend, Myra. After texting her about my horrible day yesterday, I whine about needing to let loose a little, while not spending a dime because of all the sudden expenses I have that I wasn't counting on. We agree on a girls' night in tomorrow. I'll provide the nachos, she'll bring the alcohol.

One issue down.

Seven hundred and forty-three to go.

Or somewhere around there...

Let's move on to the issue of my car.

There are very few people in this world that I can count on. Other than Callie, there's Myra, Michelle, my brother Calvin, and... Yeah. That's it. Myra is working tonight. Michelle is on a date. Guess I'll try door number three, since Callie is out for the evening.

Genny: Got stranded in town last night. Any chance you can give me a lift, then help me change a flat and install a new battery in my car?

The chances of Calvin being able to help me on a Friday night are slim to none, but I have to *try*.

Calvin: I'm at a concert. I can help tomorrow afternoon?

Genny: I'll let you know if I need you. Thanks anyway!

Do I have any right to text my new friend? The one who is anything but?

I've literally got nothing to lose at the moment.

Genny: Hey, Just Friend Walker. Thanks again for helping me out yesterday.

He doesn't reply right away and I hide my disappointment by getting some housework done. I scrub the kitchen, the bathrooms, the floors. I fold two loads of laundry and think about how pathetic I am. Twenty-nine years old and my Friday night consists of cleaning the house. At least I won't need to worry about doing it later this weekend.

Just friends Walker Kelley: That's what friends are for, Genny with a G. Your car is still in town. Need a ride?

He's a mind-reader.

Genny: Can you make my car drivable again?

Just friends Walker Kelley: If it's just a flat and dead battery, yeah. Do you need a new battery, or should I bring jumper cables?

Genny: If you don't mind driving me around, a new battery. But if you don't have time, no worries. My brother said he can help tomorrow.

No worries? Wow. I'm totally failing in the not-caring-if-he's-on-a-date department. Hopefully he can't see through my flimsy attempt at indifference.

Just friends Walker Kelley: I'm free right now. You at home?

He didn't say he didn't have a date. I try to pretend I didn't notice.

Giving an affirmative reply, I hurry back upstairs to make it look like I'm not trying, but I still look good. Extra coat of mascara? Check. Shiny pink lip gloss? Check. Run a brush through my hair so it looks soft and touchable? Check. Change out of my cleaning shirt? Check.

Just friends, my ass.

A million questions are running through my head about him. What kind of car does he drive? What does he do for a living? Why is free at seven on a Friday evening? Will he kiss me tonight, or make me wait until the next time I see him?

I push it all aside, focusing on the fact that I got paid today, so I can afford this new battery Walker's going to take me to get. I have no idea how much a new battery costs, but I doubt it will be cheap. Nothing is cheap when it comes to cars. Except the car itself, sometimes.

I'm upstairs when he knocks on the door. After yelling that it's open, I casually meander down the steps, like I don't have a care in the world and I wasn't just checking out my own reflection, anticipating his arrival. Walker stands just inside the back door, eyeing me cautiously. Probably trying to determine how dangerous I am today, since I can see and no part of me is numb. I almost wish I couldn't see him again. It would be much easier to keep my hands to myself if I wasn't aware of how good he looks in that Green Day t-shirt stretched taut across his pecs and arms, and that stubble he's sporting that instantly makes me wonder how it would feel scraping across my inner thighs.

As I very obviously check him out, he does the same, his eyes sweeping down, then back up my form in a way just friends don't do. I'm hoping the knowing smile he's wearing when his eyes make it back to my face is in appreciation.

"Hey Friend," I offer in greeting, amazed at how breathy my voice suddenly is.

"Looks like you're feeling better."

Shit. He probably saw me at my worst last night. I didn't even think about that. I hadn't showered in almost two full days, and I was crying.

Come to think of it, I'm surprised he came back today.

Maybe there's something to this *just friends* thing. None of my boytoys would've offered me a ride unless it was back to their place. And they wouldn't have stopped to check on me at all, had they seen me crying.

"Yeah." I cringe inside, hoping *better* is more like fantastic. Or sexy. Or hot and overdressed. I'll gladly take my clothes off for Walker. "Thanks again for, ya know, everything yesterday."

"You ready?" he asks, holding the door to my own house open for me. Is he in a hurry? I try to blow off that question as I climb into his car. It's a Subaru with dark tinted windows all the way around. It looks sporty and fast, and I remember how comfortable it was as I slide inside.

There's an uneasy silence as he climbs in the driver's seat and starts the engine. I have no idea where to go with it; I've never been just friends with a guy before. After Paul, I let guys become a means to an end, a way to find release, to give me what I needed to help me deal with my stressful life before I went back to the real world, leaving them behind completely.

Have I been using them? Sure. But they've been using me, too. We both get what we want, so what's the harm?

If you were with Myra instead of Walker, what would you talk about?

I can work with that. Looking at the man driving me around and doing me more favors than I have any right to ask, I attempt a *just friends* conversation. "So, um. How was your day?"

He side-eyes me, a smirk playing on his lips. "Good. How was yours?"

"Short. But a lot better than yesterday."

Yeah... That didn't last long. Now what?

What else do I talk to Myra about? Mostly our sex lives. How life would be better with a man to do all the housework. Or how life would be better after winning millions in the lottery. Both are about even in our minds, since both would be a once-in-a-lifetime jackpot.

"Wanna tell me about your stressful day yesterday?" he asks, avoiding my lingering gaze. "Since we're now *officially* friends."

Thinking about what I can tell him from yesterday, I mindlessly chew on my bottom lip. He doesn't need to know how boring my job is. He doesn't need to know where I woke up yesterday. He doesn't need to know that I went to work without brushing my teeth, getting a shower, or even eating breakfast. I already told him about my ordeal at the pharmacy... I guess I could tell him about my evening. But that happened because I had to stay late at work.

"There was that power outage yesterday." He nods and I take that as encouragement to continue. "That made work suck, and I had to stay really late to finish up everything I needed to get done."

"Where do you work?"

"At the hospital, registering radiology and lab patients. What about you?"

"The distribution center," he answers easily. The distribution center is half an hour outside of town. I've heard they're pretty good to work for. I wonder what exactly he does there. What shifts he works. If he works weekends. What does he do on the weekends if he's not working? "How late did you have to stay?"

My mind snaps back to the conversation, instead of wondering about every single aspect of Walker's life. "Almost two and a half hours. It was brutal."

He turns to flash me that brilliant smile while laughing at me. I tell him a little bit more. About how I didn't eat yesterday, not until he watched me devour my dinner. About how I was almost late to work, but not *why*. About how I got pulled over.

"Your ex is a cop? I thought you didn't date."

How clever of him to notice.

"I don't anymore," I quickly explain. "I did a long time ago. Paul helped me figure out that dating's not worth the effort."

"I have some bad news for you," Walker informs me as he pulls into the auto parts store. After parking, he turns my way to study me. He reaches out, tucking a strand of my unkept hair behind my ear. "You had more than one parking ticket on your car when I drove by. Maybe if you go down to the police station and plead your case, they'll drop it back to just one. As long as you're not asking your ex. Sounds like you'll have to sit through a date or two to get any kind of sympathy from him."

"Not gonna happen. I'll pay a thousand parking tickets before I go out with him again."

"Because you don't date or because it's him?"

His eyes are so intent on mine it's hard to focus. It feels like we're totally alone in this car. It's quiet, and with the darkened windows, everything outside is muted, like it's existing in a different plane. I can watch it without taking part in it. It would be easy to forget everything except what's right here in this car.

I *like* what's in this car.

It's my turn to reach towards him, but I have no reason to other than I want to touch him. His eyebrow arches in silent question, but he doesn't try to stop me. Tracing him with my fingertips, I outline the hard line of his cheek to his jaw, the stubble I admired from afar earlier is rough under my palm. My thumb follows his bottom lip, and his is breath hot as it rushes across my skin. Raising my eyes to his, I wonder briefly what he's thinking.

"I'm not gonna kiss you, G."

He wasn't *thinking*. He was reading my mind.

There's a whole world outside of this car, I remind myself. A world where I'm already fucking two point five guys (Chad only counts as a half, because the sex requests only go one way, not both), and I don't need to add another one. Especially one as dangerous as Walker.

"Of course not," I assure him, cursing silently when I have to clear my throat. "We're just friends."

"That's right. Just friends. It might be easier to stick to that if one friend stopped touching the other."

Like that's gonna happen. Giving him a sly smile, I open the car door, throwing over my shoulder, "You should try it. You might like to touch, too."

Lord help me, if he does.

I head right towards the counter in the store. I have no idea where anything is and I wouldn't know what I was looking at even if I read the signs. The man behind the counter sighs when I tell him I need a new battery, then asks what kind of car I have. I answer him and he asks, "What year?"

A helpless shrug works my shoulders, and Walker banters back and forth with me and the clerk, deciding on a battery that *should* work. If it doesn't, Walker's going to be spending the entire evening with me, running me back and forth to the auto store.

Maybe I should've lied about how old my car possibly was... Spending more time with Walker wouldn't be a hardship.

After ringing up my shiny new battery, the clerk gives me a total of just under two hundred dollars.

Two hundred dollars?!

What the hell is this world coming to?

Luckily, I brought along my no-matter-what neutral expression that I've mastered over the years.

Walker carries the battery out to his car while I trail behind him, trying to figure out why a damn battery costs so much, and also how I'm going to afford to get a new tire on top of it. Hopefully I can wait until my next paycheck to take care of *that* problem.

I've still got around seven hundred and forty-two problems left to go.

"You never answered why you won't go out with the cop again. Because of your no dating rules, or because it's him?"

My seat belt clicks into place as I think back to our conversation. I know what he's trying to get at, but it's not going to work. I won't break my rules for him. I might sleep with him because my body has a way of doing what it wants with or without my permission, but I won't date him.

"Because of who he is. Also because I don't date anymore. Double whammy."

"Ouch." Walker winces. "Poor guy. He shoulda tried to be just friends with you first."

"I won't break my rules for just friends either, Walker."

"Course you won't. I'm just saying he would've gotten to spend some quality time with you if he was your friend. Since we're just friends, and I'm really curious, if we were to say, go out to eat sometime... Are we going Dutch? Or can I pay because I'm a guy and you're a girl, and it just feels right to let the guy pay?"

"We're not going out to eat together."

"Friends go out to eat together all the time."

He's almost as stubborn as I am. And it *almost* breaks my neutral expression.

Avoiding his side-eyed skepticism, I look out the window, choosing to watch the tinted world go by. I have a feeling Walker wants the real thing, dating and getting to know someone and falling in love. He'll never get that from me. My life is already busy and complicated. I don't need anything or anyone to make it any more tangled than it already is.

"Ok, we won't go out to eat," he relents, sighing at *my* stubbornness. "Too early for that, I guess. How about I come over and bring takeout? You offered me some of your sub last night, takeout can't be off limits."

"Maybe," I answer, giving him nothing concrete. "Do you like movies? We could watch a movie."

Where the hell did *that* come from?

"I like movies. But if I have to sit through some romcom, you have to agree to watch another movie with me, one that *I* pick."

Silently laughing at his willingness to watch a romcom with me, I sneak a glance at him out of the corner of my eye. He's sitting in the driver's seat looking totally relaxed. He seems to be easy going, laid back, and fun. If I weren't so attracted to him, I could easily be friends with him.

"I think I can agree to those terms."

"Great. So, we'll do takeout and a movie. When?"

He's for real. He's setting up a date with me, even if we're both going to pretend it's not *really* a date. I decide to go with it. As much as I want to deny it, I can't. I like him. I like spending time with him. I don't know him, but I *want* to.

Almost as much as I want to get him out of those clothes...

Callie's schedule with work, school, and clinical can by crazy. I pick the night she's least likely be home until late. Fridays are best. Next would be Saturdays, but tomorrow I've got plans with Myra.

"Next Friday."

He wants to argue, wants to push me for sooner, but he wisely keeps his mouth shut. "Ok. Next Friday it is."

Smart man.

"How do you know about cars, Friend?"

He chuckles, enjoying his new nickname. "I really don't know that much about cars. I know the basics. You just know *nothing*, so I can see how you'd be confused about that."

Gasping, I pretend to be offended at his verbal jab.

"My dad tinkered on them when I was growing up and I'd hang out with him in the garage. I picked up all my knowledge that way."

"Are you close with your dad?" I ask, wishing I could be close to mine. I wasn't the best kid, and I wasn't close with *any* of my family when my parents died.

"Yeah. I'm close with my whole family. You seem pretty close to yours, too."

I try not to roll my eyes as I think about my brother and sister. I didn't exactly have a choice in the matter. I love them both to death, but sometimes I could strangle them just as easily as tell them I love them. Not enjoying where this conversation is going, I decide to change it. I decide to make it much more interesting. And I watch closely for his reaction. "I'm gonna go the place I shouldn't, but how do you know Chad?"

Walker's expression doesn't change. Either he figured this would come up at some point, or he doesn't think Chad is a threat to his *friendship* status with me. He's right about the friendship thing. I know nothing about Chad except what he can make me feel and his address. I don't even know his last name. Walker here, knows more about me than Chad does, and I've been fucking Chad every time he texts me for over a year.

And making eyes at Walker for the same amount of time.

"Chad is my sister's ex. When she moved out, he needed help making the rent and had a spare room. I was looking for a place to live. It just made sense. I didn't think he was going to have quite so many... *visitors* in and out at all hours of the night, but it hasn't interfered with whatever I've been doing in the four years I've lived there."

Wait a minute. His sister's *ex*? He's been living there for four years? And his nephew is *how* old?

Narrowing my eyes, I ask another question, hoping I'm piecing this together all wrong. "When did Chad and your sister break up?"

"Four years ago."

"And Zeke is four?"

He catches my eyes, knowing exactly where I'm going. "Yeah..."

"Is it obvious and you don't wanna talk about it, or am I missing something?"

Walker lets out a deep breath, running his hand through his hair and reluctantly explaining, "Chad is Zeke's biological father. Chad wanted nothing to do with him. That's the whole reason he and my sister broke up."

"And your sister was ok with you *living* with him?"

"She wasn't thrilled about it, but she thought Chad might change his mind if he occasionally saw Zeke. He didn't. Reese was heartbroken for a while, but she got married a couple years ago to a guy that loves her like she hung the moon and the stars. She told me yesterday it's about time I get my own place, so I think she's getting sick of the reminder that Zeke isn't her husband's."

Mulling that over, I admit, "I had no idea."

As my car slides into view through the window, Walker explains, "I'm pretty sure Chad doesn't want anyone to know."

Because it proves he's a really shitty person!

What am I going to do the next time he texts me? It's not like he's gonna knock *me* up, I'm on birth control and we use condoms every time, but knowing he already knocked someone up and he basically said, *too bad, deal with it*? That's *harsh*.

My door opens and Walker smiles, holding his hand out to me. I take it, still in my own head and not paying attention to how much of a gentleman he's being. He leads me to my car and I lean against it, still wrapped up in the implications of what I just learned.

"G?" Walker asks, pulling my attention out of my own little world and back to him. He's wearing a small smirk that says he's enjoying watching me while I'm stuck in my head. What was I thinking? Walker can have my attention. Walker can have *all* my attention. "I kinda need your keys to get under your hood."

Is it wrong that I instantly love his nickname for me? Or that he even *gave* me a nickname? "You wanna get *under my hood*?" I ask dramatically. With fluttering, innocent eyelashes and everything.

"I do," he nods, his voice low and hopeful. "I'll *really* get your motor running, if you give me half a chance."

This is very dangerous talk. My body is responding to his words and their dirty meaning like the word *friend* was never mentioned. I'm pretty sure that's exactly why he worded it the way he did. He's smirking like he knows exactly how hard my nipples are.

I risk a downward glance.

Yep. Totally visible.

"Focus, Genny," he murmurs, his eyes drilling into mine. "I need your keys to do anything to your *car*."

Oh yeah. My *car*. Totally forgot about *that*.

Glad to have something to distract me, I dig through my purse until I hit pay dirt. He slips them from my hand, his fingers warm and lingering, his eyes still on mine, that cocky smirk still on his lips.

Matt's going to be getting a hell of a lot more texts from me.

Watching Walker work, I admire the way his hands know just what to do. They move effortlessly from one thing to the next, removing bolts and cranking rachets, not caring how dirty or greasy they might be getting. Thinking about those dirty hands against my clean skin is almost more than I can bear right now, so I make my way back to his car, instead.

Maybe I'll be useful and take this new battery to him...

Holy crap! Maybe if I could lift this thing without pulling a muscle and falling over, I would! After struggling for several seconds, I finally get a hold of it, keeping it close to my body to try to make it as light as possible. I'm still standing there cradling this two-hundred-dollar plastic box full of bricks when a set of hands land on my shoulders. Walker slowly turns me around, laughing at my expression before stepping back and crossing his arms. "Want some help with that?"

What I want are his hands back on my body, but I'll also take what he's offering now. "Yes, please."

His hand slides along my belly, and he easily takes it from me.
In one hand.
Like it weighs nothing.

Trying not to drool, I consider some other things he could carry around so effortlessly. Namely, *me*.

Just friends, I remind myself with a deep breath, closing my eyes to make it a little easier to convince myself.

Maybe, if I think it often enough, my body will begin to understand what my mind is saying.

Or maybe, if my body keeps responding this way, my mind will give in and ask him to take me home and fuck me until the sun comes up.

Giving an involuntary groan at even that *thought*, I wonder what Callie's doing later. How freaked out will she be with a strange vehicle in the driveway and sex noises coming from my bedroom?

Totally can't happen.

"Genny? Battery's in. You wanna try it?"

Yes! I definitely want to try it!

Wait. He means my *car* again...

I climb in, turn the key, and crank the engine. It revs right up, solving my transportation problem. Cutting the engine, I jump out of the car and throw myself into Walker's arms. "Thank you, Friend! You're amazing!"

His head tips down as he watches me with very dark eyes. His arms wrap around my body, his hands awfully close to my ass. My still-hard nipples are pressed into his chest, and leaning on him like I am, I finally have proof that he's just as affected by my presence as I am by his. Those eyes of his land on my mouth, and I might *die* if he doesn't kiss me. Running my tongue along my bottom lip, I send him a silent invitation, praying for him to accept.

He doesn't.

Walker steps *away* instead, swallowing forcefully, dropping those eyes away from me completely.

Invitation not accepted. RSVP of zero. Disappointment starts raining on my parade.

"Now that we've got your motor running," he tells me in a gruff voice, "I'll work on that tire."

Fuck the tire!

I actually totally forgot about the tire, but I seriously don't care anymore. "We can always take care of that in the morning," I offer, not even trying to hide the want in my voice.

He doesn't look at me as he rejects my brilliant suggestion. Pulling the spare from my trunk, as well as some tools that I had no idea were in there, he easily replies, "I've got plans in the morning. And you're not available to hang out with me until next Friday, remember?"

Of course, he's a man who *listens*! I wasn't even sure they existed, thinking they were some myth that an imaginative girl thought up hundreds of years ago, and it's such a great concept that the female species has passed it down through the generations, hoping and praying that some man might take it as a challenge and attempt to make it true. Now that I want Walker badly enough to take him back to my house and defile my sister's ears, he has to be one of those magically rare guys who prove that myth is based in some strange sort of reality. And of course, he remembers what I said at the most inopportune moments.

"Right. I forgot," I admit lamely, too annoyed to come up with a witty or seductive remark.

"If your schedule opens up, you should let me know. I'd love to see you again before next week."

He'll meet my eyes for *that*.

I like his eyes. It's getting dark out, but the lights are on in the parking lot, shining down on us and allowing me to see the sparkle in his green eyes. They're not as green as mine. His are more hazel; green mixed with a hint of brown. They're kind of hypnotic.

"I'll do that, Walker Kelley."

"I don't suppose you ever checked the pressure in your spare, did you? This one is almost as flat as the one we just took off."

"That was all you, not *we*. And no. I never check my tires. There's an indicator light for that."

Walker shakes his head like that's the silliest thing he's ever heard. "There's a gas station a few blocks away. I'll follow you there, ok? I'll fill up your tire, then let you enjoy your night."

Meaning, he has things he wants to do. Maybe *someone* he wants to do, someone that's not *me*. Maybe he has a date, and I'm making him very late. I also got him all turned on for her. Lucky bitch, whoever she is.

I try not to sigh in frustration, disappointment, or relief.

Just friends...

Thanks to Walker and his mad mechanic skills, my car again starts right up. Walker talks to me as he fills up my spare tire, telling me I can't run this like my normal tire. I need to go slow, and I need to get a new one as soon as possible.

Standing up, the task at hand finished, he looks regretfully at my mouth. I want to tell him to just *do it* already. I've never had to beg a guy to kiss me before. If I thought begging would make him give in, I'd do it in a heartbeat.

"I'll see you next Friday, G. Let me know what time to show up and what kind of takeout you want."

"Walker..."

He shakes his head, answering my question without me ever voicing it. "Just friends, G. Nothing more."

I try to not huff at his comment.

I mostly succeed.

I *think*.

"I'll see you Friday," he says again, obviously not knowing how to end this. A kiss would be good. A kiss would be *great*. Instead, he takes a few steps toward his car, turning back to me once he's a safe distance away. "It was fun seeing you tonight."

"It was *mostly* fun, Friend."

Walker climbs in his car, chuckling at me and my obvious annoyance at his stubborn stance on our relationship status. I don't realize that I never thanked him for changing my stupid tire until he's gone.

He never thanked me for the hard-on he's taking to someone else, though, so it's all fair, right?

Climbing into my car, I grab my phone.

Genny: Busy?

Matt: Give me an hour.

Walker

Genny: What're you doing?

I wonder at Genny's random text on my way home. After spending most of the day fixing a couple things at my sister's house with her rambunctious boys, I joined Chad and a bunch of other guys for an impromptu soccer game. We played until it was dark, and Genny's text was waiting for me, patiently, until I got home and took a shower.

Laying on my bed staring at the ceiling, I contemplate my answer. Do I tell her? Do I make something up? Do I go for vague? Do I ask what *she's* doing?

Walker: Why?
Genny: Myra and I were talking about you. Thought about inviting you over.
Walker: Who's Myra?
Genny: Bestie.

A picture accompanies her text, showing Genny and her best friend in pajamas, drinks in hand, smiles on their faces. They look buzzed, which make me wonder what kind of drunk Genny is. Is she a happy drunk? A horny drunk? A mean drunk?

Walker: What're you saying about me?
Genny: We're just friends.
Walker: Is that a random comment, or what you're telling Myra about me?
Genny: Both.
Walker: How drunk are you right now?
Genny: Come over and find out...

Really bad idea. Alcohol often makes girls bolder than normal, and Genny doesn't have a problem being bold on a regular day.

Even if she wasn't drunk, I refuse to be another one of the guys she screws with no emotions involved. Reese is right. I'm almost thirty. I want a semi-nice girl to settle down with. To fall in love with. To start a family with. To grow old with. I want the real deal, and I'm not going to find it by screwing every girl who looks at me with that look in her eyes.

Love doesn't come from sex. I've been around long enough to know that. I've seen and heard enough from my apartment to know that.

Walker: Love to, G. But not tonight.

She responds with an angry emoji.

I think about getting ready to go to the pool hall where I'm meeting my friends later. I think about going to see Genny and torturing myself all night by trying to make her keep her hands to herself. I think about sitting here on my ass trying to make up my mind because this girl has me thinking about things I really shouldn't be considering.

I get up and get my shit around to go meet the guys. A couple games of pool might keep me from thinking about her for a little while.

Genny: Did your date enjoy the hard-on I gave you last night?

Laughing out loud, I stop myself from telling her I didn't have a date last night. She doesn't need to know that. What would she say if she found out I came home and watched a movie by myself, then went to bed early, doing my best not to think about how good she felt in my arms? Or that look on her face when I told her I'd get her motor running if she gave me half a chance. Or that expression she wore when I left her at the gas station, the one that was begging me without words to *kiss her already!*

After typing out a response, I lock the screen, not sure if I should send it. I think on it while making my way to the pool hall, realizing she might be drunk, but she's letting me know exactly what's going on in her head. I decide to go with it, hitting send as I walk into the bar, wondering what else I might be able to find out from her tonight.

Walker: That was only a semi, G. And no one enjoyed it but me.

Genny: Did you at least think of me while you enjoyed it?

So glad I didn't go over to her place.

I really like this girl. I like her smart mouth, her sarcastic remarks, the way she touches me without any hesitancy. It just about kills me to let her do it. I *almost* showed her how fun it would be if I touched her back, but I have *some* restraint. She's testing it at every turn, and I wonder how much longer it'll last, but it's still in place as of right now.

It wouldn't be if I'd gone over to see her. There's no way she'd keep her hands to herself while asking me these very personal questions, and my self-restraint would crumble after the first few exploratory touches. There's something there, between us. Something that's really hard to ignore. But I will, no matter how hard it is, until she wants more than casual sex. I need more than that and I refuse to share her, or any other girl, with anyone else.

Walker: Are you gonna regret this conversation in the morning?

Genny: Probably. But it's not morning yet.

Walker: Ask me that question again in the morning.

Genny: Come over. I won't have to use the phone to ask you.

Walker: Not tonight, G.

This time she doesn't respond.

Zander, one of my friends, comes over to join me as I lean against the wall, watching Alex and Kane start a game. "Hey, what's up?"

"Not much. You?"

"Heidi's family reunion is tomorrow," he complains, rolling his eyes. "I don't understand why she wants me to go. I'm not family yet."

"She thinks you are. Besides, it'll make her happy."

"True. And when she's happy..." he trails off, not buzzed enough to finish that sentence. Zander swears he doesn't talk about his sex life, but get a couple beers in him and he doesn't shut up about it.

A few games and beers later, I take a break, sitting at a table and pulling out my phone. I missed another text. I would bet my next paycheck it's from Genny. Staring at that little icon on my phone, I debate opening it. She's just going to argue with me about going to see her. Kane comes over, tipping his beer toward my phone. "Who's that? Got a new girl?"

"Not exactly," I tell him, wishing there was an easy answer. "We're saying just friends, but she's drinking and begging me to come over."

"Why're you saying just friends?"

Taking a long swallow of beer, I stall, trying to come up with some answer that isn't as awful as the truth. He won't buy it, though, so I give him the disturbing truth with a long sigh. "She's one of Chad's regulars."

Kane raises his eyebrows. "That's a new one for you. Never figured you'd go for his sloppy seconds."

"Neither did I."

He finishes off his beer, a thoughtful expression on his face. "At least read her text. How bad is she begging you?"

Unlocking my phone, I bring up her latest text, staring in shock at the picture she sent. It takes me a long minute to remember anything else, even that Kane is looking over my shoulder and staring at her photo, too. I lock my phone as quickly as possible, staring at the blank screen, cursing her in my head as I hear Kane bust out laughing beside me.

I *really* wish he hadn't seen that...

He slaps his hand on my shoulder, rocking me forward on the bar stool. "I'm gonna say she's begging you *bad*."

"Or she's telling me I shouldn't bother coming over anymore."

Grinning, he admits, "Or that."

Genny

Sunday morning, I quickly remember why I swore I'd never get wasted again. Myra agrees we might have gone a little overboard last night, and after stealing my sunglasses and some ibuprofen, she sneaks out of my house and into the sunshine to go home and back to bed.

I get set up in the kitchen, prepared to make a couple meals for throughout the week. Stuffing some green peppers, I cover them with foil and slide the dish into the oven. There's also some frozen chicken thawing in the fridge for Calle and I to grill one night this week with a salad. Two meals taken care of. Left overs or salad on the other nights. Perfect.

I'm trying to set the timer on my phone when a new text comes in, distracting me.

Walker: Am I correct in assuming someone else took that photo of you?

What photo?

Scrolling through my phone, I suck in a hard breath, staring in disbelief at a very risqué picture of myself. I'm in only my bra and a pair of pajama shorts, my hand disappearing down those shorts, and an expression on my face that says I made it to Orgasm-ville all on my own.

Holy shit! I sent that to *Walker*?!

"Oh *Lord*," I breathe, trying desperately to recall exactly what Myra and I did last night.

"Oh Lord *what*?" Callie asks, joining me in the kitchen.

"Ah, nothing," I reply nervously. I stuff my phone in my pocket and give her my undivided attention. "How's the paper going? Did you find out how you did on that test last week?"

She eyes me suspiciously. Maybe I'm being too careful?

"Good so far, and not yet. I'm not even halfway done with the paper, though, so it's too early to know for sure."

"It's not due until Friday, right? You've got plenty of time. What's your work schedule like this week?"

"I work Monday, Wednesday and Sunday." Under my fixed gaze, she finally gives me a questioning glare. "What's with you? You're acting funny."

Too careful, for sure. Shrugging, I try to brush off her comment. "Just worried about your finals coming up, that's all. They're only a few weeks away, right?"

"Nah, that's not it. What were you *Oh Lord*ing when I came in? What're you hiding on your phone?"

I wave my hand dismissively, trying to go back to what I was doing. But what, exactly, was I doing? Oh yeah. Setting a timer. For that I need my phone. "Just setting a timer for the peppers. It was set for only a few minutes. I was trying to remember what I used it for last."

That should get her off my case. I turn away from her as I unlock my phone and pull up the timer.

Callie opens the fridge, grabbing a stick of string cheese. "I don't believe you for a second, Genny, but I don't have time to figure you out right now. Would you mind making me a salad? I've been working on this stupid paper and I forgot to eat lunch."

"Callie, you know you have to eat every few hours," I scold her, looking her over for any signs that we're about to be in the middle of an emergency. "Are you feeling ok? Do you need a soda?"

"I'm all right. I just need to eat."

Shooing her out of the kitchen, I throw together a salad for both of us. I didn't eat lunch or breakfast, because I was too sick to even think about eating this morning. Speaking of feeling sick, I need to talk to Myra again to figure out how that picture was taken. It'll have to wait until after lunch; Callie's already suspicious.

After sitting with her at the cluttered dining room table to eat, I ask, "What time did you get in last night?"

"It wasn't late, you were still up. You and Myra were trashed! And loud! I could hear you two giggling all night long. What were you up to?"

"Ugh, I don't even remember. It's all a bit of a blur. She wasn't kidding when she said she was bringing the alcohol. She usually brings wine, I didn't expect her to show up with *tequila*."

Callie smiles around her fork. "Oh, you and tequila! I should have joined your little party, so I could watch..." she shakes her head with a dreamy look.

On the first anniversary of our parents' death, I got wasted on tequila. I was twenty, and that was the only bottle of alcohol in the house when they died. I thought Callie and Calvin were asleep when I started drinking, but they both came out of their rooms, and I bawled my drunken eyes out about how much I loved them, how they deserved so much more than I could give them, and how I hoped I wasn't screwing up their lives.

We cried together then, all three of us. And eventually, we told stories, laughed, sang, and even reenacted some of our favorite memories of our parents.

That was the first night I felt close to my siblings. That was the night we all started leaning on each other and stopped being so lonely and lost in our grief and pain. It's also a tradition we carry on every year.

It's also generally the only time I drink tequila, because tequila is my truth serum. And the anniversary of our parents' death is the only time I'll allow myself to cry in front of my siblings. Or anyone else. I don't really do *feelings* unless I'm all alone with no chance of anyone interfering with my pity parties.

"What kind of shenanigans did you get into that you're regretting today? That's probably what the *Oh Lord* was about earlier."

"You caught me," I mumble, hanging my head. "I was drunk texting. I didn't get a chance to look through them yet. I *can* tell you that I scare myself sometimes."

"Who were you texting?"

Hmm. What do I tell her? I haven't talked to her about Friday yet. Normally, she doesn't get home until late on Friday nights, so there's a chance she won't ever know that I had company. If it's one of those random times where she *does* come home, she's going to find a surprise when I'm here with Walker.

I don't bring guys here. Ever.

I should give her *some* kind of a heads up. "A new friend."

She gives me a judgey look, cocking her head to the side and narrowing her eyes. She knows I have a sex life. There are times when I don't come home. She always notices, and I always tell her I was with a friend. Right now, I do my best to plead my innocence. "Not *that* kind of friend! Really, *just* a friend this time."

Despite my efforts to change it, Walker and I are just friends. We haven't done any touching at all. Other than that hot-as-fuck hug when he fixed my battery. The fact that he can turn me on with just his words and a look or two is beside the point.

Callie stands up, acting like she's reaching for my empty salad bowl, then grabbing my *phone* and running from the room, instead. "Will your texts confirm that claim?"

Shit!

Running after her, I curse myself for never changing the password after she broke into my phone the last time she stole it. "Callie, *please* don't open that! I don't even remember-"

"Eww!" she gasps, stopping in her tracks. "Why didn't you tell me it was a picture of you doing *that*? I never would have looked! I need to scrub my eyeballs! Genny, that's so gross! And totally not something you send to *just a friend*!"

"Give it back!"

"Wait!" she cries, holding up her hand as she scrolls through my phone. I swear to God, I'm gonna kill her. *I* don't even know what I said to him yet. "Jesus! Are you always this forward?"

"Callie, come on! Give it back!" I yell, fuming. As I make my way around the island, she catches my movements in her peripheral vision and moves to keep me on the opposite side. This is the most childish thing she's done in years.

Maybe it's the first time I've had something to hide.

Her jaw hits her chest before she looks up at me in shock, then she dives back into my private life. "You had Ben Wednesday, Matt Friday, and you were trying to hook up with this Walker guy last night? When did you turn into such a whore?"

Whoa. That hurts. That really fucking hurts.

I'm *not* a whore.

I'm a twenty-nine-year old girl who has way too many responsibilities, way too many bills, and not nearly enough time for a real relationship because I'm too busy taking care of myself and supporting my sister while she goes to college. I'm a girl who does what she needs to do to sometimes feel like a *human*. To get rid of stress and remember that touch can sometimes be specifically for my pleasure, instead of something that gets passed out to everyone else. I'm a girl forced into a role with my siblings that I didn't want. I'm a girl who does the best she can in a world that's done nothing but crush my dreams and take away any chance at a future of my own choosing.

Fighting the rage and shame colliding in my heart, I walk away from her and my phone, huffing my way out of the room and the house. I need to go for a drive. Get away from this life and my annoying, ridiculous, can't-mind-her-own-business sister. After slamming the car door, I spin my tires in the gravel driveway, before remembering that it's a stupid fucking *spare*, and I need to be *careful*.

I drive around, thinking of my many limitations, and I *hate* that spare tire. All I want to do is get on the highway and *go*. In the early days after my parents died, when it was just me and I had so much more and less to worry about at the same time, I would drive hundreds of miles a day. The music would be at full-blast as I cried my eyes out, trying to figure out what the hell I was going to do and how the hell I was going to do it.

Gas was so much cheaper then. And I had four real tires that didn't slow me down.

Gripping the steering wheel, I make a quick decision and head straight to Myra's. I don't know if she's busy. I don't even know if she's home. But I can't be in my own house right now with a sister who judges me so harshly after everything we've been through, and I don't want to cry. Which means I need to be around people. If I indulge in a pity party all by myself, the tears will come.

Myra pushes me onto her couch, her eyes wide as she takes in my anger.

Like I said, I don't do feelings, and Myra's not quite sure what to do with me.

After swallowing nervously, she asks, "What's going on?"

"Callie called me a whore."

Myra sucks in a breath, betrayal and anger on her face. "She did not!"

"She did," I nod. "She stole my phone and looked through my texts." After remembering what those texts showed my little sister, I add, "What do you remember from last night?"

"Oh girl," she sighs, rolling her wide eyes dramatically. "Not a whole lot. What did we do this time?"

"I think you took a picture of me while I paddled the canoe."

Her shocked face tells me she remembers no such thing. Until she cocks her head to the side and really thinks about it for a long minute. "Hmph. I think you're right. Holy shit, we were wasted!"

We sit there, trying to remember more of last night for a couple hours. Now that I've got her thinking about it, she won't shut up about me touching myself in front of her. I knew I had to have been feeling bold to send that picture to Walker, but to be bold enough to let Myra even *take* it? What is this guy doing to me?

Maybe I *am* a whore...

I've already got two guys on speed text. And I answer speed texts from Walker's roommate!

He's right. We need to just be friends.

And no more getting drunk unless someone takes my phone away from me.

When I get home, my phone is lying on the island and the peppers are covered in the fridge. After changing my passcode, I tap out a message to Walker and hit send before I change my mind.

Genny: After much investigation, I discovered that someone else did, indeed, take that picture. I fear my actions from the previous evening were spurred on by mass quantities of alcohol, and my embarrassment and regret took top priority today. Please accept my sincere apologies at attempting to push this relationship past the friendship status we agreed upon.

Just friends Walker Kelley: Apology accepted, but I'm keeping the picture.

Typing away, I try to reason with him.

Genny: For the sake of our budding friendship, it would be best for both parties if the picture in question was deleted immediately.

Just friends Walker Kelley: For the sake of any future hard-ons you give me, semi or full, I think it would be best for me to KEEP the picture in question.

Oh, Lord! Scrolling through our texts from last night, I read exactly what I sent him and exactly how he replied. What was I *thinking*?!

Ok, it's *obvious* what I was thinking. I wanted Walker in my house and in my bed. But did I have to ask him about his hard-on?

And seriously? That was just a *semi*?

Genny: Does this mean you DID think of me?

Just friends Walker Kelley: Not filled with TOO much regret today, I take it.

Genny: You're avoiding the question.

I can't believe I'm texting him this way. I can't even say I'm drunk today! Talking about Walker having a hard-on specifically because of me is turning my brain to mush.

Just friends Walker Kelley: Not avoiding, just trying to keep things in the friend zone.

Genny: Then you should agree wholeheartedly to delete the picture.

Just friends Walker Kelley: I'm still a man, G. One who appreciates a girl who isn't afraid to make herself feel good and is confident enough to take and send a picture like that.

I slip my phone in my pocket and search out my sister, trying to forget all about my so-called *friend*. Callie's passed out in her room, snoring softly, laptop on the bed beside her. Closing the computer and plugging it in so she'll have it charged for class tomorrow, I watch her sleep, reminding myself that I love this pain-in-the-ass. No matter what she says, or how badly she hurts me, I'll still worry about her and be there for her in every way I can be.

There's a final text from Walker as I'm climbing into bed. This one makes me smile as I fall asleep, thinking of him again.

Just friends Walker Kelley: Of course, I thought of you, G. Having a hot friend comes in 'handy' at times like that.

Walker

Genny is incredibly specific about what she wants for takeout and *how* she wants it. She doesn't stop at telling me wants pizza. Instead, she tells me what toppings she wants, where I need to get it, and that I have to take it directly to her house. No stopping for *anything*. Not to fill up my car, a flat tire, red lights, or even an accident or emergency blocking the road.

If she asks, I'll disappoint her, because I did stop at two red lights. I'm not a complete idiot.

Knocking on her door, I wait patiently for all of zero point three seconds before she opens it with a smile and steals the pizza box, disappearing into her kitchen. I try not to get offended that she didn't even say hello.

Mental note: Genny loves her pizza.

"Nice to see you too," I offer sarcastically, stepping into her house and closing the door. She moves to me in a rush, handing me a plate and dancing back to the box of melted cheese and goodness.

"It's *amazing* to see you, Walker."

That's more like it.

"Oh, *Lord*," she moans, chewing her first bite. I try not to laugh from my seat on the stool next to her at the island, still busy taking my first piece from the box.

"I take it you like pizza..."

"No, Friend," she mumbles around another bite. "I *Love* pizza. Specifically, *this* pizza, and love with a capital L. It's right up there with orgasms and buy-one-get-one-free specials."

"That's some serious love," I answer, trying to engage her in conversation. I haven't texted, seen, or heard from her since Sunday. I want to hear what's going on in her head. I want to know what her week was like. I want to know if I was in every other one of her thoughts like she was in mine.

"Stop talking. We can talk later."

Genny must not be very good at multitasking.

With every second or third bite, her eyes roll back in her head, and I start wondering if I somehow wandered onto the set of a porn movie. I'm not one to keep up with the latest trends, but I'm pretty sure what I'm witnessing is a food-gasm. The many groans and enthusiastic whispers of *this is so fucking good*, have me double checking to make sure she's still eating, and not trying to take another picture of herself to send me later.

There's not a chance in hell she lets Chad see her like *this*.

After two slices, she pushes her plate away, turning in my direction and finally give me some attention. "Thanks for dinner."

"Entirely my pleasure," I chuckle, trying to think myself out of a hard-on. As she takes her plate over to the sink to rinse it, I admire the short shorts that hug her ass as she bends over to put the plate in the dishwasher. She smirks as she walks back to her seat, knowing exactly where my eyes just were.

"So, Friend. Tell me about your week. Any new stories about Zeke?"

Most of my stories outside of work revolve around that little guy and his family, so I'm glad she likes hearing about him. "Zeke got a hamster this week."

"Oh," she breathes, her green eyes widening in excitement. "Is it still alive?"

"So far. He got it Wednesday, so it's only been a couple days."

Leaning an elbow on the counter, she holds her head in her hand as she watches me eat and talk. I tell her about how Zeke had an adventure with me in his basement when I changed his mom's dryer vent on Saturday. How, much to Reese's horror, he asked if he could keep a mouse if he caught one that came out of the hose. He begged to go searching in the basement for his new pet until Reese took him to the store and bought him a hamster instead.

"Calvin had a hamster once. He fell asleep playing with it, like, the third day. We never found the little rodent until we discovered it's skeleton when we moved."

"Calvin's your brother?" I ask, since she hasn't mentioned him by name before.

A lock of her long brown hair falls into her face as she nods, and my hands itch to tuck it behind her hear. She absentmindedly beats me to it. "Hold long after he lost it did you move?"

"Six or seven years," she giggles. "Most of its skeleton was broken into tiny little pieces. It was disgusting." Her eyes light up like it wasn't disgusting at all, like maybe she thought it was really cool instead. "That's the only pet we ever had. I was into music and Callie did the art thing. Calvin loved his animals from afar after that. He has a small zoo now, though."

"Any new artwork from you sister since I was here last week?"

"I don't think so. We had a fight last weekend and I stormed off instead of strangling her. She's thanking me for that kind gesture by giving me the silent treatment."

"Sounds like a long week."

Scoffing, Genny says, "When she's not talking to me is about the only time she minds her own business, so it's not as bad as it sounds." She takes my empty plate, repeating the process of putting it in the dishwasher. I repeat the process of checking out her ass.

I really wish I had more dirty dishes...

"I doubt she's been painting, though. She had a big paper worth twenty percent of her grade due today. And she's only got three weeks left of class before finals, so she's been pretty busy."

She wanders into the living room, and I get up to follow her. After she grabs a couple remotes, she flops on the couch, sitting in the middle, making sure I'll be close to her no matter where I might choose to sit.

"Did you go to college?" I ask, sitting on her right, closest to the door.

She does that thing again, the thing where she bites her lip, looking vulnerable and sexy as hell, all at the same time. "Briefly. It didn't last."

The TV flickers to life a second later. I get the distinct feeling she doesn't want to talk about her *brief* stint at college. Taking a deep breath, because I have no idea what's a safe topic with her, I let my arm rest on the top of the couch, leaning back and getting ready for an entertaining evening no matter what might happen. After side-eyeing me, she cautiously leans back against the couch, very aware of my arm above her shoulders.

"What do you wanna watch?" she demands, her eyes and focus on the screen in front of us.

"Give me some options. What genre are you thinking?"

She brings up the new release list. "I was thinking horror, since I don't want to bore you with a chick flick so soon into our friendship. What do you think?"

"That'll work. There's one that came out a couple weeks ago about an exorcist-"

"On the creepy little girl? That's the one I was thinking of, too!"

There's that happy smile. If we weren't just friends, I'd kiss it off her face. When I don't, she gives a small sigh, settling back into the crook of my arm and letting me slide my arm off the couch to rest on her shoulders. Out of nowhere, she stands up, turning to look at me and my confused expression. "I almost forgot. Do you want something to drink? It's been a while since I've played hostess."

"Sure, what do you have?" I ask, glad she wasn't jumping away from me because my arm landed across her shoulders.

"Not a whole lot. I got some Miller Lite. I don't know if you drink it, but I saw it in the fridge at your place once, so I took a chance."

She saw it in my fridge because she was fucking my roommate. I rub my temples as I close my eyes, trying to get rid of the reminder. "Yeah. That'll work. Bring two, if you don't mind."

She hands me a bottle, placing another one on the coffee table with her water. Settling back into the couch and my half-embrace, she sits a little closer this time. And when I curl my arm around her to open my beer, she doesn't act like being pulled closer to me is a problem.

The movie starts. We're introduced to the characters and the plot thickens. And Genny slowly gets more and more comfortable against me. At one point, she pushes off me to grab a throw, but then settles in again, tucking her feet underneath her ass and pulling that blanket over both of us. I'm anything but cold with her against me, but it gives me an excuse to pull her in tighter against my chest.

The back-door slams open, startling us and causing Genny to scream in surprise. Throwing a disgusted look in our direction, the girl who just scared us stomps her way into the house, flicking on every light possible.

This must be Callie, Genny's sister. She looks a lot like a younger version of Genny.

"Lord, Callie! Are you trying to give me a heart attack?" Genny scolds her, climbing off the couch and away from me as quickly as possible.

"You need to call the pharmacy," Callie sneers, ignoring her sister's question.

Genny's response is immediate. She drops the stern expression she was wearing and turns concerned in half a second. "Why? What's going on?"

"They sent out my script *today*! Even overnighting it, it won't get here till Monday! And it won't be any good then!"

Rubbing her forehead, Genny glances at the clock. "How soon are you gonna need more?"

"I'm good until the middle of the week, but if the stuff I get is bad-"

"Stop," Genny insists, waiting until Callie takes a deep breath to go on. "I'll take care of it, ok? You won't run out, I promise."

With a huffed response, Callie visibly relaxes and stalks her way into the kitchen.. "Can I have some of this pizza?"

Genny follows her sister after throwing a look of apology my way. "You know you shouldn't."

"Yeah, well, you know you shouldn't have one of your boytoys in the living room right now, either."

Genny replies something in a harsh whisper that I don't catch.

This got interesting fast. Genny gets weird migraines and Callie needs some medication overnighted that's going to be bad by Monday? And why does Genny need to take care of it? Why doesn't Callie take care of it herself?

And just how many boytoys does Genny have?

Coming back into the living room, Genny grabs her phone off the coffee table. "Do you mind? I think they're open until nine, so I have a few minutes to call them."

"It's fine," I reassure her. "This seems kind of urgent."

"Thank you. I'm sorry for anything she says to you."

She disappears up the stairs to get some peace and quiet, since Callie is still mumbling to herself in the kitchen. After plating a piece of the pizza she shouldn't have, Callie flops onto the other side of the couch, eating in a much less dramatic way than Genny did.

"I take it you're Walker? The guys she's supposedly *just friends* with?"

"That's me. I take it you're the sister, Callie."

Her eyes roll back in her head as she cynically replies, "God, what did she tell you about me? I'm some ungrateful brat that's ruining her life?"

My eyebrows raise in surprise, and I think about the very little Genny's said about her sister. "She hasn't said too much about you. You're in college. You like art, any I see here is yours, and you guys had a fight last weekend. That's pretty much all I know."

"Oh. I thought she would've told you how awful I am to her."

"She never mentioned anything like that."

Callie sighs, looking up at me with resignation in those eyes that look so much Genny's. "I shouldn't be awful to her. She's pretty amazing considering everything."

"What's everything?" I wonder out loud, hoping Callie will be more forthcoming than her sister.

"Don't you know about our parents?"

"I know they're dead," I hesitantly reply.

Chewing on the inside of her cheek, she regards me with her made-up eyes. She wears a lot more makeup than Genny does, but it only highlights that green color. Even without the stylish makeup, both Genny and her sister are gorgeous.

"When our parents died, Genny dropped out of college and gave up her whole life to take care of me and my brother. She got a job she hated, bought a smaller house we could afford, and a minivan she didn't want. She kept us together and took care of us." Callie's eyes move to the ceiling, and she lets out another sigh. "She's *still* taking care of me."

No wonder Genny didn't want to talk about college. She probably loved it, and it got taken away from her in the blink of an eye, just like her parents did. She was just a kid when she became responsible for her brother and sister, paying bills, making sure everyone was fed, making sure everyone went to school and appointments and extracurricular activities. Genny got forced into the role of mom when she was just stretching her wings and testing out her freedom.

"When did all this happen?"

"Umm..." Callie takes a minute to think, biting her own lip. I guess it's a family trait, not one Genny uses just to torture me. "I was twelve, so Genny would've been nineteen."

"What medication are you on that will be bad by Monday?"

Looking down at that half slice of pizza on her plate, she sets it aside with another heavy sigh. "I have type one diabetes. The insulin needs to be temperature controlled, and it'll most likely be bad when it gets here in three days, sitting around in a truck or warehouse without regulated heating. And Genny's right. I really shouldn't be eating this."

"How long have you had it?"

"*Forever.*" Rolling her eyes, she gives me a small smile. "I was diagnosed when I was eleven."

Wow. And taking care of a sick sister on top of everything else? Callie sees my expression and closes her eyes. "I know! She's amazing and I'm a brat. Did she tell you why we fought last weekend?"

"No."

"Good. I take back what I said to her. She's still just putting me first. Sometimes I forget."

She carries the pizza back to the kitchen and makes another plate of food. Whatever she's heating in the microwave smells delicious, and when she comes back to sit on the couch with it, I ask curiously, "What're you eating now? And what *can* you eat?"

Pointing at her plate, Callie tells me, "*This* is a stuffed pepper Genny made Sunday before I was mean to her. I should stay away from sugars and carbs. Genny usually cooks a couple meals on the weekend so I have stuff to eat all week long."

That means... "No pizza, subs, or desserts?"

"Not usually."

"What about drinking?" I ask, wondering if she's even legally able to do that.

"I don't drink much. There's no way to know how my body will react to it."

"What about Truth-or-Dare Jenga?"

Her cheeks fill with color in a much more exaggerated way than Genny's do. Callie's blush fills out on her neck and chest, going all the way out to her ears. "I don't drink when I play."

"How do you play that game and *not* drink?"

"You make sure you're with a very close group of friends. And it helps if everyone *else* is drunk. Then, no one remembers much except me."

I shake my head. "I don't think I could handle being diabetic."

She glances up from her food with an amused grin. "I don't even know if *I* could without Genny. She does all the grocery shopping, making sure there's always something I can eat without giving it much thought. She never cooks anything I shouldn't eat, and we never have alcohol here." Eyeing my beer, she corrects herself. "Well, we *didn't*."

The steps creak at the other end of the room and Callie and I both look toward them, watching Genny come back downstairs. She drops onto the couch between us, pulling the beer from my hand to finish it with one long pull. "Throw out whatever comes Monday. More should be here Tuesday, ok?"

Callie softly says, "Thanks Genny. For taking care of it *and* for putting up with me. I'm sorry for what I said on Sunday."

Genny's back stiffens and she looks back and forth between me and her sister. Her eyes hold questions she doesn't voice, so I shrug my shoulders, causing her to relax a bit. "Um, thanks, Callie. Are you feeling all right?"

"I'm fine. Sometimes I forget the world doesn't revolve around me, but I just remembered. I'm gonna go upstairs to study and let you guys finish your movie. Nice to meet you, Walker!"

Genny eyes me skeptically, whispering, "What did she say to you?"

I whisper back, keeping things suspenseful and secretive. "She told me you're an amazing sister who cooks her special food and takes care of her problems."

Scoffing and shaking her head, she gets up and moves to the kitchen, bringing back another beer and flipping off light switches on her way past them. The only light in the room is now coming from the paused scene on the TV. "I don't really believe you, but she apologized for Sunday, and that's *huge*. So thank you for whatever happened while I was upstairs."

I try to suppress my victorious smile as she settles back against me without a second thought. After I twist off the cap of the beer she brought me, she steals the bottle, taking a drink and handing it back before resting her head on my chest with a sigh. "I forgot to get the remote."

"Want me to get it?" I offer, even though moving is the last thing I want to do right now.

"No." Laying her hand flat on my chest, she holds me down, just in case I wasn't planning on listening. "I like where you're at. I'll get it, I just wanna take a minute to enjoy how good you smell."

I wrap my arm around her shoulders again with a chuckle, really glad I put on cologne tonight. "Tell me about your sister."

"What do you wanna know?"

"Describe her to me. Her personality. You probably know her better than anyone."

She sighs, chewing on that bottom lip, and it affects me in a very different way than when I watched Callie do it. They might look alike, but I'm not drawn to Callie. Genny, however, is like my beacon of light in the darkness of a storm. She's all I can see, the only thing I'm pushing toward.

"Callie's smart and curious. Too curious for her own good. But she's usually really thoughtful and compassionate. She's someone who can argue both sides of any situation, ya know? She can put herself in anybody's shoes."

"You sound proud of her." I'm not surprised that she says nothing about Callie being ungrateful. Nothing about Callie being a brat or ruining her life.

"I am. She's almost done with her nursing degree and she wants to get some real hands-on experience before applying for PA school. Sometimes it's annoying to come home after a long day and pick up after her and take care of all the stupid little things that she just forgets about or doesn't know how to take care of. But then I think about how she's creating this amazing opportunity for herself and I know it'll all be worth it in the long run."

"What about your brother?"

"Calvin's the funny one," she explains, her fingers trailing circles on my arm. "He can make anyone smile, no matter what's going on. And he's the social butterfly, always at some event or party. He knows *everyone*. He probably knows you somehow. He's does HVAC work, and he just got his second promotion in three years. He's a hard worker, but it's only so he can play even harder during his time off."

"How would you describe yourself?"

She scoffs. "An enabler. Cynical. Boring. Stand-offish."

Pushing the hair away from her face, I stop her pity party in its tracks. "How would *Myra* describe you?"

"Myra?" Genny pushes up from my chest to look at me. "She says I'm kind, determined, and focused. That it's really hard for me to let people in. I've heard her call me a survivor before, but I think that's crap. We're all survivors. We all do what we have to do to get through each day."

"Would everyone go as far as you do?"

"Probably," she says with a shrug. "What about you?"

"How would *I* describe you?"

"I meant how would you describe yourself, but sure."

Looking in her eyes, I think about the very little I know about her. She's told me almost nothing. Her sister told me more tonight than Genny has. But can I figure some things out from the conversations we've had?

One thing's a definite. "You're stubborn."

She grants me a smile, and I continue on. "You don't like to mix business and pleasure, even though you can't always tell the difference between the two. You'll do anything for your sister, even if it's depriving yourself from a food-induced orgasm because she shouldn't eat the food you love. You know nothing about cars but talking about them turns you on. I would bet you like kids, or maybe what they represent. And I would guess the reason you're so straightforward at times, is because underneath it all, you're overly sensitive and insecure."

Glaring at me for the *sensitive and insecure* comment, she grabs the beer out of my hand, taking another drink. She offers it back to me, and I watch her eyes as I do the same, wishing I could taste her lips instead of the beer. Those green eyes dart back to my mouth as I hand it back to her. She may be offended by what I said about her, but it doesn't stop her from wanting me to kiss her.

And with my limited experience with her, I know she's now either going to sigh in disappointment when I don't, *or...*

Her hand gently lands on my face, cupping it as she switches which hip she's sitting on. Leaning on top of me, her back to the TV, her palm on my cheek, her gaze moves back and forth from my mouth to my eyes.

"Didn't we talk about you not touching me?"

"You talked. I ignored you."

Very true. She likes ignoring any of my comments about how she shouldn't touch me. About how I'm *not* going to kiss her. About how we're *just friends*.

"What's your game plan here, G? I feel like maybe you're trying to alter our relationship status again. Do I need to keep you away from alcohol altogether? You didn't have much, but your reaction tonight seems to be a milder version of Saturday night..."

Her lips twitch into a smile as she admits, "I love how you call me G."

"I love how you keep pretending there's nothing between us, even when you try to make us more than *just friends* every time I see you."

The smile turns into a smirk, but her eyes don't waver. "I wanna kiss you, Friend."

"That's not a good idea."

Her eyes narrow in self-doubt before she asks, "Are you seeing someone else, Walker?"

"Are *you*?" I counter, knowing she sees more than *one* someone.

She looks away, but not for long. "I'm not seeing anyone like I see you."

"Not good enough, G."

"I can't even *kiss* you until I'm not seeing anyone else?"

She says it like it's physically impossible, so I try to look at the big picture and get some perspective... Nope. Still can't do it. I'm not gonna budge on this, not while she's sleeping with other guys. But maybe if I understood *why* she's so intensely set on her reasons, I can help her move past them.

"Why don't you date, Genny? Tell me that."

She *visibly* gives in. It's like she's defeated, lost the battle *and* the war. Her shoulders slump, her face goes slack, and she leans on me fully, not even bothering to try to support herself. "It's *too much*, Walker. I've got so much to worry about. I work full-time. I cook and clean the house. I take care of everything Callie needs me to. Appointments, medications, insurance... I make sure her uniforms are clean for work. I make sure she's doing her homework and she has time to be a kid because I wish to God I had someone telling me to do that when I was her age. I pay all the bills, I do the grocery shopping, I try to have half a life by going out once or twice a month with Myra. I don't need to worry about any*thing* or any*one* else. I already have too much on my plate."

"What happened with the cop?"

"Paul?"

"He was your last boyfriend, correct?"

She groans in annoyance, flopping back against the couch. I instantly miss her warmth, but I'm more interested in getting her answer than having her body back on top of mine. That's too much temptation, and only one of us in interested in *not* rushing into sex.

Rubbing a hand down her face, she looks at me through the crack between her fingers. "If I jump through all your hoops, you'd better be the best damn kisser there ever was."

I can't help the smile that takes over my face. Her answer means she's at least considering jumping through *all my hoops.*

"Paul told me I was only enabling Calvin and Callie by helping them through college. That it was time I either kicked them out, since Calvin was over eighteen and Callie was almost eighteen, or that I moved in with him and let them fend for themselves. He wanted to ask me to marry him, and he thought that telling me to stop being there for my family would let me know he was serious about starting a life with me. A life for *us,* as he put it."

He thought telling Genny that giving up her family would prove he was serious about her? Maybe Genny didn't tell me, but Callie made it very clear that family is Genny's number one priority. And the way Genny jumped up to call the pharmacy about her sister's meds only proves it.

"He didn't want to prove he was serious about starting a life with you. He wanted proof you were serious about *him.* He wanted you to put him first instead of your family. There's no other reason for him to ask that of you."

"Thank you!" she cries, obviously not used to having someone on her side.

"First of all, I would never ask that of you, Genny. *Never.* Family comes first to me, too, whether it's my parents, my sister, or my nephews. Second, you don't have to worry about me. I'm twenty-nine years old and have been on my own for ten years. I'm pretty self-sufficient at this point. You don't need to take care of me, or worry about my feelings, or what I'm thinking, because I'll tell you. I respect that you have other obligations and can't give me all your time. I'm not asking for a lot, G. I'm just asking for you to give me a chance."

"To give you a chance by not seeing *any*one else, in *any* way, and *dating* you."

"Yes."

"Do you realize how crazy I'm going to get without any kind of stress relief?"

I pull her back against me, the way she was, with her back to the TV, facing me. "When you say *stress relief,* are you talking about your *boytoys,* as Callie put it?"

"Yes. They're my stress relief."

"Is that all sex is to you?"

"Yeah." She shrugs without an ounce of guilt or shame.

I might have my work cut out for me with this girl. There's got to be another way for her to cope with stress, though. Wait, there is, isn't there? "I thought you were a girl who could take care of that yourself."

"It's not the same," she states with wide, innocent eyes. "Not even a little."

"I could understand that if you had an emotional connection with these guys, but if you're just using them for sex... Don't some girls prefer their battery-operated boyfriends to the real deal?"

"I don't have anything like that."

An idea pops into my head. "What if I get you one? Try it out and let me know if you think you can give up the boytoys then. And when we get to the point where I'm your *only* boytoy, you can show me how you use it."

She chews on her lip again, considering that idea. I should turn away, stop staring at the way her teeth are so white against the pink of that soft flesh. Stop imagining what it would feel like to pull it into my own mouth.

"You wanna buy me a vibrator?" she cautiously asks, clarifying my offer.

"If it'll help you stop seeing other guys, yes."

"I'm pretty sure friends don't buy friends vibrators."

"I'm trying to be *more* than your friend, G," I explain gently. "In a way we can both live with."

Watching her stare move from my eyes down to my mouth, I pray she agrees to this, because I'm dying to kiss her. And knowing how badly she wants me to isn't helping.

"So, if Chad texts me..."

"Ignore it. Better yet, text *him*. Tell him you're seeing someone, so you're no longer available."

"And I can try out this vibrator before making up my mind."

Doing my best to not picture her *trying it out*, I tell her, "Yeah, but don't take too long."

"If I agree to this, can I kiss you tonight?"

Will I be able to kiss her and let her go if she doesn't stop fucking Chad and whoever else she texts? Will I be able to stop *seeing* her? Because let's face it, I won't have to just stop kissing her. I haven't known Genny as her own person, instead of one of the girls that randomly waltz in and out of my apartment at odd hours, for very long. But there's something about her that makes me feel like I have to figure out all her secrets. That I need to know everything about her.

I wonder if taking this fork in the road we're on right now is detouring us away from a disastrous ending, or taking us closer to it.

"Not tonight, G. Once you promise me you'll stop seeing whoever else you're seeing. Then you can kiss me."

"I'm not really *seeing* anyone..."

I correct myself for *her* sake, even if we're both very aware of what I meant. "Then not until you stop *fucking* everyone you're fucking. No sex. No kissing. No dates or secretive texts. I'm not gonna share you, G. In *any* way. You're either all in this, or you're not in it at all, but that's for you to decide."

"You're awfully demanding for our first date."

The corners of my mouth tip up in a smile. Now I *know* I've got her thinking the way I want her to. "I thought you didn't date."

"There's this guy..." she explains with an exaggerated sigh and roll of her eyes. "He's pretty strict with his dating rules, but he might be the world's best kisser. I'm considering breaking *my* rules to find out if he is or not."

"Yeah? He sounds like a pretty lucky guy if you're willing to do that for him," I tell her, showing her I know this is a big step and I'm not unappreciative of her possible sacrifice.

"He also said he'd buy me a vibrator. Ya know, to help with my stress levels. I get really bad migraines if I get too stressed out, so it had better work damn well."

"I'll bet he'll gladly give you a hand with that after you prove he's your one and only."

"Considering how turned on I get whenever he's around, he'd better be taking me to get this vibrator soon."

Chuckling at her confession, that she's not at all nervous about admitting, I let her eyes stare into mine. She's making a point, making sure I understand that she's agreeing to my terms, but I need to make it happen fast.

"I'll take you tonight, G. Or tomorrow. Or the day after that. Anytime you want, we'll go."

"Take me tomorrow," she concedes, turning away from me to grab the remote. "I can try it out tomorrow night and let you know how it goes on Sunday. I'm gonna let you know in person, though, so if it works out, I can finally kiss you. I'm sure you can make time in your schedule for a measly five minutes to kiss the girl who's giving up all her stress relievers *and* breaking every one of her rules for you."

"It'll take longer than five minutes, G. But I'll definitely put you on my schedule."

She settles back into me with a smile, starting the movie again. I don't care about the movie anymore. I'm thinking about Genny in an adult store with me. Or Sunday, when I'll finally get to kiss her.

There's no way that kiss won't happen. I'm gonna buy her the best damn vibrator there ever was, just to make sure I get her mouth on mine.

Genny

My sister is being strangely nice to me this morning.

She made me *breakfast*. She brought it to me while I was still in bed. She knocked quietly on my door, and when I answered, she came in with a smile on her face and scrambled eggs on a plate. There's even a steaming hot cup of coffee.

"Morning, Genny. Are you hungry?"

"Ah, sure..." My eyes roam over the tray she's placing in front of me, then back up to study her face. "What's going on? Are you in trouble for something?"

"I just thought I'd do something for you for a change."

She doesn't react to my intense stare, so I verbalize the accusation running around in my brain. "Why are you acting so weird? What did you and Walker talk about last night?"

Her legs join mine under the covers. "Not much. He asked about my meds, what kind of food I could eat, and how I handle all of that in this crazy grab-and-go world we live in. Made me remember how much you do for me every single day."

"Aw, Callie..." I sigh, shaking my head at her grateful words. "I want school to be what you focus on, not what there is to eat. I'm just trying to make it easier for you to make a good life for yourself."

"Which is something you never got to do," she reminds me quietly, knowing I hate talking about anything I gave up to keep my family together.

It wasn't a *choice*. It was something I *had* to do, whether I wanted to or not.

"I may have eavesdropped on you guys for a couple minutes after I told you I was going upstairs. I don't deserve to be described the way you did after I called you a whore. I'm sorry. I know you don't let yourself have real relationships, so you can focus on taking care of me."

My sister leans her head on my shoulder, wiping at her eyes, and I wonder what the hell has gotten in to her. Callie hardly ever apologizes, at least not to *me*. Squeezing her against my side with my arm around her shoulders, I tell her, "Thank you for saying you're sorry. You really hurt me when you said that."

"I like Walker. Why are you pretending to be just friends with him? He seems really nice."

"What did he say to you?"

Shrugging at my question, she eyes my coffee, and I hand her the mug. "He didn't say much, but he talked to me like I was an equal. Like what I said was worth something. He didn't act like I was stupid just because I'm a kid letting my big sister take care of my problems."

I haven't heard Walker talk to a lot of people, but I'm glad she pointed this out to me. Paul was always a bit patronizing to people he thought were in less desirable jobs than he had. Like they weren't as good as he was. And he always spoke to my siblings like they were just kids, like their opinion didn't matter, even though Calvin was an adult and Callie almost was.

I forgot about that.

"I really like Walker, too," I finally admit.

"Are you gonna give up your boytoys to give him a chance?"

Narrowing my eyes at her word choice, I turn to fully look at her. "Just how much did you overhear last night?"

"Enough to know that you have plans today... And later tonight."

Trying not to feel embarrassed about my sister knowing I'm going to be testing out a vibrator for the first time tonight, I reach over and pinch her arm. "Then you already know I'm going to give him a chance, brat!"

She rubs her arm with a smile as she gets out of my bed. "I love you, Genny!" She sneaks out of my room, taking my coffee with her.

I love that noisy girl, too.

Genny

"Will this be your first vibrator?"

Last night, it didn't seem this personal while we were talking about sex and various toys to help achieve my favorite kind of stress relief. But today, in Walker's car, with the sun shining brightly down on me through the sunroof and windshield, it seems like an *incredibly* personal conversation to have with a guy I haven't even kissed yet.

If he's buying this toy for me, does that give him a right to know? Deciding it does, I answer with my eyes planted firmly on anything outside the window, as far away from his as they can get. "I've never had or used any sex toys."

"Have you ever been in an adult store before?"

"Once," I admit, scowling at the memory. "It was a long time ago, when I was in college. On a dare, I had to go in and buy something."

"What'd you buy?"

That was another life. One where I was only partially responsible for any consequences I ran into. One where I had dreams and friends and fun times. I didn't give the purchase much thought at the time. I thought it would be one daring memory among many. "A set of dice, I think? They were at the checkout counter and the first thing I saw."

Walker laughs, side-eyeing me again. "This is gonna be fun," he promises with a grin.

How often does *he* frequent the adult store? How many *other girls* has he brought here? Does he make a habit of buying girls sex toys before he'll kiss them?

Here I thought I was special...

After parking, Walker holds my hand as we cross the asphalt to the entrance. How sweet is that? I didn't know people actually held hands anymore. There's something to it. I like the way his hand wraps around mine, how it feels against my skin. I like the way his hand is bigger than mine. It makes me feel like he's protecting me and leading me. No one leads me. At least not before Walker. I've been on my own since my parents died, stumbling down the wrong road just as often, if not more so, than picking the correct one.

The door to the store has a warning sign on it about needing to be of legal age to enter and how we're under video surveillance. Awesome... *Nothing* about this is in my comfort zone. Now, I'm really glad Walker is holding my hand, because as soon as we get past the door, I'm clutching it like it's a lifeline. Like if he lets go, I'll melt into a puddle of embarrassment on the floor, just for stepping foot in a place like this.

He looks back with a knowing smirk, since he's practically dragging me along behind him. "You ok back there, Genny?"

When he uses my name, I cringe. Which only makes him laugh harder. "What're you so nervous about?"

"I don't want people to know me here."

"Why not?"

"Because they'll think that I..." Looking around, I shrug my shoulders, not wanting to say the words out loud. "Ya know..."

"Have sex?" he asks with a raised eyebrow. "Oh no! Not *that*! Everyone, look! This gorgeous girl holding my hand likes sex!"

Desperately trying to hold onto the warm feeling that flooded my body when he called me gorgeous, I turn away from the guy standing at the end of the aisle, who's now smiling in a very creepy way at us. With the nod of acknowledgement he sends our way, any warm feeling I had turns quickly into mortification.

"Lucky you," he tells Walker, his eyes begging my clothes to fall right off my body. Crossing my arm over my boobs with the hand that's not currently clutching Walker's, I force them to stay firmly in place.

"Yes, lucky me," Walker replies, his voice low and directed at only me. His eyes are sparkling with humor and his lips are twitching into a reluctant smirk. After our new stalker leaves the aisle, Walker does his best to reassure me. "Everyone has sex, G. There's nothing wrong with being in this store and experimenting with different toys so you can take control of your own orgasms."

"Fine," I hiss, wanting to be done with this conversation *and* the task at hand. "That doesn't mean you have to broadcast it!"

"That was just for fun."

I bravely shoulder my way past him, so we can get out of this house of debauchery as quickly as possible. "Oh, *Lord*," I whisper, eyeing the huge selection of plastic dicks spread out before me. "I didn't know there would be so many... And in such different sizes. Holy smokes!"

My eyes pass over a huge black dildo that would never fit inside a normal vagina. It's bigger than my *fist* and I shudder at the thought of anyone coming anywhere near me with that thing. "How am I supposed to pick one of these? There's like a *million* here!"

"Perfect!" a chipper voice tweets from behind us. "I can help with that. It's kind of my specialty."

Who the fuck specializes in helping people pick out vibrators?

When I turn around, I catch sight of the unique *expert*. She's a little older than Callie, with jet black hair that hits the tops of her shoulders, and a confident smile. She's wearing a name tag that reads, *Hi! I'm Maggie!*

"Will this be for both of you?"

Raising my wide-eyes to Walker, I find him wearing a very happy grin. He's obviously enjoying my discomfort. "Just for Genny," he replies. "At least for now. It'll be her first one."

"Oh, great!" Maggie chirps, excitement lighting up her brown eyes. "There are some things you should always consider when buying any toy. First, what's it made of? Silicone is what I usually recommend, but a hard plastic is also super easy to clean. The silicone feels more realistic, though."

"I have to *clean* this toy?"

Maggie smiles at my naivety. "Considering how you'll be using it, you wouldn't want to use something that wasn't clean, right? Having sanitary toys is as much a part of safe sex as using condoms."

"Ok," I breath, already feeling like I'm way out of my element. And I thought I was an expert at all things sex. I was *so* wrong. And I'm not sure I'm ready for whatever else I'm going to learn from this young, outgoing girl. "What else should I consider?"

"What kind of sensations do you like most when you're getting it on?"

What did she just ask me?!

Is this for *real*?

Walker squeezes my hand, and I turn to look at him with an incredulous stare. My normally easy-to-find neutral expression has abandoned me. *His* expression is one of amusement because he's enjoying this. *Really* enjoying this. "I think she's trying to find out if you like external or internal stimulation," he informs me with that mocking grin.

"That's a good start," Maggie agrees. "But also, do you prefer localized sensations that are more intense, or stimuli that's spread around? Do you follow a specific routine when you go to town, or do you browse a different shop every time?"

How I'm possibly going to answer these questions in front of Walker? It's going to be hard enough to give Maggie such intimate knowledge about me, but with Walker standing right here, listening to my every word?

This isn't at all how I pictured today going. I figured there would be a selection of vibrators, sure, but not a whole damn *wall* of them.

Realizing we're still attached, I open my hand, trying to let Walker go. He holds on, that knowing smirk only growing wider. "You wouldn't be willing to walk away while I have this incredibly personal conversation with Maggie, would you, Friend?"

"Hell, no, G. This is way too much fun. Consider it my way of doing some research for our future endeavors."

Figured that wouldn't work, but I had to try.

I push him partially behind me to at least *pretend* he's not listening to this conversation. That he's not hearing exactly how I touch myself alone in the dark while probably thinking of him and all the things he won't yet do to me.

"Let's start over," I shyly suggest to my vibrator guide. "One question at a time, please."

A patient smile crosses Maggie's face. "Let's start with where. Inside, outside, or both?"

"Umm, both," I admit quietly. Hopefully quietly enough that Walker can't hear. "Flying solo, usually more external, though."

"If you get something for external use only, you can't use it inside, but massagers for inside can be used inside *and* outside. For vibrators that work best internally, there's a few different types to narrow down. There's just the basic vibrator in a ton of options," she says, pointing to a specific section. "Then there's ones for reaching the G spot." Another section. "And last, but certainly not least, the ones for dual action. These provide you with external stimulation while they're inside you," she explains while pointing to yet *another* section with an even wider variety of choices.

This category must be the winner of the popularity contest.

"This is too much," I tell her, instantly overwhelmed. "I like sex. Real sex with real guys. This is just to get me through life without casual sex until *this guy*," I say, pointing my thumb over my shoulder at Walker, "decides he's made me wait long enough to do the deed with me."

Maggie purses her lips in thought, considering my confession. "Let me get a few options around for you. Just to narrow it down so it's not as overwhelming. I'll meet you at the front whenever you're ready, ok?"

"Sure."

Turning away from her, I find Walker watching me with cautious eyes. His hand is still holding mine and after realizing I'm squeezing it tightly, I relax my fingers without letting go.

"How do *you* do stroke it?" I demand, wanting to level the playing field a little.

He doesn't even flinch. "With a firm grip."

Smothering a grin, I press for more. "Do you like soft and slow or hard and fast?"

"Depends on how close I am," he says, a smile hinting at his lips. "What do you prefer?"

"Depends on what I'm looking for. Am I in a hurry and I just need to just get off, or do I have all day and I want to relax and really enjoy myself?"

Walker tugs me closer by our enclosed hands, sliding his free arm around my waist and leaning towards me. My breath catches in my throat, thinking *maybe* he's going to finally kiss me. Instead, his face moves past mine to whisper in my ear, and I suppress a sigh of disappointment. "Do you have any idea how much I'd love to see you *really enjoy yourself?*"

"Do you have any idea how much I want you to kiss me right now?"

"Yeah," he answers with a smile. "I *do* have an idea about that. Tomorrow, G. After you enjoy yourself tonight."

Sliding my hand out of his, I lock my arms around his neck, enjoying how close he has me pulled against him. "I have an idea," I murmer as he crooks an eyebrow up.

"What's that?"

"How about *you* enjoy yourself at the same time *I'm* enjoying myself tonight?"

He chuckles quietly against me, shaking his head in disbelief. "So, we'll just blow right past kissing and copping a feel, and move straight to mutual masturbation?"

"It's not like we'll be able to see or hear each other. Knowing you're doing it too, will help me feel less... afraid to try it. And if it were up to me, we'd be kissing pros by now, so blowing past that is totally your fault."

His eyes twinkle as he contemplates my proposal. "If I'm at home, and I know you're trying out your new toy, you won't be able to stop me. I'm going to be thinking about how you're using it and wondering how much you're enjoying it. I have a picture on my phone to help get me started if my imagination can't keep up for some reason."

I try not to blush at the fact he kept that picture and is planning on referring to it to help get himself turned on later. "That's a yes, right?"

"It's a most likely," he corrects me. He rests his forehead against mine and I marvel at how close we are without having done *anything* physical yet.

This guy is *trouble*. This guy is working all my secrets from me and using them against me before I even realize he knows what they are.

Walker presses a kiss to my nose and I glare at him. That's not the kind of kiss I want. Not even close. Smiling at my reaction, he whispers, "You're adorable when you're mad at me."

"You're a tease, and it's not adorable at all. It's incredibly frustrating."

"You like me anyway." He unlocks my arms and puts his hand back around mine. "Let's go pick out your new toy. Gotta make sure you don't stay frustrated. And I can't wait to see what I'm picturing you using tonight."

In the end, I pick out a smaller, curved, purple wand. I like that it doesn't look like a penis. I like that it's simple and uncomplicated. Maggie says it's a great option because it's waterproof, wireless, and rechargeable, plus it comes with a cleaner, so it's everything I need with one purchase.

When she tells us the total, my eyes nearly pop out of my head. The cost of this vibrator rivals that of the car battery I purchased last week.

"Holy smokes! Are you kidding me?"

Maggie and Walker share a smile as my new toy is boxed up and put in a discreet bag. Walker, ever the gentleman and buyer of expensive sex toys, holds the door for me on the way out, then takes my hand again as we make our way through the sparse parking lot.

"I don't know how comfortable I am with this anymore."

"Why?" he demands, holding the car door open for me, as well.

"Because that little... *toy*! Is really expensive! You shouldn't be spending that much money on me when I don't know if I'll be able to give up the real thing for an overpriced plastic dick and date you like you want me to."

"I'm willing to bet you will. And given enough time, I'd bet good money you'll even thank me for it."

Rolling my eyes as we pull out of the parking lot, I consider the fact that today, he's proving to be somewhat arrogant. Not that I mind. I like a guy who gets a little cocky occasionally, as long as he can back it up.

That's what I'm questioning.

How can he be so sure that little massaging wand is going to make me come so amazingly that I'll be willing to give up three guys who know just what to do to get me off?

Walker doesn't know it's three, at least I hope he doesn't, but thanks to Callie's comments, he definitely suspects it's more than one.

"Besides. It's already yours," he reminds me. "You may as well see what kind of job it can do."

"This is the weirdest date I've ever been on, just so you know."

"Good. I like knowing I'm memorable."

"You're memorable, all right," I promise as I slowly get more and more comfortable the farther we travel from the store we just left.

He slides his hand back over mine. "If I'm so memorable, when was the first time you ever saw me?"

I pull my hand free, letting my fingers fall in the space between each of his, my palm to the back of his hand. Uncomfortable silence fills the car, and his fingers squeeze mine as he waits for my answer.

"That night at the bar," I whisper, keeping my eyes on our hands. "The first time I went home with Chad."

"Hmph. I didn't think you'd noticed me."

"I did," I admit, remembering him and that night easily. I was more interested in him than Chad, but Walker's eyes held so much more than lust. Walker's eyes held *questions*, and all I wanted was a trip to Orgasm-ville.

"Then why'd you go home with *him*?"

"You're not the type of guy who would fuck me the same night we met."

"Oh, Genny," he sighs. "How long have you been doing this? Since you broke up with the cop?"

"Not quite. I took some time to get over him first."

"You go home with a lot of strangers, or do you stick to your regulars?"

"Are you judging me?"

"Not at all. I'm trying to figure out how many guys I'm up against to convince you that a real relationship is better than what you're used to."

Tucking my hand into my lap, I stare out the window. He says he's not judging me, but I didn't believe him the first time he said it, and I still don't now. "I think I'm done answering your questions about my sex life."

He sighs, staring out the windshield before turning his gaze back to meet mine for a second. "You wanna ask me some, instead?"

Jumping at the chance, because it's been almost entirely one-sided so far, I ask the first question I think of. "Were you in a relationship with the last person you had sex with?"

He side-eyes me with a shake of his head. "No." Shooting him a hypocritical look, I watch as he shrugs his shoulders. "I was looking for one, but it didn't work out."

"When was the last time you had sex?"

"Last year."

"*What?!*"

He simply looks at me, knowing I wouldn't be able to give an answer anywhere near as acceptable considering our circumstances. Thinking about how attractive he is, how confident and sweet, arrogant and funny... Why are girls not throwing themselves at him?

They probably *are*, he just doesn't want them.

Why is he after *me*?

Does he like the chase, the challenge of something unattainable? What happens when he catches me? Does he get bored after he's won the prize? Or is he as attracted to me as I am to him? Am I something he's wanted for a while, but always thought was out of reach, and now that we're getting a chance to explore this, he's making sure I'm giving him a *real* chance, instead of just a half-assed one?

"Wait," I ask, repeating his explanation. "If you wanted a relationship, but it didn't work out, does that mean that even if we end up not being compatible, you'll have sex with me?"

"We're compatible, G."

"You don't know that. We barely know each other at all."

"If we weren't compatible, you wouldn't be afraid of how this is going to end."

I had already forgotten about that. I remember it now, the tension in the air when he was just trying to give me his number, the way I hesitated, somehow knowing that he was going to change me in ways I didn't think I was ready for.

I'm still not sure I'm ready for it, but he's already doing it.

Matt texted me last night, and I *ignored* it.

If it had been Ben, ignoring a text wouldn't be that much of a surprise. I ignore his texts half the time, because sex with Ben is always a process. But Matt? I hardly ever ignore his texts. Just like he hardly ever ignores mine.

And this bag between my feet?! I'm going to take paddling the canoe to a whole new level for the man next to me. And I'm going to talk about it to him, a guy I like. Hell, I've already talked about masturbation more with Walker than I have with anyone in my *life*. And I sent him a *picture*! Of *me*! With my fingers in a very inappropriate place! Even if he couldn't see my fingers, there was no question what they were doing.

I guess I have no one to blame except myself for where this *relationship* is going. I'm the one who pushed it into any kind of sexual territory.

He's right. We *are* compatible. In a very scary, but very real way.

And I really like him.

Plus, I wanna find out how good of a kisser he is.

Pushing the bag around the floor with my feet, I let myself imagine what it might feel like when I use my new toy tonight. What something other than a dick attached to a real human will feel like. Will the vibrations really make it as good, or even better? Will the fact that I'm in control of every little move make me enjoy it more, or will it just frustrate me? I can't imagine it'll be as good as actual sex with an actual guy, but I'll try it.

To get a kiss from Walker, I'll try almost *anything*.

"What else are you doing today?" I ask, knowing I'm drastically changing the subject.

"I was thinking of taking you out for an early dinner if you don't have anywhere you need to be. Then I'm watching my nephews, so Reese and her husband can have a night out."

A small smile washes over my face as I think about Walker watching his nephews. His face lights up when he talks about Zeke and all his little boy adventures. I wish I could see him with them.

It's way too early for that, though.

If I'm thinking its *way too early* for anything, then I'm already thinking we're going somewhere...

"If we don't go down in flames, can I meet these kiddos someday? You make them sound pretty spectacular."

"Definitely. You can meet my whole family. We usually all get together at some point every weekend."

I miss that. Family get-togethers. Calvin moved half an hour away and is usually so busy he can't make it back into town whenever Callie and I have time off together. Summer's coming, though, so Callie won't have classes. She'll be working more, but maybe I can arrange something so the three of us can get together. We're a small family, but we're all we have. I'll have to text him and see when he can come see us. It'll probably be easier for Callie and me to work around his schedule.

"You're not seeing anyone else, are you?"

Walker smiles in my direction as he reaches for my hand again. "Only you, G. I love that you were jealous."

"I wasn't jealous," I huff pointlessly.

"You're a rotten liar. Do you have time to go to dinner with me?"

"Yes."

"Good. My friend, Kane, manages a restaurant I wanna take you to, and we're almost there."

Fidgeting in my seat, I try to hide my nerves. "I'm gonna meet one of your friends?"

Walker tries and fails to hide a grin. "He's already a big fan of yours, so you don't need to be nervous."

"Why is he already a fan of mine?"

He hesitates for a second, trying to act like he's focusing on traffic as he pulls into a Barbeque joint, but I know better. There's a reason. Walker just doesn't want me to know about it yet. Instead of an explanation, he offers, "Why don't we go find out?"

While he's parking the car, I glare at him across the console. He smiles, and I remember he thinks I'm adorable when I'm mad. Damn it all to hell. I'm gonna have to work on my mad face. It didn't work on Callie this morning, and it has the *opposite* effect of what I'm aiming for with Walker.

Walker leads me inside, where he walks up to the bar and says something to the bartender. The guy behind the counter gives him a large grin and a high five. We find a seat while the bartender disappears to find Kane, and the hostess makes her way to us with eyes only for Walker and a flirtatious smile on her lips.

"Walker," she purrs, totally ignoring me. "It's been a while. How are you?"

"I'm good, Chloe. How're you?"

Chloe. I instantly hate her.

Deep down, I know it's not her, but the easy way Walker smiles at her. They make useless small talk for a minute before Walker introduces me as his date, which somewhat calms my racing heart, but does little to settle my desire to kick her pretty little face in.

"Genny," Chloe sneers. "Nice to meet you."

"Likewise." I flash my best smile her way, hoping she can see from my eyes the way I'm giving her a slow, torturous death in my mind.

A chuckle breaks through our murderous stare-down and Chloe and I both disengage our weapon of choice to eye Walker. It only causes him to break into a full-blown laugh, the chuckle easily forgotten. Watching Chloe stomp away from our table in her stiletto heels, Walker tries to calm himself, and *me*, down. "Put your claws away, G! There's nothing there for you to worry about, I promise you."

"I was trying to be *nice*," I grumble, glaring at her long after she disappeared out of sight.

"Nice, like a panther stalking her prey."

"Whatever. She was flirting with you while I'm sitting *right here!*"

"Walker!" a booming voice echoes around us, followed by a very tall, very broad, very dark man I can only assume is Kane.

Standing up from the booth, Walker and Kane partake in some weird handshake that looks second-nature to them. They've probably been friends for decades, I decide from their ritualistic greeting. Eventually, Kane turns in my direction and his eyes easily roam my face and all of my body exposed above the table.

"Hey, it's your girl!"

"Hopefully," Walker replies as I narrow my eyes. "We haven't reached a definite conclusion on that yet."

Ignoring the fact that Walker's apparently already telling people I'm his, I stand up to introduce myself. "I'm Genny," I offer, holding out my hand in greeting. Once Kane wraps his large paw around mine, I ask so very sweetly, "Why are you a big fan of mine, Kane?"

A grin takes over his entire being, and Kane looks back at Walker. "She doesn't know?"

Walker simply shakes his head with a sheepish grin.

Kane sits beside me, pushing the menus Chloe brought us out of his way. He starts telling me a story, using his giant hands to help him get his point across. "Last weekend, me and two of my buddies are out playing pool, waiting for this sorry excuse of a man to show up. Walker here has been pretty boring lately, so when he showed up late, we all figured he was out with his nephews, wishing he had some rug rats of his own to chase around. But then he's on his phone half the night instead of playing with us. Worked in our favor, because he sucked, and he had to buy drinks all night long."

Walker scoffs, but doesn't deny anything.

"Anyway," Kane continues, pulling my eyes his way again. "He was sitting at the bar, looking all depressed as shit, caressing his damn phone. I figured I'd better find out what's wrong and cheer him up a little."

Walker rolls his eyes and shakes his head at Kane's description of their outing. He catches me watching him and gives me a smile, but there's a tightness about his eyes. Where exactly do I fit into this story that has him nervous? I turn my attention back to Kane to hopefully find out.

"Walker tells me there's this girl he likes, but she's drunk-texting him, begging him to come over and play with her."

Ok... From my texts, I get that I may have been begging, but I never said I wanted him to *play* with me. It may have been implied, but still...

"He's staring at his phone, caressing this dark, locked screen like some pathetic douche. He's got the icon telling him he has a text, but he doesn't know if he wants to open it. See, he really wants to go play with the girl, and he's tired of resisting, right? I finally tell him to just open it anyway, cause I want to know how bad she wants him."

I wanted him so badly I did things I never would have dreamed of...

"He eventually grows a pair and opens her text. Well, hot *damn* if she didn't send him a picture of just what he was missing out on when he refused to come over. You are one confident, sexy-as-hell woman, Genny!"

Wait. *Kane* saw it?! *Kane*? Oh my fuck!

My eyes flash to Walker; he's trying not to laugh. Doing my best to keep control of my neutral expression, I slowly look back toward Kane, who also has a huge smile on his face and is still talking to me. "I'm wishing you'd taken off a little more; that bra was pretty, but I'm betting what's underneath is even prettier. I have feeling Walker is damn glad you didn't, though."

I have no idea what to think, let alone *say*.

As far as I can tell, I have two options, here. I can drop my head in my hands and cry, or I can laugh with these two, who are now in a very small group of people who've seen me in a very intimate position.

At least he called me sexy, right?

"I guess I'll have to send a warning text from now on before I send Walker any half naked photos of me."

Kane laughs. "That'll take all the fun out of it for me, Miss April."

Walker just raises those beautiful expressive eyebrows, silently asking if I really plan on sending him more.

"Miss April?" I ask, turning my attention back to Walker's friend.

"You should be the centerfold of the month, Genny girl. You made me so hard in that half second I got to see your sweet little body..."

"Oh Lord," I finally cave, giving up my couldn't-care-less act. "Erase that from your mind! You weren't supposed to see it! Had I not been wasted, Walker never would have seen it either! The picture never would have been *taken*!"

"Never, April. I'll be picturing you like that as you walk down the aisle at your wedding."

"Whoa, whoa, whoa!" I abruptly hold up both hands to stop this at *once*. "I'm just starting to consider *dating* again! Let's not ruin this night with talk of weddings or marriage, please!"

Kane gives me a manipulative smile. "I'll only stop if you give me that menu. You don't need to even look at it. I'll make sure you get the best food you've ever had. I'll be seeing your O face again tonight, but it'll be covered in my signature barbeque sauce!"

And I thought Walker was arrogant! Handing over the menu, I try to hide the grin that's taking over my face. Kane may be crude, but he's still giving me compliments. And he's funny. And he's Walker's friend. Walker is a good guy. I can't see him being friends with a total dickhead.

Kane pushes himself out of the booth. "You want a drink to go with your meal?"

"Right now, a drink sounds great."

"Awesome. I'll make sure it's a good one. I know you have to be drunk to take half naked pics of yourself."

"Go away!" I beg with a laugh, physically pushing his leg to get him moving away from our booth. Shaking my head, I look over to find Walker quietly laughing at me as his friend walks away.

"So, that's Kane."

"You let him see that picture?"

"I didn't *let* him see anything. It just happened. A warning before pictures like that would be *great*."

I shake my head. "I doubt I'll be sending anymore pictures like that."

"Don't stop because of me. I thought it was a great picture. Some people don't photograph well, but you? You looked amazing. And as long as you give me a warning, Kane will never see another one. Neither will anyone else. I don't like to share, remember? Ya know, you should take another tonight, while you try out your new toy."

"Shut up," I hiss, not wanting anyone to hear about what I'll be doing later.

Nudging my foot to get my attention, he tips his chin and eyes to the bar. The bar where Chloe is sitting and watching us. When my gaze locks onto hers, she tosses her long hair over her shoulder and directs her attention to something somewhere else.

"You think she was flirting with me, huh?"

"Please. We both *know* she was flirting with you."

"Didn't peg you for the jealous type, G."

"Are you kidding me? With all the work I'm going through to get a freaking kiss from you, there's no way I'm letting some other girl swoop in here with her bleached blonde hair and trampy, little black dress to steal you away!"

Walker's eyes meet mine over the table as he gives me a proud smile. "Trampy doesn't do it for me, G. I like fiercely stubborn, overly protective, straightforward yet secretly sensitive girls, who ask me to masturbate at the same time they do."

"Gotta bring that up, don'tcha?"

Moving around the table, he sits on the bench seat beside me, dropping his arm around my shoulders, his thigh pressed tightly against mine. His eyes are intense as he looks down at me and I do my best to control my breathing.

"I'm about ready to tell you to take that toy in the bathroom and try it out *here*, because I'm betting kissing you the way I want to right now would easily convince you that Chloe is not a threat."

"Or," I whisper breathily. "You could just kiss me. You seem pretty sure that toy is going to sway me in your direction. Why wait?"

Walker leans down, his mouth so very close to mine, and my lips part automatically. I tilt my head up with closed eyes, granting him the easiest access I may ever give him, depending on how good a kisser he turns out to be. Our breath mingles between us, steaming up the space between us with anticipation.

Feeling a feather soft touch against my bottom lip, I sigh in relief, expecting his mouth to press against mine.

But relief doesn't come.

He's watching me closely when I open my eyes. His fingers brush across my face, finally touching me like I told him to last weekend. Cupping my cheek, he runs his thumb softly across my bottom lip. When his eyes move from mine to my mouth, I close my lips over the tip of his thumb, and a lustful smile plays across his face as I suck him farther into my mouth.

"You're right," he whispers, pulling his hand away from me. "Touching *is* fun. I didn't know you would be so wickedly indecent."

"I'm not indecent."

"Just so impatient, you'll put any part of me in your mouth that you can get that pretty little tongue on."

Frustrated beyond belief, I grab his shirt and pull him as close to me as he was a second ago. "Walker, just kiss me already! Please! I'm begging you."

His mouth suddenly closes over mine, feeling like a tall, cold glass of water after I've been stuck in the desert for two long, hot weekends with no liquid in sight. Later, I'll be horrified at the moan that burst from me the second his lips touched mine, but right now, I don't care. Right now, I'm opening my mouth and pulling him closer, locking my arms around his neck and threading my fingers into his hair.

His tongue slips past my lips, instantly tangling with mine as he drags me onto his lap so he can kiss me more thoroughly.

I cling to him, my breathing ragged as he kisses me over and over. One of his hands is on my back, holding me close, but the other is on my face, cupping my cheek as he devours my mouth, pushing slightly on my jaw so he can deepen the kiss, then coming back again and again for another taste.

I wonder if somehow I died and went to heaven, because his kisses taste so impossibly, amazingly good.

Someone clears their throat beside us, and Walker breaks away from me, his breathing just as labored as mine. Hiding my face against his chest, I hear some glasses being placed on the table and Kane's voice as he quietly asks, "You know you're in public, right, man? I don't have to ask you to leave for acting like a horny teenager, do I?"

Walker's hand moves to my hair, cradling the base of my skull before he presses a kiss to the top of my head and slides me off his lap.

Clearing his own throat, Walker answers, "It's a little hard for me to control myself when someone's begging me, but I'll pull it together."

"Ah, April's a beggar. Nice! Here I thought you were exaggerating last week."

I rub my cheeks and take a deep breath before looking over at Kane and his knowing grin. "April, got a shot here for ya that'll help loosen you up. Walker, buddy, just remember to send any pictures my way."

"Not gonna happen." Walker's hand finds my thigh, caressing me in a way that lets me know he's very sorry our kiss got cut short.

Good Lord, so am I.

Kane promises our food will be out shortly, walking away and leaving us alone again.

"Jesus Almighty," I whisper. "You know, you could've just kissed me like that and I would've promised to see you and you alone without any further negotiations. Another few minutes and I think you would've gotten me off just with just your tongue in my mouth."

Laughing out loud, Walker squeezes my leg until he gets himself under control. He's still chuckling when he answers me. "You'll promise right now to give up your boytoys?"

"Yes. That toy could be amazing or a total dud, I won't be able to tell tonight because you have me so damn turned on a good breeze will send me over the edge. Who the hell needs boytoys when I could just ask you to kiss me again?"

"Well then, send me a picture of you trying out your new toy and I promise I'll kiss you in private tomorrow."

"It's gonna come with a warning," I tell him, narrowing my eyes and side-eyeing him.

"Good, I'll make sure I'm alone and no one's looking over my shoulder when I open it."

"And you'll kiss me with no interruptions?"

"Definitely no interruptions," he answers, a gleam in his eye that can only be interpreted as desperate anticipation. "I need time to kiss my new girl long enough to convince her she'll be glad to be rid of any toys that don't remind her of me."

Walker

Genny: Warning: The following content is intended solely for the viewing pleasure of recipient, Walker ? Kelley. By agreeing to accept the content, you are granting permission for sender, Genevieve Rose Stotler, to inflict severe and lasting damage to recipient's seemingly impressive manhood, should sender ever discover that recipient shared the following content in any way, whether it be intentional or accidental. Please respond as to whether you agree or disagree to this totally non-legally binding, completely informal, textual contract.

Chuckling at her very formal warning, I send her a much simpler reply.

Walker: You didn't wait for me?

Genny: Couldn't. You had me too worked up.

Walker: ? is John, and I gladly accept any and all terms Genevieve Rose Stotler can come up with.

I'm not in the best place to receive what is certainly another photo she doesn't want anyone but me to see. Not because someone may accidently see my phone, but because I'm still at my sister's, watching two little worn out boys. They're upstairs asleep, but I don't exactly want Reese walking in to see me sporting a hard-on while her children are upstairs sleeping and I'm supposedly watching the game.

I still wait anxiously for the content Genny feels the need to warn me about.

Holy *fuck*, is she *serious*?

Walker: G, you sent me a VIDEO?! And were you in the shower?

Genny: I was in the shower; Maggie assured us it's totally waterproof. As for the video, is it too much? I thought it would be ok because it's short... Delete it and I'll send you a picture instead, since you're so unhappy.

Walker: There's not a chance in hell I'm deleting it or that I'm unhappy. I'm also not watching it until I get home.

There's no *way* I can watch that now. A video of Genny, using the vibrator I bought her, in the shower? I need to be at home, by myself, preferably in bed, to watch this video.

I'm suddenly dying to be at home.

Picking up the device that holds such temptation, I read more of her words, hoping it will somehow distract me from thinking of how that video ends.

Genny: Suit yourself. I've decided the toy you bought is definitely worth another test ride. The initial results were better than expected, but I'm questioning if it's because of my general reaction to you from earlier. The second set of results will hopefully give me a more accurate idea of what it can do for my stress levels.

Walker: *How much of your initial test run is on that video?*

Genny: *Only the most important part, Friend.*

Walker: *What do you consider the most important part?*

Genny: *My first ever, Walker-induced orgasm.*

Christ, how am I supposed to have any restraint after *that*? And does that mean she was thinking about me, or just that I'm the one who bought her the vibrator? Either way, I'm considering that vibrator worth every penny, since I now have a video of the show I can't wait to see.

Summoning what I consider super-human strength, I resist a little while longer. Maybe if I keep texting her, I'll be able to distract myself until Reese and Steve get home.

Walker: *I must be amazing if I can give you an orgasm from ten miles away.*

Genny: *Judging from the way you kiss, I wouldn't put it past you. Be forewarned, I'm now expecting fireworks when I get my first orgasm directly from you.*

Honestly, if we ever get there, so am I. That kiss we shared was like none I'd ever experienced before. Pretending I'm afraid of not being able to give her those fireworks, I type back a response and press send.

Walker: *Nothing like a little pressure...*

Genny: *I'm sure you can handle it. So, tell me. Is begging your kryptonite?*

Hearing Genny beg did something strange to me. It didn't matter that we were in public, at Kane's restaurant for God's sake! It was just her and me, and so very little space between us. And when I gave in and kissed her like she begged me to? The feeling of her lips under mine, so soft and sweet, so willing, so *eager*? Nothing else even *existed*. Resisting her might turn out to be the hardest thing I'll ever have to do, but I will. At least for a little while longer.

Walker: *I decided the night we agreed to be just friends that I wouldn't kiss you until you begged me for it.*

Genny: *And now you have me not only begging you, but dating you as well. Well played, Friend.*

Walker: *Thank you, G. I thought it was fool-proof.*

Genny: *Please tell me you also decided you wouldn't have sex with me until I begged for it...*

Walker: *Do you really expect me to reveal all my secret strategies?*

Genny: *Not at all, but a girl can dream.*

Does that mean she's dreaming about sex with me? Does that mean I *was* the person she was fantasizing about when she gave that toy a test spin in her shower? Needing to know when I can see her again, I type out another question.

Walker: What're you doing tomorrow? When's a good time for me to come claim that uninterrupted kiss?
Genny: Anytime you want. I'm doing chores around the house and will be home all day.
Walker: One last question. Does this video contain sound?

There's a long pause while I watch the TV but don't see a single play of the game Reese recorded for me. Finally, my phone announces that I have another text and I refocus my eyes, so I can find out how she responded.

Genny: Ya know, I didn't check for sound. Callie wasn't home during my test ride, so there's a good chance you might hear a sigh or a moan here or there.

A sigh or a moan? While she's having an orgasm? There's no way I'm going to be able to wait to watch this video now...

Just keep texting her! I remind myself. *For as* long *as you can.*

Walker: So, you're not a screamer?
Genny: I thought the previous question was your last.
Walker: You just wanna leave me guessing, don't you?
Genny: It's surprising how well you've gotten to know me in such little time. Have a good night, man I'm currently dating. Think of me when you get home.

Like that's something I could possibly resist...

I scroll up through our conversation, letting my thumb linger over her video. I have no idea when Reese and Steve are planning on coming home, but I'll see their headlights when they pull in the drive. Zeke and Finn are upstairs sleeping. No harm in taking a look, right?

Deciding to go for it, I make sure the sound is turned up to max and the image is covering my whole screen. Hesitating again, I look around. Am I really going to watch it *here*? It's not a good plan, but I simply can't stop myself from hitting play.

The sound of running water rushes to my ears as Genny's face lights up my screen. I can only see her head and the tops of her shoulders and I wonder where her hands are, how her legs are positioned, whether the toy is inside her or not. Her head is tilted forward, her eyes are closed, and she's letting out little whimpers as her breaths come faster and faster. A breathy *Oh Lord* pushes past her lips. And then her head falls back as she moans out loud...

"Uncle Walk? Whatcha watching?"

Shit!

Fumbling to lock the screen, I shove it in my pocket before I realize I can still hear Genny's deep moans as she comes in her shower for me. After yanking it back out of my pocket, I struggle to stop it, or turn down the sound, or turn the whole damn thing off! Something!

"Nothing buddy. Why aren't you sleeping?" I demand absentmindedly, still hitting buttons on my damn phone. Why the *fuck* aren't you sleeping?

Finally, the video either ends or I get it stopped. Standing up, I toss it on the couch, rushing up the steps to usher him back to his room. Halfway up the stairs, headlights splay out on the far wall of the living room, announcing his parent's arrival. I'm glad they're home. Zeke isn't always easy to get back to bed when he wakes up.

As I'm about to walk into Zeke's room, the sound of running water suddenly comes from downstairs. Glancing over the railing and down into the living room, I freeze when I realize I didn't get Genny's video stopped at all. Instead, it's starting over from the beginning.

On Reese's big screen TV.

Holy *fuck*, are you *shitting* me?!

I push Zeke roughly into his room and slam the door, then turn around and sprint down the stairs. I'm not even close to the couch when Reese and Steve walk in. They're laughing, happy, oblivious to what's playing on the TV in front of them.

Please don't look up! Please don't look up!

Mentally, I cross my fingers. They're talking back and forth, still on a high from enjoying an evening together without the boys. It looks like I might still get out of this.

Until that breathy *Oh Lord* comes from the TV speakers.

Genny is going to *kill* me.

Reese is going to kill me.

Reese's head snaps toward the TV as I'm finally able to grab my phone. I still have a huge problem, though. I have no fucking *clue* how I got it onto the TV in the first place, so how the hell do I get it *off* the TV?

I start hitting buttons, again searching for anything that might stop this nightmare from playing out even further as I attempt to block out the angry words being expelled from my sister's mouth at an alarmingly fast rate. Growling in frustration, I eventually just grab the remote to the TV and hit the off button.

The entire room goes dark and blissfully silent.

For about two seconds.

Zeke starts crying from the top of the stairs. Reese yells at me for streaming porn while her boys are under the same roof. Finn wakes up and starts screaming from his room. Steve starts laughing his ass off.

Fuck me and my weak restraint.

Collapsing on the couch, I drop my head in my hands and wonder exactly how Genny is going to inflict severe and lasting damage to my manhood. No matter how impressive she thinks it might be, she's not going to be ok with this. Maybe I should wait to tell her. Maybe I *shouldn't* tell her. How else is she going to find out?

If we don't *go down in flames*, as she put it, maybe we'll be able to laugh about this someday.

Reese stomps her way up the stairs to put the boys back to bed. I try to figure out how I got the video on the TV in the first place, so I can undo it.

"I gotta ask, who's the girl?" Steve says, sitting beside me on the couch.

"I don't know how this got on the TV, how do I stop it?"

Taking the remote from me, Steve turns the TV back on, where Genny's video seems to be playing on an endless loop. Thankfully, Steve mutes it, his eyes fixed on the TV and the image of Genny doing something she wanted only me to see.

Me! Not my brother-in-law!

Two seconds later, the TV is back to playing the Yankees game.

Afraid to touch my phone and trigger some new set of horrors, I push it deep into my pocket, rubbing my hand over the back of my neck. Steve starts laughing again, and I avoid his knowing stare.

"Tell me who she is and get out of here. I'll calm Reese down. You should really call her tomorrow before your parents come over, though."

He's giving me a life line. I don't know Steve very well, but in this moment, I love him like a brother.

"Genny's the girl I'm dating."

"I thought Reese told you to find a nice girl."

Shrugging my shoulders, I try to hide my sheepish smile. "She did, but who wants nice all the time?"

"I hear ya. You'll never believe how not nice your sister can be."

"Come *on*, man! She's my *sister!*"

He laughs while standing up to shake my hand. "Thanks for giving us an evening off. Next time, you might want to make sure it ends a little differently."

Doing my best to not run, I hurry out of my sister's house. I *will* be thinking of Genny tonight when I get home, I'm not sure if it's in quite the way we were both hoping it would be, though.

Hell, who am I kidding?

I still need to watch the end of that video.

Walker

I have a plan.

It's a *coward's* plan, but a plan, nonetheless.

Chad threw together another soccer game today, same teams as last weekend. It starts at three, and I'm here at Genny's at quarter after two. Which means I have, at *most*, a half hour here. As much as I want that uninterrupted kiss to last all day, I also want to leave with my manhood intact and unharmed.

My morals and good conscience say I can't *not* tell her. Telling her as I run out the door, is, *technically*, telling her.

Foolproof, right?

Callie answers the door, surprised but happy to see me. After inviting me in, she yells up the stairs for Genny. Something is in the crockpot on the counter that smells amazing. Maybe, in a few weeks, when Genny forgets the fact that I can't seem to view her pictures or videos in private no matter how hard I try, and if I'm not dead or dying because of an infection from however she doles out her lasting damage, maybe Genny will invite me over for one of these meals she cooks for her sister.

Smiling at me from the staircase, Genny beckons me to her. Callie watches me move toward her sister, and I can't help but think she's rooting for me. I give Genny my undivided attention, watching her disappear up the stairs, obviously wanting me to follow her.

I like this game. I can play this game all day...

Well, at least until I have to leave.

She's swinging open a door when I hit the top of the stairs and I quickly follow her in, not at all surprised when she throws herself into my arms in what I think is a bedroom. Her mouth is on mine before I can even close my eyes. Forgetting all about what I need to tell her, I wrap my arms around her and kiss her with everything I've been holding in since I watched her video all the way through for the first time last night.

And again this morning.

And *again*, before I came over.

That video should be deleted. I'm a little obsessed with watching it.

Or maybe I'm going to save it in an email, so I'll always have a copy as long as I've got internet connection.

Genny steps backward, pulling me with her as she sucks on my bottom lip, lowering herself onto a bed and forcing me down on top of her. As much fun as I know this will be, I certainly don't have time for anything more than kissing. "G, we can't-"

"Shut up and kiss me, Walker."

Dipping my tongue back into her mouth, I feel her legs lock around my waist. The seam of her yoga pants is hot and insistent, rubbing against my zipper, where my cock is straining to get as close to her as it can through all our clothes. I push my arms under and around her, moving us farther back on this mattress before rolling us over. If she's going to make it this hard for me to walk away, I may as well have the best seat in the house for the show. On my back, with her on top of me.

Once she's in control, she slows down. Her kisses aren't quite so frantic or needy. They turn sweet, slow, and deep. Her breaths come fast and shallow. Her eyes flutter as she rubs the apex of her thighs against my erection, and she tips her head back, savoring the feeling.

As I bite back a groan, I try not to compare what I'm hearing and seeing to what was in that video.

"Walker," she pants, her eyes snapping open to find mine. "I need... Will you..."

Not knowing exactly what she wants, I pull her closer, pressing her mouth to mine again. Her hands move into my hair as she moves her tongue past my lips. When I slide my hands to her hips, she grabs them, shoving them between us to cup her breasts under her shirt.

"Jesus, Genny," I growl. I wasn't expecting to move this fast with her.

Once my hands are on her, they have a mind of their own, and they aren't moving away from exactly where she put them until they get their fill. Cupping and squeezing, I explore her soft flesh over the lace that's keeping me from feeling her bare skin and pebbled nipples. My palms rub over the tight little buds, and I can't help but smile as she gasps and arches her back, pushing her tits more firmly into my hands.

She suddenly pushes her hips down, grinding on my dick, and I hear a familiar moan coming from the back of her throat. Her pelvis moves, rubbing fast against the bulge in my shorts, and out of nowhere, I get to see *in person* Genny having an orgasm.

Holy shit, I was not expecting this.

Holy shit, she's coming on me and we're both fully clothed!

Holy shit, is she gonna be pissed when she finds out what I accidentally did last night...

When the last of her moans are over, my hands lower her and her tits down to my chest. I kiss the top of her head as she catches her breath, my mind reeling. Where the hell do we go from here? I wasn't planning on getting this physical with her yet. On second thought, all I really did was kiss her and lay here. And cop a very nice feel of her tits through her bra.

No, scratch that. All I did was enjoy the show.

Yeah, *that's* what I'm gonna go with.

"Mmm..." Genny murmurs against my neck.

"You weren't kidding about getting off from just kissing me, were you?"

She stretches out against me, her legs tangling with mine. "Whatever gave you that idea?"

Chuckling in her ear, I let my hands travel her sides, overtop her clothes. It's a peaceful aftermath, even if I'm hard enough to be incredibly uncomfortable. It's nice just holding her. And letting her lay on top of me like it's her job.

She's really fucking good at it.

"I don't wanna be an asshole," I murmur against her hair. "But I need to go soon."

"You can go if you have to. I'm good now."

What?!

She's *good* now?

Does she think she can just use me and send me on my way? I know it's been a while since she's dated or been in a relationship, but that's pretty callous, and it pisses me off.

"I'm not one of your boytoys, G. I don't want you to just use me to get yourself off."

She rolls to face me, obviously feeling very at home draped over my body. "Does that mean I can get *you* off?" she asks with a wide grin.

"No! Look..." Shaking my head, I try to come up with a good way to tell her how I'm feeling. To let her know that what she just said was the exact thing you should *never* say to someone you're dating. "I just don't wanna feel like you're using me, and when you say shit like that, that's how I feel."

Genny slides down my body to stand at the edge of the bed, watching as I stand up next to her. Her words are rushed and strained as she explains herself. "I wasn't trying to make you feel that way. Honestly, I was joking when I said it, because what else do I say when you tell me you have to leave two minutes after you get me off without even touching me? The way you affect me is a little embarrassing, and I really don't know what to think right now."

"That's a much better response. And whatever you're thinking is ok. As long as it's not 'I got mine, so you can go.'"

"Ok, well, I'm thinking that was kind of crazy and amazing at the same time." She shoots me a shy smile with a shrug of her shoulders. "What're *you* thinking?"

"A couple things. That was possibly the hottest thing I've ever had happen while fully dressed, so don't be embarrassed." Wrapping my hands around her waist, I pull her back to me. "And I need you to kiss me again."

"Gladly, Friend."

"Don't get as carried away this time."

"I can't promise that," she whispers, her words hot as she breathes them over my lips. Brushing my mouth against hers, I focus on not letting her devour me like she did five minutes ago. It *kind* of works. I pull away at the first sound of that sweet whimper.

"I have something to tell you that's gonna make you mad."

Those green eyes meet mine expectantly and she pulls slightly farther away. "What?"

"You shouldn't have sent me that video while I was watching my nephews."

Her eyes round out as she thinks about the possibilities of what may have happened. I have a feeling whatever she's thinking is nowhere near as bad as what actually happened.

"Did that poor, innocent four-year-old hear it?"

I hold her tight against me, cringing as I prepare to tell her the truth. "It's a little worse than that. Did you know there's a way to put a video from your phone on the TV? I knew it was possible, but I don't know how to do it."

Her hand covers her mouth and she lets out a giggle. "You didn't!"

"I did," I tell her, nodding. I take her in just like this, memorizing her happy, lazy expression as she's in my arms. Because I'm a little afraid of how she's going to react to what I'm about to tell her.

"And Zeke saw it? Oh Lord! I'm a child corrupter!"

"I don't think Zeke saw it..."

Her eyes narrow as she quickly puts it together. "Who saw it, Walker John Kelley?"

"You have to believe me, I didn't know how to stop it! I *still* don't know how it happened!"

"Walker, who saw me having an orgasm meant only for your eyes?"

Unable to look at her face, I look between us, hanging my head. "My sister and her husband."

Gasping, she pushes out of my arms, staring at me with her arms crossed over her chest. After a minute of stunned silence, she huffs out her disbelief, tapping her foot as she tries to figure out what to say to me.

"I can't *believe* you!" she finally yells, throwing her hands in the air and pacing the room. "I even gave you a warning! What more do you need?"

"Maybe some lessons on how to use my phone?" I shrug sheepishly, rubbing the back of my neck. She's not immediately going for my manhood. I'm a little surprised, but so very glad. Maybe it's a good thing she got off right before I told her. Gives her more incentive to keep me in working condition.

"Good Lord!" she cries, spinning to look at me. "Where's your phone?"

Reaching into my pocket to protect it, I ask, "Why?"

"Because we're deleting not only the video, but the picture, too. And you're definitely not getting anything new to look at because you'll probably accidently put it up on a *power point* during your next meeting at work somehow!"

"No."

"*No*?! What do you mean, *no*? Give me your phone."

I grab her outstretched hand and pull her to me, kissing her hard for as long as I dare, because even mad, she still kisses me back. Then I step out of her reach and move backwards toward the door. "I gotta go, G. I'll call you to set up a date for next weekend."

"I swear to God, Walker, if anyone else sees anything..." she yells as I head down her stairs.

"No one else is gonna see. But you're not deleting them."

That didn't go as badly as I thought it would.

In fact, it went a whole hell of a lot *better* than I imagined.

Genny

I hand Michelle the coffee I picked up for her and toss my purse into the filing cabinet at the booth I'm stationed in today. Then I work my way down the aisle, stopping in to say hello to all my coworkers.

I'm working the late shift today. Which means, not only did I get to sleep in, but everyone is already here by the time I show up fifteen minutes early. Michelle's in the booth next to mine, and she glares at me from around the partition separating us.

"What?" I ask, reaching for my hair. Is it sticking up? I didn't spend a lot of time in front of the mirror this morning.

"You brought me coffee."

Dropping an eyebrow, I reply, "Sorry, I thought you'd like it."

I guess she's in a bad mood?

"How was your weekend?" she barks as I log into the computer.

The corners of my mouth tip up and I realize my smile has been there all morning. Probably even since yesterday or Saturday night. It's not new, it just keeps getting bigger, especially as I recall everything I did this weekend… And who I saw this weekend. "It was good," I reply, sharing a secretive smile with my computer screen. "What about you? Did Sam take you out again?"

"He did. What's with your chipper mood this morning? Did you see Chad this weekend?"

I shake my head when she looks at me questioningly, and I breathe a sigh of relief when we both get patients.

Mondays are usually busy, and if we get to talk, it'll be a disjointed conversation. At least until the afternoon when it slows down. Forgetting all about her and my secret weekend adventures, I make small talk with my patients, finding out a little bit about each person's life before sending them on their way.

After calling in my last patient before lunch, I look up to find Matt standing in my booth. Hmph. This could be interesting. "Hey," I offer. "Are you here for labs?"

His eyes take me in as he stands in my booth, clearly surprised to see me here. "Yeah. I didn't know you worked here."

"Of course you didn't. Exchanging the details of our personal lives wasn't exactly our thing."

His lips tip up into the smile that first attracted me to him years ago.

Handing me his paperwork, I find out his last name and pull up his chart number, verifying his insurance and date of birth, since I'm already very familiar with his address and phone number.

"Busy weekend?" he asks, referring to his unanswered text from Friday night. How exactly do I play this? Do I say it was and let it go? Do I do what Walker suggested and tell him I'm seeing someone? That's probably the best thing to do. Talk about awkward, though.

"Yeah, ah... Sorry about Friday. I started seeing someone and... Well... I kinda want to see what happens, ya know?"

Wow, that was harder than I was expecting it to be.

Matt says nothing, slowly nodding. After scribbling out his signature where I tell him to, he meets my eyes. "I didn't think you wanted anything more than what we were doing."

"I didn't. It just kind of... happened."

"Huh."

He stands and turns to go. I watch him leave.

I'm kind of sad. Matt was fun. Matt helped me get through a lot, even if he wasn't aware of doing it. I'm not sad I'm giving him up to see what happens with Walker, but I'm kind of disappointed in how this ended.

Flipping off my light, I lock my computer and stand up to stretch. Michelle pops her head around the partition, causing me to scream in surprise and clutch at my chest. "What the heck are you scaring me for?!"

"What the heck did I just *hear*?! And that was *Matt*? Honey, he's hot!"

"I know he's hot, why do you think I slept with him for the better part of three years?"

"Because he's *efficient*."

Rolling my eyes, I clock out and make my way out of my booth. "I'm serious!" she insists, stopping me in my tracks. "Did I hear you say you're seeing someone?"

Grinning widely with my secret, I walk off for lunch, leaving her to question her sanity at my unusual comment.

After thinking hard about it, I stop outside the department and lean against the wall. I don't know if I'm making the right move or not, but I can't leave things like this. Not after all this time. Matt sees me as soon as he steps out of the department. "Hey."

"Hey, can I walk with you for a minute?" I ask. He shrugs with indifference and I fall into step beside him. "I don't want things to be weird between us."

"Then don't let them be."

"That's hard when I feel like you're disappointed in me."

Turning to me with a sigh, he shakes his head. "Don't do this, Genny. We don't do feelings. We had a good time but it's over now. No big deal."

"That's it?" I ask, feeling like it's a much bigger deal than he's making it out to be. Am I crazy, though? Sure, we had a standing invitation going for a long time, but maybe I really was nothing to him.

"That's it, Gen. See ya around."

Wow. Walker's right.

For the first time, I feel used.

It feels like shit.

Genny

I set three plates at the island and grab an extra stool. Since the dining room table was taken over by Callie's studies four years ago, the island has become where we usually eat. She's almost done with her bachelor's degree, and I have no idea what life holds for us when she graduates. Is she going to move out and leave me here alone? Is she going to stay here and save up money while she gets a few years' experience under her belt, so when she applies for PA school, she doesn't have to take out a million loans? Is she going to turn my entire world upside down because I no longer know what role to play in her life?

Yes. The answer to the last one is a definite *yes*.

Callie bounds down the stairs, grabbing a bowl and standing in front of the stove to put together her chicken taco salad. Myra already has hers in front of her at the island. After making myself a bowl, I join them.

Callie's already on her phone, seemingly oblivious to anything Myra and I might talk about, so when Myra asks me what's new, I don't hesitate to tell her. "I cut it off with Ben and Matt."

"Whoa... Seriously?"

"Mhm," I mumble around my food. "I promised Walker no one but him and the magic wand he bought me."

Myra cracks up laughing. "What're you talking about? What *magic wand*?"

Over our meal, I tell her about my agreement with Walker and how he introduced me to sex toys. And how I was amazingly bold after being called the centerfold of the month, and sent him a video of me using my new, fun toy. And how he let his freaking sister and brother-in-law see it. I think Myra spit out more food from laughing so hard than she actually ate.

"Oh my God, Genny! How many people have seen pictures or videos of you pleasure cruising?"

Groaning into my empty salad bowl, I try to count them all up in my head. Walker, of course, his friend, Kane. His sister and her husband. Callie. Myra. Do we count little Zeke? Walker said Zeke didn't see anything, but he heard it, so does that count?

"Possibly around the same number of guys I've had sex with."

"That's fantastic!" Her eyes sparkle and I dread whatever is coming out of her mouth next. "What are you gonna do when Chad texts you? Are you giving him up, too?"

"Oh my God, there's *another* one?"

Myra and I look at Callie in surprise. "How long have you been listening, little girl?" Myra asks her.

She blinks, feigning innocence. "Not long, promise."

I roll my eyes, scoffing. "Like I'm gonna believe that."

"Answer the question, Genny. Are you gonna give up this other guy, Chad?"

"What's it to you, little sister? You're very interested in my business all of a sudden."

She gives me a small smile, poking my side with her finger. "I like Walker. You should be good to him."

"You think I should be good to him after he showed half his family a video of me having an orgasm?"

"I do," she nods. "I think you're an idiot for sending videos like that in the first place, and it's your own stupid fault other people saw it. He's trying to get you focused on learning how to date again, and getting to know you, and you keep shoving sex in his face. Be good to him. Be good to *yourself,* and give him a real chance."

Blinking my surprise, I turn to stare at Myra, completely stunned into silence. I look back at my little sister, trying to fight back the proud tears that are threatening to cloud my vision. With very few exceptions, my parents' anniversary being many of them, I can honestly say I hardly ever cry in front of my siblings. I've always had to be the strong one. I'm not going to start crying in front of her now. "Who are you? Are you sure you're related to me? Are you sure I'm the one who's been trying to teach you about life for the past ten years, because you seem much wiser than I am right now."

"You taught me right, Genny. You just forgot what was right about love and sex after Paul broke your heart."

"Oh Lord," I whisper pulling her in to a tight hug. "You weren't supposed to know Paul broke my heart."

"Paul's an ass."

"Yes, Paul *is* an ass," Myra seconds. "And Callie's right. You need to give Walker a real chance."

"Boo to you both for ganging up on me! I was gonna give him a real chance anyway, but now you'll never believe me."

And then, doesn't the man himself call me. After a bunch of excited oohs and ahhs from the two girls in the kitchen, I take my phone and slip up the stairs to talk to him in private.

"Hey," I say once I get to my room.

"Hi. Are you busy?"

"Not too busy to talk to you."

"Aren't you extra sweet tonight?" he teases, making me chuckle as I realize I'm not usually sweet at all. "Does this mean you're not mad at me anymore?"

Maybe Callie's right. Maybe it *is* my own fault. And maybe I've been using sex as an excuse to keep my heart locked up for too long. "I'm not mad at you."

"I'm really glad to hear that. How's your week going?"

"Umm... Interesting."

"Why's that?"

"I told my boytoys that I'm seeing someone and won't be playing with them anymore."

"Yeah?" he asks, a smile in his voice. Rolling over onto my stomach, I kick my feet in the air behind me, feeling every bit the typical high-school girl on the phone with her big crush.

"Yeah. One of them made me feel like crap, so I'm really sorry if I made you feel used on Sunday."

"We talked about it, G. We're good. You don't need to apologize again. Can I ask, does that mean you told Chad?"

"Mmm. No," I venture, trying to explain. "I never really considered him one of *mine*. It was more I was one of *his*. Does that make sense?"

"Wow. Ah, I don't know if that makes sense..."

Walker's voice sounds stressed, and I try to think of a way to make him understand. "I never contacted Chad, it was always the other way around. Just because I didn't tell him I'm seeing someone doesn't mean I'm going to answer him if he texts me. Why does it matter? I promised you I wouldn't see anyone except you."

"It matters because I'd love to bring you to my place and have it not be weird."

"Oh." Taking a deep breath, I decide we need to talk about something else. Anything else. "How was your game on Sunday?"

"Good. We won three to two."

"Maybe sometime, I could come watch you play."

"You could. It might be weird. Chad's on the other team."

Well, that didn't work out like I was hoping, did it?

"Walker, I'm trying here, ok? I wouldn't even know what to tell Chad if I texted him. He'll probably text back asking who I am."

"He knows exactly who you are, Genny. And while he may not remember your name if he saw you on the street, he'd remember *you*."

Pretty sure Walker's wrong about that one, but whatever. I'm not going to argue with him about whether some other guy remembers who I am in the light of day. After a heavy sigh, I say, "Tell me something good. I don't like fighting with you."

"Something good?"

"Mhm."

After a moment of silence, he informs me, "No one has seen you on my phone since I saw you last."

"That *is* good!" I chuckle. "When can I see you again?"

"What're you doing Thursday? I was thinking of introducing you to my sister. She's very eager to meet and judge this girl I'm dating that sends me videos like yours."

Rolling my eyes, I try not to jump at such an invitation. "Well, when you put it that way..."

"I'm kidding! Sort of... Seriously, though. I want you to meet her and my nephews."

"Tuesdays and Thursdays are kinda my dinner-with-Callie nights."

"So, I *am* interrupting," he guesses, inaccurately.

"Callie was just telling me she likes you and I need to give you a real chance, so I think she's ok with it."

"Then come over Thursday. Tell Callie I'll make it up to her."

"How're you gonna do that?" I wonder out loud, already smiling at the fact that he would *try* do that.

"Don't worry about it, G. That's between me and your sister."

"Well, if that's the way you wanna play it, you can ask her yourself." I get up and head for the stairs, hearing his deep chuckle in my ear. "I have a question for you the next time I see you. Just you, no one else."

"Why don't you ask me now?"

"Because I wanna see your reaction when I ask you."

"Now I'm curious," he says in my ear, the smile in his voice pulling another one from me, even if my question is enough to make my palms sweat.

"Good. I hope it keeps you up at night."

"Nah, I've got a great video of you that'll help me get to sleep."

Rolling my eyes as I step into the kitchen, I reply, "I'm glad to know I'm so boring that I help put you to sleep. Now keep your dirty thoughts to yourself, here's Callie."

She takes my phone with a look of confusion. "Hello?"

I don't know what he's saying to her, but she's smiling and nodding her head. Her bright eyes turn to me as she lets out a little laugh, holding her hand in front of her mouth. "I'd love that! Yeah, I'll tell her. See you later, Walker."

She hangs up and hands my phone back to me with a smile. "You're gonna meet his sister and nephews on Thursday."

"What was the rest of that conversation?"

"Nothing you need to know right now." Callie shoots Myra a sly grin and I sigh dramatically, knowing from that look that Callie will be telling my bestie about her secret conversation with the guy I'm dating.

Walker already has them collaborating against me.

Is it wrong that it only makes me like him more, knowing that he's pulling my sister into this? It proves how different he was from Paul. Paul didn't even like picking me up here at the house because he would have to *put up with* Calvin and Callie. Here Walker is making deals with Callie behind my back. And I love it.

Callie's absolutely right. I need to be good to Walker.

I just feel like I'm assuming way too much if I text Chad. Assuming he'll remember me. Assuming he'll give a shit. Then again, what do I care if he doesn't give a shit? Wouldn't it be better that way?

Am I just nervous to tell him because then I'll really have no one to have sex with?

Or is it because Chad is the best I've ever had?

Maybe Walker is even better than Chad. He certainly kisses better than Chad, but what if that's his best talent and he's not amazing when it comes to the actual sex part?

Walker got me off with his hands on my boobs and all our clothes in place. *That* was an impressive feat. Was it just all the buildup though? All the talk of sex and masturbation and the videos and pictures and sex toys?

How horrible am I that I wish there was a way to *know* before officially giving up Chad?

I've got a lot of thoughts to sort through tonight.

Walker

Genny still hasn't replaced her spare tire when I show up Thursday evening to take her to Reese's. Is money an issue, or is it the time it takes to go and get it fixed? She doesn't live far from where she works, but she really needs to get that taken care of. If she has another bad day, she's gonna be stuck along the side of the road without a spare. I'll gladly come and get her, but what will we do with her car?

She answers my knock with a hesitant smile. "Come on in. I'm almost ready."

"You all right?" I ask, missing the enthusiasm of the last greeting I got when I saw her.

Looking over her shoulder as she makes her way towards the stairs, she admits, "Just a little nervous."

I find Callie studying at the dining room table. She looks up as I walk into the room. "Hi, Walker."

"Hey, Callie, how're you doing?"

"Good. I've been working on our plan. I may have tweaked it a little."

"Excellent."

I chuckle, before hearing how she *tweaked* the plan. Or changed it altogether. My plan was simple. Hers is rather involved and is more a surprise for Genny, instead of being a way to make up for me stealing Genny from Callie. It's supposed to be for her, though, so I shrug my shoulders and roll with it. "Maybe we should exchange numbers, so I don't have to ask your sister to talk to you about this. Is she going to kill me or love me after our she finds out about this plan?"

Scribbling her number on a piece of paper, she remarks, "I thought for sure she would've killed you for showing that video to your sister. But you're standing in our kitchen, upright and breathing, so I'm not sure what to think."

"She told you about that, huh?" I rub my hand along the back of my neck with a cringe, wishing *no one* knew about that. Instead, it seems as though *everyone* does. No wonder Genny's nervous. I really screwed up there. I'm still not quite sure how I did it, and that's the scariest part. I could accidentally do it again.

"She didn't exactly *tell* me... I may have been eavesdropping when she told Myra."

Punching Callie's number into my phone, I send her a quick text. "You do that a lot?"

She gives me a sly smile, admitting, "More often than Genny thinks. It's become a lot more interesting lately. She was pretty boring before you came along."

"Glad to be of service, I guess."

"How exactly are you servicing my sister?" Genny asks from behind me, horrified.

"I was thanking him for making you happy again. This week has been fun with you," Callie answers, saving me from a very awkward conversation. Callie must be very sneaky. She's way too practiced at seeming innocent when she gets caught.

I'll have to try to keep that in mind when I'm here with Genny.

Genny stares skeptically at her sister, who just shrugs and goes back to her laptop. Genny must be used to the way Callie twists the truth. I hope Genny *has* been happier with me around though, because I'm happier being around her.

Genny grabs her purse and walks with me to the door. "We need to talk about your tire," I tell her.

"I know! I have an appointment to drop it off tomorrow morning. Callie's getting up early to take me to work."

"Good," I chuckle at her exaggerated response. "Thanks, Callie. See ya."

Callie sends a little wave in our direction before dropping her head back into her studies. Grabbing my hand once we're on the porch, Genny drags me behind her to my car. But she takes a shaky breath as I open the passenger door for her.

She must be really nervous. I wish I could tell her it's gonna be fine, but I have a feeling bringing it up will only make her anxiety worse. And I don't honestly know that it's going to be fine. Reese wants to meet Genny, but only so she can size her up. She's already thinking poorly of Genny simply because of that video. I told her she needs to think poorly of *me*, for making such a bad judgement call and playing it when I did, but my stubborn sister is still placing all blame solely on the girl who took the video in the first place.

I made Reese promise to be nice, but with Reese, *nice* can be a very subjective term.

"Wait," Genny says, stalling, as she stands between the car and the door. She tugs on my hand, pulling me close enough that I know exactly what's on her mind. *This* is more along the lines of the greeting I expected tonight. Cupping her face with both my hands, I don't wait for any more of an invitation. She breathes a sigh against my mouth as my lips find hers. Tilting her head up to mine, she makes it easier for me to deepen the kiss, and her hands snake around my waist.

Part of me is whispering that I need to keep this short and sweet...

I really wish that part of me would shut up. No matter how right it is. In the end, I listen, because I don't need Genny crawling her way up my body to have an orgasm right here in her driveway.

Her hands hold mine in place on her cheeks as I pull away. Her eyes are still closed, like she's cherishing the feeling of me on her lips even after I'm gone. This girl can turn me on in less than a minute. I don't think begging is my kryptonite, I think maybe *she* is.

"Hi, G."

A smile plays on her lips before she finally opens her sparkling green eyes to look at me. "Hi, Friend. I like the way you say hello to me."

"My words or my actions?"

"Mmm," she murmurs in appreciation. "Both."

Dropping her hands, she finally climbs in the car and I shut the door behind her. Right now, I don't care if Reese loves or hates Genny. I don't care what anyone thinks about her. I like Genny enough to know I'm probably already in trouble. Everyone else can fuck off and leave us alone.

Maybe I'd prefer that. I really like what happens when Genny and I are alone.

Genny takes my hand after we leave her driveway, lacing her fingers through mine. She's not looking at me, focusing instead on our hands. I wonder just how nervous she is, because not only is she not looking around or bouncing in her seat with whatever thought is in her head, she's also quiet.

Squeezing her fingers in mine makes her look up, and I catch her eye. "You ok over there?"

She presses her lips into a thin line, nodding and watching me as I drive. "Where are we going?" she finally asks, breaking her silence.

"To my sister's. She lives across the street from the pharmacy. I figure we can all walk to the park, that way we won't be stuck at the scene of the crime."

I'm rewarded with a small smile from her, but it doesn't reach her eyes. "Can you pull over somewhere? I wanna ask you a serious question and I don't want to do it there."

Maybe the reason she's nervous has nothing to do with my sister...

When she told me the other night on the phone she had a question for me and me alone, I didn't think it was a *serious* question. Honestly, I didn't know what to think about it, but Genny seems to shy away from any serious questions unless backed into a corner, so I figured it was anything but.

Finding a random parking lot, I pull in and take my hand out of hers to cut the engine. I find her watching me again, fully facing me with her back to the window when I turn to her. "Talk to me, G. What's your serious question?"

She bites her lip, thinking hard before letting the words rush out of her all at once. "Do I shove sex in your face?"

What?

Seeing her this nervous about such a weird question, I ask for some clarification before I even consider an answer. "Where is this coming from?"

"Someone told me you're just trying to get to know me, and I'm constantly shoving sex in your face. It got me thinking, ya know? That's what we talk about the most, and I sent you stuff that was totally about sex, I just... I don't know, I guess I'm sorry. I really like you, and I don't want this to be just about sex. I want the whole relationship thing that you're offering, but I don't really know how to go about getting it."

I watch her closely, trying to figure out how to answer. She's fidgeting in her seat waiting for whatever I have to say, so I reach out and offer her my hand, which she gladly takes. It calms her down a little.

"I don't think you're constantly shoving sex in my face. Do we talk about it a lot? Sure. But I think that's because sex is a big part of who you are. I like that you're confident enough about yourself to send me pictures and videos. I like that you're not afraid to talk about it, and that we can tell each other exactly what we expect."

"What do we expect?" Genny asks, a grave expression on her face.

I give her a playful smile. "You expect fireworks and I expect you to see only me."

"Oh," she breathes with a giggle. "I already got some fireworks."

"That was more like a sparkler," I inform her, giving her an arrogant smirk. "You haven't experienced fireworks yet."

Genny's eyes shoot up to her eyebrows. "Is that right? *Now* who's putting unnecessary pressure on you?"

"Like you said, I can handle it."

Taking a deep breath, I push on. She's the one who brought it up, so hopefully she won't be offended. "I think you're more comfortable talking about sex than anything else. I *like* that you're so open about it, and I don't want you to change that, or stop bringing up sex because of whatever this person said. But I would love for you to open up a little more about *other* stuff, too."

"Like what?" Her voice is quiet again. I have a feeling it's going to be tough for her at first, but if she wants the more of an honest-to-God relationship like I want, she's gonna have to push through it and really talk to me.

"Stuff about your past. Like your parents. Like college. Like why you take care of Callie like you're more her mom than her sister."

"Hmm," she murmurs. "That stuff is a *lot* harder for me to talk about."

"I know. But if you want the whole relationship thing, you have to let me in."

Settling back against her seat, she thinks that over as she studies the traffic rolling by outside her window. Eventually, she looks my way, meeting my eyes cautiously. "Ok."

"Ok?"

"Yeah," she says, taking a deep breath and letting it out slowly. "I'll do that for you."

Feeling the corners of my mouth tip up in a smile, I start up the car. "You *must* like me."

"Or I'm looking forward to finding out what real fireworks feel like."

There she is. I'm laughing as I pull out of the parking lot, because Genny's back in all her splendid glory, no hint of nerves in sight. Genny's a very sexual person, and she flaunts it because it's the only part of herself she's comfortable with. I'm fine with that as long as she slowly lets me get to know the rest of her, too.

Pulling into Reese's driveway a few short minutes later, Genny's nerves come back, but not like when she was scared to talk to me. I'm glad to know she was more nervous about the seriousness of our relationship than she is to meet my sister.

"Can you kiss me again before we go in?"

"I can, but Zeke will probably be running out the door in less than a minute."

"Then quit wasting time."

I meet her over the console, sweeping soft, lazy kisses along her mouth until she grabs my shirt and murmurs against my lips, "I want your tongue in my mouth, Friend."

Christ, the things she says to me... I can't imagine not giving in to her, no matter what it is we're talking about when she says things like that. Kissing her the way she wants me to, I quickly get caught up in the taste and feel of her. *So* caught up in her, I don't realize Zeke is watching us until it's much too late.

"Eww, Uncle *Walk*! You're kissing a *girl*!" His little hands slap against my window and I press one last kiss to Genny's sweet, hungry mouth. My offended nephew glares at me through the glass, like I'm a traitor to boys everywhere for even *thinking* about kissing a girl, much less doing it.

Picking him up and hanging him upside down, I slam my car door shut and lift him over my shoulder, letting his legs hang down my back. "Am I supposed to kiss boys, instead?"

"No," he giggles. "You're only supposed to kiss your mommy!"

"My mommy doesn't want my kisses. I had to find the prettiest girl around, so I could kiss *her* instead. Don't you think Genny's pretty enough to kiss?"

Zeke studies Genny, who's cheeks are filling with color as she walks around the car to join us. "Is she the girl from the TV?"

Maybe Zeke *did* see Genny on the big screen. "Yeah, but you weren't supposed to see that."

"You're pretty when your face isn't messed up," Zeke proclaims, totally not understanding how much of a privilege it was to see Genny with a *messed-up* face. Holding back a laugh, I watch to see how Genny will react to him.

"How was my face messed-up?" she asks innocently.

"Like this," he says, and I look over my shoulder to see my very young nephew mimicking Genny's orgasm face, laughing out loud at how wrong this entire conversation is on so many levels.

"Well that's not how I *wanted* to look," Genny explains seriously. "I wanna be a movie star, ya see, but I'm not very good at it. I was trying to look scared. Can you show me how to look scared?"

"Sure," he says wiggling in my grasp. "Lemme down, Uncle Walk." When I set him on his feet, he grabs Genny's hand, tugging it until she's on his level. Then Zeke gives her his best scared face.

"Wow, that's *really good*," she praises him with wide eyes. "Can you teach me how to do it that way?"

"Yeah!" His little face lights up with joy at the prospect of teaching a grown up something, instead of always being the student. "You gotta make your eyes real big."

"Like this?" she asks, her eyes going even wider. Zeke's little hands move to her face, pushing on her cheeks till her jaw drops.

"Do this with your mouth," he instructs, his mouth forming an "o." Genny does as she's told, and Zeke gives her a smile. "That's better. Can you do other faces?"

Reese's head peaks around the corner of the screened door. "Are you guys coming in or what?"

"We're coming," I yell back, loving what's happening between Genny and my nephew.

Genny stands up but takes Zeke's hand. "I'll probably need your help with my other faces, Zeke. You seem a lot better at this than me."

"Cool! I gotta go tell my mom!"

He takes off, running toward the back door, and I steal the hand he was holding. "I think you have a new friend."

"Let's see if his mom is that easy to win over," she mutters, bumping her shoulder against mine. Moving her mouth close to my ear, she whispers, "Thanks for the kiss."

"My pleasure, G. Anytime, anywhere."

As I hold the door open, Genny takes a deep breath, entering Reese's kitchen with a forced neutral expression. Reese is busy getting the baby gear around and doesn't immediately turn around to greet us. Zeke's rambling, telling his mom a very animated story about how he's going to help his new friend become a movie star, and Reese is half listening to him, nodding her head and making appreciative noises as she packs up the stroller. When my sister stands up to face us, her expression isn't very welcoming, and I roll my eyes in annoyance.

"Well, if it isn't the up and coming *movie star*," she sneers, sarcasm dripping from her voice. Genny clears her throat, obviously uncomfortable.

Reese is going to hear some not very nice things from me when this is over.

"Yeah, that was kind of an audition clip that wasn't meant for the general public," Genny explains. "Zeke tells me I wouldn't have gotten the part, so I'm sorry you were subjected to the torture of watching my very poor performance."

Reese simply stares before trying to hide the smile she's suddenly wanting to give in to. "I don't know about the quality of your *performance*, I just didn't like it being on my TV."

"I didn't like hearing about it being there, let me tell you! It's entirely my fault, though, so again, I'm sorry. I knew Walker was here with your kids and I sent it anyway. It was a really bad call on my part."

"Hmph," is Reese's only response.

I think I love Genny a little bit just for rendering my sister speechless. Reese always has something to say, especially about anyone I'm into. She had plenty to say an hour ago when I called to confirm that she still wanted to meet the girl who graced her TV with such an unforgettable *performance.*

"Reese?" I catch her attention, giving Genny a brief reprieve. "What can I help you with?"

"Can you get Finn from the living room and I'll attempt to get this stuff out the door?"

It's *probably* safe to leave both girls in the kitchen while grabbing my youngest nephew. I'm pretty sure Reese isn't going to be a bitch to Genny after that introduction. Hell, I think my sister almost *likes* Genny, since she's taking full responsibility for my blunder, and she didn't shy away from the awkwardness of what happened, just accepted it and apologized first thing. I listen closely anyway as I leave the room, ready to step in if necessary.

"Since you're here with Walker, I'm going to say your performance couldn't have been that bad. He gave you the lead role for this part of his life."

"I think there's a lot of lead roles in Walker's life," Genny replies as I grab Finn from his pack and play. He's clapping his hands and standing against the rail, gurgling his excitement at seeing me. If he's standing up like this, he's gonna be walking in no time. Reese is going to have her hands full then, for sure.

Finn and I make our way back into the kitchen where Genny has the diaper bag slung over her shoulder. Zeke is pouting, his little fists crossed over his chest as he voices his distaste at having to hold his mother's hand once they're outside.

"I don't wanna hold your hand, Mommy!" he yells in their driveway. His little angry stance has me trying not to laugh, but Reese just puts her hands on her hips and stares him down.

"It's either hold a grown up's hand, or we go back inside and don't go to the park."

"I wanna hold *her* hand!" Zeke says, pointing at Genny.

Genny glances at Reese, who's obviously not happy about the turn of events, and holds up her hands, showing him they're full. "I'm pushing the stroller, Bud. Maybe next time, ok?"

Reese grumbles under her breath, grabbing the stroller with more force than is necessary. "It's fine, just hold his hand tight. He likes to run away when he gets half a chance."

After glancing at me, Genny hesitantly releases the stroller and reaches for Zeke. He gives her a huge grin as he takes her hand and holds on like he's trying to steal her from me. I'll have to watch out for him. I know for a fact he's can steal a heart in about half a second when he's trying. It's impossible not to fall in love with him.

Once getting the ok from his mom, Zeke pulls Genny across the street ahead of us, chattering to her about God-only-knows-what as she attempts to listen to every word that comes out of his mouth. She looks back at me with wide eyes and a happy smile before they disappear into the park, leaving Reese and I in their dust.

"Your girlfriend just stole my first born."

"She'll bring him back to you. She might love kids, but she has enough to deal with right now."

"What's that supposed to mean?" Reese demands curiously. She's shielding the sun from her eyes as she looks at me and I wonder if I should tell her anything about Genny. Genny may seem really open, but I'm finding out the opposite is true.

"She just hasn't had it easy. Don't judge her until you get to know more about her."

My sister simply rolls her eyes before zeroing in on Zeke and Genny already on the playground. *"No one's* had it easy, Walker."

"Exactly. *You* should know everyone has their own story to tell. She knows about Zeke, and she's not judging you."

Gasping, Reese turns around to punch me on the shoulder as I'm stretching out the blanket for us to sit on. "You told her about Zeke?"

I rub my arm, wincing. "Are you working out, sis? When the hell did you get strong enough to hurt me?"

"Don't change the subject!" she warns, getting Finn settled on the blanket, then turning to glare at me.

"She knows."

Reese eyes Genny cautiously now, getting a little nervous herself. "What did she say?"

"She wondered how you could've been ok with me living with him."

"Hmph."

Twice now, Reese is speechless. I definitely have to keep bringing Genny around.

Zeke comes running over, holding up something green between his fingers. "Mom, Uncle Walk, look! Genny says I'm really lucky!"

Genny walks slowly behind him, her hands in her back pockets, which only draws my eyes to the curves of her breasts pushing against her shirt. She shrugs, a small smile on her face. "When he fell down, I explained he was in the perfect spot to look for a four-leaf clover. He knows his numbers really well. He counted out all the three leafed clovers before he found the lucky one."

Zeke beams up at Reese with Genny's praise. "We made up a song, too, Mom. Wanna hear it?"

"Yes," Reese confirms, looking over at me. *He didn't cry?* she mouths, while Zeke breaks into a song about swings and snakes and four-leaf clovers. Then Zeke takes off, pulling Genny behind him as he races to the monkey bars.

Zeke has been crying over every little thing since Finn was born. Reese tells me it's because Zeke no longer gets all the attention, and crying is his way of forcing people to fawn over him.

On the second rung of the monkey bars, Genny tickles him until he lets go, falling right into her waiting arms. My sister watches Genny with a laughing Zeke, finally admitting defeat a few minutes later.

"Dammit. I wanted to hate her."

"Impossible, isn't it?"

Reese side-eyes me, glaring out of the corner of her eye. "I'm gonna try a little harder. I'll get back to you."

Finn's standing next to Reese and using her knee to steady himself. Holding my hand out, I guide him along as he stumbles his way to me, dropping quickly onto his butt once there. He lets out a high-pitched squeal and Reese looks over, holding up her hands, just out of his reach. After pushing himself back onto his chubby bow-legged feet, he reaches for her, taking a single step on his own before falling down again.

Reese sighs. "He's so close…"

"You should start catching up on your sleep now. You're gonna be exhausted when it happens."

The next time Zeke comes running over, he falls face first into my chest. "Uncle Walk, Genny won't push me high enough on the swings… Will you push me?"

"I'm better than Genny at something? *Finally*! I thought you weren't gonna play with me anymore!" Jumping to my feet, I catch Genny around the waist and deposit a quick kiss on her surprised mouth. Then I race after Zeke, letting him beat me to the swings. Hopefully, Reese doesn't try too hard to hate Genny when she's sitting right there with her.

Pushing Zeke on the swing as he chants *Higher, higher!* I watch my sister with Genny. I want them to get along. I want Reese to enjoy Genny's company because I want to bring her around. A lot. I want her to meet my parents and join our family gatherings. I want to weave her into every part of my life.

The things I want with Genny are a little shocking. Normally, it's months before I let anyone I'm dating meet my family. Normally, even when I let it happen, I'm only doing it because it's expected. And I usually know them a lot better than I know Genny.

It feels like I've known Genny for a long time, but I really haven't. When I'm thinking about her, it'll take me by surprise that I have no idea what her favorite color is. Whether or not she wore braces as a kid, or what she meant when she said she was *into music*. Does that mean she liked to listen to music, or did she play an instrument?

I *feel* like I know her. I can guess her reaction to things, I can tell when things offend her or make her happy even when she doesn't show it. Maybe I know Genny as a person, but I don't know all the details that made her who she is.

I know she was horrified to find out Kane saw her picture, but she played it off like it was no big deal.

I know she really wants Reese to like her.

I know that not knowing what Callie and I are planning is secretly killing her.

And I know that she's afraid to tell Chad she won't have sex with him anymore

Knowing how she's treated sex for the last three years, I can understand how it would be scary. She gets weird migraines when she's stressed, I've seen how weird they can be, so I can understand how it would be really convenient to have someone on speed dial when life gets stressful. But why is Chad the only one she's afraid to tell?

I don't know the answer to that question, but I need her to give him up in order to trust that she's really in this. That she really wants this.

I turn my attention back to Zeke, who's pumping his little legs as hard as he can, trying to go even higher than I'm pushing him. As he swings back to me, I grab the chains and ignore his grumbling complaints when I slow him down. "Hey, Zeke, you like Genny, right?"

"Yeah," he answers, enthusiastically nodding his head as he looks around. "She's almost as pretty as Mommy, but she's funner than Mommy."

"That's because mommies can't always be fun. I bet if Genny had to yell at you for misbehaving, you wouldn't think she was as fun, either."

"Genny won't yell at me. I'll be good for Genny."

Ruffling his hair, I tell him that's good to know. Maybe I'll have to convince Reese to let Genny come over the next time I watch the boys. It'll take a hell of a lot to convince her to let that happen, but I can try, right?

"I think we should go back and tickle Genny until she surrenders, what do ya think?"

"Yeah!" Zeke yells, taking off again for home base.

I jog after him, wanting to get there about the same time, hearing him giggle at our secret plan before he's even half way there. Reese yells for him to watch out for his brother, so I pick Zeke up in my arms, falling to the ground beside Genny. Zeke immediately reaches for her and she holds her arms out to him. That's when the sneaky little guy gets out his tickle fingers and pushes them against her belly.

"Hey!" she laughs, trying to push his hands away. My nephew is relentless, though. When I join in from the side, she starts squealing in between her laughs. She tries desperately to move away from us, but with Zeke on top of her, she can't roll away. Finally, she yells, "*Stop!*"

Zeke freezes, thinking he's in trouble, but she wraps her arms around him and holds him close as she tries to catch her breath. She whispers in his ear and he nods his head against her breast. She whispers again, and he breaks out into a smile, obviously reassured he's not in trouble.

Lying on my side facing her, one arm still on her thigh while the other props up my head, I watch as Zeke climbs off Genny and comes at *me* with his tickle fingers. Genny wasn't telling Zeke he wasn't in trouble. She was telling him to get me next.

Genny isn't as comfortable touching me under my sister's watchful eyes, so it's easy to push Zeke's hands off me and roll away from her. I jump up and jog away from them, turning around to find Genny chasing me and Zeke rolling on the blanket laughing.

Perfect. I have no problem with Genny catching me. But first, I run far enough away that Zeke won't see what I do to his new friend. Running around the corner of the restrooms, I catch Genny as she follows me. After shrieking in surprise, she melts into my arms as I cover her mouth with mine.

I can't even keep my hands off her when I'm at a playground with my sister and my nephews. I'm in trouble.

The *best* kind of trouble.

Genny leans into me, her tongue becoming more insistent as her hands lock themselves around my neck. In the back of my mind, there's that same little voice whispering that this is already getting out of hand, but I don't care. Right now, I want her in my arms, nowhere else.

Pulling her with me, I lean against the side of the building and slide my hands around her waist under her shirt. She groans at the feel of my skin on hers, her hips pushing against mine. Moving one hand south, I grip her ass and feel her break the kiss to tip her head back. Ever the opportunist, I take advantage of having her long, elegant neck exposed, taking my first taste of her that doesn't come from her mouth.

"Walker..." she whispers, one of her hands moving from my neck up onto my scalp, her fingers pushing through my hair. Kissing my way back up her neck, I take her mouth again, gripping her ass in both hands and pulling her against me.

I don't have much time left, if any, so I spin us around and pin her against the wall, capturing her mouth one last time. "You never told me how the second test ride went."

Her eyes fly open, glassy and confused as I take her mind somewhere it doesn't want to go. A smile slowly works its way onto her flushed cheeks as she answers. "Better than expected. But I was still thinking of you, so I don't know if it counts."

"I wasn't there. It counts." Running my hand up her side, I squeeze her ribs lightly, letting my fingers trail along the outer curve of her breast. She moves her arm, encouraging me closer to the middle, tipping her head back and closing her eyes as I brush over her nipple.

"This isn't a good place to be touching me like this, Friend."

"What? Thinking about being inside you while you're up against the restroom building in a children's park isn't a good idea?"

"Not the best you've had, I'm sure."

Genny cocks her head to the side, listening. Sure enough, Zeke's voice is getting louder as he yells for *Uncle Walk!* and *Genny!* "You give me some very bad ideas, G."

"You should see the ideas that take place in my head when I get out our toy."

I step away, adjusting my very tight pants, as Genny pulls her shirt back down and fluffs her hair. "*Our* toy?" I ask, wishing more than ever that I could take part in how and when she uses it. There's no way we're there yet, though. "I wanna hear all about these bad ideas."

"Be good and maybe you will."

"What's your definition of *good*, G?"

Zeke runs around the corner screaming our names and Genny catches him mid-stride, picking him up and spinning him around.

"What're you guys doing? You were gone a long time," he whines.

"I got stuck. Your Uncle Walk made sure I wasn't hurt, and that I felt *really* good before he got me unstuck," she tells him, making eyes at me the whole time.

Zeke eyes us curiously, not quite believing Genny. "Where'd you get stuck?" he demands skeptically, looking around to see what anyone could possibly get stuck on back here.

"Zeke, get away from Genny. If you can," I offer, trying not to laugh as he squirms in Genny's arms. "I trapped Genny like she's got you trapped."

His eyes narrow in suspicion and he glares at Genny's flushed face. "Uncle Walk kissed you again!"

"And now that I have *you* trapped, I'm gonna kiss *you!*" Genny promises, smothering his face with a hundred kisses. At first, he pushes her away, not wanting any gross kisses from a *girl*. But by the time she's done, he's laughing and kissing her right back.

See? I'm not the only one who can't resist her and that sweet mouth she has.

Once Zeke forgets he's mad at us for being gone so long, Genny puts him down and he walks between us. We're each holding one of his hands and he's running ahead and jumping into the air, letting us swing him up and back before his feet touch the ground again.

Reese packs up when we get back to the blanket and Zeke says he wants Genny to hold his hand on the way home. My sister just shakes her head with a long sigh.

Back at Reese's, Zeke pulls Genny up the stairs, asking her to read him a story since Reese told him very sternly that it was bedtime. Reese shoos them along with her free hand, Finn still planted on her hip, slapping her boob and singing a nonsensical song only he knows.

Genny easily won over my nephew tonight.

"I thought I was going to be Zeke's number one girl until he was at least in middle school, so I can honestly say I hate her for stealing him from me," Reese informs me.

"He told me you're prettier than she is."

"Aww," Reese says, her hand going straight to her heart. "He said that?"

"You're still his number one. She's just a shiny new friend. Let her watch them with me some time. When she scolds him, I'm sure she'll drop below you in his mind."

"And find her giving another *performance* in my living room when I get home? No thank you!"

I knew it wouldn't be easy. "I promise we'll keep our clothes on."

"Sure, they'll be on, they'll just be pushed out of the way. Not happening, Walker. I don't feel like taking the time to disinfect my house after a night off."

"What if we watched the boys at Genny's house?"

Reese stops what she's doing to stare at me. "Why would you want to spend a night with your girlfriend watching my children?"

"I don't know," I admit with a shrug of my shoulders. "Today was a lot of fun. I like seeing her with Zeke and I'm betting she'll have just as much with Finn. What's the big deal?"

"Oh my God," Reese says slowly. "You're nuts about her, aren't you? You like seeing her with the kids you love, because it makes it easy to picture your future with her."

"What? I'm not thinking anything like that yet. I'm just thinking today was *fun*. I love spending time with the boys, and I love spending time with Genny. I'm just putting two things I love together."

"You love Genny, huh?"

"I love spending *time* with her," I correct. "It's way too soon to figure out if I could love her or not."

"Uh-huh," Reese mutters, a sly smile covering her mouth. "Sure, Walker, whatever you say."

Rolling my eyes, I steal Finn and move into the living room, where I let him stand on my legs as I sit on the couch, his little hands wrapped around my fingers. He's babbling, trying to tell me how much he thinks his mom is crazy, I'm sure. I tell him he's absolutely right, his momma's a bit of a whack job. The way he smiles when I say it tells me we're on the same wavelength.

I don't tell Genny I offered her house and her assistance in watching the boys. It didn't seem like Reese was very keen on the idea. Sometimes I talk without thinking, and my mouth gets me in trouble.

Luckily, when I drop Genny off at the end of the night, talking is the last thing she's interested in doing. Using my mouth to kiss Genny gets me in a different kind of trouble, but I like *this* kind of trouble. I'll take this kind of trouble as often as I'm able to get it.

Genny

"Are you sure you don't want me to take you out tonight?" Walker asks from my couch a week and a half later, and I reassure him *again*.

"Very sure. You can take me out next weekend," I tell him for the third time. Maybe if I give him a better explanation he'll leave it alone. "This week is gonna be weird and I just want to relax tonight."

"Why's it gonna be weird?"

Bringing a bottle of beer over for us, I settle on the couch next to him. "You know about my migraines. Remember when I said I usually get them?"

"When you're stressed out."

"And when I'm hormonal."

"Oh-kayy."

This is awkward. How do I say, *Walker, I'm gonna get my period, so I'm going to have another episode*? I was hoping he'd be able to figure that out on his own, but apparently, he needs a little coaxing to help him put two and two together.

"I'm going to be hormonal this week, which means I'm gonna get another migraine. Probably tomorrow. So, if I you try to get ahold of me and I don't answer your texts or calls for a couple days, don't worry about it. I'm just sleeping off my migraine *and* my cramps."

"*Oh*," he says, finally getting it. He stares at me quizzically before taking a drink of the beer I just gave him. "What's wrong with your brother?"

"What? Where did that question come from?"

"You get these weird migraines, Callie's diabetic. What's wrong with Calvin?"

"Nothing," I laugh. "Calvin's perfect, health-wise. Lucky bastard!"

Walker slides his arm around me and pulls me close. His mouth moves oh-so-close to mine before he stops and eyes the stairs. "Where's Callie tonight?"

Callie... Of course, *she's* the reason Walker's tongue isn't in my mouth right now.

"She's *supposedly* in her room."

"She's a sneaky one, isn't she?"

Nodding in agreement, I pull him back to me, but he just smiles against my lips. Damn it all to hell. If he won't kiss me, maybe I *do* want him to take me out. Somewhere we can be alone, and I can get him to kiss me the way I want him to. The way *he* likes to. I don't care if he blames it all on me, there's no way he can honestly tell me he doesn't enjoy every second of our tongue wrestling sessions.

There's always my room.

Hmm. Would I be able to resist him if I get him on my bed in a horizontal position with his tongue inside my mouth again? I'm curious to see if I spontaneously combust like I did the last time I rolled around with him up there. Is it something that happens every time, or was last time just beginner's luck?

The thought of trying to figure that out really turns me on.

Trying again to kiss Walker, I roll my eyes at his closed mouth. "You're no fun," I complain.

"You're *too* much fun. If you weren't quite so responsive, I wouldn't hesitate. We don't need Callie to see your *messed-up* face in person, do we?"

"Can we take our little party up to my room then?"

Walker's expression tells me he likes that idea very much, but he's still reluctant. "I was hoping to spend tonight getting to know you better. If we go to your room, I doubt we'll do much talking."

"Compromise?"

"I'm listening..."

"We can write down questions we want to ask each other. If you answer one of my questions completely and honestly, as a reward, I'll kiss you. Then we'll switch, and it'll be my turn."

"Hmm," he murmurs. "So, you're going to be extremely open and honest because you want as many of my kisses as you can get... I think that sounds like a fun game. Can I add a rule? For my own personal protection?"

"Why do you need protected from me?"

"Yes or no, G."

Rolling my eyes, I tell him, "Yes, within reason."

Walker chuckles before finally opening that sweet mouth and sliding his tongue between my lips. He tastes like beer and promises. Promises of all the good things yet to come. Promises of *fireworks*.

"We have to keep our clothes on," he whispers in my ear. "All of them."

"You're *definitely* no fun," I whisper back, already wishing I could shed some, or *all*, of mine. "But since that was my plan all along, I'll agree to it for tonight."

Stealing some paper and pens from Callie's studying station, we make our way to my room. "Does it need to be an open-ended question?" I ask.

"Any question you want. We should probably have roughly the same amount though."

"Eh," I shrug, while tapping the pen against my mouth to help me think. "You kissing me, me kissing you... As long as our mouths and tongues are fused, I don't care who's turn it is."

Scoffing, he reaches out to slide his hand along my skin under my shirt. I'm very ok with it, encouraging it even, until he tickles me, his hand torturing me and making me squeal in laughter until I can get away from him. Walker's a fan of tickling. I'll have to make sure to tickle *him* the next time he lands me on top of him straddling his hips, with the erection I love to feel between my legs.

"So that means if you only have ten questions for me, but I have fifty, once you're done asking yours, I get to ask you question after question until all mine are answered, right?"

I didn't consider that, did I? I was focusing on the kissing part. "Ok, we should have the same amount. And I'm adding a rule." Walker arches an eyebrow from his leisurely spot on my bed. "No more tickling me."

"No more tickling you *tonight*," he agrees.

"I'll take it. Don't get me wrong, I love your hands on me, but next time do something with them that doesn't make me squirm, please."

"I don't know, I've seen you squirm in a way that tells me you *love* the way I'm touching you."

"No more tickling," I demand, pointing my pen at him. Smiling, he goes back to his question making.

Can I just mention, really quickly, how amazingly good he looks sprawled out on my bed the way he is? Walker relaxed and happy, taking up a huge amount of space on my queen size bed, has me coming up with all kinds of fun games. And none of them require pens or clothes.

Scribbling out a few more questions, I look up to find him watching me. Maybe he's ready. I quickly tally up the things I most want to know.

After comparing totals, I write out a couple more, just whatever comes to mind first. I want my questions to be random, so I mix up the cards they're written on and tell him to pick one. Walker reads the first question silently before studying me. He's thinking, trying to come up with a good answer. "What's the coolest thing you've done that no one knows about?" His eyes flick back to mine before he adds, "We should make another rule."

"*Another* one? This is supposed to be a simple game! We're making it kind of complicated."

"This is a good question and I wanna steal it. I was thinking our new rule should be that we both have to answer each question."

"My questions for you might not be questions I want to answer," I complain. I definitely didn't pick out my questions thinking *I* would need to answer them.

"Then no kissing after that question."

Glaring at him, I'm not sure what to hope for. Do I want his questions to be easy for me to answer, or a fun way to learn about him? "Ok, fine, but you'd better have some good stories to tell me. Now what's your answer?"

Walker looks back down at the paper. "I was there when Zeke was born. My mom was supposed to be in the delivery room with Reese, but he came a couple weeks early, and I was the only one who could get there in time. I got to cut the umbilical cord. It was the most amazing moment of my life."

"Wow," I whisper. "That's a good story. No wonder you're so close with him."

"Yeah, I love that little rascal." Walker beams a proud smile, turning the tables on me. "What about you?"

"Nothing like *that*," I complain. Thinking back, I try to remember anything cool that I've done. It's been so long since I've done something that wasn't just another part of ordinary everyday life. There has to be something I did that was fun. What about way back in high school, or college? There's gotta be *something* from then, right?

"I don't know if it's cool, but back in high school, there was this guy," I start, a little nervous because this story definitely isn't *cool*.

"Oh God," Walker mutters shaking his head.

"Relax, it's not like that. He was really sweet, but a total nerd. We were lab partners my junior year, so even though he wasn't someone I'd normally ever associate with, I got to know him. When it came prom time, someone asked him to go and he said no because he was too nervous that she'd want to kiss him, and he'd never kissed anyone before. So, I taught him how to kiss. And he took her to prom and eventually married her."

Walker ruins my story by *laughing*. "Are you trying to take credit for someone else's happily ever after?"

"Oh Lord! I'm just saying I helped out a friend without telling anyone. He was actually a pretty good kisser once he gained some confidence."

"My story's way better than yours," Walker comments, his eyes lit up like Christmas morning. "I guess that means you need to kiss me, right?"

Oh yeah! I forgot about the kissing part of this game. Deciding I should keep it short and innocent since we're just getting started, I lean into him nice and slow, taking my sweet old time. When my lips finally touch his, I feel him opening up, very ready for things to get hot and heavy. Instead, I let my lips linger on his for a few seconds and pull away before our tongues wander out of their respective homes, pulling a question from his pile with a smirk.

"You're gonna pay for that little trick, G."

"I hope to, Friend," I confess, shooting a smile his way and grabbing one of the cards from my pile. "Now. Your question for me. If I could have any job in the world, what would it be?" I think about all the dreams I had before my parents died. I was so young, so naïve. My dreams were simple, but apparently not simple enough. The greedy hands of fate stole them in the blink of an eye.

"I wanted to be a music teacher."

"*Wanted* to be? Is that what you'd still choose if you could do anything?"

"I guess, if things were different. It's been a long time since I've thought about what I'd do if I could do anything. Usually, I'm not thinking about what *I* want, ya know?" I shake my head, trying to rid myself of the useless nostalgia trying to take over my emotions. "What about you?"

"I don't know, I like my job. When I was a kid, I wanted to be a famous football player or a mailman. Yes, a mailman," he confirms, seeing my surprised face. "But I like what I do now. It's not mentally stressful, so at the end of the day, I can leave it all there. I don't bring problems home, like what I didn't get done, or what I have to do the next day. I don't have emails coming in at all hours. I go in, do my job, and leave."

"What exactly do you do there?"

"I drive a forklift, loading and unloading trucks."

"Really?" I ask, more excited than I should be. "I've always wanted to do that. Not the loading thing, I've always wanted to drive a forklift. I think it would be fun."

"It's not all that thrilling when you do it day in and day out, but it's not bad, either."

"So, you're saying you'd do exactly what you're doing now?"

Walker shrugs his shoulders, explaining, "I don't want to be famous and I don't want to deliver mail in the snow or rain, so, sure."

"Well then, my answer is better than yours this time, so you have to kiss me."

"Good," he mumbles, eyeing me sitting across from him on my bed. "Come here."

"I need to come to you?"

"No, but you should. It'll be a lot more fun if you're closer."

Rolling my eyes, I move towards him, crawling on my hands and knees as he smiles seductively at my progress. Once I'm practically on top of him, he closes that beautiful mouth over mine, kissing me with enough intensity to make me feel like I'm drowning in a sea of want for him. His hands push past my face, up into my hair and he pulls me closer still. Soon, I'm sitting on his lap, my legs around his waist as his tongue invades my mouth, making me ache for him in a way that will surely drive me insane until he leaves, and I get to play with our toy.

Walker lies back on my bed, pulling me down with him until I'm straddling him again. His hands find their way under my shirt to slide up my back, his touch igniting little fires along my skin that lead straight between my legs.

Suddenly, I'm on my back, with Walker on top of me.

Yes. *This* I like. *This* I can get used to, clothes or no clothes. His mouth leaves mine for a second, then comes right back at a different angle, one that allows him to kiss me deeper. Rocking my pelvis towards him, I groan at the contact, at the hardness pressing between my legs, wanting so much more, with so much less in the way.

Then he's *gone*.

Blinking my eyes open, I look around, dazed, wondering exactly what happened to stop that fun ride. Walker's standing at the side of my bed, looking down at me with a grin on his face and a very hard bulge straining against his pants.

Oh, that jerk! He probably thinks that was suitable payback for my short kiss to him earlier.

"I'm changing my mind about that last answer..." he says, his voice rough and uneven. "I want the job of turning you on and getting you off as often as necessary. I have a feeling I'll have to pull overtime every day, but I think I'm the best person for the job."

Flashing a smile, I change my mind, too. "I want to be your supervisor."

He chuckles, shaking his head slightly. "Course you do."

"No," I tell him, letting an idea play in my mind. "I really did change my mind."

He raises an eyebrow, waiting for my new answer, even though I'm terrified to say it out loud. Can I voice it? Can I admit it to him? I suppose if I'm going to admit it to anyone, it should be him, since I agreed to let him in. Sitting up, I drastically change the subject and admit something I never even fully admitted to myself. "I wanna be a mom. That's the job I want more than any other."

"It seems like you kind of already are a mom."

"Only a substitute. And I was totally unqualified when I got the job."

"You'd want to have your own kids, then? I thought maybe you'd be sick of taking care of other people, no matter how old, and want to focus on yourself."

"No," I assure him, feeling like this is way too early in our relationship to be having a talk about wanting babies. "I want my own kids, eventually. Now that I'm not a kid myself, anymore."

He simply nods before reaching into the messy pile of cards on my side of the bed. "Next question," I vaguely hear him say. "What is the best compliment you've ever received?"

He lays on the bed next to me, getting comfortable once again. "I've got two answers for this one. The first one is when this girl I really like had an orgasm just from kissing me. And the way she did it? Like she had no control, like getting kissed by me turned her on *so* much, her body just took over and *bam!* She was coming apart in my arms and looking like the most beautiful thing I'd ever seen... *That's* the best compliment I've gotten, by far."

Smiling at my heated cheeks, he goes on, doing his best to prove my secrets are safe with him, "But if anyone other than you should ask, it's when my sister told me I'm gonna be an awesome dad. Your turn. What's the best compliment *you've* ever gotten?

After side-eyeing him, I roll onto my side and prop my head in my hand, mirroring Walker and his lazy position. "Callie gave me some really wise advice the other day, and I couldn't believe it was coming from her. I feel like such a screw-up when it comes to her and Calvin, but she told me that I taught her *right*, and it almost made me cry."

"How long have you been teaching your siblings about life?" Walker asks quietly, his eyes intent on mine.

This is it. This is when I either let him in, or keep shutting him out.

It's been a really long time since I've told anyone the truth. I didn't even really tell Paul. I only ever told him parts of it.

Walker deserves *all* of it.

Reaching out, I take his hand and move closer, laying my head on the arm that's propping up his head, his eyes still watching me. Once I'm comfortable, I begin my story.

I don't leave anything out. I start with the day I got the news, that fateful last class I was ever in. The phone call that interrupted the entire lecture hall and had the professor cursing and glaring at me as I walked out, trying to figure out if what I'd just heard was real or some kind of cruel, sick joke. The tearful drive home from school, the one I never should have taken, because to this day, I still don't remember how I got to my car, let alone home in one piece. Trying to arrange the funerals, and deal with the onslaught of questions and advice from neighbors and friends who thought they knew what I needed to hear to grieve and move on with my life. Feeling so very alone and scared and lost. Being told that Callie and Calvin would be put into the foster system if I didn't step up and take legal guardianship of them.

I even admit how I *didn't* step up at take legal guardianship of them. Not at first. I was too young and stupid to take care of myself, how could I take care of them, too?

But then they were *gone*, and I literally had no one. And that was even more terrifying than the thought of trying to take care of them was.

Walker's silent the entire time, his eyes letting me know I've got his undivided attention. He doesn't interrupt me or ask questions. He simply lets me tell my story, and occasionally squeezes the hand he's still holding. And when I'm done, he has the best reaction anyone ever has when learning about even part of my story. He tells me he's proud of me, and that I did the right thing. Then he says I'm amazing, strong, and brave.

I've always wondered what would've happened if I hadn't done it. Would Callie and Calvin have gotten better opportunities, would they have had better lives with someone else? We weren't that close before our parents died, and my younger siblings suddenly having to listen to me was a rough transition. And me suddenly having to make decisions for all of us instead of just myself was the *hardest* transition, at least for me. I tried really hard to not let anyone see that.

While Callie, Calvin and I are close *now*, I've always prayed that was enough of a trade-off for how much better their lives might've been. I was just a young, scared kid, who had no idea what I was doing with them. I just knew I was going to screw them up somehow. It was inevitable.

Somehow, we all turned out ok.

It feels so good to hear someone tell me I did the right thing. And it's been so long since someone has told me they're proud of me that my eyes go cloudy with unshed tears.

I don't know what to do with these emotions in front of Walker. When he lowers his head to mine, I gladly accept his kiss, the one that tells me he's here for me and he believes in me, although I don't know how he can. His thumb brushes away the moisture on my cheeks, and he moves so he's behind me, wrapping his body around mine and giving me space to come to terms with my emotions, while still being here if I need him.

It's everything I've ever wanted and didn't know how or who to ask for it from. And with Walker, I don't even need to ask, he just somehow *knows*. He somehow knows *me*, even with me telling him very little about myself. Is it possible that maybe he's simply *right* for me? That maybe we won't go down in flames, like I originally predicted? Maybe we'll get our own happily ever after, instead?

Pushing aside all my crazy thoughts, I pull Walker's arm closer around me, focusing on the here and now. I'm thankful beyond words that he's still here, and that he knows exactly what I need to feel less vulnerable after pushing through my fears and telling him my story. Lacing my fingers through his, I pray he knows how much I trust him. And I fall asleep that way, feeling safe and *protected*, for the first time in as long as I can remember.

Walker

Genny's story blows me away. Callie's version was simple, to the point, matter of fact. Genny's was full of emotion, the biggest one being fear. Fear of letting me see how she felt, but also the fear of regret. How she could still be questioning whether she did the right thing for her siblings ten years later lets me know just how unsure of her role with them she is. But Callie seems like a well-adjusted, happy college student, and Genny has so much to do with that. I haven't met Calvin, but I would bet he turned out just as well.

Her tears break my heart. The fact that she's embarrassed to cry in front of me tells me how rarely she lets people in. But she did for *me*, and I try to show her that I'm here for her in whatever way she needs me to be. When she falls asleep in my arms, I lie with her, thinking, for a long time. Way longer than I should.

I have no idea what time Genny has to get up for work. Pulling out my phone, I text Callie to see if she's still awake. She seems to be a night owl, always up late. She promises she'll get Genny up for work and I try to slowly extricate my body from Genny's. It's a lot harder than I thought it would be, simply because I know she gave me her trust tonight, and pulling away from her is the last thing I want to do.

There's some left-over paper on her nightstand and I grab one of the pens we were using for our game to write her a quick note, referencing the first text I ever sent her. When she asked me how I knew her name would be spelled different from the normal Jenny. I'd texted her then that I had a feeling she was one in a million. My note tonight is simple, telling her now I *know* she is.

Callie's downstairs at the table after I sneak out of Genny's room. Arching her eyebrow, she declares, "You're either boring Genny to sleep or you gave in and had sex with her. I really thought you'd last longer, Walker."

Chuckling at her directness, I disappoint her even further. "None of the above, Cal. She told me about your parents. About everything she felt and how scared she was to take care of you and your brother after it happened."

Callie freezes, eyeing me with suspicion. "Are you sure? She doesn't talk about that stuff. Not even to Myra."

"I'm sure Myra knows, you probably just weren't eavesdropping during that conversation."

She shakes her head with wide eyes. "Myra knows what happened, but she's asked *me* how Genny dealt with all of it, because she was different after it happened. Different than she was when they went to school together. Genny doesn't talk feelings, Walker."

Not knowing what to do with that statement, I watch Callie and her expressions. She looks so much like Genny, just younger. Her lips aren't quite as full, her nose is turned up just a bit more. Callie's a little shorter, her hair longer and lighter. Genny's not quite as toned, but it just makes her curves softer and more fun to touch.

These girls are gorgeous. It's easy to see how Genny had her regulars. Who in their right mind turns down a girl as beautiful as her when she asks for sex only?

Me. I'm that fool. It's turning out better than I ever imagined it could, though.

"You're the one who told her she was shoving sex in my face, aren't you?" The blush that highlights her cheeks and neck confirms my theory. "I don't know if she's told you, Callie, but Genny's so proud of you."

She bites her lip, confessing, "I know, but not because she told *me*. Because she told *you*."

Walker

The week drags by without a word from Genny. I miss her random texts, her challenging comments, her sassy mouth. Wednesday morning, I text Callie to make sure Genny's ok. She responds quickly, saying Genny's migraine is much worse than normal.

Thursday, it's pouring down rain outside, and Reese invited our parents over to our weekly meet. I love when my whole family can get together, especially since I still get to play with the boys. Even Steve is home this week, and I make a mental note to ask how to get things from my phone to the TV and back again if I get a minute alone with him.

I brush the rain from my shirt after letting myself in the backdoor, and I'm immediately grabbed by a little pair of hands around my leg. Pretending to try to shake him off like I did the rain, I smile down at Zeke's laughter. Even with his easy grin, he's looking through my legs out the door.

"Who ya looking for, Zeke?"

"Genny."

Oh... It makes sense, she's been coming here with me on Thursdays since that first one when she met him. She's fallen in love with my nephews almost as quickly as they fell in love with her. I'll bet Reese hates her even more now that his new routine is apparently to watch out the door for her every week. Picking him up, I gaze into his sad little eyes and resist the urge to pull out my phone and text her yet again. "Genny's sick, so she's at home in bed."

"Genny's sick?"

"Uh-huh. Hopefully she can come next week, though." He gives me a thoughtful look as I set him back on his feet. After kissing my mom on the cheek, I reach around her to grab a glass. She side-eyes me in a very familiar way that says I'm in trouble, although I have no idea why. Maybe I can get out of it. I try to sneak away into the living room, but luck is *not* on my side tonight.

"Walker, I heard about your news from your *sister*. You know I don't like to feel out of the loop, are you deliberately keeping me in the dark?"

Unsure what she's talking about, I look at Reese, who's pulling a casserole from the oven. She rolls her eyes at my confusion, mouthing, *Genny*!

"Mom, you know I'd never keep you in the dark about anything important. What did you supposedly hear?" Hopefully I can find out exactly what Reese told our mother about the beautiful, smart-mouthed vixen I'm dating.

"You don't think news about you finally having a girlfriend is important?"

"We're dating, Mom, nothing's official yet."

"The way Zeke talks about her, you need bring her to meet me. And if she's as great as Reese says, you need to *make* it official."

Arching my eyebrows at Reese, I smile in her direction. "Funny, Reese has only told me she hates Genny for stealing her first born every time she comes. I didn't think she'd be giving her a thumbs up. Zeke's trying to steal her from *me*, so I know *he's* saying good things about her."

"Your nephew has been staring out the door all night, hoping she was coming with you. I was hoping for that, too," Mom says, pointing towards the door. "Wait, where'd Zeke go? He's probably heartbroken she isn't here."

"He took off towards the living room when I told him Genny wasn't coming."

"Well go find him, it's time to eat."

Finally having permission to travel farther inside the house, I set out to look for Zeke, checking all his favorite spots before finding him in his room upstairs. He's huddled over his small desk working on something so hard he doesn't even bother to look up when I come in.

"You ready to eat, Zeke? Gram says it's time."

"In a minute," he mumbles, eyes totally focused on whatever masterpiece he has on his desk.

"Whatever you're working on, we can finish it after dinner, Bud. You don't wanna make Gramma mad, do you?"

Zeke lets out a frustrated sigh, scowling up at me. "I'm making a picture for Genny. It'll make her smile and then she'll feel all better."

Chuckling at how eager he is to see her, I squat down next to him and look at what he's working on. "I think your picture *will* make her feel better. You don't wanna rush it, though. Let's go eat and then we can come back and take our time on it, so it'll be perfect, how's that sound?"

His eyes are so kind and thoughtful when he looks up at me, it makes my heart hurt. Zeke is all his mother, none of that asshole roommate of mine. Reese is doing an amazing job with him.

"Will you give it to Genny when it's done?"

"Yeah, of course. She's gonna love it."

His eyes narrow as he stares at me, obviously not happy about something. "No kissing when you give it to her. Not in front of my picture."

That's not happening, but he doesn't need to know that. Ruffling his hair, I tell him "Whatever you say, you're the boss." After getting what he thinks is my consent, he finally relents and walks down the stairs with a frown.

I don't think he believes me about the no kissing rule...

Dinner is almost over when my phone vibrates in my pocket. Reese and my mom both have very strict rules about no phones at the dinner table, so I check it *under* the table, trying to be secretive about it, only needing to know if it's Genny or not. I haven't heard from her since leaving her place Sunday night and her silence is killing me. Zeke catches me from his booster seat, pulling on my arm and asking in a hopeful voice, "Is that Genny?"

Busted.

Mom and Reese glare at me. Steve shakes his head with a smile and Dad just keeps on eating. Nothing phases my dad. He's seen and heard it all, someone in trouble for checking their phone at the table isn't anything new. Even if it's been years since it's happened.

"Umm, yes. It *is* Genny," I answer carefully. "But I'm not going to check it right now, because it's rude to check your phone at the table."

Reese and Mom turn their attention back to whatever it is they were talking about, but they're now keeping their eyes on me. Great. Just what I need. Thanks for tattling on me, Zeke.

Dinner now can't get over soon enough. Which of course, means it drags on and on. Reese never makes dessert, so when the dishes start being cleared, I think I'm free, but *no*. Mom brought dessert.

Zeke is excused, running back upstairs to work on his picture for Genny.

Sure, *he* can go think about Genny, but I'm forced to sit here, barely even listening to the conversation because Genny finally feels well enough to text me, but I have no idea what she said, and the desire to find out is killing me.

"Walker, would you mind checking on Zeke? He's been gone a while and he's a little too quiet up there," Steve requests, smiling slyly in my direction.

"Yes!"

I practically jump from my seat, surprising everyone except Steve. He somehow knows exactly what I'm going through. He doesn't need me to check on Zeke, but I'm definitely glad to get away from this table and the idle chitchat my mother and sister can spend hours doing. My phone is out before I even hit the living room and I sigh in relief at the sight of Genny's words.

Genny: I'm feeling human enough to accept any offers of attention you may wish to give me.

Walker: Is that your way of asking me to come see you?

Genny: Kinda, but not exactly.

Walker: What exactly are you saying, G?

Dots pops up on my phone, letting me know she's typing out a reply. It's gone by the time I sit down behind Zeke to admire the picture he's showing me, but there's no new text for me to view. When she still hasn't sent a reply a minute later, I add some encouragement.

Walker: *I miss your smart mouth, G. Talk to me.*

The dots pop up on my phone again, but this time she sends it.

Genny: *I miss YOU. I would love for you to come over, but I don't want you to feel like you have to.*

Walker: *Seeing you is never an obligation. I'm at my sister's, can I stop by when I leave?*

Genny: *YES!*

Capital letters *and* an exclamation point. I'm gonna say she's excited to see me. Thank God, because I can't wait to see her and that delicious mouth I can't stop thinking about. It doesn't take me long to say my goodbyes to my family and make my way to her backdoor.

The smile that brightens her face when she swings it open is enough to make my week. Before I sweep her into my arms, I give her Zeke's drawing, which is kept safe from the rain in a Ziplock bag. She looks it over, her eyes sparkling with an unspoken question.

"Zeke wanted to make you feel better. He drew this and put it in the bag himself, so it wouldn't get wet. That's you on the swing next to him, but he's higher, so he's winning... He also said no kissing in front of his picture."

"Tell him I love him to pieces, but I can't follow that rule."

"No? Are you gonna kiss Callie in front of it?"

Callie raises her eyes from the dining room, obviously not finding my joke amusing. Genny simply shakes her head, a smile tugging at her lips as I step in closer to her. "You gonna call Myra over and kiss *her* in front of it?"

She shakes her head again, pulling me against her body and wrapping her hand around my neck. "Try again. One last guess."

"Am I the lucky winner? Are you gonna kiss *me* in front of his drawing?"

"Ding ding ding!" she whispers, pulling my face down to hers. She kisses me like her sister can't see us. I briefly wonder what that's about, although I certainly don't stop to ask. Instead, I let my tongue invade her mouth, wrapping my hands around her waist and holding her tight.

After a couple minutes that disappear in the blink of an eye, she leans her forehead on mine, taking a moment to catch her breath. "Let me put this on the fridge. Can you tell Zeke thank you? It's really sweet that he thought of me."

"I will, but you can do it yourself if you want. Reese wants me to watch the boys again tomorrow night. I didn't know if you wanted to help me with that?"

"Really? I didn't think she wanted me in her house without her being there."

"Ah, she doesn't really," I admit, busted for the second time this evening. "I was thinking maybe we could bring the boys here and have a sleep over."

Genny spins around, pausing her task of putting Zeke's drawing on her fridge to stare at me incredulously. "You want to bring two young boys here, to a strange place, to spend the night? Have they ever had a sleepover before? Will it be their first time not sleeping in their own house, if what you're suggesting happens?"

"I don't know," I shrug. "Does it matter? It's gonna happen at some point, and at least I'll be here. Or you. Zeke isn't going to want anyone but you."

"Where are we all going to sleep?" she cries, shaking her head.

"Wherever you want. Finn has a pack and play, and Zeke can sleep on the couch, he won't care."

"They can sleep in my room," Callie offers. "Now that Genny isn't a zombie anymore, I was hoping to go to the beach for the weekend with a couple friends. They're leaving tomorrow morning."

Genny looks back and forth between me and her sister. "When were you going to tell me about this, Callie?"

"I was gonna tell you Tuesday night, but you weren't really in the best mind space to have a conversation with me. When your pills didn't help, I told my friends I wouldn't be able to go. But you're better *now*, so I'm bringing it up. I promise I'll be good. We're staying on the boardwalk, so we won't have to worry about driving drunk. Unless we *want* to. And my plan is to just stick to the soft-core drugs and only give oral for money. I promise I won't be a full-blown prostitute addicted to crack when I get back."

"Lord, Callie. If I didn't know you better..."

Callie grins at her sister. "Yeah, but you do."

Turning back to me, Genny pokes her finger into my chest. "If I say ok to this sleepover, where are *you* gonna sleep, Friend?"

"I was hoping with you. With the boys here, we won't be able to shut the door. That way, maybe you won't rape me in my sleep."

Scoffing, Callie says, "Good luck with that."

"Hey!" Genny yells, offended. Callie opens those big green eyes, looking every bit the part of an innocent angel. Genny and I both know better. All three of us also know that it's going to be hard for Genny to keep her hands to herself. If she agrees to this, it's something I'm really looking forward to.

"Callie, just make sure you write down where you're staying. And take your tester, and extra insulin, just in case. And text me every hour so I know you're alive. Maybe every half-hour."

"Already on it, but let's limit the texting to twice a day," she suggests, holding up a list she's working on. "You don't need to worry. I just wanna lay on the beach, listen to the waves, and get a tan."

Genny's caving. Not only do I get to spend some time with her and the boys, I get to spend a night with her in my arms. And now I know Genny will have the house to herself all weekend. I was wrong earlier. Today *is* my lucky day. Maybe I'll test out our will power and see how she feels about me staying with her Saturday night, too, without the boys down the hall to make sure we behave.

My pants are getting tighter just thinking about it. I tell my dick to slow down. One thing at a time.

"Ok."

"OK?" Callie asks, obviously excited.

"Yes, ok. To both of you, ok."

Pulling her in close, I press a kiss to Genny's forehead before reluctantly letting her go to text Reese. It took some convincing for Reese to consider leaving the boys under my care for a whole evening, night, and part of the next morning. But Steve, my new best friend, was there encouraging her, reminding her that they haven't had a whole night to themselves since their honeymoon. I don't want to think about *that* in any way, but I'm glad I get to watch the boys with Genny.

Reese thinks it's weird, saying that I'm trying to play house with my girlfriend. Maybe I am, I don't know. All I know is that it's going to be a hell of a lot of fun.

Callie runs up to her room to pack, leaving Genny and me alone in the kitchen. After stealing another long, steamy kiss, she holds my hand, looking up at me with eyes that let me see deep into her soul as she tells me she's sorry about not getting back to me for so long.

I could look into these eyes for years and still not get bored.

"You told me it would probably happen. Callie said it was worse than usual?"

"Yeah. The pills didn't work at all this time. I had to go see my head doctor."

"Your *head* doctor? Should I be concerned about this?"

There's the smile I was hoping for. "No," she chuckles. "He switched my meds and gave me a guan block. I've never had one of those before, so it was interesting."

"What's a guan block?"

"It's basically a nerve block for migraines. They stuck a big needle through the back of my neck, all the way down to the nerve, and injected this stuff that blocks the receptors from telling my brain that I was in pain. I went in on the fourth day of a horrible migraine that wouldn't let up, and walked out feeling amazing."

A needle down to the nerve? That's a little terrifying to think about. What happens if they hit something they shouldn't? What happens if she moves while the needle is inside her neck? Doing my best to suppress a shudder, I pull her into my chest. "That was today, I take it?"

"Yeah. Thank God I have FMLA set up for my migraines, or I probably would've been fired."

"Is bringing the boys over tomorrow a good idea? Is it too much, too soon?"

"No, I'm good now. Just make sure you're here. You're changing all the dirty diapers."

I shake my head, chuckling. I'll easily agree to change all the diapers if I can be with her. If I can sleep with her tucked into my side like she was Sunday night, I'll do just about anything she wants me to.

Pulling Genny out onto her back porch with me, I steal several goodbye kisses, promising myself that tomorrow night they won't be to say goodbye, only goodnight.

And I can kiss her good morning, when we wake up the next day, too.

Genny

"Genny," a little voice whines, pulling me from the glorious dream I was having. "Genny, I'm hungry."

Small, insistent hands lands on my face, prying my eyes open, letting me see Zeke's intense blue ones staring back at me. Walker wasn't kidding when he said Zeke only wanted me. If I had a fan club, Zeke would be the president, CEO, and owner, all wrapped up in one tiny little body.

Thinking of Walker, where is he? He was supposed to be sleeping with me.

"Genny, get *up*. You been sleepin' a *long time*."

Opening my eyes on my own, I roll onto my back, stretching and yawning, trying to convince myself that kids are not little devils. It's not their fault they go to bed early and wake up even earlier. It's not their fault that I stayed up much too late playing my favorite kissing game with Walker. If he wasn't such a good kisser, it would've been much easier to stop playing and go to sleep with his body wrapped around me, keeping me safe. If he was *still* here keeping me safe, I'd be using him as a shield from this beautiful little boy's very persistent morning mood.

"*Gen-ny*," he whines again.

"Ok, ok! I'm getting up."

"Yes!" Zeke pumps his fist in the air, and I try not to laugh. He shouldn't be making me laugh this early. He shouldn't have the *ability* to make me laugh this early. But if I'm honest, I would admit that my cheeks are sore from how often he and Finn made me laugh last night, so I should really only expect more of that to happen this morning.

Standing at the top of the stairs, Zeke announces to the entire house, "Genny's *finally* getting up!" in a very dramatic, loud voice. I hope everyone else is already awake, because if not, Zeke is probably their unwelcome alarm clock.

After grabbing my phone, I make my way to the bathroom, shutting the door on Zeke's following feet, and locking him in my bedroom while I pee and brush my teeth. What is he talking about, *finally* getting up? It's not even seven in the morning! How long has *he* been up?

He's waiting right where I left him when I come out of the bathroom.

Lord, I need coffee. I love this little kid more than I should, but I need coffee to deal with him this early in the morning.

When Zeke figures out I'm moving to the stairs, he grabs my hand and leads me through my own house, down to the kitchen where I find two other beautiful males. Walker's at the stove in a pair of sweatpants, making breakfast with Finn on his bare hip. He shoots a knowing smile in my direction and hands me a coffee mug that's only half full.

I cringe at the sweet taste after finishing it off. "How do you drink your coffee?"

"That's sugar, G. It makes sense you don't like it, you're already pretty sweet all by yourself."

Mumbling at his endearing comment, I make us another cup while Zeke tugs on my pajama shorts. "Genny, will you play blocks with me? Please?"

Walker saves me from the little devil that's almost pantsing me at this early hour. "Zeke, I think Genny needs some coffee to wake up before she's able to play with anything or anyone, ok?"

It's Zeke's turn to grumble as he walks away to play with the *blocks* he found in Callie's room last night. It's a good thing he can't read yet, or he'd be getting quite an education from Callie's Jenga game. That's just what I need. Zeke running home to ask his mom how to play the grab-ass game.

Sitting at the island with straight black coffee, just the way I like it, I watch Walker in my kitchen. Let's clarify that; I watch Walker *shirtless* in my kitchen, with a baby on his hip, while he makes us breakfast. I've drooled over much less and now I'm seriously questioning why. After this stunning sight, I'm going to have to adjust what my level of drool-worthy is.

He catches me watching him and walks over, handing Finn off to me with a delicious coffee-tasting kiss. I don't mind his sweet coffee nearly as much *this* way. He steals the mug, sipping the hot black liquid while moving back to the stove.

Yes, I could get *very* used to waking up like this. Even with very little sleep.

A couple minutes later, Walker calls Zeke back into the kitchen, serving all of us scrambled eggs. I keep Finn on my lap, feeding him and myself while Walker takes care of the little pouter, who's suddenly decided he doesn't *like* scrambled eggs. At *all*.

"What's your favorite breakfast food, Zeke?" I ask, trying my best to distract him. If someone else is making me breakfast, I don't care what it is, I love it simply because I'm not making it. But I'm an adult who takes care of herself and others. I'm quickly finding out that sometimes I just want to relax and let someone else take care of me.

"Pancakes! With sausage!"

"I like that, too," I tell him. "If you eat all your eggs, I promise next time we have a sleep-over, you can wake me up early and I'll make pancakes and sausage for you."

"I don't *want* eggs!"

"Good," I sigh in relief. I really didn't wanna get up early the next time he's here anyway.

Walker reaches out to take my hand, pulling it up to his face so he can kiss my palm. He's being extra affectionate with me this morning and I love every single touch, glance, or hint of a smile. But it also pisses Zeke off. How dare his uncle willingly kiss a *girl*? Zeke starts screaming, which causes Finn to start crying. Rolling my eyes at both of them, I calmly take another sip of coffee, offering it back to Walker. He does the same, placing the mug of coffee between us when he's done.

"What time did you wake up?" I ask over the noise of Zeke throwing himself on the floor to start a full-blown tantrum.

"Five thirty," he answers easily. "The boys and I are used to getting up pretty early."

"Wow. Thanks for letting me sleep."

"I figured *one* of us should be able to. Getting out of bed was really hard, though, if you know what I mean." Zeke's screaming starts to get softer and I catch Walker's eyes to assure him I know *exactly* what he means. "I feel like I could crawl back into that bed with you right now."

I pretend to think about that, cocking my head to the side and staring at the ceiling with pursed lips. "I could do that... With all this noise coming from the kitchen, no one would be able to hear anything we might do up there."

"Don't tease me, G."

"Friend, I'm pretty sure out of the two of us, *you're* the tease."

He smirks, knowing exactly how frustrated I was every single time he stopped us last night. By the time he stripped down to his boxers to sleep, I was ready to get out our toy and show him how well it worked, since he wasn't willing to help me get where I really, *really* needed to be. But he wouldn't let me get that far. He watched me get it out, acted like he was going to help me use it, then hid it somewhere in this house that wasn't in my room.

I'll have to remember to ask him where it is before Callie comes home.

After all that, when I was ready to resort to the old-fashioned method and use just my plain old fingers, he wrapped his arms around me and held my hands close to my chest, stopping even *that* from happening. And he was just as turned on as I was. His erection was rubbing against my ass all night. Or at least until I finally fell into a restless sleep in his very strong arms.

It was the most fun I've had sleeping with anyone.

Also the most frustrating.

Zeke groans loudly against the floor, either bored with not getting any attention or tired after wearing himself out. Finn is happily bouncing on my knee, clapping his hands on my boobs. Finn's going to be a boob man when he grows up. I wonder if I'm the first girl he's felt up besides his mom and grandmother.

"What're our plans for this morning with these two screamers?"

"Are *you* a screamer?" Walker chuckles, a curious glint in his eyes. This isn't the first time he's asked that particular question. It also isn't the first time I've evaded answering him.

"Definitely not today. Zeke's screamed enough for all of us today," I very expressively tell Finn as he watches my face. He leans forward, putting his tiny little hands on my cheeks and laughing when I puff them up with air to push his hands out.

Walker arches an eyebrow, but I still leave his question unanswered. Tilting the empty coffee mug towards me, he watches as I nod, answering *that* silent question, and he gets up to make us another cup. "Reese said she'd be here around nine for these little monkeys. I bet she shows up early, though. When I asked if this was their first overnighter, she teared up and told me it was."

"Mommy's coming?" Zeke asks excitedly, watching Walker from his spot on the floor.

"She is. In a couple hours. What do you wanna do until then?"

"Play blocks." He's a stubborn one, that Zeke. Still stuck on those dirty blocks.

"As soon as we clean up breakfast, we'll play blocks."

Zeke sighs and rolls his eyes. He must not be a big fan of the cleanup game.

He doesn't help us, but he stays out of the way as Walker and I clear the plates and load the dishwasher. Walker lets his hand rub along my back as he walks by, sweeping the hair off my shoulder before kissing my neck while I'm rinsing off the plates in the sink. Then he leans on the counter, waiting for me to finish up while he watches me with that beautiful smile and delicious coffee.

Taking a sip of that coffee, I realize it's not delicious. He made it the way *he* likes it this time.

Call me a sucker, but I still like sharing coffee with him enough to drink it the way he makes it.

"Zeke, go get the blocks," Walker instructs his nephew. "The rest of us will be in as soon as we're done here." As soon as Zeke is out of sight, I'm in Walker's arms with his mouth warm and insistent on mine. Finn is back on Walker's hip, but he only squirms, wanting down or attention. Right now, he's not getting either. Walker's giving me all his attention and I'd be ok with all of us going down. Finn to his pack and play, and me and Walker on each other. But Walker's not gonna let that happen. No matter how hard I beg him.

Plastering myself against the only other adult in this house, I let Walker know with my body just how much I like him in my space this early in the morning. He gets the message loud and clear, telling me with *his* body that he really appreciates me sharing my space with him this early in the morning. We might be on the verge of getting a little carried away when the sound of wooden blocks crashing against each other makes it way to us in the kitchen, and we finally break apart. But not before he whispers in my ear how much he wants me right now.

Join the club, Friend.

I've wanted him that much since the first time he kissed me.

I didn't miss the fact that Walker didn't tell me what *he's* planning on doing after Reese picks up the kids. I'd love to say I thought his plan was to do *me*, but I'll settle for him just sticking around for a while.

After a half-hour, I'm all blocked out. Zeke is *not*. He loves these new blocks. Walker's lying on his side on the floor, mostly watching Zeke push the blocks around the carpet before adding them to the growing tower he's building. Finn is doing his own thing with a very noisy xylophone toy, sitting near Walker's knees.

"I think I'm gonna hop in the shower... You got these rascals for a bit?" I ask. His eyebrows shoot up and I hope he's thinking about what it would be like to join me.

"Yeah, I got 'em," he grumbles, clearly not happy about my plans.

"Would you want to tell me where you hid something last night, that would make my shower a lot more... satisfying?"

Walker chuckles, insisting he's *definitely* not telling me where he hid *anything*. I sulk my way up the stairs to shower alone with no toys. At least he can't stop me from finding a release by myself the old-fashioned way this morning.

Coming down the stairs a half-hour later, I'm fully dressed and somewhat satisfied. Walker obviously doesn't like my wardrobe choice, probably because I'm now wearing a bra, and clothes that cover a lot more of my skin. Or maybe he's glaring at me because of my orgasm-induced flushed cheeks and much more relaxed mood.

I gave him plenty of opportunity to help me take care of it and he chose not to. What did he think was going to happen?

Walker's talking about going upstairs to take his own shower when someone knocks on the door. Reese is early. Zeke throws himself into his mother's arms and she wipes away tears as she hugs him tight. Steve follows her in, and I'm so glad I showered and got dressed before they arrived.

Walker's still shirtless in sweatpants that hang low on his hips, making me think of all kinds of ways to touch every square inch of him.

I kinda hope he stays shirtless. Like, *forever*.

Steve and Walker bumps fists while Steve thanks him for giving him a night alone with his wife. Walker happily tells him we'd love to do it again sometime.

Reese dries her tears, turning to me, asking, "Were they good? Did they sleep? I was so worried about them all night. I'm sorry we're early, but I just couldn't wait to make sure they were ok."

"They were perfect. Zeke threw a little fit this morning, but other than that, he was great. Finn is an angel. If he was up in the middle of the night, Walker got him because I didn't hear a thing."

"He usually sleeps all night. Zeke never did till he was almost two, but Finn's a good sleeper."

Reese holds her youngest up to blow on his belly and he squeals in joy, laughing forever. It's a beautiful sound and as soon as they leave, this house is going to suddenly be very, very quiet.

"God, I missed these boys," she says, hugging them both to her chest. Zeke struggles to get out of her grasp, just so he can continue playing with the blocks, his joy at being with him mom again entirely forgotten.

Oh, crap. The *blocks*!

Glancing up in horror, I watch Steve pick up one labeled truth, reading the words on other side. He side-eyes Walker before picking up another one and reading that. Then another. And another.

"Interesting game you've decided to let a four-year-old play with."

I wait for Reese to see what they're talking about while watching Walker trying to hide a smile. He tells his brother in law, "I hear it's a real blast."

In my head, I kick him in the shin.

In real life, I tell Reese I'm going to go upstairs and collect the boys' things from Callie's room. She offers to help, and I tell her to just relax. I honestly just need a minute to myself before she sees that damn game and hates me again.

Luck is on my side this morning. Reese doesn't notice the blocks, and Walker doesn't put on a shirt.

He attacks me with his mouth as soon as we're alone. He half pushes me to the couch. Only half because I'm also dragging him there. When the back of my legs hit the cushions, I let myself sink down, pulling him with me, until I'm on my back with him above me. With his mouth still fused to mine, my hands explore his very naked chest, back and arms as he pushes my shirt up to the bottom of my boobs and splays his large hands across the bare skin of my back.

I really like this skin on skin thing. A *lot*. I want more of it.

Before he can stop me, I pull my shirt over my head, then cover his surprised mouth with my own. It only takes a fraction of a second until he kisses me back, shoving his knee between my legs, causing a moan to burst from my lungs at the rough friction. Then he finally lowers his chest onto mine.

Mmm, *yes*. If only I didn't have this damn bra on, we'd be skin on skin from the waist up.

See? I don't need *everything*. I'm not *rushing* this. I just want his skin on mine. As much of it as I can get.

"How hard did you come in the shower?" he asks, his lips trailing over my collarbone.

"Not as hard as I would have if you'd been there," I breathe, running my hands over his head, through his thick, dark hair, making it stand up on end. He somehow looks even *more* attractive like this. Maybe it's just knowing that he slept here, he's just out of *my* bed, and it's *my* hands that gave him that look.

"If you'd waited, I might've. You tortured me all morning, G! Running around in those little shorts with nothing on underneath. The way your nipples got hard in that cami every time I kissed you, or a dirty thought entered your head… You think a lot of dirty thoughts, G."

"They all involve you, Friend."

He moans, taking my mouth again. He's torturing *me* now, and I can't take it. I've gotta at least try. Wiggling my hands between us, I pray he thinks I'm trying to touch *him*. Instead, I unclasp the front of my bra and pull the cups to the side, hearing his sharp intake of breath when he realizes what I just managed to do without him stopping me.

"Genny," he scolds, reaching to cup a breast with each hand.

"Lord, yes," I whisper. "I just wanna feel you. Your skin on mine. Nothing else, I swear."

"I can't do that, G."

Huffing out a sigh, I accept defeat and close my eyes. He moves off me, probably to cover me with my shirt or push my bra back into place or *something* to ruin the amount of skin to skin contact we were achieving.

When his lips close over my nipple, I gasp loudly in the silence of the room, totally shocked.

"There's no way I can see these beautiful tits and not taste them."

I hold his head in place over my chest with my hands fisted in his hair. My head falls back, and I push my chest into him, lost in the feelings that are taking over my entire being.

Walker Kelley does things to me. He makes me feel things that are so intense it's like I've been living underwater my entire life. The moment he kissed me that first time, he hauled me up from the deepest, darkest part of the ocean, and I'm now experiencing everything he does to me at a level I've never felt with anyone else. A level I never even knew *existed*.

The thought that he's so different from everyone else I've ever known makes me dizzy, even with my eyes closed.

Walker picks me up, holding me in his arms as he sits on the couch and pulls me down to straddle him. His mouth is back on mine, his hands on my boobs as I push myself down to feel that beautiful cock of his between my legs.

"I can't have sex with you, G. Not yet. But I wanna watch you come on me again."

I don't need any more of an invitation than that. Pushing my tongue into his mouth, I let my hips take over, feeling him so hard and so close to where I need him. I reach under my clothes, opening my folds as much as I can, so I can feel even more of him. Walker groans when he watches my hand disappear inside my shorts, his fingers tightening on my nipples.

I pull my hand up and rub my wet fingers across his bottom lip, so very close to coming undone at how dark his eyes are while he watches me move on him. When his tongue moves hesitantly over my fingers, slowly sucking them into his mouth, my eyes close involuntarily, and I prove myself a liar as I scream out his name in ecstasy.

I'm *totally* a screamer...

When my body stills, he wraps his arms around me, pulling me close, so I feel nothing but glorious skin on skin from our waists up. His hand strokes my hair and I let out a sigh as I lay against him.

"The next time we do that, can we wear less clothes?"

Walker presses a kiss to my head, laughing out loud as he lets his hands slide down my back and inside my shorts. He grips my ass, squeezing gently before picking my bra up from the couch beside him. "Probably not," he sighs, pulling the straps of my bra over my shoulders. "Let's get you somewhat covered before I lose control again."

Pouting, I deliberately sit up, so he gets a good look at what he wants covered. "Aw, Genny," he breathes, moving his hands to feel me again.

"Let's go upstairs and take a nap instead."

"Are you really gonna sleep? Or just tempt me?" he murmurs, his eyes watching his thumbs run lazy circles around my nipples, which are quickly turning into taut peaks once again.

"Why don't you take a shower? Find your own release, since you don't want to find it with me, then crawl back in my bed and we'll sleep. I was really hoping to wake up with you, but instead, I woke up with a little blue-eyed monster prying my eyes open."

"He *can* be a monster, can't he?"

Walker leans down to flick one nipple with his tongue. Arching my back, my breast gets shoved into his mouth and he smiles against my skin.

"I think you shouldn't talk about your nephew with your mouth on my boob, Friend."

"I think I can feel how wet you are through my pants, G, and it's driving me *insane*."

"You're more than welcome to take off your pants, so you can feel it firsthand. In fact, take off all your clothes and just sit there. I'll find a way to make us both feel good."

Groaning against me, he raises his head to claim my mouth, pulling me back down against him as his tongue tangles with mine. "Ok," he whispers against my lips.

My eyes open in astonishment, unable to believe he finally gave us the go-ahead. When he sees my reaction, he chuckles, making my chest vibrate with his amusement. "Ok, I'll take a *shower* and we can *nap*. Not, ok I'll sit here naked while you do what you want. I guarantee neither one of us will be just sitting still when I let you have your wicked way with me."

"When's that gonna happen?"

"I don't know. But we're definitely getting closer; I don't know how much longer I can resist you."

"I don't know why you resist me at all."

"That's part of the problem, G. I keep forgetting why I'm trying to."

Pulling the straps back off my shoulders, I throw my bra on top of my shirt on the floor. Callie isn't here, and I have a very hot, very hard man on the couch with me. I really don't see the need for all these clothes. I kiss him slowly before climbing off a very turned-on Walker and walking topless up the stairs. While he's in the shower, I'll change out of these shorts and into clean underwear, but that's all I'll be wearing for our nap. Feeling as much of Walker's bare skin against mine is my new mission in life.

When Walker comes to bed after his shower, he doesn't complain about my choice in sleepwear. Instead, he slides the front of his body tight against my back, throws an arm over me, and quietly chuckles as his hand very firmly cups my breast.

Genny

Waking up the second time today is so much sweeter than the first. Not that Zeke waking me up was *bad*, it was just *early*, and I had been hoping to find Walker in bed with me. Now, there're no small children in my house and the best kisser in the world is pressing his very hard erection into my ass, as his fingers ever so lightly rub my nipple.

I wonder if he's awake and fully conscious of what he's doing. Or maybe he's having a really good dream starring the one and only me. That's a fun thought.

Carefully pushing my arms up and my legs down, I stretch gently while still in the warm, delicious circle of Walker Kelley. I could wake up like this every day for the rest of my life and be a very happy girl.

"Mmm. Do that again," his gruff voice commands.

This time, I'm not as careful. I stretch a little farther, pushing my ass hard against him, my boob directly into his waiting hand. I'm rewarded with a low groan, deep in his chest. His fingers flex on my boob and he lands his mouth on my shoulder, biting me as I cry out in surprise.

It doesn't hurt, it's more *shocking*... But *Lord*, does it turn me on.

"Do you have any idea what you're doing to me?" he asks. His elbow is resting on my hip and he holds me in place as he pushes that fantastic feeling erection even harder against me.

"I have a pretty good idea," I murmur lazily. Wiggling my hips, just a little, I hear another groan push past his lips. My hand covers his, moving it on my boob, torturing myself like I just did to him. When I pull his hand up to my mouth, his face moves over my shoulder, watching me. Taking my time, I slowly lick a long, wet line up his palm and return his hand to my boob, sliding that wet flesh across my taut nipple and pushing into it.

"Christ, G. You're making it so damn hard," he complains directly into my ear, his voice on edge. I wonder if I can push him over that edge. How far can I get him to go with me, right here, right now?

"I know," I murmur, wiggling my hips against him again. "I can feel you."

"Not what I meant, but yeah. That, too."

"I can make it better for you," I half tell, half ask him. While he's thinking that over, I move his hand south, sliding it down my stomach, inching us towards the waistband of my lace underwear.

"Genny," he warns, his voice soft in my ear. But he wants this. I can feel it in the way his hand doesn't stop mine. When my hand slows, his doesn't. It moves over the satin and lace, right down to that sweet spot between my legs, where his fingers explore exactly how wet I am underneath the fabric keeping him from really touching me.

Holding his hand in place, I roll onto my back and let my legs fall apart. I want to see him. I want to see his face when he touches me for the first time. And when he's lost in watching just how much his touch affects *me*, I want to touch *him*.

This new position makes it so he can kiss me, too.

His hand freezes as his tongue explores my mouth. He's stalling while he makes up his mind, kissing me like this while he cups my most sensitive area with his large, very able hand. I help make his decision a little easier, pushing my hips against him, his fingers sliding easily across the wet material of my underwear.

Walker chuckles into my mouth, pulling slowly away. His fingers finally start moving, though, stroking a deliciously soft line up through my folds. "I'm starting to think you're the devil in disguise."

"Funny, I think you're an... Oh!" I gasp out as his fingers graze over my clit. "An angel."

"Why an angel?" he murmurs, settling in to enjoy the show while his fingers move over me.

"Because the way you touch me kills me. And when you finally let me come, it's like I'm in heaven."

"How're you gonna feel when those little sparklers turn into a whole damn fireworks show?"

Pushing my pelvis up to make him touch me harder, I sigh in relief for half a second before he pulls back. "Show me and I'll to tell you."

"I think I wanna get to know you a little better first."

Closing my eyes in frustration, I try to not pant as his fingers move in a lazy figure eight around my entrance and my clit, never quite touching either through my underwear. "We've already gone through all of our questions."

"I've got a couple more."

"Ask whatever you want, but then touch me! *Please*, Walker!"

His fingers settle over my clit, rubbing lightly, causing me to cry out and arch into him. Then his fingers are back to their slow, torturous figure eights, his voice gentle in my ear as he whispers, "I *love* it when you beg."

"That's not a question, Friend."

"It's not, is it?"

He nips my earlobe with his teeth, sucking on it for a couple delicious seconds. It must have a direct line to my clit, because that part of me is now throbbing in time with the tugging of his mouth. "Let me get right to it, then. Who's your favorite band or singer?"

"I couldn't pick just one," I grind out through clenched teeth. He's killing me here. He knows it; he's even *enjoying* it.

"Ah, but you have to, my sweet Genevieve."

No one has called me that since the last time I was in trouble with my parents. Hearing it on his lips does something to me, pulls me up even higher. I might spontaneously combust when he finally touches me the way I need him to. We'll go down in flames, just like I predicted, but it'll be a hell of a lot more fun than I thought it would be.

"Maroon Five!" I cry out, the first band I can come up with when taking my full concentration off how he's making me feel.

"I went to a couple of their concerts," he replies conversationally. "They're good. Not my favorite, but-"

"Next question!" I growl at him.

Walker chuckles and dips that beautiful smile to my lips, sweeping his tongue in for another taste, teasing me by pushing into my mouth, not down where his fingers are. "Ok, ok," he murmurs against my lips. "What's one thing you want to do before you die?"

"Have sex with you."

"That doesn't count."

Jerk! That's a perfectly acceptable answer and he knows it. Moving my hand over his again, I desperately try to make him touch me where I need him to. He only laughs at my efforts, easily able to deter me. Concentrating hard, I come up with another answer. "I want a real vacation."

"When's the last time you went on one?"

"Spring break. Eighteen."

"Good. See, these questions aren't that hard. Just answer honestly. What's your favorite color?"

"Red." His fingers move in tighter circles, getting closer to where I need him by such a small distance it's almost immeasurable. But he *is* closer, so I'll answer his questions. I'll answer as many damn questions as I have to.

"Favorite author?"

"Ken Follet."

"When's the last time you had sex?"

Wincing, I keep my eyes closed tight, not wanting to see his reaction. "The night you changed my tire."

"Did you think of me?"

133

"Yes."

"Did you wish it *was* me?"

"*Lord*, yes..." I breathe, knowing it's true and seeing in his eyes just how much my answer pleases him. He's gotta touch me now, it would be inhumane to keep teasing me like his is.

"Favorite season?"

What the *hell*?! Groaning my frustration, I bite out, "Spring."

"How much do you like me?"

"I think I might love you."

Walker's mouth is on mine before those words register in my mind. When I stiffen under him, shock and mortification washing over me, he changes everything by slipping his hand under the wet material separating us and sliding his fingers through my heat, directly to my entrance. Then, the only thing I think about is how good it feels as he finally pushes inside me.

My hips move to meet him halfway as I groan directly into his mouth. His fingers thrust into me, filling me, finally easing that ache that was slowly taking over my entire body. Walker moves his mouth to my breast, sucking my hard nipple into his mouth as his thumb brushes across my clit. I gasp a harsh cry as fireworks light up my entire world behind my closed eyelids.

After coming back down from that glorious high, I eventually remember that I wanted to touch him. I'm still breathing heavily, but I'm thinking halfway clearly, so I roll into him, forcing him onto his back as I push my tongue into his mouth as a thank you. His hands are on my hips when I straddle him, one of them still very wet on my skin, and I reach between us to rub him through his boxers.

His moan is the sweetest sound I've ever heard.

I sit up and move slightly lower, so I can touch him properly. His eyes are on mine and they hold a warning I chose to ignore as I push his boxers over the bulge I desperately need filling my fist. He springs free, popping up into my hands, and Walker's fingers find a home on my thighs, gripping me in a way that lets me know he's still not sure we should be doing this.

Too late. After all he's done for me, it's only fair I get him off *once*.

Besides, there's not a chance in hell of me letting him go right now.

Gripping him with both hands, I slowly pump up, then back down, watching his face to gauge his reaction. His head is tipped back, but his eyes are on my hands locked around his cock. "Faster," he grinds out through a clenched jaw, and as I heed his desperate plea, I can't help thinking we really need some lubrication. His eyes close while I experiment with the firmness of my grip and rhythm, trying to find which combination gets the best response from him.

His hands move off my thighs to wrap around mine, showing me exactly how he needs me to move. Letting him guide most of my movements, I slowly slide farther down his legs to lower my head over him.

"Genny, *no*." He says it very clearly. He's very sure he doesn't want us to go where I'm trying to take us. Not yet.

Lifting my eyes to his, I can *see* how tortured he feels as his body tries to convince me he needs this, even as his mind and voice are stubbornly trying to dissuade me. I stick my tongue out to lick the tip of him, *needing* that drop of precum in my mouth, even if he doesn't want me to taste him yet.

The second my tongue makes contact, his hands are in my hair, holding me in place as he thrusts his hips up, shoving himself into my mouth. I anchor myself against his sudden, forceful movements by slamming a hand onto the mattress, fully enjoying him and the way he's now fucking my mouth like it's the best thing he's ever felt. Using my lips, my tongue, my hand, I let him take what he needs. Soon, he's groaning out my name, his hands holding my head still as he fills my mouth.

Swallowing him down, I move up the bed to lay in his arms, hoping with everything I have that he's not mad at me. He should be. I pushed him farther than he wanted us to go. He told me *no*, loud and clear, and I totally ignored him.

I also told him I think I might love him...

He could be mad at me for a lot of things.

His arm sneaks around me, holding me close as he catches his breath. When his heartbeat slows under my ear and his hand is slowly rubbing my arm, he lets out a small laugh. "You *are* the devil, aren't you?"

"Are you mad at me?"

"I *should* be, but I'm not. More proof you're the devil in a very sexy disguise."

Cringing, I push myself up to look at his face, relaxed and sated, happy in the aftermath of everything we just did. "Should we talk about it?"

Laughing, he pushes the hair out of my face. "Talk about how you don't listen worth a damn?"

"No," I argue shyly, doing my best to meet his eyes when all I want to do is look away. "About what I said."

His face immediately softens, and he slightly shakes his head. "Not if you don't want to."

I settle onto his chest, letting out a relived sigh. "As long as you don't get weird or run away screaming, I *really* don't want to."

"I promise when I leave, I won't be screaming."

"Are you gonna come back after you leave?"

"Yes." Walker's hand smooths out my hair before he lets it run through his fingers. "We're good, G. We're *very* good."

Walker

A lot.

More than I wanna admit.

Not at all if you don't stop torturing me!

I was prepared to hear any of those answers. I was *not* prepared to hear her tell me she thinks she might love me. I also wasn't prepared to feel like the happiest man alive at the sound of her words. Or to want to give her anything she might ask for in return.

Reese is right. I'm playing house with Genny. Trying to figure out if she's my future.

The way Genny's whole body stilled under me once those words were out of her mouth tells me she was just as shocked as I was. And the way she asked me later if we should talk about it let me know just how scared she was of how I was going to react.

We lay in a very comfortable silence for a while. I feel like I could lay here with Genny forever, simply sharing the same space. Talking, laughing, touching. It doesn't seem to matter what we do, it's all fun, and sweet, and something I want to do a lot more of. But I have a game in... an hour. Putting my phone back on her night stand, I sigh, realizing I'm going to have to leave her a lot sooner than I thought I would.

"Got somewhere you need to be, Friend?"

"Another game today. I have a little time yet."

"You do that a lot. Every weekend it seems."

"Yeah, we kind of have an unofficial team. It's usually a lot of fun, but today I'd rather stay here with you."

"You can, ya know," she whispers, still unsure about how much she should say after her confession earlier. "Stay here with me tonight. If you want to."

Honestly, I have no idea what I'd tell her if she told me again, right now, wanting to actually see my expression when she says it. I know it doesn't freak me out, which is surprising. But I don't know what I'd say in response either.

"Are you *asking* me to sleep here again? Without my nephews?"

"Maybe," she admits, hiding her eyes from me. "It's not like I have an empty house very often."

I love when Genny gets shy. It doesn't happen too often. Wanting to take advantage of this rare moment, I roll us over, letting her take some of my weight, catching the slow smile tugging at her lips. "So, you're just an opportunist."

"No," she insists, reaching up to run her fingers along my face. "I like sleeping with you."

"Are you gonna stick to some rules if I stay here again, or are you gonna blow them outta the water like you did today?"

"I'll be good," she promises. "I'll be really good."

Chuckling, I kiss her fingertips as they pass over my lips. "I already know you're really good, G. I'm asking if you'll stick to some *rules* this time."

Her quick smile confirms she was trying to be sneaky and manipulative with her previous answer. "I'll stick to your rules. Even if you tell me I can't touch you at all, I'll listen."

"I'm not saying that by any means, but we'll go over rules when I get back. Sound good?"

"Very. Should I make you dinner?"

"Let me take you out."

"Ok."

It might be the easiest agreement I've gotten from her. Climbing over top of her, I reluctantly get out of her bed and start pulling on clothes. Today, I want to get this game over with so I can get back here. And seeing Chad is the *last* thing I want to do. God, I hope he doesn't try to ask me about her during one of the breaks.

Maybe seeing Chad will reinforce my rules about sex with Genny, though. She's pushing all my boundaries. And after feeling her mouth on me? I don't know if I'm going to be able to tell her we can't do that again.

Genny pulls her pajama shorts on over her soaking wet panties. Her cami gets pulled on next, and it takes everything in me not to pull her back into that bed, so I can watch her nipples harden under my gaze.

"What're you gonna do while I'm gone?"

"Make sure Callie's still alive. Maybe see what Myra's up to. Any idea when you'll be back?"

"Three or four hours, probably."

"Am I dressing up or down for dinner?"

"Not as down as you are right now, but definitely down."

She smirks as her arms move around my waist. She reaches up on her tiptoes to kiss me and run her fingers through my hair. I try to resist her sweet mouth and seductive charms. I'm about ready to give in to her again when she breaks away, dragging me out of her room and down the stairs.

"I need you to promise me something," she demands as she starts picking up Zeke's blocks.

I stop myself from telling her I'll promise her anything she wants me to, watching her bend over repeatedly in those teeny tiny shorts. "What?"

"Promise me you'll tell me where our toy is before Callie comes home."

"I promise."

"Can you tell me when I'll find out what you're planning with her?"

"Nope. Although speaking of that, I need to talk to her."

"Of course, you do," she admonishes, rolling her eyes.

"If I promise you'll like it, will you stop worrying about it?"

"Probably not." She gets all the blocks back in the box before standing up again, complaining, "I thought you were supposed to be doing something for Callie?"

"It morphed into something else. Don't worry, she's excited about it."

Settling on the couch, we talk about random things until it's time for me to go. Genny doesn't try to seduce me again, and I'm glad. I wasn't kidding when I said it was getting harder to resist her. Maybe what we did today will be enough to keep her satisfied for a while. It only fueled my libido for her, touching her, feeling how wet she was for me, how ready, how needy. She's not ashamed or shy. It's one of the hottest fucking things I've ever seen, and it only has me imagining what she's going to feel like when I'm finally inside her.

She may not seduce me before I leave, but she does kiss me like she's drowning and I'm the only thing that can save her.

She probably knows it only makes me want to get back to her that much faster.

∞ ∞ ∞

Sunday night when I get home, Chad's in front of the TV. I toss my keys into the bowl next to the door and throw my bag in my room, trying to suppress a sigh. He usually works Sunday nights. I was hoping I wouldn't have to see him. It must be his weekend off.

Sucks for me.

"Hey man," he greets from the couch.

"Hey."

"You've been gone all weekend. Tell me about this girl."

There's no good excuse for me to walk back into my room and ignore him. Grabbing a bottled water from the fridge, I walk into the living room and sit on the recliner to catch the score of the game he's watching. "Her name is Genny," I tell him, glad she has a common nickname.

"*And...*"

"And she's sweet and thoughtful and selfless. She loves watching my nephews and arguing with me. She gets shy when things get personal, and knowing she's finally starting to trust me makes me feel like maybe I'm not good enough to deserve her."

"That's not what I'm asking," he mumbles, his eyes on the game.

"I know what you're asking, I just don't care. A girl's body doesn't describe who she is. That's something you'll probably never understand because you don't take the time to get to know anyone."

"The fuck is your problem?" he barks, my harsh tone making him give me his undivided attention.

"I don't have a problem, Chad. You do."

He glares at me from his seat on the couch. I shouldn't be starting this fight. This has nothing to do with him. It has everything to do with the fact that Genny won't tell him she won't see him anymore. She trusted me enough to tell me about her parents, to tell me about everything she's been through, everything she's given up keeping her family together. Why won't she give up this asshole who doesn't care about her at all?

"Does this have something to do with that kid?"

What a fucking piece of *shit*. I knew what was going on with him and Reese and Zeke. I stayed out of it, not wanting to be in the middle, but right now, listening to him talk this way about my favorite kid in the world, I can't believe I've stayed out of it for as long as I have. "He's not *that kid*. Until you sign the fucking papers, he's *your* kid. You want nothing to do with him. Sign the papers so Steve can adopt him, and he can finally have a dad that loves him."

"Gimme a break, I pay the child support."

"You think that makes up for everything else?" I demand, not really expecting an answer but needing to voice my opinion.

"I don't know what's with you tonight, but stay outta my business. I don't need to deal with this shit."

"Not a problem," I mutter, making my way back to my room. I don't need to deal with his shit, either.

Reese is right again. It's time to start looking for a new place.

It doesn't surprise me when some girl is standing half naked in the kitchen later, when I go out to get something to drink. Her name is Alison or Alyssa. It starts with an A, but that's all I can remember.

At least it's not Genny.

It's only been a few hours since I left her.

And I already miss her.

Walker

Genny: Wanna come over later? Callie's home and I'm making dinner...
Walker: Is that the only reason you're inviting me?

It's only Tuesday and she's asking me to come over. Maybe she misses me just as much as I miss her.

Genny: You forgot to tell me where you hid our toy.

Shit!

Being with Genny makes me forget things. I'm still typing out it's hidden location when another text comes in from her.

Genny: Plus, I'd love to see you.

There's my girl.

After finishing my text, I hit send and get ready to leave. I went for a run when I got home from work and was just trying to figure out what I wanted for dinner when Genny's text came. Chad's working, so I don't need to worry about running into him. We're not being very civil to each other right now. Genny said dinner was in an hour, but I'd much rather spend the time with her and her sister than being cooped up in this apartment with nothing to do.

Callie lets me in, her eyes bright, her skin a tanned, glowing brown. "You're early."

"Couldn't stay away," I confess, stepping past her to wrap my hands around Genny's waist. She's using a meat mallet to pound away at some chicken on the counter, but she gives me a smile and a chaste kiss. She's back to little-to-no touching in front of her sister, I guess. Either way, I just want to be near her.

"How was your trip, Cal? Looks like you got some sun."

"It was amazing! So much better than I remembered. Maybe I need to move to a beach town once I'm ready to settle down..."

A scowl takes over Genny's face. She's going to have a hard time dealing with Callie moving that far away. Especially since Calvin doesn't live very close, either.

"Wanna look at some pictures?"

"Sure," I answer, getting up and following Callie into the living room. She's going to cast them to the TV. Maybe Callie can show me how that works...

After laughing at my ignorance, she does just that. And then she shows me how to make it stop. That's what I really needed and I'm grateful to have the knowledge, even if I needed it a while ago.

As Callie's showing me her pictures, I feel like a pervert, looking at Genny's little sister and her friends in bikinis on the beach. But she changes the subject to talk to me about our plans for Genny, thankfully dragging me out of my thoughts.

"Myra said she'll keep Genny out of the house one evening after work in a couple weeks. And I'll stay with a friend that night and let you guys have the house to yourselves again."

"You don't need to stay anywhere else, Callie."

"You're still not having sex with her?"

Chuckling, I don't confirm or deny her assumption. "This has turned into something for you and your sister. You should be here. It has nothing to do with me anymore."

"No, no, no. You're not getting out of this. It was your idea."

"My idea was nothing like what you're now planning. I think it's a great idea, but it's a family thing and I'm not family."

"Walker, please," Callie insists, resting her hand on my arm. "She'll appreciate you being a part of it and so will I. She's different with you around. She's more fun than she's been in a long time. And she's gonna need some extra moral support. Every time I try to talk to her about what happens now that I've graduated, she changes the subject."

"What *are* you planning?"

"I got a job at the hospital. I start in two weeks. I want to move out at the end of the summer and let Genny have her own life again, but I don't know if she's going to be able to handle it. She's grown so accustomed to having someone else to take care of. I don't know if she'll even remember how to figure out what *she* wants. I think you can help her with that."

"Me?"

"Yeah."

Genny calls us from the kitchen, letting us know dinner's ready. Suspicion is in her eyes, but it only makes Callie smile. We sit at the kitchen island while we eat, Genny occasionally holding my hand under the table.

"Genny, this is awesome. Thanks for finally inviting me to dinner."

"I offered to cook for you before," she argues.

"Yeah, but I don't want you cooking *for* me. We made breakfast together Sunday, and that was great. Cooking for Callie and inviting me is also great. What is this, by the way?"

"I'll keep that in mind," she tells me, rolling her eyes. "It's just spinach and mozzarella wrapped in chicken. How's your week been so far? I heard all about Callie's trip, what's going on with you?"

Do I tell her about Chad? She knows Zeke is biologically his. It's not like I'll be giving anything new away. And telling Genny is the same as telling Callie because Callie will just eavesdrop on whatever conversation I have with her sister anyway. I would love to get it off my chest. And if I'm honest, I'll admit that I would love to tell Genny about it.

"Things are a little awkward at home right now. Chad and I got into an argument Sunday."

Callie practically chokes on her food before looking between me and Genny. "Chad, like the Chad Genny *knows*?"

"Yeah," I admit, nodding my head, wishing Callie didn't know quite so much about Genny's sex life. "He's my roommate. And my nephew's biological dad."

"That's twisted," Callie declares with wide eyes.

Ignoring that, because it's true and I have no idea how to respond to it, I tell Genny and Callie how Reese had papers drawn up when Steve asked her to marry him. When Steve proposed, he said he'd also like to adopt Zeke and raise him as his own. Reese presented them to Chad. He said he'd think about it. It's been *years*, and he still refuses to sign them *or* acknowledge Zeke as his own.

"If Chad signs the papers, he doesn't have to pay child support anymore, right?" Callie asks.

"Right."

"Then why wouldn't he *want* to sign them?"

"We have no idea. Just to be a dick, I guess."

Genny's quiet through my story and Callie's questions. Her hand is in mine, but she won't look at me. I hope she knows I'm not judging her for what she's done with him. She didn't know anything about him then. I have a feeling if she had, she never would've given him a second glance.

"Would Reese have to get a job if the child support stopped coming in?" she asks later, after the dishes are cleared and we're sitting in the living room. Callie's in her room or eavesdropping on the stairs, no way to know for sure.

"Maybe. It would definitely make things harder, but it's a problem they would love to have to deal with. Zeke has Chad's last name. Reese, Steve, and Finn all share a last name. When Zeke starts school, there's bound to be questions, and Reese didn't want to have to deal with it. Especially when he's too young to really understand."

"I can't imagine having to worry about that," she says, snuggling into my side. "Your sister's pretty awesome."

"Yeah, she is. Kinda like you."

"No, she's way more awesome than me."

"You should let Reese in a little bit. I think you might find you have a lot in common with her."

She pushes up off me, demanding, "Because I slept with Chad?"

I did *not* see that one coming. Pulling her chin up so she has to look at me, I try to correct the mistake I had no idea I was making. "Because you're both incredibly stubborn and fiercely protective of the people you love."

She studies me, wanting to believe my words but having such little regard for herself she's finding it difficult. I could ask her now, to please text Chad and tell him never again. But I really don't want to fight with her about anything tonight, let alone her past sex life. I don't want to hear her excuses about how she never contacted him, and he might not remember who she is. We both know that's bullshit.

She has to know by now that's the main reason I'm holding back from having sex with her. I haven't told her that specifically, but how could she not know? I told her, she had to be with *only me*.

She promised she wouldn't have sex with him or anyone else while she was with me. Maybe I should be satisfied with that, but her hesitancy to cut the cord with him has me wondering why she won't officially let him go. I guess that's why I need her to tell him before we go any further.

"I'm sorry," she says eventually. "I guess I'm a little touchy about the fact that I had sex with such a dickhead."

"It's all right. You're not gonna do that anymore."

"No, I'm not. Never again," she promises, resting her head back against my chest.

At least there's that. Whether she texts him or not, I don't need to worry about her actually having sex with him. Maybe that *is* enough. Maybe I just need to trust her about sex like she's trusted me with the side of her that no one else ever sees.

"Do you want me to turn on the TV?"

Genny's head moves against me and I look down to find her shaking her head. "I don't really like TV. I'd rather just talk with you if it's ok."

"I don't mind at all."

But she's quiet. We sit on her couch together, lost in our own thoughts. I feel close to her right now anyway, just sitting with her in my arms. I think about how Reese told my mom Genny was almost perfect for me. I think about how I can get Genny to meet my parents. And how to get her to meet the rest of my friends.

This past weekend may have ruined me. Now, everything I do, I want her with me. Spending almost a full forty-eight hours with her has me spoiled. I want to sleep with her in my arms. I want the lazy morning conversations we have over shared coffee. I want the games we play before bed. I want the way we worked together in the kitchen to make breakfast or lunch, or whatever. I even want cleanup, if I get to share it with her.

"Really? The coat closet?" she asks with a smile I can feel against my chest, breaking me from my thoughts.

"Last place you would've looked, right?"

"Definitely. How about next time you help me *use* it, instead of hiding it on me?"

Letting her hair run through my fingers, I hold her tight, thinking that really isn't much more than we've already done. "That sounds like a good plan. Let me know when you have the house to yourself again and we'll take it for a test ride together."

"I might have to encourage Callie to get a new hobby now that school's out."

"I might help you with that."

Walker

Kicking the ball back and forth between my feet, I weave my way down the field, keeping my eyes on my teammates' positions. I quickly pass it to Sean, who's set up, ready, and waiting, right in front of the goal. Sean leans left, faking out the goalie while kicking the ball into the net, then raising his hands up into the air victoriously. Goal!

We're seriously kicking the other team's ass today.

The other team wants a quick break to regroup. It's not gonna help them, but I head to the sidelines to get my water bottle anyway. The hardness of Chad's sudden glare makes my skin itch, but it quickly moves off me to scan the goal line. What the hell does he think I did now? Or is he just pissed because I'm covering someone and playing offense, making it that much easier for my team to crush his?

Callie's near the goal.

As soon as I'm looking in her direction, she starts waving, walking toward me. I get it now. Chad thinks it's Genny. They look so much alike, from this distance he can't tell it's not her.

No wonder he's pissed. Now he's going to think I stole one of his many girls. God forbid I have one all to myself when he has a dozen...

I meet her halfway down the field. "Hey, Cal. What're you doing here?"

"I was in town and saw your car. Figured I'd stop by to say hi. You're pretty good."

"Thanks," I laugh.

"I finished my painting for Genny today. I'm super nervous to give it to her, but excited, too. Thanks again for doing this."

"You're gonna make Genny cry, you know that, right?"

"No way," she insists, shaking her head. "Genny doesn't cry."

Genny *does* cry. I've seen it and I know how much Callie's gift and words are going to affect her sister. "Wanna bet on that?"

"About Genny crying? Absolutely."

"If she does, you have to enter one of your paintings in that art competition I told you about."

There was a flyer up on the bulletin board at work. It's for local, amateur artists, and the winner gets an art show displaying all their artwork. The pieces can also be sold if the artist is open to selling any. I told her about it when I picked Genny up to hang out with Reese and the boys this past Thursday, for our normal Thursday night date.

Callie wasn't very receptive to the idea.

She still isn't. Her face goes white at even the suggestion. "No, I don't show anyone my paintings."

"Guess you're not too confident about winning."

That steely reserve I saw in her and her sister pushes through from behind the nervousness in her eyes. "Fine. I'll take your bet. When Genny doesn't cry, you have to have sex with her."

I shake my head with a laugh. "You realize that's not exactly a hardship for me, right?"

"I don't know if it is or not. You're afraid of something and it's holding you back. She told me a while ago she doesn't think you trust her. I thought she was crazy, but now that I know what I'm looking at, I think she's right."

That turns my good mood into something else entirely. Holding out my hand, I tell her, "I'm still gonna win this bet."

She takes my hand, shaking it firmly. "No, you aren't."

She turns and starts to walk away, getting halfway across the field before she cups her hand around her mouth to yell back at me. "I'm staying with a friend tonight, Walker. You're welcome!"

Everyone on both teams watches her walk away. I can already hear the questions they're gonna ask. She's a gorgeous girl in her early twenties and we just laughed and joked like she's my kid sister. Once she's out of sight, everyone's eyes turn to me.

Everyone's except Chad's.

His hard, unforgiving eyes have been on me the entire time.

Genny

Looking in the mirror again, I take a deep breath before nervously fingering the bracelets on my wrist. It feels like too much. I have on a fun, flirty dress, that showcases a lot more cleavage than I'm used to, but also my long, toned legs. I also have makeup on, my hair is done, and Callie lent me some jewelry. It all feels foreign, like I'm trying way too damn hard.

"Stop fidgeting! When you relax you look fantastic, but when you keep touching everything, you look self-conscious."

"I *am* self-conscious!" I inform Callie.

"Why? Walker loves you. His friends are douches if they don't, too."

I calm my racing heart and tell her again, for what feels like the hundredth time, "Walker doesn't love me. He *likes* me, but he doesn't *love* me."

"Semantics." She her hand dismissively at my statement. "He will soon enough. I'm calling it now, you wait and see. Besides, tonight you're worried about his *friends* judging you. I promise they're only going to be judging *him* and asking why he hasn't tapped that yet."

"Why *hasn't* he tapped that yet?" I mumble, wondering when the hell he's going to quit making us wait. It's been six weeks already. Two weeks since he finally gave in and started helping me with my orgasms for real and not just in my imagination. I haven't waited this long for sex since I was in high school.

I keep reminding myself he's worth it. I'd do just about anything at this point to prove to him I'm all in this. I just don't know *how* to prove it to him.

Callie stands between me and the mirror, pulling me out of my thoughts for a second. "What *exactly* is making you so self-conscious?"

Tugging at the dress, I try to pull the hem down so my ass doesn't feel like it's hanging out. As soon as I do, I feel like I'm flashing Callie. "This dress is too revealing."

"Really? Why'd you tell me I looked great in it a few weeks ago?"

"Because you're twenty something!"

"Ha!" she says, pointing a finger in my face. "You're still twenty something for a month yet! You're just not used to showing *any* skin. It's not too revealing."

"You can see my boobs!"

"Anyone can see your boobs no matter what you're wearing. That's kind of what happens when you've been blessed in that department. It doesn't come close to showing your *nipples*, so you're fine."

Growling at her logic, I attempt to keep my hands off the dress. They move instead to my face, covered in simple but tasteful makeup that brings out the green of my eyes. Callie helped me with it. Ok, she didn't *help* me, she did it all. I don't do dress up. I don't know how to do this, how to *be* like this. The only makeup I ever wear is mascara and shiny pink lip gloss.

Next is the jewelry. I kinda like the necklace. But the bracelets are driving me nuts. Every time I move my arm, I feel like I'm caught on something, and they fall up my forearm when I lift my hand above my waist. Plus, they're so noisy! There're eight thin, silver bands, and Callie pulls most of them off my wrist, leaving only three. It's better. Still weird, but better.

"Here, put these on," she demands, shoving a pair of heels into my hands. It's only a small heel, only two inches, probably the smallest she owns. "You need to walk around in them. Get comfortable. You don't want to fall in front of his friends, do you?"

"No." I squeeze my eyes shut tight, panicking at adding one more uncomfortable thing to my already drastically foreign ensemble. "I can't do the heels. I'll do everything else, but I need either a wedge or flats." She grumbles, disappearing back to her room to find me something else.

I'm terrified. Downright *terrified*. Walker knows me. We've talked about everything under the sun several times. But I'm meeting his friends tonight, and there's this pressure for me to impress them. I have to make them think Walker is lucky. I have to make them think I'm good enough for him.

Because *I* feel like I'm not.

I know I'm pretty; I've used my looks to my advantage many times. But rarely do I ever put *this* much effort into my appearance. It's been a long time since I've felt like I *had* to. Tonight, I feel like that. And *that* makes me incredibly nervous.

Callie comes back with some strappy sandals that should work. They have a wedge heel, but again, it's not high. I've cursed Callie's shoe collection many times over the years, but tonight, I'm grateful for it. Sliding my feet into the sandals, I stand up and do a little twirl that lets way too much air breeze across my ass. Callie nods her approval. "Out of curiosity, you have a sexy pair of underwear on, right?"

My eyes search for her as I spin around to face her. "You told me it wasn't too short!"

"It's not. But you do, right?"

"Of course! Whenever you have a dress on and you're out with a guy, you have good underwear on. Did I teach you nothing?"

"About guys and sexy underwear? Not really. You were always telling me that guys only want one thing and you should never, *ever* give them that one thing."

I'm so nervous and scared that I'm horribly emotional on top of everything else. Looking at my little sister, who really isn't little at all, I suddenly pull her into my arms and hug her tight. "I'm sorry I've been such a hypocrite. You're not totally screwed up about guys and sex and love, are you?"

"Are you fucking crying?" she asks, a horrified expression on her face.

"Why are you swearing at me?"

"You never cry, Gen. *Never.*"

"I'm not," I insist, letting her go while I blink back any moisture that may be clouding my vision. "Why are you avoiding my question?"

Callie crosses her arms over her chest, mad at me for some unknown reason. She finally sighs, rolling her eyes to the ceiling. "I'm not *totally* screwed up. Just a little."

"Aww, Callie... I'm so sorry!" I gush, the tears almost spilling over onto my cheeks.

"I was joking! And you *are* crying! What the fuck! Just when I thought I could *count* on you..." She throws her hands in the air and stalks out of my room.

Shit. I obviously screwed up somewhere...

Moving back to the mirror, I try to wipe my eyes without smearing my makeup. Callie did an awesome job and I *do* look fantastic. I'm just feeling super vulnerable, and now I'm crying, so I'll look fantastically *emotional* with red rimmed eyes.

A knock at the back door comes a few minutes later, and I hear a brief exchange between Walker and Callie. One of the first things out of her mouth is an incredulous *She's fucking crying!* Walker chuckles, making me wonder what the hell is going on with those two. Never did I think Walker would laugh at hearing that I was crying. Maybe I'm wrong about all of this.

Maybe I'm wrong about *him.*

Then he's knocking on the open door of my room, leaving me no time to consider that heart-stopping thought. Wiping my now-dry eyes one last time, I turn around to find him staring at me like I'm a stranger.

"Holy shit, G. You look amazing. Are you trying to pick up someone else tonight? You don't have to dress up like this for me."

"I want your friends to think I'm good for you."

"Genny, my friends are gonna thing you're *too* good for me." He walks into my room, his eyes looking me over again as he gets closer. "Can I kiss you? I don't want to ruin your makeup."

"If you *don't* kiss me, I'm not going."

There's that smile I love. His hands are gentle on my face, pushing into, but not through my teased and curled hair as his lips meet mine. "I missed you," he whispers against my mouth and I resist the urge to tell him I missed him, too.

Maybe that was my big mistake. Telling him I thought I might love him. Most guys would be running scared after that. He's still around weeks later. I just need to reel in my emotions and my clinginess.

"You just saw me last night, Friend," I remind him between soft, sweet kisses.

"Yeah, but not this morning or all day today."

These types of comments melt my heart. I lock my hands around his neck, pulling him closer and pressing my entire body against his. "Are you staying tonight?"

"I would tell you yes, but after seeing you in this dress, I'm gonna tell you there's not a chance in *hell* I'm letting you out of my sight until you're showing a hell of a lot less skin. And I wouldn't mind some time in between now and then when you're entirely naked, but only if we're alone in this house when it happens."

His fingers skim the bottom of my ass underneath the hem of this short dress. Pulling his mouth away from mine, he grabs my hand. "We need to get out of this room or we won't be going anywhere tonight."

Once we get out to his car, he opens my door for me, but catches both my hands in his. "Are you ok? Callie said you were crying."

This is much more the response I would expect. "I'm a little emotional tonight."

"Why?"

I silently remind myself it's nothing. Walker doesn't act like he isn't interested in me. Walker acts like he's head over heels in *like* with me. It's just all my insecurities trying to sabotage everything I'm feeling for him. "I'm just nervous to meet your friends. I want to make you look good."

"Genny, they're gonna love you. Kane already loves you. And if the others don't, they can go fuck themselves. I don't really care what they think, ok? You're amazing and *I* know that. That's all that matters."

I nod, trying to convince myself as well. "You're right."

"Are you sure that's all that's going on?"

"Yeah. I'm good now."

He doesn't believe me.

He *shouldn't*.

It's the first and only time I've lied to him.

Regret immediately overwhelms me, making me feel like I just broke my own heart by lying to the person I've come to trust more than anyone else. He must see it on my face, because he sits me down in the passenger seat of his car and squats in front of me, searching my eyes. "What's going on, Genny? This isn't you."

"I'm sorry," I hiccup. *Stupid fucking tears!* "I just lied to you."

"I know. I just don't know *why*."

The first few tears get swept away by his thumbs while I try to get myself under control. It's not working, though. I'm too worked up. I can't even swallow around the lump in my throat that's only getting bigger with each breath I take to try to calm myself down. My chest is tight with emotion that I need to let go of and I'm practically hyperventilating before I realize what I *need* to do.

I *need* to let it all out.

I'm going to ruin my makeup and Walker's going to think I'm a psycho, but it's the only way I'll be able to stop the emotions that are threatening to consume me.

"I just... need... to cry," I manage to get out. "I'll explain... why... after."

"Whatever you need. Just don't lie to me."

Nodding, I tuck my chin and let it out. I sob and cry, my breath hiccupping in my throat, my tears dripping down my cheeks. Walker pulls me out of the car, sitting in my seat and cradling me onto his lap, holding me tight as I cry.

And cry.

And *cry*.

Talk about embarrassing. This is *not* wheeling in my emotions or my clinginess. This is flaunting all my insecurities and bawling like a freaking baby.

But it lets me get to a point where it's *over*. Where I finally feel like myself again. I'm no longer nervous, I'm no longer questioning everything, I'm no longer wondering if Walker actually likes me or is just playing some game with my heart.

His hand is stroking my hair when my tears stop and my breathing finally returns to normal. He looks down at my red, streaky, most likely racoon-ish face. I hurt him. I can see it in his clear, hazel eyes that are looking so worriedly at me. Not knowing where to start or how much to tell him, I swallow nervously.

"I think I messed up," I achingly confess.

"You did. When you lied to me five minutes ago."

"No, before that."

"Come one, G. Out with it. You've got me really worried, and we don't have all night to figure out whatever it is you're trying to tell me." His words are harsh, but his tone is soft. His hands are gentle, holding me close, protecting me from whatever I might need him to. He doesn't know what I'm afraid of, but he's still here to shield me from whatever it might be

I'm totally and completely in love with him.

Letting my fingers run over his face, I realize just how much of an idiot I was. "I started to question... this. Us. And it's because I'm stupid and insecure and sensitive, just like you told me I was."

"I never said you were stupid, G. Far from it."

"Yeah, because you're perfect. And I'm this messed up girl who uses sex as stress relief and doesn't let anyone in because then they might *know* me and all my weaknesses. But if I don't let anyone in, I'm never gonna find out what love is. And if I don't wait for you, I'll never know how great a real relationship could be."

Walker presses his lips against my forehead, totally confused. "When did you mess up, Genny?"

I'm not making any sense. I don't know how to tell him what I'm just figuring out. I don't know how to put it into words. So I'll just talk until it makes a *little* bit of sense, because that's all I know how to do right now.

"I thought if you liked me, you'd have sex with me. But you won't. And I got it in my stupid head that maybe you *didn't* like me, not really. You liked me a *little*, but not enough. You were just testing out the waters, getting your feet wet, so to speak. And I went and told you I might love you, and then I pushed you into doing things with me that you didn't want to do that soon. So, maybe the reason you were holding back was because I wasn't good enough for you. But if I impressed your friends tonight, maybe they would tell you I *was* good enough, and maybe *then* you'd have sex with me."

"Genny, sweetheart, if this is all about sex-"

"Shh." I hold my finger up to his lips, not done with my explanation yet. "But then I lied to you. And I *hate* myself for that. I don't want to lie to you, I trust you! If I'm so screwed up in my head that I'm forgetting *that*, something is wrong! And you were so sweet to me, all the time *and* just now. You let me cry, and you held me and protected me like no one has done since... since... well, since it wasn't just me that took care of everything."

Blinking my eyes, I try to figure out what exactly I'm trying to tell him. His eyes are still mine, still worried, still confused and I shake my head against them; I'll search his eyes forever if he lets me and that won't get us anywhere.

"You're wonderful to me, Walker. Really, the best thing that's happened to me in as long as I can remember. It doesn't matter why you won't have sex with me. It can't be because I'm not good enough. I let you see the real me and you stuck around anyway, so you must like me."

He's trying to figure out what I'm getting at with my rambling, but he's still lost. He's still worried about me, too, the sweet, caring man that he is. But, I'm good now. I understand it. It took a while, but I've finally figured it all out.

"Genny, I still don't understand when you messed up."

"My whole adult life," I admit, wondering why I never realized it before.

"And that has you crying tonight?"

I can't help the small laugh that bubbles out of me. Sometimes talking nonsense is exactly what you have to do to get it straightened out in your own head, even when it doesn't make sense to anyone else. "Yes."

"Can you tell me why again? I'm still not sure I understand..."

"You not having sex with me made me think you didn't like me. But now I see that you're just better than any guy I've ever known. You have your reasons. I don't know what they are and that's ok. It doesn't mean you don't like me."

"So, you were crying because you thought I didn't like you?"

"Pretty much," I nod, confirming his suspicions and smiling into eyes that're suddenly questioning my sanity.

"And because I held you when you were crying, about me possibly not liking you, you realized just how silly you were being?"

"Exactly."

Walker fights the smile forming at the corners of his mouth. He doesn't want to laugh at me. Especially after the crazy emotional episode I just had. It's funny, though. I beat him to it and laugh out loud, feeling so much better now that I've cried and gotten it out and let it all *go*.

"Oh, Genny," he laughs softly against my hair. "I might think you're a little weird at times, but I promise you, I really, *really* like you."

I thread my fingers through his and pulling our hands close to my chest. "I'm sorry I lied to you."

"I'm really sorry you thought I might not like you."

"You never did anything that would indicate that. That's just my own craziness running loose in my head."

"I'm still sorry," he whispers, his eyes intent on mine.

"Thanks for letting me cry, I probably ruined your shirt... Crap, I probably look like hell. Callie's gonna scream at me, she spent forever on my makeup."

"Your makeup is pretty messed up, but I still think you're one of the most beautiful things I've ever seen."

I relax back into his chest with a sigh. "You need to stop saying such sweet things to me, Walker."

He gives me a huge grin. "Why do I need to stop saying sweet things?"

Hugging him with all my strength, I pray this isn't the last time I get to feel his chest against mine as I tell him the exact thing I've been trying *not* to say this entire evening. "Every time you do, I want to tell you I love you."

"No *I thinks* or *mights* this time?"

He's not freaking out. He's not pulling away.

Instead, he's making a *joke*.

"No. I'm totally in love with you, Friend."

"I'm not quite there yet, G," he quietly confesses, regret obvious in his voice.

"It's ok."

"Thanks for telling me..." Walker presses his lips against my temple, his hands sliding down my sides to my hips. "Can I come in with you, so you can wash your face?"

Callie's in the living room when I open the door. Her eyes go to my hand, wrapped up in Walkers, then up to my face, before shooting over to Walker. "You don't have to rub it in! I get it! She cries! You know her better than I do, God!"

"What's wrong with you?" I demand. It's my turn to be confused. She's been acting so strangely today.

"Callie, I would never intentionally make Genny cry."

The way Walker and Callie are talking to each other and completely ignoring me pisses me off. I have no idea what they're talking about, but it has something to do with me crying. "What the fuck is going on with you two?" I ask loudly, glad when both their eyes zero in on me and they stop glaring at each other.

Callie tosses the book she was reading onto the coffee table, crossing her arms over her chest. "*You* tell her. She likes you better."

Walker rolls his eyes, shoving his hands into his pockets. "We have a bet about the surprise we're planning for you. She bet you won't cry. I know you're going to."

"You're taking bets on whether or not I'm going to cry at some surprise? Are you guys going to hurt me?"

"No!" they say in unison.

"They'll be good tears," Walker explains. "You'll like the surprise."

"Oh, Lord... I've gotta go wash my face."

They continue arguing as I head up the stairs, but Walker's waiting for me in my room when I'm done in the bathroom. All the makeup is gone, and I leave my face bare. I pull off the bracelets and change out Callie's wedges for my flat sandals. I'm pulling out shorts and a t shirt when Walker's hands slide around my waist from behind.

"Leave the dress," he whispers, his voice hot against my ear. "It's gonna get us out of there and back here a lot faster."

When he puts it *that* way...

Spinning in his strong arms, I look into his eyes, seeing no hint of the hurt that was there earlier. He watches me, studying me like he always does. If telling him I'm in love with him is making him act or think differently towards me, he's hiding it really well.

"Walker?" I ask hesitantly, not sure if what I'm about to offer is something he's even interested in. "Would you want me to drive, so you don't have to worry about watching what you drink?"

"You trying to take advantage of me, G?"

"No." I shake my head, enjoying the humor sparkling in his eyes. "I promise I won't let us do anything more than we've already done. I just want you to relax and be carefree tonight. I want you to let go a little. I want you to feel as happy tonight as I always do with you."

"Can I trust you with my car?" His eyebrow arches and I huff out an offended breath. He laughs, though, assuring me with another scorching kiss that he's joking. "I'll give you my keys once we get there. You know the guys are going to assume we're late because I couldn't keep my hands off you, right?"

"Is that bad?"

"No." He shakes his head with a smile. "I just don't want you to be surprised if they make some... *inappropriate* comments."

"Should I let them know your girl had an emotional breakdown instead?"

Walker presses a kiss to my nose before grinning at me. "Say that again."

"That I had an emotional break down?"

"No. Call yourself my girl again."

I grin at his joy in the simple things, leaning back into his arms. "I'm your girl, Walker. I'm all yours and *only* yours."

"Damn straight," he replies, claiming his girl's mouth with his. "And you can tell my friends whatever you want about us being late. I really don't care what they think. I'm just glad you're back to being the Genny I know."

Genny

"April!" Kane shouts, heading our way as soon as we're through the door. "You're look almost as hot in that dress as you do topless."

Kane is over-the-top obnoxious, but at least he's always giving me compliments while he's doing it. "Nice to see you again, too, Kane."

"I haven't seen you in ages, doll. I asked Walker for another pic, but he forwarded me the warning you sent him instead. Nicely played. A man's gotta protect his manhood, even when it means denying me."

"Don't you have girls tripping over themselves to let you see them topless?"

"Yeah, but it's not the same as a picture. A picture can't nag you or ask when you're gonna see them again, and you can look at it as often as you want."

"Wow, Kane. That's just about the sweetest thing I've ever heard."

"Come on, April. What do I have to do to get that picture?"

Shrugging my shoulders, I look toward Walker, who's talking with two other guys I've never met. "I guess convince Walker he doesn't need his manhood to function."

"Awww, girl. You're breaking my heart," he cries, holding his chest like he's in pain. "Give me a chance, Miss April."

"Can't. I'm already taken."

With that, Kane pulls me into a bear hug, squeezing me hard enough he almost takes my breath away. "You're a good one, April. I'm glad he caught you."

Walker's beside met, eyeing Kane cautiously when I'm finally released. He slides his hand to the small of my back, ushering me over to a tall chair next to the pool table his other friends are already at. "The guy in the Mets hat is Alex. He's the quietest of the four of us. Kane, obviously, is the loudest. Zander is the guy playing Alex, and this is his fiancé, Heidi."

A girl waves to us from the next table. She's bouncing in her seat, and the smile she's wearing tells me she's bored and I'm the next lucky contestant to be her new best friend. Walker stands next to me as I lower myself into the chair he pulled out, then offers his beer to me. Seeing Heidi hop off her chair to head my way, I gladly accept it.

"Hi! You're Genny, right? I'm Heidi, Zander's fiancé." She holds her left hand out, fingers together, palm down.

The best position to admire her engagement ring.

I make appreciative noises while mentally rolling my eyes. "We haven't picked a date yet, how do you feel about a fall wedding?"

"Oh, ah..." I raise my eyebrows, looking over her shoulder at the guy she'll be with until death do them part. "I'm pretty sure you should be asking *Zander* that, not me."

"Please, he's a *guy*. Guy's don't want any part of wedding planning. I was thinking fall, but spring might be nice, too. I just can't decide what time of year I want. The venue is booked out for almost a year and a half, so I really need to make up my mind and get on the list."

Turning to Walker with wide eyes, I quietly ask for his beer back. He laughs at my discomfort, wandering off to the bar to order another. How can Zander put up with this girl? I've known her for a full two minutes and I already want to strangle her.

Oh Lord, what if Zander's just as bad?

Heidi prattles on about how strenuous it is to plan a wedding, and how she's already *so* stressed out and it's probably two years away yet. By the time Walker comes back with a shot, I down it without a second thought.

I really should've asked what it was...

Kane and Walker both laugh their asses off at my sour face, then toss back their own. The burn makes its way down my throat and settles in my stomach, and I wonder how they're willingly drinking whatever that was. I raise my middle finger in a casual salute to both of them before turning to see what Heidi is talking about now.

"-can't decide on how many bridesmaids I should have. I was originally thinking eight, but if I ask Melanie, I have to ask Daphne and Susan, too, or they'll unfriend me. But then that's *ten* bridesmaids. and that's kind of a lot, right? I don't think Zander can come up with ten groomsmen! I guess if I cut Melanie, it would only be seven, and Zander can come up with *seven*, I mean who doesn't have seven close friends? I don't like odd numbers though, so I'll probably just go with eight-"

When Walker pushes his beer into my waiting hand, Zander comes over, sweeping Heidi off her feet and into his arms. She lets out a shrill scream, making everyone in the vicinity cringe as she giggles in his arms. "Hey beautiful," he smiles at her. "Making new friends?"

Heidi gets quiet and I can finally hear myself think again. Once Zander and Heidi are done with their mini-reunion, Zander holds out his hand for me to shake. "I'm Zander. Sorry if Heidi was talking your ear off, she can't shut up when she's nervous." He flashes a smile in her direction and her face turns bright red.

"I'm Genny. Heidi is really excited to marry you."

"You mean Heidi is really excited for *her* wedding day. I keep telling her we can just elope, but she wants all the attention of a really expensive, unforgettable day that leaves us penniless."

"Every girl spends years dreaming of her wedding," I reason. I don't know why. Out of the two of them, I'm choosing Zander's side of this debate.

Zander glances at his fiancé with a grimace. "And every guy prays he doesn't spend decades paying for it."

With that, he moves back to Heidi, who's anxiously awaiting his return. I'm glad he's here, though, because she's quiet when he's near her.

Walker's next to me again, smiling and happy, calling Alex over to us. Alex must be shy. He nods in acknowledgment when Walker introduces me, his eyes meeting mine before he softly tells me it's nice to meet me. Kane and Walker are moving towards the pool table and I turn to Alex with a pleading look. "Sit with me? I don't think I can take Heidi sitting here all night." He gives me a knowing grin, sliding into the chair across from me.

"I was watching you and Zander play while pretending to listen to Heidi. You both seem pretty good."

Alex, Mr. Shy Guy, nods at my words.

"Have you been playing a long time?"

Another nod.

"Are you in a league or anything?"

A *shake* of his head. At least that's different, right?

"I've never been good at pool. My sister, Callie? She's really good. I have no idea where she got it from. My brother likes to play, and I know he started teaching her, but she surpassed him in what seemed like seconds. I was always too busy to really learn, but with Callie and Calvin both done with school, I think I'm gonna have to find some new hobbies."

Right then, I realize how scared I am of the future. I didn't mean to babble on like that to Alex. He probably thinks I'm just as bad as Heidi. Risking a glance at his face, I find him studying me like I'm a science project. "What? Did I accidently say something not nice?"

I'm rewarded with a stunningly handsome grin from under his baseball cap. Alex shakes his head and I think we're going right back into our pattern of me asking questions and him giving non-verbal answers, but he surprises me. "What's your last name?"

His voice is quiet, and I strain to hear him over the clack of the pool balls bouncing off each other and the general bar noise. Taking a sip of Walker's-turned-*my* beer, I wonder why he's asking. "Stotler."

"I thought you looked familiar. I know Calvin. And your sister looks a lot like you, right?"

"Yeah, it's creepy how much she looks like me. How do you know my brother?"

"We went to school together. He took HVAC, I took autobody. How's he doing? I haven't talked to him in a while."

"I'm not sure. I've been trying to figure out a day he can come up and we can pretend we're a family again, but he's so busy." I sigh with a hopeless shrug. "I guess busy is good."

He's studying me again. It makes me self-conscious. Calvin was a good kid. Still is, although I know he'd roll his eyes and insist he wasn't a kid anymore if he heard me saying that. His college years were rough for all of us, especially at first. When Callie and Calvin were both in high school, it wasn't too bad. But when Calvin started going to college, we tried to make it work without him getting a job.

To put it simply, it didn't work. At all.

Choosing to ignore Alex's heavy stare, I turn back to the game, watching the way Walker's eyes peruse the table. He's had a few shots already, but he doesn't look too buzzed as he leans over and expertly sinks two striped balls into different pockets.

I can't ignore it any longer. "What did Calvin tell you? I feel like you're sitting over there judging me."

After a quiet chuckle, Alex admits, "He thought you were over-protective. A control freak."

"That sounds about right," I mumble, remembering all the fights we had back then. I'd like to think I wasn't as bad when it came time for Callie to start college, but honestly, I don't know if I was or not.

"He also said he thought you were doing the best you could." Alex smiles at me, his very white teeth glowing against his dark skin. "He didn't say that until we were almost out, though."

"Of course not! He let you think poorly of me until the end."

"You should give him my number. I'd love to hang out with him again."

Getting my phone out of my purse, I type out a text to Calvin, adding Alex's phone number when he gives it to me. My brother's reply is instantaneous.

Calvin: What're you doing with Alex?

Genny: He's a friend of Walker's.

Calvin: Walker is your boyfriend Callie's been talking about?

I type out an affirmative answer, smiling and looking up to find that boyfriend watching me. He must be talking about me, because Kane is also watching me. Walker's eyes roam my body, heating me up in all the right places. The grin he flashes next says he knows exactly what he's doing to me.

I like Walker a little buzzed. I like when he's as forward as I am. I like when his mind is exactly where mine is.

I'm *so* ready to get out of here.

I came here to meet his friends. I've met them. I've chatted briefly with all of them and even found out that Alex knows my brother.

Now, let's go home and get naked.

Walker's reading my mind again because he slowly shakes his head and mouths *not yet*. There's an underlying tension hiding in his stance, his eyes never leaving mine. Maybe he's expecting me to put up a fight?

Letting out a quiet huff, I drink the rest of his beer, turning back to Alex...

Who's *also* watching me closely.

Risking a glance towards Heidi and her fiancé, I find them watching me as well.

Why is everyone watching me?!

Am I unknowingly flashing everyone?

I check to make sure all my girly parts are covered. Yep. Nothing inappropriate showing.

Are my nipples hard?

Well, of *course* my nipples are hard, Walker just undressed me with his eyes.

Other than that, I don't see anything that would make them all stare at me like they are.

Lost as to why I'm getting so much attention, I grab my purse to head up to the bar, intending to get Walker/me another beer. Looking over my shoulder, I double check their eyes.

Still locked onto me.

What the hell?

A hard body stops my forward progress, almost knocking me over after I slam into it. I reach out, grabbing onto an arm to keep myself upright. Maybe I should've been watching where I was going. After side-stepping whoever I just ran into, I'm in the middle of mumbling an apology when his cologne hits me. Blue eyes the same exact shade of Zeke's collide with mine next, causing an unwelcome gasp past my lips.

Maybe Walker's friends didn't know he and I weren't having sex yet, but apparently, they all know I had sex with his roommate. And that's why they were watching me so closely.

To witness my reaction when I realized he was here.

A wicked smile peeks out from under those familiar blue eyes and something inside me twists painfully, causing me to wince as I look away. After letting go of Chad's arm, I walk around him in a daze, wondering what I'm supposed to do with all these feelings that are suddenly in the very forefront of my mind.

Walker

Why the fuck is Chad here? He's been watching Genny since he walked in ten minutes ago. She's been oblivious, thank God, but I know he's gonna do something to change that soon.

We haven't talked, haven't had any real conversation at all, since the night I yelled at him for not signing over his rights for Zeke. He was still talking to me after that, but just barely, until the day Callie showed up at the soccer field and he figured out who Genny was to me. And to him. He hasn't said a word to me since.

She turns around after grabbing her purse and runs right into him. She's shocked he's here. And she doesn't seem happy about seeing him, but she doesn't push him away, either. Now, he's sitting next to her at the bar, and I'm wishing I hadn't told her we couldn't leave yet. Maybe if I'd told her we could, we'd be out the door and she'd have never known he was here.

But I'm a selfish prick. A *buzzed* selfish prick. One who thought I wanted to see what would happen when she saw him. I want her to choose me, but that's stupid. She's already chosen me. She told me a couple hours ago she's in love with me. I think I'm right there with her, but I wasn't a hundred percent sure, so I told her I couldn't say it back. Right now, watching her at the bar with Chad, I'm wishing I'd said it a hundred times. I'm wishing I'd trusted her and had sex with her. Not only because I've wanted to every single time, but because I know she's frustrated with me for *not* having sex with her. She may have said she knows I have my reasons and she doesn't need to know what they are, but she had an emotional breakdown earlier today because of it.

She *has* had sex with Chad. And she didn't want to give him up. I'm also pretty sure she still hasn't told him she wouldn't have sex with him anymore. Even if she promised me she wouldn't.

"Hey, man. You ok?"

She wanted me carefree and happy, which I undoubtedly was before Chad walked in the bar. Now, I'm full of emotions that are anything but. I'm pissed. I feel guilty. I feel a little drunk. I feel dread and anticipation splashing around in my gut. I feel like I'm gonna be sick, and it's not from the alcohol.

I shrug my shoulders at Kane before looking back at the pool table. It's my turn. It's been my turn for a while. I told Genny we couldn't leave because I was in the middle of this game. I suppose I should finish so we can.

But I couldn't care less about the game anymore. After completely missing my shot, I watch Genny and Chad while Kane runs the table. She looks torn. That's the *last* expression I want to see on her face. Why would she be torn if she loves me?

Just throw your drink in his face and come back over here, I tell her telepathically. *Come back to me.*

Now they're *arguing*. What the hell do they have to *argue* about?

Maybe she's telling him she's with me and she's not interested in seeing him ever again. He'd argue with her about that, wouldn't he? Before he knew she was with me, he probably wouldn't have. He has plenty of other girls he can text at all hours of the day. Now, he probably thinks it's a competition.

"Just go over and talk to her," Kane tells me.

Maybe I should. She'd know I'm there to back her up and maybe Chad would leave her alone. Now that I think about it, why the hell am I still over here? Why didn't I follow them over as soon as she figured out he was here? She probably thinks I'm letting her fend for herself, not trusting her to make the right decision.

That *is* kind of what I'm doing, though, isn't it? Figuring out once and for all if I can really trust her. Figuring out if she'll break it off with him and be all mine.

Chad gets up, walking angrily towards the exit and I breathe a sigh of relief. Genny can come back to me, now. She can come over here and kiss me, lean into me, reassure my drunk ego that I was overreacting and she's still in love with me and I'm the only person she wants.

She glances my way, her eyes tight with some emotion I've never seen on her before. Disappointment? Maybe she's upset I stayed back here and just watched?

Where the fuck is she going?!

Lowering her eyes, she follows him out the door in that very short dress I convinced her to leave on.

Fuck.

My chest feels like there's a ton of bricks sitting on it. I close my eyes and try to come up with *any* reason she'd be going outside with him and it wouldn't be to let him fuck her. To let him take care of the frustration I've been forcing on her for weeks. I come up empty. I can't think of a single reason she would be following him outside if she was planning on keeping her promise to me.

Or if she loves me.

Kane, Alex, Zander, and Heidi are all watching me carefully. I didn't think it would matter if they knew she'd been with Chad. I thought it would give me an excuse for taking things slow with her, and it did. But now, it also means that everyone knows my business, and that my girl, the one I was so excited about them meeting, is going outside to fuck my roommate instead of me.

Dammit!

Throwing my pool stick onto the table, I start walking to the door, but Kane gets in my way, blocking me from going anywhere and grabbing my arm as I stumble to a stop in front of him. "There's gonna be a good explanation for this, just wait and see."

"Fuck off! What the hell kind of explanation could there be?"

"I don't know, but she's a great girl. She wouldn't go out there to fuck him when she's getting it from you."

"She's *not*!"

Kane's face contorts to an expression of disbelief. "Say again?"

"She's not getting it from me."

He thinks about that for a few seconds, maintaining his position that blocks my way. "There's still an explanation. She loves you, Walk. Anyone with half a brain can see that. She's not gonna do that to you."

"She just fucking did."

"Huh-uh. I'm not buying it. You should have a little faith in your girl. Sit down. Have a drink. Let her explain when she comes back."

"*If* she comes back," I grumble, unable to come to terms with what I just let happen.

"She's coming back. For *you*. *To* you. She's *your* girl, Walker." Kane pushes me into the seat where Genny was sitting with Alex. Picking up the beer Alex was sipping, I throw it down my throat, needing something to numb the anger that's tearing me up inside. It doesn't work. I think about getting another shot, instead, but I can't. I have to find out what she's doing. I have to find out if she still wants me. I have to find out if we're still an us.

Us. As in Genny and me.

Genny, the girl who gave me her heart today, and I told her I didn't want it yet.

And me, the asshole who simply *watched* while the guy she used to fuck started an argument with her.

Fucking Goddamn it all to hell.

I stand up and barrel toward the exit, needing to see if she's still here, and what she's doing with him if she is. When I slam the door open, Genny stumbles backwards, her fingers on the handle as it flies toward her. She looks up at me in surprise, her cheeks flushed, her eyes wide and nervous, and my heart bottoms out in my stomach. I reach up and grab the doorframe, to steady myself and block her entry.

"Walker..."

Her voice is breathy, and one hand moves to smooth her dress down over her ass.

"Really Genny?" I demand, my voice low and hard with rage.

"Really *what*?"

"You couldn't wait for me? Had to go fuck my roommate in the parking lot because I wasn't giving you quite enough? Couldn't keep your legs closed another week or two?"

Gasping at my words, her eyes show me just how much I hurt her before turning as cold as mine. She stares me down, not denying a word I said.

"You never trusted me at all, did you?"

"How the hell could I? You just proved I couldn't."

She closes her eyes, furious at the truth I spelled out for her. A single tear rolls down her cheek and I can't help but be glad she's feeling even a little bit of the pain that's ripping *my* heart to shreds.

The second her angry eyes meet mine, I know it's over.

Completely over.

And it's just as disastrous as we both predicted it would be.

Throwing my keys at my feet, she sneers, "Go to hell, Walker."

She turns around and walks out of the bar, out of the parking lot, and out of my life.

Walker

Living in this apartment with Chad is killing me, even though I'm doing everything I can to avoid him. I saw him Sunday, at the game. I usually play defense, but I switched positions again, so I could kick his ass on the field. He didn't seem to care one way or the other, but I suppose that's because he already won. He got the girl. Stole her right out from under me. While she was on a fucking *date* with me.

Right after the game, I started seriously looking for a new place. There's not a whole lot available in my price range. If my parents hadn't turned my old room into a home gym, I would ask if I could move back in with them just to get away from him.

Today is Tuesday, the day Callie and I were going to surprise Genny. It started out simple. I said I'd take them both out to eat, since I was taking Genny away from Callie for an evening. Callie said she wanted to cook us a meal instead, to show her appreciation to Genny, who's done so much for her. Not only since their parents died, but especially while Callie went to school, to get a degree, something Genny wasn't able to do.

Then it morphed into Callie wanting to make a painting for Genny. She was going to present it to Genny before the meal, but then Callie wanted out. She wanted me and Genny to enjoy the meal like it was a date. I didn't like that idea. I thought it should be about Callie and Genny, but Callie was hooked on this idea, and she wouldn't let it go.

She's stubborn, just like her whore of a sister.

Callie: Where are you? You were supposed to be here half an hour ago!!

Genny must not have told Callie what happened.

Callie and I had gotten close over the many times I'd seen her, just like Genny had gotten close to my nephews. Genny broke my heart, but Callie didn't. And I don't want to ruin her image of her sister; I don't want to be the one to tell her that Genny fucked someone else while out with me. And Callie is going to want details, she's not going to accept this easily.

It's still pretty fucking hard for *me* to accept.

Walker: I'm not coming, Cal. Genny and I aren't working out.

I go for short and sweet, already knowing there's no way it'll fly.

Callie: Bullshit! You guys are perfect together. What do you mean it's 'not working out?'

Walker: Genny and I over, Callie. If you ever need anything, let me know. But as for why it's not working out, you'll have to talk to Genny.

Genny: Don't worry, I will.

It sounds like a threat, and coming from Callie, I think it is. They're close, so I don't think Genny will lie to her. But that would also mean Genny will have to admit she was the one who fucked this up, and I don't know if she can do that. She'll probably blame it on me. I shouldn't care what Callie thinks of me, but I do. I don't want her to think I was the one who hurt Genny. I don't want to be the bad guy. Not to anyone, but especially not to Callie.

Kane and Alex both think I should've let Genny explain, that there had to be a different explanation. But I'd seen enough to know. I don't need her excuses or her lies.

Zander's on my side. And Heidi. God, Heidi is a pain in the ass. I loved Genny's reaction to Heidi. Hell, I loved *Genny.* I *still* love Genny, and I hate that it took me losing her to figure that out. But I can't get over this. I can't forget this. I can't *forgive* this.

Needing something to do, I head over to Reese's. I don't know if she's busy, but I don't care, either. Zeke can always make me smile. He's one person I can count on to not fuck me over.

Except when I get there, he's begging me to text Genny and ask her to come over. I tell him no over and over until I snap, and he's standing in front of me crying, because I hurt his feelings and all he wanted was to see Genny.

Reese isn't appreciative of me yelling at Zeke for my own screw ups. I don't tell her it wasn't my screw up. I don't tell her anything at all. I just leave.

Deciding to give up and go to bed early, I'm almost asleep when I get another text from Callie.

Callie: You're a fucking asshole. And she didn't cry. Thanks to you, she's back to showing NO emotion.

Guess Genny lied to Callie after all.

Walker

Saturday, my entire family is at Reese's. Zeke and Finn, who's finally walking, are in the kiddie pool laughing and splashing each other until one of them gets mad and they both start screaming. Steve is seated in a nearby chair *supervising* and interfering very little. His parenting technique is to let the boys figure it out. I think Finn's a little young for that, but what the hell do I know? They're not my kids.

Zeke is still asking for Genny. It's only been a week and I know he's going to be asking for her for a long time. I miss her, despite being mad as hell at her, and that pisses me off. I should be able to hate her after what she did. Part of me does, but there's another part, of equal size, that loves and misses her, and *that* part is making me fucking miserable.

Reese is inside with my mom, preparing who knows what to eat. It'll be delicious, but I won't taste it. My anger makes it impossible to enjoy anything, even the things I usually love. Dad is at the grill. He tried to talk to me but left after I snapped at him.

I'm lashing out at everyone. I'm *trying* to control it. It's not going so well. Which means, I'm sitting under a tree in the shade, all by myself, surrounded by my family members that I'm slowly pushing away from me.

Fan-*fucking*-tastic.

It's been a *long* week.

Next week promises to be more of the same.

Can't fucking wait.

Walker

Stepping into the pool hall Friday night, where I'm supposed to meet the guys, I almost stop breathing when I see them. For a second, I think it's *her*. But it's not. It's her younger look-alike.

Callie's talking with Alex. Someone else is with them and it slowly dawns on me that it's Calvin, their brother. I never got to meet him. I wanted to. I wanted to know her whole family and everything about her. I wanted her to meet my parents and go to all my family functions. I wanted her to be a part of every single aspect of my life.

Alex, Calvin, and Callie are all laughing about something. They seem at ease, like they know each other, like they're comfortable with each other. Callie must feel my eyes because she turns around and looks directly at me. She shakes her head while glaring at me, obviously believing whatever Genny told her instead of the truth she's probably never heard.

She taps her brother on the shoulder, saying something to him and pointing me out. I'm still standing in the doorway watching them. He sizes me up, saying something to Callie while watching me.

I don't need this shit.

I don't need them telling lies about me, making me out to be the person who was in the wrong. Turning around, I walk back out to my car. I have no idea where I'm gonna go, but I'm not staying here.

I get a text late that night from Alex. Reading it, I delete it, then turn my phone off completely. They've got him against me now, too.

Alex: You should really let Genny explain.

Genny

"Do you wanna know how it went?"

My eyes snap shut. I swallow thickly around the lump that's now constantly stuck in my throat. It takes all my willpower to summon my neutral expression, but it's firmly in place when I turn to my sister Saturday morning. Calvin's on the couch still sleeping. It was nice to wake up with my entire family under the same roof, but I've been reading on my phone and drinking disgustingly delicious, u*n*sweet coffee, dreading the moment one of them would wake up and tell me about their evening.

Ready or not, the time is here.

"Yeah, of course. Did you have a good time?"

The sound of the coffee machine fills the silence and Callie waits until she and her mug of coffee are seated with me at the island. She gives me a smile, but her eyes are sad. Which means I know exactly what's coming.

"Walker was there."

My lungs squeeze as every last molecule of air is sucked out of them. I raise my coffee so she can't see the devastation written across my face. My neutral expression doesn't have near enough power to remain in place when a storm stirs up the wreckage of my heart every time his name is mentioned.

Even when my neutral expression slips, I can usually still hold all that wreckage inside. If anyone's good at pretending everything's ok when it's clearly not, I am.

At least when anyone is around.

Callie's been working so much she's hardly ever here. This is the first I've seen Calvin all summer, and he's asleep. Myra's busy. Michelle and Sam are an official item in the throes of new love, spending every spare minute together. And those are all the people on the I-care-about-Genny-Stottler list.

When my parents died, everything was suddenly my responsibility, and I had *no* experience with responsibility. Zero. *Zilch*. The loss of my parents, the loss of my dreams, the loss of *me*, as an individual, the loss of the certainty and confidence I'd always had but disappeared as quickly as my parents' lives ended, had me reeling in a sea of numb confusion.

I was *lost*. I had no one to lean on, nothing to fall back on, no idea how to make everything work. I forced myself through each minute, focusing on one little thing and pushing everything else to the back of my mind until it was the most pressing thing in it's *own* moment. When that got comfortable, I worked toward ten minutes. Then a half hour. Then an hour. It was slow, agonizing progress, but it was *progress*.

With this break up from Walker, I'm experiencing loss in a whole new way. I know how to be responsible. I know how to get shit done. I know that it's imperative that I form a routine and follow it to a T, to make sure I get through the day on autopilot.

But I'm not *numb*.

I wish I was. I wish, more than anything, that I could stop *feeling*, because then I wouldn't feel like I was back underwater. I'm in a place where all I see is my tiny little world. But this time, I'm very aware of the world outside my line of vision and *nothing's* muted. My emotions are here, live and in color. I was floating when I was submerged before, but these emotions are so strong they're like a giant boulder trapping me on the bottom, so I can't get to the surface. And I *have* to get to the surface, because not only do I know how great the surface is, but here on the bottom, I can't *breathe*.

Breathing underwater isn't possible. I must've had a tank of oxygen strapped to my back before I met Walker. Because I lived underwater, and I somehow still *breathed*. It might not ever have been as full a breath, not anywhere near as cleansing as the fresh air above the waterline was, not nearly as satisfying and effortless as being happy and thinking that I was finally moving toward a future of my own choosing.

But I still was able to *breathe*.

And I *can't* breathe anymore.

I make a show of it. I pretend I'm ok. No one believes my act, but they let me keep pretending, because the few people in my life that are left that care about me, know that I *need* the act to survive. If I give in to the pain, to the feeling of losing my dreams again, of losing *myself* again, or at least the happiest part of myself I've ever found, I don't know that I'll ever come back from it.

The pain is too overwhelming.

The person I was becoming with Walker was too happy.

The dream I thought I was going to get was too perfect.

Every time I start to think that my life is moving in the right direction, somewhere I *want* it to go, somewhere that *I* chose, not fate, or life, or the Lord up above who apparently hates me with a passion I will never understand, reality slams the door to the future I was creating.

I don't have control over my future.

The only thing I have control over is how I react to the shitty hand I'm always given.

"Yeah? How's he do-"

My voice cracks. My shoulders bounce. My throat closes completely.

I clutch at my throat, trying to hold it all in, but it can't be contained. The façade is over.

A sob breaks through the confines of my chest and tears stream down my cheeks as I double over at the pain twisting my soul. It twists my soul like a chain, doubling up on itself, then tripling, then quadrupling. I become smaller and smaller inside this shell of a body. My soul is a shy, terrified being hunched in the corner, trying to become invisible so it doesn't have to suffer its way through yet another blow.

Callie's arms surround me, and her breath is shaky as she tries to comfort me. "Genny," she whispers, her anguish almost as easy to hear as mine. "I'm so sorry."

I've always been the strong one. The only time my siblings have seen me cry, before right now of course, was on our parents' anniversary. I need to find the strength I once had. Maybe it was a different kind of strength. Maybe it was for a different reason. Maybe it was because they depended on me, and needed me, and they don't anymore. But there's got to be *some* of that strength left. I have to find it. I have to hold onto it. I have to somehow rebuild it into something I can find whenever I need it.

My parents' died and I had to take on the role of responsible adult when I was anything but. This is hard, but it's just a fucking *relationship*. Relationships end all the time. Isn't that why I avoided them in the first place? Maybe what I had with Walker was exponentially more intense than anything I've ever felt with anyone, but I need to keep going. If what I went through ten years ago didn't kill me, Walker's words and easy dismissal certainly won't.

"If I'd never given him a chance, you never would've won that contest," I reason with her. Swallowing thickly, I wave my hand at all the missing artwork on the walls. "You're in high demand, little sister. You're officially an artist, and now that you're graduated and have a real job, you'll have the time and money to create the pieces you've always wanted to. And people will spend good money on them because you're so talented."

Her face crumples, which is not what I was expecting. She grips my hand and regards me with tears in her own eyes. "It's *my* fault this happened. I told you to give him a chance. I thought he was a good guy. I only wanted you to be happy, I swear."

"Oh, Callie... Walker *is* a good guy, and this is no one's fault but my own." My voice threatens to give out on me again, so I stop and take a shaky breath. I wipe my eyes. I lick my dry lips. I clutch her hands in mine, wishing things were so very different. Then I meet her eyes again and give her the truth.

Even though we're both adults, and I never wanted to be her role model, it doesn't change the fact that I'm still looking out for her. "As much as it hurts now, I wouldn't give up the time I had with him for anything."

"Really? Even after what he said to you?"

Drastically switching topics, I ask, "You know Mom and Dad called me that night? The one before the accident?" Callie shakes her head. "Mom told me she embarrassed you in the food court and you got mad at her. But she also told me that you donated your allowance for the whole month to a little girl that couldn't walk because of some illness she had."

"I don't remember that."

"She couldn't believe how generous you were. How you were so worried about this other person you'd never met. You said something to her about how you couldn't eat candy, but that wasn't nearly as bad as not being able to walk. She couldn't get over what a big heart you had."

"I hated every second of that day," Callie gushes, guilt and despair all over her face as she gives me her confession. "I was such a brat. She brought up sex right in the food court, where anyone could hear, and I told her she was ruining my life. When we got home, I slammed my bedroom door and wouldn't talk to her for the rest of the night. I was still mad at her the next morning, and then it was too late. She was gone."

Callie was just starting to get boobs, and mom took her out to try on and buy bras, had the period talk with her, and started bringing up sex. Mom called me that night and told me about it. It was a rare moment for me, because I just laid on my bed and let her ramble on, actually listening to everything she was saying. Dad talked to me, too, and I got to tell them both I loved them before I hung up. I never thought it would be the last time I talked to them. I never thought I wouldn't get to hear their voices again. I never thought I'd be so grateful that I answered the phone that night, instead of just sending it to voicemail like I did so often in those first few weeks of school.

I was a brat, too. Just a much older one.

"Do you think Mom would've given up that last day with you?"

"No," she chokes out, her tears overflowing now. "She wouldn't have given up a second of her time with me. Even the days when I was an ungrateful little bitch."

"Because she loved you, Callie. So much."

Just like I loved Walker. But the time to make a point is over. It's now time to console my sister, so I pull her into my arms and hug her as tightly as we wish we could do with both of our parents.

Callie sobs into my shoulder, making my own tears fall harder. "I never got to tell her I was sorry. I should've told her I loved her. I should've told her she was the best mom ever. I should've told her how much she meant to me!"

"She knew you loved her. So did Dad."

"What did Dad say?" Calvin says, his voice low and unsteady as he makes his presence known. I don't know how long he's been standing there listening, but I don't care. I reach out and grab his hand with a watery smile. I should've shared this with them years ago, but my last moments with my parents were so much better than theirs. It didn't seem right to shove it in their faces.

"Dad was bitching about you not wanting to hunt with him." Calvin scoffs and we all let out a small laugh. "But he said he wished you could understand it had nothing to do with killing the animal. It had everything to do with sharing that time with you. He had no idea how to connect with you, because you two had nothing in common. You lived for animals, while he loved hunting and fishing. But he thought you could relate to the beauty of spending time in the woods and admiring the animals on their own turf. He didn't care if you both went in the woods and didn't even take a gun. He just wanted that time with you."

Calvin sniffs and squeezes my hand, then leans into our little Stottler mountain. "You're not the only one who regrets their last words, Cal. I called Dad a murderer."

It's the little things we do that we think nothing of, that end up hurting us the most. The things we believe because we don't want to even realize there's another side to things, another perspective. We believe there's always time to make things right. We forget that tomorrow isn't guaranteed. We forget that everything we love can disappear in the blink of an eye and we should cherish every second we have.

"Guys," I pull them both in closer, kissing Calvin on the cheek, then Callie. "In case I don't ever get the chance to tell you, or I forget, because I'm really bad at expressing my feelings, I want you to know I love you. So much. I'm so proud of both of you. And I know I fucked up a lot over the years, and most of the time things weren't easy, but I'm so glad we stayed together. I'm so glad we have each other now. I'm so glad we're closer now than we were before."

"I'm so sorry you had to give up everything for that to happen," Callie whispers, and I take my own unspoken advice. I shift perspectives. I force myself to look at it from a different angle. I force myself to see the silver lining, instead of the dark cloud hovering over my small, little, saturated world. The dark cloud *will* move on. It can't rain every single day for an eternity. It's not possible. Mother nature doesn't work that way, and neither does life. There are ups and downs, and it's my choice how I react to any of it.

"Maybe what I gave up wasn't nearly as great as what I gained."

A miniscule amount of oxygen gets sucked into my desperate lungs.

My new perspective gave me a coffee stirrer. I'm still underwater, but there's a tiny hose giving me just enough air that I can breathe a little. That must be the secret. The answer. The way to keep surviving. *That's* what I have to focus on.

The silver lining.

Everything happens for a reason. I have no idea what the reason is that Walker and I ended as horrifically as we did, but eventually, *there will be a reason*. Until then, I'll keep searching for my inner strength and my silver lining.

As many times as I have to.

Walker

"I'm sick of you acting like this! Either tell me what's going on or get out of my house!"

Rolling my eyes at my overly dramatic sister, I prop my feet up on her coffee table and proceed to ignore her to watch the game. It's Thursday night and it's storming outside. I hung out with her and the kids until the kids went to bed. I should leave, but I don't wanna go home. Chad's off today. He'll be there. I don't want to see his face ever again.

"Dammit, Walker, what happened with you and Genny?"

I drown out the sound of her voice by turning up the volume. Maybe she'll get the hint.

"If you wake the boys up, I'll kill you myself."

Turning the volume back down, I continue ignoring her.

"If you don't talk to me, I'm gonna tell Zeke you broke Genny's heart and he'll hate you for life."

"Everyone else thinks it's my fault, why not him, too?"

Reese sits beside me on the couch, grabbing the remote from my hands and muting the TV. "I don't think it's your fault. I don't know *what* to think. All I know is you're miserable, you're making *me* miserable when you're around, and Zeke misses his happy Uncle Walk. Which you are *not*. Tell me what happened."

After Callie and Calvin's little trip to the pool hall last week, even Zander and Heidi are against me. *Everyone* thinks it's my fault. But I know what I saw. And if someone wanted me to believe what I saw wasn't what it looked like, she should have denied it the moment she came back in the bar after being outside with my roommate.

"She cheated on me."

Disbelief registers on Reese's face, and I briefly wonder if I should've said anything. "Oh my God, really? I never would've thought she'd do that. She was crazy in love with you."

"Not crazy in love enough," I mumble. Being pissed off and angry at everyone and everything makes me mumble a lot. The problem is, I don't care if people hear me.

"Did you catch her in the act? I mean, could there be any other explanation?"

174

"Close enough to it."

"Aw, Walker... You really liked her. Is there anything I can do to help?"

"Yeah, find me a new place to live."

She freezes, her eyes slowly raising to mine. Her head shakes back and forth, slowly at first, but then with more urgency. "It wasn't with Chad." When I don't respond, she lets out an anguished moan. "Walker, I'm so sorry. Chad's messed up everything for us. I swear he's like our own personal demon. You think you've moved on, that you don't need to worry about him anymore, and then he does something else. What does he have against us?"

"I don't know, Reese."

I do, though. Maybe not in Reese's situation, but in mine it was because he thought I stole Genny from him. And he wanted to get her back, only to prove that he could. That he can get any girl he wants, even if she's *my* girl.

Reese doesn't tell me to leave. She tells me I can sleep on the couch whenever I want.

Walker

It's been a month. I still think about her every day. Somedays aren't so bad. I don't think about her for a while at a time. Like fifteen minutes if I'm lucky, but I have to stay busy. If I'm not busy, she's in almost every thought I have, so I make *damn* sure to stay *damn* busy.

Today's her birthday, though. And I can't stop thinking about her no matter how busy I make myself.

It's a Wednesday night, and I decide it wouldn't be that awful to drive by her house. I have no idea why I'm doing it. What do I expect to see? Her car in the driveway? Callie's van in the driveway? Maybe I'll see a *different* vehicle in the driveway. Maybe she's seeing someone. Maybe she's *fucking* someone. Or even a couple someones. Maybe it's really bad idea.

I do it anyway.

There's a fucking *for sale* sign in the yard.

What the hell? Where is she going? Did she get a new job? Did Callie move out like she wanted and Genny's moving closer to either her or Calvin? Did she find some new guy and she's moving closer to *him*? Moving *in* with him? Is she so sick of this town that she needs to get away from it? Does everything, everywhere remind her of me and she can't take it anymore?

That's how *I* feel.

Telling myself it doesn't matter, I head back to Reese's. I've been staying there whenever Steve is out of town. I'm still not happy Uncle Walk yet, but I'm starting to be able to fake it better. Maybe when Genny's gone and I can't find her, it won't hurt so fucking bad.

Yeah... I don't believe that either.

Walker

It's been six weeks since I've seen her. Since she cheated on me. Since she made me realize how much I love her by shattering my heart. I'm tossing and turning in my own bed in my own apartment because Steve is in town. I'm glad for him, Reese and the boys.

I'm not glad for *me*. Chad's working, so I don't need to deal with him tonight. I will in the morning.

It's not like I haven't seen him. I have. I just want to shove his head through the wall every time I catch even a glimpse of him.

The guys have been bugging me, sending me messages, asking me to hang out with them again. Asking me to even just *talk* to them again. I've been ignoring them since they all told me it was my fault. Assholes. They just want to believe a pretty face.

It's early. I shouldn't be lying in bed, but I don't have anything else to do. I went to the gym, went for a run after the gym, made dinner, watched TV, did the dishes. It's Friday night. I should be out on a date, trying to find a different girl to love, since the one I fell for couldn't be trusted. I can't, though. I compare everyone to her. She's ruined me in so many ways.

I still can't fully hate her. *That* pisses me off to no end.

Hearing my phone vibrate on the nightstand, I reach for it, hoping for any kind of distraction. After unlocking the screen, I stare at my sister's text for a long time, unsure of how to respond.

Reese: I saw Genny today at the hospital. You'll be happy to hear she looks like hell. I told her what an awful person she is and that I hope she gets what she deserves.

It doesn't feel as good as it should. It actually kinda hurts.

Walker: What did she say?

I shouldn't ask. I shouldn't care. I should thank my little sister for having my back and go to sleep. But thinking about Genny looking like hell and getting yelled at by Reese just makes my heart twist in a way I wasn't expecting.

Reese: It was really weird. She asked if I'd heard from Chad.

Walker: Why?

Reese: I have no idea.

Walker

"Walker, hey..."

Glancing over at the girl who's talking to me, I stop on my way out the door after work. It's not like I have anything to rush home to.

"Hey, Sam. How's it going?"

"Good, um. I was wondering if you might want to go to a concert with me? It's tomorrow night. My friend that was supposed to go, bailed. I know it's really short notice, but I didn't know if you were free or not. Or if you'd want to go or not."

Sam's cute. She's nice. She's had a crush on me since forever. She's not my type, though. Before it was because she's too nervous, too nice, too eager to please. She backs down from anything even remotely looking like a confrontation.

Now, it's simply because she's not Genny.

On second thought, she's everything Genny isn't... Maybe I should give her a chance.

"Ah, I might be able to swing it. Who're you going to see?"

"Maroon Five. They're my favorite. I have every song they've ever recorded memorized."

Trying not to sigh, not to close my eyes, not to clench my fists and curse out the girl I love that's ruining even *this* for me, I very calmly ask Sam for her number. "I'll see if I can rearrange some things. I can't promise anything, but I'll let you know."

"Great! No pressure! I mean, I know its last minute and you probably had plans, so... Just let me know. Either way is totally fine."

"I will, Sam. I'll text you tonight."

I go to the damn concert and think of Genny the entire time. And I kiss Sam goodnight, feeling absolutely *nothing*, even though she's so excited I know she's jumping up and down and dancing in her front hallway as soon as I'm gone.

I'm lying, I *did* feel something.

Regret.

At least it got me out of my apartment for a while.

Genny

I'm still up when Callie gets home. Calvin's right on her heels and he motions with his chin for me to move off his temporary bed as soon as he's in the door. He heads upstairs to the bathroom while Callie beckons me to the kitchen. It's the only room not cluttered with boxes.

Callie's trying to move out, and I can't live in this big house all by myself.

Even if moving is the last thing my heart wants to do.

Callie and Calvin go out to the pool hall with Kane and Alex once or twice a month. The nights they go are always rough for me to get through. I've been going out to the bar Chad works at every weekend to keep myself distracted. Usually once during the week, too. I'm so tired of it, though. I'm so tired of staying up late, of seeing his face, of hearing his voice, of watching him hit on *so many* girls. It's truly amazing how many girls he tries to dazzle with his beautiful blue eyes and panty-dropping smile.

I told myself, tonight, I can take a break.

So tonight, I'm dealing with the heartbreak of my ruined relationship with Walker instead. Because Callie always brings news of him after seeing his friends.

Kane never mentions Walker to me. Kane only mentions Walker if I ask, and I'm way too chicken to ask.

Kane has been amazing to me. He gave Callie his number the first night Callie went out with Calvin to the pool hall, telling her to make me call him. I don't know why I listened, but I'm glad I did. *Someone* had some faith in me, even if it wasn't the person who mattered most.

Kane challenged me to prove that I wasn't moping around my house. And that was exactly what I was doing. It took me a while, but I realized me settling into a depression would only give Walker the knowledge of how badly he hurt me if he ever found out. I took Kane's advice and started trying to live again, even if only by talking to Kane and letting him practice his drill sergeant skills on me. Walker doesn't need to think he broke me. Walker doesn't need to think he matters to me at all.

Even if he always will.

"Genny... Kane wasn't sure if he should tell you or not, so he told me to do whatever I think is best."

"What's he afraid to tell me?" I ask, already preparing for the worst. Walker's rejoined their group. Walker's back to living again. Walker's doing ok, while I'm still pretending half the time when my inner strength evades me and that damn silver lining is winning the game of hide-and-seek. I tell myself to swallow down whatever emotions come, because that's what I do. When I'm tired and I don't have the desire to keep searching for that silver lining, I swallow all my emotions, so I can get through the rest of the day.

The silver lining isn't always easy to see. And leaning on my inner strength constantly has seriously depleted my supply.

But this news is so much worse than I was expecting.

"Walker has a new girlfriend."

Tears burn my eyes as my heart skids across the inside of my ribs, screeching to a halt that steals my breath a few seconds later. I should've pretended again tonight. I should've waited until tomorrow to hear this news.

No. I should've waited *forever*.

It'll take me that long to get over it.

Walker

I've been seeing Sam for a month now, which means it's been almost three months since I saw Genny last. The for-sale sign in front of her house is still there. I still only see her car and Callie's van in the driveway. I still lie to myself and pretend I don't care.

Sam is boring. I take her out every weekend. I kiss her good night. She's invited me in, invited me to stay without words, because she's too afraid to ask for what she wants. I've done some heavy petting, taken off some of her clothes, but I'm not into it. She doesn't turn me on. Not even a little.

She's afraid to touch me. She won't reach for my hand. She won't wrap her arms around me when we're kissing. She has no desire to go anywhere near my dick. She's afraid to touch any part of me unless I move her hand somewhere.

The exact opposite of Genny.

It's driving me crazy.

I always feel dirty when I leave Sam's place. I've never stayed, even though she wants me to. I would rather go back to my apartment and risk dealing with Chad than stay with her, and it's finally getting through my head that I need to end it. I have no desire to fuck her. I have no desire to kiss her. I have no desire to take her out, or even *see* her, ever again.

Work is going to be really awkward when I end whatever it is I'm doing with Sam.

It's funny. A month with Sam feels like forever and I still hardly know her. A month with Genny felt like a blink of the eye and I felt like I'd known her for years.

I still fucking miss her.

I still fucking *hate* her.

I still fucking *love* her.

Walker

"That's it! I've fucking had it with your psycho girlfriend!" The door slams loudly in our small apartment and I blink a few times to figure out that I fell asleep on the couch. Chad stomps through the room, kicking his door open before slamming things around in there, as well.

I have no idea what he's talking about. He doesn't know Sam and I wouldn't call her my girlfriend. Isn't it kind of a requirement to *like* your girlfriend? Or feel anything towards her at all? Besides, I told her last night I couldn't see her anymore. I figured her having the weekend to deal with it would be better than seeing her at work the next day. She cried and told me it was ok. That she understood. I didn't give her a reason, but she understands? She can't even get upset about *that*? She can't stand up for herself and demand a reason?

Honestly, I feel sorry for her. And disgusted with myself for letting it go as far as it did. I knew it was never going to work. I knew I would never like her. I knew I was nowhere near ready to date again. I'm a fucking bastard for seeing her even once.

Chad's grumbling and cursing in his room. It sounds like he's kicking something else now. I don't know what his problem is, but I'm not dealing with it tonight. Getting up from the couch, I head to my room, being extra careful to not even look in his direction.

"Don't close your fucking door, Walker! I'm done with this shit! Give me two fucking minutes."

"Chad, I don't know what you're talking about."

"The fuck you don't! I'm getting it, ok? Just give me two Goddamned minutes!"

I give him two minutes. Whatever has him so worked up has nothing to do with me, even if he thinks it does. Maybe he's finally lost it. Maybe he's suddenly delusional. I'll have to google different STD symptoms and figure out if hallucinations or something of the sort is on any of the lists.

Chad comes out of his room, his face red and strained, his chest rising dramatically with every forced breath. He shoves some papers into my hands before backing away. "It's *done*, ok? Tell your girlfriend to leave me the fuck alone and mind her own fucking business!"

"Who are you talking about? I don't have a girlfriend."

"Genny," he sneers, obviously hating her almost as much as I do most of the time. "Tell her it's done, and I *never* want to see her again."

Welcome to the club, asshole.

He slams the door in my face, leaving me standing there in a state of total confusion. What the hell could Genny do to Chad to have him this mad? Their relationship is entirely physical, no emotions at all, and this is more emotion from him than I've ever seen. Despite not wanting to know anything about the two of them, especially together, this weird turn of events has me curious. Stepping back into my room, I throw the papers on my bed before I think to look at them.

The packet is an old, stained, wrinkled, legal document.

My eyes roam the first few pages several times before I realize what it is.

It's the documentation for Chad to give up his rights to Zeke.

And they're *signed*.

Chad *signed* them, giving up his rights as Zeke's father! Steve can adopt Zeke and Reese doesn't have to worry about Chad fucking up her life ever again!

I don't trust myself with this. I'm going to get it wet or dirty or lose an important page; *somehow* make it so it's not legal anymore. It's late. Almost three in the morning, but this can't wait. Grabbing my phone, I call Reese. Better yet, I walk to the front door and grab my keys while holding the phone up to my ear. I'll take them to her. Right now.

"Walker?" Reese mumbles, obviously still half asleep. "What's going on?"

"Reese, I'll be there in five minutes."

"What's going on?"

"Wake Steve up, too. I'll be right there."

"Walker, what's-"

I hang up on her. I'll be there soon enough. And she'll be really glad I woke her.

Steve stands in the open doorway waiting for me, worry written in the lines marking his forehead. Reese is in the kitchen, pacing, worried sick about whatever I have to tell her that's so important I had to wake her up in the middle of the night *and* drive over to tell her in person.

I don't tell them anything. I hand Reese the paperwork and watch as it dawns on her what the gift is that she just received.

Reese's hand shakes uncontrollably as it moves to her mouth. She shakes her head, her watery eyes raising to meet mine before settling in disbelief on the paperwork again. "Walker? Is this...? How did you...? Oh my God, Steve! Steve, we can be a real family! Steve!"

He moves to her side, wanting to believe, but needing to see it for himself. They hold the stapled papers between them, looking at every page, every single signature legible and where it should be, tears streaming down their faces at their long overdue good fortune. I watch them, happy, in love, finally getting what they deserve.

The sight of it gives me more joy than I ever could have imagined I would feel tonight.

I walk away quietly, letting them have their moment, wondering how *Genny* had anything to do with making this happen.

Wondering if maybe Genny *did* have an explanation for following Chad out of the bar that night.

Wondering if maybe I pushed away the best thing that ever happened to me because I was insanely jealous, and I didn't trust her the way she trusted me.

Wondering exactly what I'm going to say to her when I track her down in the morning.

Genny

"You got this, April! Embrace the burn! Push harder! You totally got this!"

Kane's words are just what I need to spur me on, and I gather what little energy I have left to spin the pedals of my bike around just a few more times. It's the hills that get me. The biggest hill is the last one on our long ride and I might actually make it over the top this time. Risking a glance at what's ahead, I realize I'm closer than I've ever been before. My chin lands against my chest as I focus on nothing other than slowly forcing these pedals in one last rotation.

He's right. I *got* this. I'm fucking *conquering* this hill today.

When the bike starts rolling on it's own down the hill, Kane lets out a loud, victorious whoop, and I lift my head to feel the wind on my sweaty face as I raise my hands in pride. Gravity can do the rest. I don't know if I could push the pedals down again if my life depended on it. I'm wiped out. Exhausted. In need of a huge glass of water and a bed. Maybe a shower when I wake up from a nap.

No *maybe* about that last one. I definitely *need* a shower. I'm disgusting. I'm just not sure my rubbery, overused legs will hold me up long enough to get my gross body clean before I crash for a while.

Slowing to a stop in front of my house, I walk my bike around the corner to discover a car in my driveway that really shouldn't be here. After leaning my bike against the house, I turn around and walk back to the front, where Kane is slowly doing circles in the road, showing off his impressive skills to Callie, who's hanging halfway out her window.

Kane calls Callie June, since that's the month he met her, telling her that she's his centerfold for *that* month. She didn't know that he called me April until after her new nickname had stuck. Kane and Alex both call her June now.

Zander hasn't jumped on that bandwagon because Heidi would kill him.

"April, what's up?" Kane yells and I flinch at how easily his voice carries through the still morning air. Pulling off my helmet, I wonder what I'm supposed to do in this situation.

Scratch that.

I wonder what I *want* to do in this situation.

"There's a bit of a problem in my driveway."

His eyebrows fold together as he taps his biking shoes on the pavement. He has funny shoes that click into his pedals. He swears it helps him with his cycling skills; I tell him it makes him look feminine. It's an ongoing argument I love to have with him.

"What kind of problem?" he asks as Walker steps around the corner of the house. Kane sighs, immediately understanding what kind of *problem* I'm asking him to help me with. "You got it, doll. Just slip around the back. I'll text you my schedule for next weekend."

"Thanks, Kane. You're the best."

Walking the wrong way around my house, I swallow the lump of emotions that's already trying to crawl out of my heart and up my throat. I don't have time for this. *Wrong.* I have tons of *time.* I don't have the *energy* to deal with this. Emotionally or physically.

"Walker, what're you doing here, man?" Kane asks, blocking Walker from following me.

"What the fuck are *you* doing here?"

"Going on a bike ride with my favorite girl. What's it to you?"

"She'll screw anyone I know, won't she?" Walker's voice growls. The things he thinks I'd do instantly pull tears from my eyes, and all the barriers I've put up to protect myself from my emotions concerning him come crashing down all at once.

"Fuck you, Walker. That's totally uncalled for. If you weren't such a dick-licker you'd have figured that out by now."

I was really hoping to not hear anything Walker has to say, but they're following me around the house, and I can hear every word. These new words hurt me just as much as the ones from that night in the bar. The night his eyes got hard and he treated me like I wasn't his girlfriend, just a cheap whore.

I told myself I would *not* cry over Walker Kelley ever again. He's not worth it. He doesn't deserve my tears after the way he treated me.

But my body refuses to listen, and I try my damndest to hold in the desperate sobs trying to escape my lungs, at least until he's gone. Until he can't hear how he still affects me.

"Look, you're right," Walker sighs, his words already tinged with regret. "I'm a total asshole. I just want to talk to her."

"Leave, Walker. She doesn't want you here."

I shut the back door firmly behind me and sink to the floor in front of it. Callie's on the stairs, watching me, but I don't have the energy or the desire to move. I don't have the motivation to get myself under control this time. Walker does something to me. He always has. He brings out the best and the worst in me. He makes it so I can't hold back my emotions. He makes it so I can't ignore what I'm feeling.

"I just want to tell her one thing. Come on, Kane! I thought you were my friend!"

"You've ignored me for *months*. And Genny wanted to tell you *one thing* the night you broke her heart, but you wouldn't hear it. Why the hell should she give you the time of day after the way you talked to her?"

"Fuck!" The entire house vibrates after Walker's loud growl reaches me. I don't know how he's making it happen, what he's doing on my back porch to make it shake hard enough for me to feel it while I'm inside, but it only makes my tears fall faster. Callie's suddenly next to me, her arm around my shoulders, doing her best to comfort me as we listen to the conversation between the love of my life and the guy who helped convince me to try to live again after said love of my life treated me like shit.

Or whatever is *worse* than shit.

Walker must give up, because the house stops shaking and I can't hear them anymore. They're talking, but they're not yelling, and my pathetic ears are straining to hear his voice again. The sound was like a sweet harmony to the beating of my heart. I just wish I couldn't understand what those words meant, because the *meaning* of those words was definitely *not* a harmony of *any* kind.

It's been three months. I was only with him six weeks. I'm nowhere close to getting over him, and I have a sinking feeling I never will. Walker and his hurtful words will haunt me for the rest of my life. I wonder if he knows how well I'm keeping my legs closed now. He must not, considering what he accused me of doing with Kane.

His words in May were angry, said in the spur of the moment, his feelings making him say things he shouldn't. It doesn't excuse the way he talked to me, but it's something I could forgive. Knowing he moved on so fast, that he couldn't wait to start seeing someone else, tells me he never loved me. Not like I loved him. He really wasn't anywhere close to feeling what I was.

"Callie!" Walker yells. "Callie, can I talk to you? *Please!*"

Her arm tightens around me and I decide I've had enough. Pushing myself into a standing position, I try to say something, *anything* to my sister, who has been so very kind to me in the recent months.

The night she asked what happened with me and Walker, she gave me a beautiful painting. It was a portrait, capturing the best version of me. Callie doesn't do portraits very often, but she's good at them. She painted me *happy*. She painted me the way I was with Walker. She told me she would never be able to pay me back for all the things I've done for her over the years, for putting up with her and the way she sometimes treated me. For giving up every dream I ever had to raise my bratty kid sister. She told me she would always look up to me, that she knew she always had someone to believe in her and push her to reach her full potential. Someone to always be in her corner, even if we were fighting.

It was beautiful and thoughtful and sweet, but I was fighting my emotions about Walker so hard, her words barely registered in my angst-riddled brain until much later. I never even thanked her properly. The painting is sitting in my room, the canvas towards the wall. I can't look at it because I know Walker was the reason I looked that happy.

He's also the reason I'm still so *un*happy now.

"You can talk to him if you want," I tell her. "You guys were close. I'm just gonna go to my room for a while."

"Genny... Maybe *you* should talk to him. Get some closure."

"I can't do it, Callie. I *can't*. I just need to lie down for a while. Forget him... Forget everything."

There's pity in her eyes. She knows I'll never get over him. It's not possible. I listen closely as I head up the stairs, but I don't hear the door open. I don't hear her voice. I only hear Walker and Kane arguing on the back porch before a car door slams and Walker's car is in the street, driving away from my house. Driving away from me.

I can finally breathe again. Even if every breath is silently choking me and it's barely enough to keep me alive, not functioning anywhere near fully, I'm at least getting *some* oxygen now that he's gone.

That's one of my last thoughts before a stress-induced migraine steals my vision.

It's just as well.

There's nothing I want to see right now anyway.

Genny

"Number thirty-four, booth three!"

Work is dragging today. It has this whole week, since Walker showed up at my house last weekend and destroyed any resolve I had to control my emotions. I was doing so good before he did that. People were beginning to think I was human again. I know I didn't do a good job of pretending to be ok, but I *tried*.

Since Walker tried to see me, he's been blowing up my phone. Sunday it was a couple texts. Monday, it was texts, missed calls, and a voicemail. Tuesday morning when I woke up to another text, I blocked his number.

Damn if *that* didn't feel like a hard kick to my guts, cutting off all contact from him. It should have made me feel *better*. Instead, it made me cry all night with a new kind of despair I didn't even know existed. Another migraine followed, just to make my night even better.

It's Wednesday now, and we're working our way through the after-work rush that comes through every day at this time. I get to leave in a half hour, and it can't come fast enough, but what do I do then? Callie's working tonight, so I have the house to myself. The house that I'm slowly packing up because Callie wants to move out, and that house is way too big for just me. I tell myself it'll be good to move somewhere else and start over. Somewhere that I don't have a memory of Walker in every single room.

A patient comes into my booth and I suppress a heavy sigh. Ready to work, hoping for a distraction from my life, even if just for a few minutes as I register this person, I do my best to plaster a friendly, incredibly fake smile on my face.

But I find myself looking into Reese's eyes, and I immediately know that I will *never* get past this. It doesn't matter where I live, what hobbies I take up, how busy I am. It doesn't matter if I get a new job or move a thousand miles away. I will *never* get over Walker Kelley.

"Genny!" Zeke pushes past the desk and throws himself into my arms. God, I miss this little boy. Hugging him tight, I put on a semi-real happy face and ask him how he's doing.

"I start school next week," he complains, frowning and crossing his arms like he has real, adult-size problems.

"That's awesome! Are you excited?"

Wiggling his little body around, he shrugs his shoulders the way Walker always did, and I scream at my heart for twisting the way it does whenever something reminds me of him. "I dunno."

"It's gonna be so much fun, Bud. You wait and see. You're probably going to be the smartest kid in class. Definitely the most fun."

Reese has been simply watching me this whole time. The last time she was here, she came alone, and she yelled at me in front of the entire department. Hopefully with Zeke here, she won't do that again. Finn isn't with her and I wonder how he's doing. He has to be walking by now. Probably starting to talk, too. He's probably grown to half Zeke's size. I watch the park every Thursday night on my way home, hoping to catch a glimpse of them. It's only happened once.

"How did you do it?"

Reese's voice cuts through my daydreaming, forcing my neutral expression back into place as I answer her question as to how I could cheat on her brother.

"I don't know, Reese. I'm just some girl who can't keep her legs closed."

"What?"

"Nothing," I mumble, knowing there's no way Walker would have told her what he said to me that night. Zeke is hanging on my arm, chattering his little mouth off about his summer adventures. The last thing I want right now is for him to leave, but I can't take Reese watching me the way she is. "Do you have paperwork? I'll get you registered so you don't have to be here all day."

"How did you get Chad to sign the papers?"

That catches my attention. I was almost ready to give up. I've been going to the bar less and less, because I thought he was never going to give in. I didn't go last weekend at all. My eyes eagerly meet her this time. "He did? He finally signed them?"

"Yes. I don't know how you got him to do it but thank you. You have no idea what it means to me. To Steve. It's a dream come true... I don't need labs, I just wanted to thank you." She wipes away her own tears as she gives me a genuine smile. I never thought I'd see that directed my way ever again. Breathing a sigh of relief, I give her a real smile back. It feels pretty strange on my face after the week I've had, but it feels good.

"I'm really happy for you. You guys deserve it. This little guy deserves it."

I pull Zeke in again for another crushing hug. He still hasn't let go of my arm and I give him a little tickle to make him let me go. He comes right back, though, proving he misses me just as much as I miss him.

"When can I come play at your house again, Genny?"

Oh shit... I was doing so good at not crying.

I haven't cried all week, not since Saturday when Kane saved me from having to talk to Walker. Blinking hard, I try to not crack now. "Probably never, Bud. I'm

Making Her Wait

selling my house. And your mommy probably wants you all to herself. She kinda likes you, ya know."

He giggles at my words, rolling his eyes dramatically. "Mommy *loves* me."

"Of course, she does. You're impossible not to love!"

Reese hands me a slip of paper. It's a card with a phone number on it. "I'd love for you to watch Zeke sometime. He misses you like crazy, and it's the least I can do after everything you've done for us."

"I don't think that's a good idea-" I start, but she cuts me off quickly.

"Maybe this weekend for a couple hours? Saturday, around two, so you don't have to worry about feeding him? It doesn't need to be at your place, you can just take him to the park. Please?"

"Yeah, please?" Zeke begs, his little eyes on mine.

Realizing she probably doesn't have a regular sitter anymore since Walker started seeing someone new, I try to ignore the way my chest suddenly feels heavy and gapingly empty at the same time. I would love to see Zeke for a while, no matter what the reason. "Ok," I reluctantly agree. It's going to be hard as hell, but I'll do it for Zeke.

"You didn't cheat on my brother, did you?"

I stay silent, refusing to answer her. It's none of her business and she doesn't need to doubt his story. He stopped talking to his friends when they found out what I really did and said to Chad in the parking lot that night. Walker felt betrayed enough by them that he wouldn't go out with them anymore. He needs to have someone hate me like he does.

The fact that Kane was with me on Saturday didn't exactly help things.

"It was great to see you, Reese. And you, too, Zeke. Will it be ok if I see you in two days? Can you handle hanging out with boring, old Genny for a little bit this weekend?"

"Yes!" he yells excitedly, pumping his fist in the air just like I remember, pulling a second real smile from me today. Maybe it won't be such a bad idea to see him sometimes. Lord knows how much I miss him. No matter how much he reminds me of Walker, no matter how much it hurts, he still makes me smile. He still tugs on my heart in the best possible way.

"I'll see you at my place on Saturday," Reese promises.

After I press a kiss to Zeke's little face, he grimaces and wipes his arm across his cheek, shooting daggers my way. "No kissing!"

"I can't promise that, you know I like kisses! I'll see you in two days, Zeke. Two days!" Holding up two fingers in a peace sign, I wave goodbye to him with my other hand. He flashes that devilish grin at me before they both disappear out of my booth.

Walker

"You really don't have *any* proof that she cheated on you?"

Rubbing my hand across my face, I try to control my frustration that's currently directed at my sister. After last weekend, when she and Steve calmed down enough to call me and ask exactly how I got those papers, I told her I had no idea what had changed Chad's mind, but Genny had something to do with it. At that point, I'd already been forced off Genny's property by my own best friend.

If that wasn't a mind fuck, I don't know what is.

Sure, I've ignored his calls and texts for months now, but to find him suddenly hanging out with Genny, taking a fucking bike ride with her? The way she looked, with sweat glistening over her entire body, dressed in only a sports bra and a pair of gym shorts? The way he *protected* her and kept *me* from her?

I had no right to assume that she was with him. Of course, I opened my damn mouth and said something insinuating exactly that, pissing them both off and digging myself even deeper into the hole I can't seem to climb out of.

Not the best way to try to ask Genny to talk to me...

I tried calling and texting her. I left her a voicemail, knowing she wouldn't listen to it. She has no reason to give me a chance to explain myself. I really fucked up this time. And last time. I fucked it all up. I don't know what to do now.

Other than sit and sulk in my own misery.

Reese is now demanding to hear the story of that fateful night at the bar, the story I never really told her. Steve has the boys somewhere, so it's just me and my sister. Reese asked me to pick up some stuff at the pharmacy and come over. She wants to figure out how Genny got Chad to sign the papers. I keep telling her it doesn't matter. They're signed. Chad is out of her life. He can no longer be her personal demon.

Now that I suspect how much of a jealous asshole I really was to Genny, it hurts even more to tell the story about that night. I told Reese anyway, hoping it would get her off my back. She should now understand why Genny won't have anything to do with me. She should understand that I'll never be able to explain what happened, because Chad is back to not talking to me, and Genny won't even hear me out.

Just like I didn't hear her out.

Karma's a bitch who loves revenge.

"No, Reese. I don't have any proof that she actually cheated on me. I jumped to conclusions and ruined any chance I may have ever had with her."

"Is it possible she just followed him out there to talk to him about signing the papers?"

"Anything is possible at this point."

Almost anything.

Getting Genny to talk to me is impossible. And if *that's* impossible, I know getting her to ever forgive me would be *out-of-this-world* impossible. *Never-going-to-happen-in-a-million-years* impossible. A fantasy that I will *forever* think about, dream about, and desperately wish for. The biggest regret of my entire life, because I know I'll never find another girl like Genny.

It was the first text I ever sent her. She's one in a million, unlike anyone else in the world. I knew it *then,* and *still* managed to fuck it up.

"What did you say to her when she came back in the bar? You just told me it was something nasty. What was it?"

"It doesn't matter, Reese. I was an asshole. I hurt her the best way I knew how."

"Was it something about her not being able to keep her legs closed?"

Cringing, I close my eyes, trying to not think about the shock and betrayal on Genny's face when she heard me say those words. It dawns on me now that *guilt* wasn't one of the expressions crossing over her face that night. No matter how hard I try not to see the emotions that were there, it's useless. Her expression in that moment is all I can see, whether my eyes are opened or closed. "How the hell did you find that out?"

"It was something she said to me when I saw her at the hospital."

The reminder of how I hurt her, how I fucked up the best thing I ever had, is too painful. I can't do this. I can't talk about it. I can't hash it out with Reese. I can't hash it out with *anyone*. I know exactly what I did now. I know exactly what *Genny* did now. I don't know how she did it, but I know she's responsible.

Genny protects the people she loves, and she loves Zeke and Finn like they're her own nephews. Thursday nights were her favorite date nights with me once she started joining me at Reese's every week. She somehow took care of the problem of Chad being in their lives. Something I wasn't able to. Something Reese wasn't even able to do.

I thanked her by proving how much I don't deserve her. But hurting her the way only I could because she didn't let anyone else in the way she did me. She didn't *trust* anyone else the way she trusted me. And I used it against her.

"Reese, I can't talk about this anymore. I'll never be able to find out how she got Chad to sign those papers. What matters is he *did*. Let's just be thankful for that and move on from this catastrophe."

"We are," she insists. "Steve and I already started the adoption process. I just wish I could thank her, ya know? I feel like she performed this miracle for me, and I've been hating her for what I thought she did to you. I almost wish I could continue hating her because it was so much easier. But I can't. Not after what she did for me. It really makes me feel ashamed of myself. I'm always telling Zeke he needs to hear both sides of the story before he makes assumptions, but I just judged her without giving her a chance."

Pushing up from my spot on the couch, I try to get her to stop talking. "Shut up, Reese. Please! If you think *you* feel ashamed, try to imagine how I feel."

"I can't. If I were you, I'd *hate* myself."

That's putting it mildly.

"Well, while you're here," she goes on, finally changing the subject. "I was hoping you could fix the sink in the boys' bathroom. It's been leaking for a while, I just keep forgetting to tell you about it."

Glad my interrogation is over, I tell her I'd love to. "Steve's tools downstairs yet?"

"They're already up there. He tried to fix it this morning before I invited you over."

"Great. So, a ten-minute job is going to take me an hour or more?"

"Probably." My sister flashes me a mischievous smile. Her husband may be her soulmate and someone who's helped me out in very surprising ways, but a handyman with things around the house, he is not.

At least I have something to keep me busy for a while. Maybe until Steve gets home with the boys. I could definitely kill some time playing with them. Playing with Zeke has been fun again since he finally stopped asking about Genny. That was about the same time I started dating Sam. God, what a mistake that was. I'm learning a hell of a lot about mistakes lately, aren't I?

Lying on the floor, with my head and arms under the sink, I hear Zeke burst through his bedroom door into his room. A smile plays on my lips as I hear him jabbering on about the pictures he's been drawing lately. This spring and summer he's really gotten into drawing. If Callie didn't hate me, I'd see if she could work with him, but I know how bad of an idea that is. She looks too much like Genny. He'd be asking me for Genny constantly again, or maybe for Callie instead. That wouldn't be *as* bad, but still too much for me to handle.

I need to find a way to forget them both. I somehow need to figure out how to move on. How to accept the fact that I will never see Genny again, or that if I do, it'll be in passing because she'll never want to talk to me after the things I said to her. After the way I hurt her.

"This one's a dinosaur. He's hungry, see? That's blood cause he's eatin little dinosaurs." The sound of rustling papers works its way to my ears, and I hurry to finish. Listening to Zeke describe his pictures it the best part of his drawings.

"This one's you and me. We're playing blocks at your house. That's Finn and that's Uncle Walk."

I suddenly find myself paralyzed, wondering if what I'm suspecting is possible.

"That was a good day, wasn't it, Zeke?"

I keep listening with my eyes clamped shut, my heart thumping wildly at the unexpected sound of her voice.

"Yeah. This one's a dog. His name's Max and he likes to lick me. That's his big tongue."

She's *here*. In this house, in the room right next to me, with my nephew. I don't know how Reese managed it, but I wonder if she has any idea how ugly this might get in front of Zeke.

Wait, Genny loves Zeke. She won't cause a scene in front of him by yelling at me. She won't ignore me in front of him either. She doesn't want him to think it's ok to treat people like that.

Maybe my sister is a fucking *genius*.

Being as quiet as I can, I extricate myself from the cabinet and cautiously step into Zeke's room.

"Do you like it when he licks you?" she asks Zeke, a small smile on her face.

She's so fucking beautiful. Reese said she'd looked like hell, but that was, what? Six weeks ago? She doesn't look like hell now, just like she didn't last weekend. She looks tanned, healthy, glowing. Maybe her eyes are a little empty, a little void of the life I'm used to seeing there, but someone who didn't know her well wouldn't be able to tell the difference.

She's sitting cross legged on the floor, with Zeke in her lap, as they sort through a whole pile of pictures Zeke drew. If they don't notice me, they're going to be here for a while. And I'm going to watch and listen for as long as I can, soaking in the sight and sound of her.

"Yeah, it tickles."

"You know that's how dog's *kiss* right? That means you like when Max *kisses* you!"

Zeke gasps, as if she's playing a mean trick on him. "Nuh-uh."

"*Yuh*-huh," she counters, tickling him in the sweet spot on his belly that makes him laugh like a maniac. It also makes him lean back in her arms, catching sight of me and holding his hands out for me to save him.

"Help, Uncle Walk," he cries when he's able to suck in enough air. Genny's back instantly goes rigid and stiff. She's holding her breath, most likely closing her eyes and trying to figure out a way to disappear through the floor. I have about five seconds before she can get Zeke off her lap. Ten if I add in the amount of time it'll take her to get down the stairs.

"Genny, can I talk to you?"

Her head cocks to the side, allowing me a glimpse of the pained expression on her face. "That's not a good idea... Zeke, Buddy, I gotta go. It was great to see you again. I'll miss you."

"Genny, don't go!" he pleads as she lifts him out of her lap. She stands up, gently pushing him away.

"I'll talk to your mom about when I can see you again, Bud. I promise."

"Genny!" He clings to her leg, giving me a little more time.

But I don't know what to say.

There's nothing I could say that will take away her pain, nothing that will erase everything I said that night. Nothing that will make things right between us.

She bends over, trying to pry his arms from her, still refusing to look at me, or even face me. She almost gives in. She falters, almost wrapping her arms *around* him instead, but her resolve is back before it takes over. "Zeke, listen to me. You know how sometimes you're really mad at someone and you don't want to see them?"

"Yeah," he says, unsure, but nodding anyway.

"That's how your Uncle Walk makes me feel right now. We had a big fight, and I need to go away before I say something really mean to him, ok?"

"No!" He pulls on her arm, keeping her on his level while he searches her eyes. "You gotta hear both sides before you get mad. Mommy says so."

"Zeke," I interrupt, hoping she'll hear what I tell him. "*I'm* the one who didn't listen to both sides. Genny did something that was really *good*, but I thought it was bad. *I'm* the one who said mean things and hurt Genny's feelings without listening to her side."

"Did you say sorry?" His eyes swing to mine, even as he continues holding her in place.

Swallowing, I look back to her. She's finally meeting my eyes, but if looks could kill, I'd be dead a *million* times over. She doesn't appreciate me using this lesson against her. She doesn't want to hear what I have to say. She doesn't want to even be in the same room as me. "I want to, bud. But I think I hurt Genny so much she doesn't want to hear it."

"Genny, you have to let Uncle Walk say sorry. And you have to forgive him. You *have* to!"

She drops to her knees, wrapping him up like she's wanted to the entire time she's known I was here in this house. "I can't, Zeke. I'm not a strong enough person for that. I gotta go, kiddo. I love you."

Zeke pushes her away, just enough so he can see her face. It's streaked with tears, breaking my own heart as well as Zeke's. He runs his fingers across her cheek,

196

something she's done to me many times. Something I desperately miss. Something she apparently taught Zeke to do to her.

This time when she gets up to leave, he doesn't stop her. Instead he glares at me, upset that I hurt his friend, upset that I made her leave, upset that I ended his precious time with her.

He glares up at me. "You made Genny cry."

"I did, Bud. I didn't want to, but I did."

Zeke's eyes turn soft, and he watches me curiously before letting out a very big sigh for his very small body. "Are you sad, Uncle Walk?"

"I am." Sitting on his bed, I rub the back of my head, wondering if I'll ever get the chance to talk to her again. "I really miss Genny."

He crawls into my lap, doing his best to comfort me. "I *love* Genny," he whispers, patting my back as his mother often does to him and his younger brother.

"I do, too Zeke. I love Genny, too."

Genny

The backdoor slams, letting me know Callie's home from looking at another apartment. Rushing into the kitchen, she hugs me from behind, letting out an excited squeal in my ear. I plaster a smile on my face as I spin around to face her, dreading the news I'm about to hear.

"I found an apartment! It's amazing! The rooms are big, the kitchen is updated, there's actual counter space in the bathroom! It's perfect!"

"That's awesome Callie. I told you it would happen sooner or later."

"It also has two bedrooms, so you can accept that offer on the house and move in with me until you find your own place."

I turn back around with a sigh, knowing *that* isn't the reason I'm dragging my feet on selling the house.

"You know you're just going to be depressed living here by yourself, Gen. It's not healthy for you to stay here alone. I know you."

"I know, Callie. You're right, I just... It's hard to say goodbye."

"Because you never did before. You didn't get to say goodbye to Mom and Dad. You didn't get to say goodbye to college because you never went back. You never got to say goodbye to anyone or anything that was important to you."

Thinking back through my life, I try to find something that will prove her wrong. I've said goodbye many times. In my head. Maybe I never got to say it in person, but I eventually come to terms with things in my own time. "Paul! I said goodbye to Paul."

"No, you didn't," she insists gently. "You walked out when he gave you his ultimatum and then texted him to never contact you again. You've never said goodbye. Maybe if you say goodbye to Walker, moving out of this house won't be so hard for you."

"You, Myra, Michelle... Why does everyone think I need to talk to Walker?" Throwing my frustrated hands in the air, I stomp my way out of the kitchen and into the living room where I stand in front of the couch, willing my tears to stay in my eyes and not fall. "It's not going to help! It's just going to make things worse. Why can't anyone understand that?"

"Why can't you try it?"

"Because it hurts so *fucking* much to even *think* about him! Seeing him last weekend just about broke me, Callie. I can't do it again. I *can't*."

My sister takes my hands and pulls me to sit on the couch with her. "That just tells me you need to. Yell at him, scream at him, curse the day he was born, but do it to his face. Let him know how much he hurt you. Listen to what he has to say. Then scream at him again. I'm not saying it won't hurt, but I'll be here for you when it's over. I'll order your favorite pizza, buy you a carton of your favorite ice cream, and sit with you all night, listening to you tell me how unfair life is. You deserve a full-blown pity party and I'll gladly be the host... At least think about it, ok?"

"I'll think about it. And I'll ask Kane to convince you pansy girls to stop bugging me about talking to Walker. I'll bet *he* doesn't think it's a good idea. Guys know it's better to stuff your feelings rather than talk about them."

"Really? Walker never talked about his feelings?"

"Shut up." The desperate plea comes out of my mouth as a harsh demand.

"That's what I thought. But go ahead and talk to Kane anyway. I'll bet he agrees with us *pansy girls*. He's a big teddy bear when it comes to relationships."

Dammit, she's right. Casey, the girl he's seeing now is always telling me about the sweet ways he shows her he cares. He's big on talking about his feelings. He just does it in obnoxious, overly exaggerated ways.

Callie sees me start to cave and gives me a smile.

"I'll think about it," I mumble miserably. "But if I decide to do it, you'd better be on call. If you skip out on me, I'll kill you before dying of a broken heart. Then Calvin will have to deal with this house. At least my funeral will be easy. Him, Kane, Myra and Michelle. Yours will be a pain in the ass to deal with. Maybe he can combine them so mine doesn't look quite so pathetic."

"You're so morbid lately." She rolls her eyes at my rare drama queen moment. "I get the keys to my new place in ten days, so I'm gonna kill you slowly and start bringing all my boxes from my bedroom downstairs. I'm expecting you to be my roommate, so let me know when I can give you the spare key without an argument."

She leaves me sitting on the couch in front of an empty TV screen. She leaves me sitting in the middle of a half-assed pity party that I've been living in for months. She leaves me thinking about Walker, which is the last thing I should be thinking about.

But the most important thing is, *she's leaving me.*

Everyone is moving on except me.

Maybe I *should* try to get some closure from Walker. If for no other reason than to be able to say that I did everything I could to move on.

Walker

Genny: Maybe we should talk.

The last thing I expected on my phone tonight was a text from Genny. I don't know how to respond. I want to talk to her more than anything, but I'm afraid whatever I say will piss her off and change her mind. Finally, I type out the simplest message I've probably ever sent her.

Walker: Ok.

Genny: It should be somewhere I can yell, and it won't offend anyone except you.

Smiling, I realize how much I've missed the way she doesn't shy away from whatever she's feeling. At least not with me. She owns it, whether it's justified or not. Whether it's *rational* or not.

If we meet to talk, everything she might say will be justified. I don't know about the rational part...

Walker: Ok.

Genny: I'm probably not going to be very nice to you.

Walker: I deserve whatever you have to say, G.

Calling her G is taking a chance. It might piss her off, it might make her cry, it might make her miss me. It might make her feel a lot of different things that make her want to shut me out again. But, God, I miss her. I don't care if she yells at me and calls me every bad thing she can come up with, she'll still be *communicating* with me again.

Part of me knows this might be it. The end. The thing she needs to move on and forget me.

But part of me is still flooded with hope that maybe, just *maybe*, she'll hear my apology and accept it. Maybe she'll realize she still loves me, and she'll give me a chance to prove that I love her just as much. That I was a fool for not trusting her. That if she gives me another chance, I won't question her ever again, because she's an even better person than I gave her credit for.

Which is kinda scary, considering how amazing I thought she was *before* she magically got Chad to sign those papers.

It takes her a long time to reply, and I start to question if I already fucked up again. I debate on typing out an apology for using her nickname, letting it go, or begging her to please meet and talk to me.

In the end, I let it go, having a feeling the more I say, the less chance I have of this ever happening.

Letting out a heavy sigh, I put the phone on the table beside me and go back to watching the first college football game of the season. I'm seeing it, but not paying attention. Instead, I'm trying to figure out how to say the things I want to say to Genny. How to make her understand how sorry I am, how horrible I feel for not trusting her. How guilty and ashamed I am of the things I said to her.

The game is over and I'm climbing in bed when another text comes though.

Genny: You know the trail that goes to Widow's Peak?

The entrance to the trail is just a few miles past Genny's house. It's a popular running trail. A lot of people walk their dogs along the trail. Some people bike it. I wonder if that's where Kane and Genny were when I saw them on their bikes.

Walker: Yes.

Genny: We can meet there. When works for you?

Walker: Anytime. Whatever works for you.

It takes her ten minutes to answer me. She's probably not sure if she's doing the right thing. I vow to myself that when she leaves after meeting with me, she'll know it was.

Genny: Tomorrow? 1pm?

Walker: I'll be there.

Walker

I'm twenty minutes early. Possibly a little excessive, but I need to make sure I don't fuck this up, and if I'm late, I'll be fucking it up from the start.

My morning was spent at Reese's, explaining why I wouldn't be there for lunch and asking what she thinks I should say. She doesn't know Genny well, but the things she ticked off her fingers were similar to the list I've already got in my mind.

She told me to let Genny talk first and to not interrupt her no matter what she says or how much it might hurt me. And to not touch her. That's all gonna be tough to do, because there's so much I want to tell Genny. I think me apologizing should be the first thing said, but Reese shook her head and made me *promise* to follow her instructions.

After promising I would let Genny talk first and not interrupt, Reese told me that may be the most important promise I've made so far in my life.

I don't know if that's true, but I'll treat it like it is. Reese is a strong, independent, stubborn girl. Genny is a strong, independent, stubborn girl. They're a lot alike and entirely different all at the same time. I'll treat anything Reese says about my upcoming talk with Genny like treasured gold. Without Reese's manipulative interference in my love life, I never would've been able to see Genny in the first place. Or tell her I knew exactly how much of an ass I had been and that I wanted to apologize to her. Even though those few heart-wrenching minutes filled me with hopeless despair, I know for a fact without that surprise meeting, I would not be standing here waiting for my girl.

Waiting for *Genny*, I correct myself. In my heart, she'll always be my girl. But I probably shouldn't call her that right now. At least not when anyone can hear me.

Remembering all the rules I need to follow for this meeting is going to be hard.

Genny's car pulls in ten minutes after I get here. I watch her from where I'm standing, giving her some space and letting her come to me. It's not what I *want* to do. It's what I think I *should* do.

I'm not used to having to think so much about every move I make with her.

Maybe that's what got me in this position in the first place. Maybe if I'd *thought* about it, I would have realized that Genny never would have fucked Chad right under my nose, let alone at all. After everything she learned about him, she was just as disgusted with him as I was.

Her hands slide nervously on her favorite pair of daisy dukes, the ones she says shows off her legs to the best advantage. She wanted some extra confidence, I guess. If she knew how stunningly gorgeous I think she is, she would know she doesn't need it.

Her hair is pulled out of her face, up in a long ponytail, probably to keep her neck cool in this blistering late August heat. She's wearing a simple V-neck shirt and hiking shoes, carrying a water bottle in her hand. I wasn't sure if we were walking the trail or just meeting here so she could yell *not very nice things* at me. It looks like we're taking the trail. I'm glad. It means her yelling at me is going to take more than two minutes.

She can yell at me for the rest of my life if it keeps her talking to me.

"Hi," she says, stopping just out of my reach. Her eyes look past me, and I resist the urge to step closer and tilt her chin, to force her eyes to meet mine. "I thought we could walk so I don't have to look at you."

Very good thing I resisted that urge.

I try to not let her words hurt me. She's just being honest. I'm sure there's a lot worse to come.

"Ok."

Starting down the trail, we walk side by side. The silence is deafening. The waiting, torturous. But I'm with her, so I tell myself to calm the fuck down. To let it happen however she wants it to happen.

A few minutes later, she starts talking. I recognize the random string of sentences that sound a lot like the rambled reasonings she gave for her emotional breakdown that last day we were together. The words and sentences are different, but what she's doing is the same. She's trying to figure out what she's feeling, what she wants, so she can try to explain it to me. I do my best to hear it all, knowing I'll be analyzing every single word later.

"Everyone keeps telling me that I need to talk to you, to get closure. What the fuck is closure, though? I looked it up. It's feeling like an emotional experience has been *resolved*. How the hell can *that* happen after what you did to me? You're always going to be my biggest regret. I mean, how easy was I? Not in the physical sense, although we can both agree I was easy in that aspect, too, but emotionally?"

She scoffs at herself, rolling her eyes toward the sky.

"You asked me to open up and let you in," she continues, telling me part of our story that I'm already familiar with. "I thought about it for all of two minutes and said ok. No one's ever wanted to know me the way you did. No one even realized they *didn't* know me. You saw past the girl I showed the world and asked for the real me. And I was so happy to finally be seen, I *wanted* to give you all of me. When you asked me questions, I was scared, sure, but you made me feel safe. You made me feel like you were going to be there for me, no matter what the answers were, that you *liked* me for who I was. And while my baggage and my past is something that would scare a lot of people, you didn't run. You made me feel like I was a good person after what I'd been through."

I *did* think she was a good person. I *still* do. And I liked *everything* about her. Everything *except* the way she handled stress.

"I can see how you might've found it hard to trust me about sex. But I promised you I wouldn't be with anyone except you. I told you when I gave up my boytoys. I was scared to give Chad up, and I realized that was because sex was my go-to. Once I cut it off with Chad, I would have nothing left, no coping mechanisms at all, and I would have to fumble my way through the stress, find new ways to handle everything... It was *terrifying*."

She takes a deep breath, letting it out so slowly before continuing.

Still without looking at me even once.

"After I told you about my parents, you held me while I cried, and I felt like someone finally wanted to *protect* me. That I wasn't alone anymore. I knew I had to do the right thing and give you all of me. So, I texted Chad the next morning before my migraine hit and told him to lose my number... I gave it all up for you. I trusted you. I wanted you. I loved you. I didn't know it at that point, but I did, I already loved you then."

She broke it off with Chad and didn't tell me? *That* long ago?!

She made good on her promise, and I never asked because I was afraid of her answer. I assumed she didn't follow through. I assumed she wasn't all in with me when she was. Almost the entire time.

"I started thinking about a future with you, Walker. About us, together, for the long term, not just the here and now. I started picturing us with a house of our own, with kids of our own, who would be close to your nephews and our siblings, and we'd be happy because we were *together*, and you made me happy."

She stops in the middle of the track, turning away from me, wiping her eyes, doubling over with emotion. "Dammit, Walker. You made me so *fucking* happy."

Genny takes a few uneven breaths, her hands on her face, covering her eyes, her back to me. It takes everything in me to not touch her, to not hold her, to not tell her she made me really fucking happy, too, and I know I fucked it up and hurt her this much. But Reese's voice is there, in the back of my mind, reminding me to let Genny talk until she's done. To not interrupt or ask questions. To not touch her, under any circumstances, unless it's a crystal-clear invitation.

It's the hardest thing I've ever done.

Eventually, Genny gets her emotions under control and stands up straight. She breathes deeply, in through her nose, exhaling out of her mouth, trying to get her head together. Then we're walking again, making our way up the gently sloping hill through the woods to the top of Widow's Peak.

"I can't say at times I didn't doubt it," she says, picking up her speech as if she never lost control. "I had to change the way I thought about *everything* for you. It's probably a much healthier way to look at some things, especially sex, but it was *new* and *different*, and it was hard to *trust* it. I'm not saying I didn't trust *you*. I did, without question. It was just hard to trust this new way of looking at things. Of how things worked when I looked at the big picture and not just the little piece of the world I knew. And that last day, I had a major emotional breakdown and you didn't freak out on me. You were *still* there for me. I found that if I could talk about it, we could figure it out together. It might be crazy but breaking down on you made it so easy for me to see that we could *make* it. We could talk things out and compromise and make things *work*. Which made me realize that it didn't matter when you finally had sex with me, because we had forever. Because I loved you, and you were the right guy for me, and we just had to keep the doors of communication open. If we could do *that*, we could get through *anything*."

She's no longer in my peripheral vision, so I stop and turn back to look at her. At where she stopped in her tracks and is *finally* meeting my eyes. Hers are red, puffy, bloodshot. But they're also confident and sure.

"And then you shut me out, Walker. You assumed the worst and didn't even ask me to explain. You said things to me that you should never say to anyone, let alone the girl who just told you she's in love with you. You always said you weren't judging me because of my sex life before we got together, but you proved to me that night you *were*. It was something *you* couldn't let go of. My past made *you* not trust *me*, even though I did everything you asked me to."

Throwing her hands in the air, she shakes her head, looking away for only a second before bringing her eyes back to meet mine. "I really don't know where to go from here. I don't know if closure is *possible*. But I know that I want to keep seeing your nephews as long as Reese allows me to, and I don't want it to be as hard as it was last weekend. I can't go through that every time."

Genny closes those brilliant, beautiful, green eyes that I miss so much, blocking out the sight of me standing before her, giving her everything I can. Here, in this moment, when I know exactly how much I've already lost, she has my trust. She has my love, my respect, my heart. She has every piece of me that has ever mattered.

"Tell me what to do, Walker. Tell me how to get past this. Tell me how I move on from you because I have no idea where to even start."

Not only do I not know how, I wouldn't tell her if I did. I don't want her to move on from me. I don't want her to find the closure she's seeking. I want us to move past this, but not in the way she's thinking.

I'm like her, though, wondering if what I want is *possible*. She's right about everything she said. Right down to the fact that we could have had forever, and I took that possibility away from us.

And everything she said just blew anything I thought might have made a difference out of the water.

"Genny, you're right. About everything. You figured it out long before I did, because I'm only realizing the root cause of all this right now. I knew I didn't trust you, but I didn't know *why*. Before I get to that, I'm sorry. I'm so very sorry for what I said, and what I thought. I'm sorry for being so jealous my reasoning skills became that of a three-year-old's. Even Zeke knows you hear both sides before saying mean things and he's only five. I'm sorry, Genny. More sorry than you'll ever know."

Fresh tears are cutting a new path down her cheeks. She didn't wear any mascara, and I love knowing that she was willing to be so open with me, so *honest* with me, that she knew she was going to cry. What I love the most, though, is how she's not looking away. She's watching me through those tears, listening to what I have to say, listening to my reasons and my apologies. Listening to me beg her to please, *please* don't hate me.

I take a step towards her, and her breath hitches in her throat. I know I can't touch her, I don't deserve to touch her ever again, but I want to be as close to her as I can. I want to smell her, I want to feel her warmth, I want to show her I'm here, more than willing to hold her if she wants me to. If she *allows* me to.

"Genny, the reason I didn't trust you wasn't because I judged you, although you're right. I did. The reason I didn't trust you is because I knew I wasn't good enough for you. You're gorgeous, smart, funny, selfless, strong, independent. You're so many of the most amazing things... I strung you along, promising sex at some point in the future because I wanted you to fall in love with me before it happened. Because I knew how you treated sex and I didn't want to be just another guy to you. I wanted to be *your* guy. I couldn't *believe* I got lucky enough that you fell for me. I couldn't believe that I got to be with this girl, this *woman*, who was so amazing she could have any guy she wanted, all she had to do was ask. When you walked out of that bar behind Chad, the part of me that hated how great you were and how much I didn't deserve you took over. It easily convinced me you weren't as perfect as I thought you were, because I *wanted* that, I wanted you to mess up. I couldn't stand knowing how flawed I am compared to how perfect you are."

She scoffs, not believing my words, just as I knew she wouldn't. Genny has no idea how the world sees her. She's always been a beautiful girl, but getting to know her, I quickly realized she's so much more than the beauty everyone else sees.

"You are, Genny. You're absolutely perfect. As soon as you walked out of that bar, I realized I *was* in love with you. I realized it just as I thought I was losing you, and it *hurt*. God, it hurt so much. So, when you looked like you did, your cheeks all pretty and flushed, like you look after you come, added to the fact that you were nervous? I just knew my worst nightmare was true. And I hurt you back before you could hurt me any more than you already had."

Sighing hard, knowing this isn't going where I want it to, I switch gears. This isn't about how I felt that night. This is about what I did to her. This may be the last time I can truly talk to her. I need to make her see that we *can* get through this.

If she wants to.

"I hurt us both," I confess, staring deep into her eyes that haven't left mine for more than the briefest of seconds since she let me see them. "The minute I realized how much I loved you, I ruined everything we had, which was the best thing I've ever experienced. I still love you, Genny. I don't want you to get over me. I want you to try to forgive me, work with me, give me another chance. I know it won't happen overnight, but if there's any part of you that thinks maybe we could still have that forever you wanted before I was such a dick to you, I'm asking you to give me a chance. Give *us* a chance."

This time, she *does* look away. She watches something far off in the distance, chewing on her bottom lip, thinking over everything I said, hopefully thinking of how great we were together. Wiping her hand across her cheek, she meets my eyes again, asking me something I never expected.

"How can you say you love me if you're seeing someone else?"

Fuck... How did she hear about Sam?

"I'm not."

She crooks an eyebrow, so I give her more. I give her everything.

"I *was*, but I'm not anymore. It was literally *nothing*. I didn't like her, I couldn't even *stand* her. I thought she might distract me from you, because she was everything you're not. But it didn't work. I thought about you every second I was with her. Compared her to you in every way."

"What about you is so flawed?"

"You're kidding right?"

At the slight shake of her head, I take a deep breath and try to not feel like a total shit for even *asking* her to give me a second chance as I scroll down through the list. "My temper, my jealousy, how I judged you, how quickly I jump to conclusions, the fact that I sometimes get so mad I forget to hear both sides of the story, how I forced my nephews on you, how I'm entirely selfish and stole you again and again from your dinner nights with Callie, how I asked you to trust me without trusting you in return, the fact that I let you believe I was seeing someone else in the beginning, the fact that I still watch that damn video you sent me because it's the only way I get to see you, even knowing that you would hate me doing it... Should I go on?"

"No... That's enough."

She sighs, still watching me. I probably shouldn't, but I don't know that I'll ever have another chance, and I feel like I owe it to my sister.

Plus, I'm curious as hell.

"How did you get Chad to sign the papers?"

The smile that spreads across her lips is genuine, and I fall in love with her all over again. She even gives a short chuckle. "I became the world's best cock blocker. What matters to Chad? Sex. That's pretty much all he cares about. I hung out at the bar where he works and showed every girl he looked at Zeke's picture, explaining that he had this beautiful child he refused to acknowledge. I have to admit, he lasted a lot longer than I thought he would."

"How did he not kick you out of the bar?"

"I'm not a complete idiot," she reasons, rolling her eyes. "I spent a couple weeks making friends with the other bartenders, the bouncers, the owner. He might need to find a new place to work, because they were all on my side and didn't think very highly of him by the time he gave in. Although they all said he was a hell of a worker, so he might be ok."

It feels like we're back to normal. I know it won't last, though. Raising my eyebrows, I admit, "I *almost* feel bad for him. I can only imagine how persuasive you are when you're on a mission."

Another smile flashes in my direction. "He really never stood a chance."

"No, he didn't."

Then she remembers why we're here and it's gone. God, it felt good, though. Maybe she felt it, too. Maybe it'll help sway her in my direction.

She looks at the surrounding woods, at the serene quiet that's enveloping us in this magical state of ceasefire. Letting out a heavy sigh, she raises her eyes back to mine.

"I miss you, Walker-"

"I miss you, too, Genny. So much."

Her hand comes up in front of her, stopping any other words from passing through my lips. "That wasn't an invitation. Is there anything else you want to say while we're both here?"

Disappointment crushes the hope I was starting to have. Now, *I'm* the one who needs closure. Because this is probably the last chance I'll ever get to talk to her unless it's in passing when she sees Zeke. Shrugging my shoulders, I tell her the only thing that really matters. "I'll always love you, Genny. If you give me a second chance, I will do *anything* to prove we're worth it. That what we have and how we feel is worth fighting for. Worth saving."

"How do you know how I feel?"

"You love me, Genny. I know you. You won't tell me because you don't trust me anymore, with good reason. But I know you love me."

She shrugs that off with a heavy breath. "As I was saying, I miss you. I miss you so much it hurts every morning when I wake up, every time I drink coffee that isn't disgustingly sweet, every time I look at the weird spaces on the walls where Callie's paintings used to hang, every time I see a kiddo running around, every time I lay down in bed. I *miss* you."

What happened to Callie's paintings? Praying I someday get the chance to ask, I push it from my mind and focus on Genny once again.

Wiping angrily at the tears still falling from her eyes, she goes on. "But I don't know if I can trust you *enough* to give you a second chance. I don't know if I can put myself through that again. I don't know if I can let myself get happy with you, only to have you hurt me again."

"It won't happen again, Genny."

"You don't *know*, Walker!" she yells. "You can't see the future. Part of being in a relationship, part of being in love, is giving the other person the ability to hurt you and trusting that they won't. People *accidently* hurt each other every day, and I expected *that* kind of hurt. I didn't expect you to *intentionally* hurt me... I don't know if I can forgive *that*."

Looking away from her for the first time, I stare up at the clear blue sky, wishing I could go back in time and fix this. Make it never happen in the first place. Make myself listen to her that night, make myself beg her for forgiveness, back when it would have made a difference. There were a thousand times I could have changed how it all went down, and I made the wrong choice *every* time. It's no one's fault but my own, and I'm doing everything I can to fix it.

But it's still not enough.

"I'll *think* about giving you another chance, but I can't promise you anything."

Maybe it *is* enough.

It's all I can do. It *has* to be enough.

"Genny, if there's anything I can do to prove-"

"There is. Don't contact me. Don't call me, don't text me, don't stop at my house. Not unless I get ahold of you first. I need some space to really think about this. There's a lot going on in my life right now, and I don't need you barging in at the worst times. Unless there's some kind of emergency that involves you, or your nephews, just give me space."

What's going on? I wonder, but it's none of my business. Not anymore. Not unless she decides to give us a second chance.

"Ok," I concede, grateful she's willing to even think about it to push for anything more. If she wants space, I'll give her space. I want her back. I want *us* back. I'll do *anything* to make that happen.

Genny suddenly fidgets on her feet, her teeth on her bottom lip, obviously wanting something before walking away from me, but terrified of whatever it is. She's back to not meeting my eyes, trying to figure out how badly she wants whatever it is she's thinking about. Her eyes are full of tears when they find mine.

"Can I touch you?"

Her voice is shaky, but she doesn't look away as she waits for my answer.

"Yes. *God*, yes."

"Can you stay perfectly still and not touch me back?"

Grimacing at her impossible request, I close my eyes, collecting myself before answering, because I literally *just* told her I'd do *anything*. "If I have to, I will."

She visibly swallows, closing her eyes as more tears escape and roll down her cheeks. "I'm gonna touch you, and then I'm gonna go. Please stay here until I'm gone. Give me a chance to leave without having to worry about you following me."

Without waiting for a response, she takes two small steps, closing the distance between us. I shove my hands in my pockets, hoping that keeps them away from her. Genny's fingers run over my face, pausing to brush across my cheekbone, my lips, my jaw. Like she's memorizing every last detail.

Like she's saying *goodbye*.

Her tears are overflowing again as she whispers, "Don't open your mouth, Friend."

Then her lips are on mine.

She didn't tell me not to kiss her back, she told me not to open my mouth.

Pressing my lips to hers, I taste the salt of her tears. I smell her, I feel her, I taste her. She's everything I want. She's everything I need.

She's *everything*. Period.

Trying my best to hold back my own tears, I close my eyes against the sight of her as she leaves. I try to not hear the sobs racking her body. I try to not feel the emptiness her departure brings. I try not to lose the sliver of hope she just gifted me by saying she'll think about giving me another chance.

But it's fucking *hard*.

Because the girl I love more than life itself, the girl that holds my entire future in her hands, is *running* to get away from me.

Genny

Thump!

Racing around Alex and Kane, I dash toward the stairs where that awful noise came from. I get there in time to find Abe inspecting a new hole in the wall. One that magically appeared after he was showing off for Callie, trying to take too many boxes down the stairs at once.

I warned him this would happen! Several times!

"Abe, how many holes are you going to put in these walls?! Quit showing off! You're stressing me out!"

"Relax, Miss April. Walker can fix that, easy peasy."

"Walker isn't here."

"That's no one's fault but your own."

Growling as I round the corner, I find Kane and Alex prepared to carry my mattress down the stairs. "Kane, I'm going to kill your little brother!"

"Don't you dare!" Callie sings from her old room. "I'm having way too much fun with him."

"Eww..." I call out after her, but I'm smiling. I like Abe for her, even if he is destroying my walls.

"How many are we up to, now?" Kane asks, speaking of the count we have on how many holes, scrapes and scratches will be on my walls, courtesy of his brother, by the time we get all my stuff moved out of this house.

"Sixteen I'm aware of. I'll do an official count when everything is out and we can see the walls clearly."

Kane shakes his head, used to his brother's antics, but amazed at how exaggerated they became as soon as he met my sister. "Walker will fix it all. You said you have two more weeks to be out, right?"

Sighing at another mention of Walker, I hang on to my resolve to not scream at everyone for talking about him *constantly* the past couple weeks. They all know I'm thinking of giving him a second chance. I met with him three weeks ago, and I still haven't given him an answer, but I've been *busy*.

Really busy.

I accepted the offer on the house the day after I met with him, but the buyers wanted everything finalized as quickly as possible. Callie moved the following weekend. I started looking for my own place after that, and found the perfect little house a few miles away. It's on the same street I've lived on for the last decade, but several miles out of town, past the trail where I met Walker. We're moving *my* stuff now, and I'm kind of excited to start over.

Part of that is because I'm leaning towards giving Walker a second chance, but I'm not a hundred percent certain. I want to talk to him again, see his face when he answers the questions I still have. See if he still feels the same after waiting for me all this time.

If he's still waiting for me.

Judging from how everyone talks about him in front of me, I'm going to assume he is. But assumptions are what got us in this situation in the first place, so I'm still hesitant.

"Two and half technically, but yeah," I finally answer. "That would really help me out if he could fix all the screw ups your brother is making."

"He'll do anything for you, doll. He's dying, waiting to hear from you."

Waving Kane off, I move to my room. Callie was right. It was easy to say goodbye to this house after I talked to Walker. I got the closure I needed. Plus, something I didn't think was possible. He told me he *loves* me.

That kinda changed everything. That kinda made me think that we *both* made huge mistakes. And now that we know what life is like without the other in it, maybe we should just jump all in and try again. With our eyes wide open this time.

But I've been too busy to call and properly talk to him. I wanted to wait until everything settled down, but it seems like nothing is going to settle down ever again. Calvin called me last week and told me he's getting married. *Married!* My little brother! He never even told me he was seeing anyone!

Calvin's fiancé is *not* like Heidi. She wants a small, intimate wedding, and she wants it as soon as she can get it. Their bridal shower is next weekend and they're getting hitched next month. And the anniversary of our parents' death is right in the middle of those two important weekends.

Picking up some random things that were hiding under my bed, I throw them in the nearest box, knowing that unpacking is going to be a bitch, no matter how organized my packing methods are. Callie took a lot when she moved out. I told her to take the living room furniture and the dining room table, the bigger things that are more expensive. I'm still questioning that decision since she makes a lot more money than I do, but if I'm starting over, I want to *really* start over. New house. New things. New furniture.

New *memories*...

Once the moving truck is packed and ready to go, I tell everyone I'll meet them at my new place with pizza and beer, plus a salad for Callie. I want a minute alone in this house that oversaw the many years, the many fights, the many hugs and laughs and conversations and decisions my small family had.

This house kept what's left of my family together.

We all live on our own now, but because we *chose* to, not because we were *forced* to. This house was good to us. I hope this house is just as good to the next family that lives here.

I'll be back. I need to clean the entire house from top to bottom. But it's nice to see it this way. Lived in, but empty. A shell waiting to be filled with love and life and everything in between.

Looking around one last time, I let my hand trail over the railing of the stairs, along the walls, and the counters of the kitchen, over the knobs of the front door. I make a loop, thinking about all the life lessons I learned here, all the things I experienced here, all the things I tried to teach Calvin and Callie here.

Then I think about Walker and all the things I learned about *myself* here.

I know what I'm going to do. I hope I'm right about how he's going to react.

I walk away from my old house with a smile, knowing I'm doing the right thing.

I don't need *closure*. I need to give Walker *everything*, and find out if he really does trust me now.

Walker

She's moving today.

I haven't heard from her since I met her on the hiking trail, but I started talking to the guys again. Kane and Alex both hang out with her on a semi-regular basis. Kane sees her almost every weekend, but I'm not worried about it after meeting his new girlfriend. He's head-over-heels for Casey, who's a tiny thing he towers over. When they stand next to each other, the top of her head barely meets the middle of his chest. I wonder how that works, but I'm not going to ask.

It was good to hang out with them again. They already knew I'd met with Genny, that I knew the truth, that I apologized to her for being such an ass. They knew the basics; the gist of the conversation we had. They don't know I told her I love her. They don't know that she cried and asked to touch me. They don't know that she kissed me and literally *ran away* from me.

Even if they only know half of the information, it's nice to know they think she's going to give me a second chance. They've all told me not to fuck it up. They've all guaranteed they'll let me know if they see me doing it, and they'll kick my ass if I don't listen to them again.

It's good to know they have my back... *If* Genny agrees to give me a second chance.

I'm over at Reese's, hanging out with Steve watching the game. We've been getting to know each other a bit more since I'm here almost all the time now. He's been helping me deflect my mother's attempts at setting me up on blind dates, and I've been teaching him how to fix things that need to be worked on around the house. It's slow going because of his schedule, but I'd trust him to fix a broken toilet lever or to clear out the garbage disposal when it gets jammed now.

Genny was over to see Zeke and Finn last weekend. Reese told me she was coming, and I stayed away. I'm giving her the space she asked for, even if it's getting harder and harder to do.

When the game ends, I get my shit around and drive back to my new home. Or at least the place where I sleep. I wouldn't really call it *home*. A text comes through as I'm parking, and I wonder what Reese forgot to tell me before I left. Knowing she probably wants me to pick something up or come back and get something, I let the engine run while I check her text.

But it's *Genny* finally getting a hold of me, not Reese.

Genny: Hey. Are you busy?

I type out a quick reply, knowing there's nothing I wouldn't drop entirely to talk to her. Even if by text.

Walker: Definitely not.

Genny: Wanna see my new place?

She's kidding right? She's talking to me *and* asking me to come see her? She's letting me know where she's going to be living, giving me the chance to know where to stalk her the way I've done off and on for months?

Walker: Yes.

She texts me an address and I briefly wonder if she's playing a joke on me. It's the same street as her old place. What did she do, move a few blocks down?

Genny: Warning: It's a DISASTER. I moved today, and nothing is organized or unpacked. There's left over pizza if you're hungry, though. Oh! And I don't have a couch. Or any chairs. Just so you know what you're walking into.

Smiling at her warning and all the memories it brings, I hope she knows she's teasing me by sending a text worded like that. I'll sit on the damn floor just to be near her. Hell, I'll stand for the rest of my life if I have to.

I'm nervous, but hopeful. If she was going to tell me there was no way she could give me another chance, she wouldn't be inviting me over, right? She wouldn't be this nice to me. She would probably just text me telling me to leave her alone. This has to be good news.

Her new house has a front and back porch. And it's out in the middle of nowhere. Her closest neighbors must be half a mile away. She has a garage now. She also has bare windows and every light is on in her small, one story house.

I'm not sure which door to go to, so I hesitate once I get out of my car. Or maybe I'm hesitating because I'm afraid to go in and have my hope crushed. Either way, Genny solves the problem by standing in front of the backdoor, her curvy silhouette blocking my view into her new house, but a sight I could stare at forever.

"Hi," she calls softly as I climb the two steps onto the back porch. She opens the door and I follow her into the house, hoping to get some kind of clue as to how this is going to go by the expression on her face. She's giving nothing away tonight. Not yet. I look around her new place, instead.

There isn't a single piece of furniture to be found. The TV stand is set up on the far wall of the living room, with the TV and Xbox on it, but otherwise there're just boxes. *Lots* of unpacked boxes.

Following Genny into her kitchen, she grabs a beer, tilting it back, swallowing its contents before tossing it into a recycling bin sitting in the pantry with the door wide open. "Do you want something to drink? Pizza?"

"No, I'm good." Or at least as good as I can be, considering I'm not sure what to expect from her. Am I staying a while? Or is she kicking me out in five minutes after breaking my heart?

"How are you?"

"Ah, good, I guess. How are you?"

"I'm good. I'm sorry it took me so long to get back to you. I sold the house, Callie moved, *I* moved, obviously, Calvin's getting married... I've been really busy."

"Does that mean you haven't had time to think about giving me a second chance?"

She cocks her head, looking at me, taking me in, trying to see something in me or on me that will answer whatever question is in her mind. "No, I've thought about it. A lot. I was hoping to ask you some follow up questions, though. I don't want to assume anything."

She's still not sure. If she wants to ask me questions, she's at least seriously considering it. Which means I still have a chance. *We* still have a chance.

"That's probably a good idea. I foolishly made an assumption a few months ago and lost everything I ever wanted."

She smiles. "I had a feeling you'd be ok with it."

I like the smile. It gives me a good feeling about all of this.

Hopping up on the counter, she gets comfortable, her hips shifting back and forth before she takes a deep breath. "Do you still feel the same way?"

"About you?"

She nods nervously, and I try not to laugh. She's asking if I still love her? And she's nervous about it? "I still love you, Genny. I still want you. I'm still sorry about what I said, and did, and I still want a chance to try to make this work again."

"Can I trust you to trust *me*?"

"Yes."

Something shifts in Genny's eyes, letting her relax and breathe a little easier. *That's* what she needed to hear. *That's* what she needed to know.

"What do you want with me?" she hesitantly asks. "Describe it."

"The *more* we talked about ages ago. I want a chance to have a real relationship with you." As every word leaves my mouth, I think of a hundred more. Maybe it'll be too much too soon, but I'm not going to lie to her. She only lied to me once, and had an emotional breakdown because of it. "I want to grow old with you, I want to have kids with you, I want to argue with you over how sweet the coffee is that we share every morning. I wanna bitch about you to my friends because you're always nagging me to mow the yard instead of playing with the kids. I wanna be thankful for you every day because life just isn't nearly as fun or exciting or *worth it* if you're not with me. I want it all, but only with you, Genny. You're the key to everything I want."

"Alex said you moved. Where do you live now?"

I rub my neck, at the quick topic switch. "I had to get out of that apartment. I was sleeping on Reese's couch for weeks whenever Steve wasn't home. My parents found out, so my dad and I fixed up the storage space above their garage. I'm still looking for something more permanent, but it got me out of there, so for now, I love it."

"Can I come see you there sometime?"

"You can come see me anywhere. Anytime."

"Even when you're at work?"

"Yes. I'll always have time for you."

Her cheeks turn pink as she gives me an embarrassed smile. "I got written up at work the first time Reese came to see me."

That's *my* fault. It's my fault we weren't together, it's my fault Reese thought Genny cheated on me, it's my fault Reese got her in trouble. "I'm sorry, Genny. For everything. I wish I could go back in time and take it all back. I wish we could start over and that it wouldn't be as messy and complicated and-"

"Walker?"

Sighing, I try to calm my thoughts, my emotions, my *fears*. "Genny?"

"Will you kiss me?"

Fuck yes.

I'm standing in front of her before she can blink. She didn't tell me to not touch her. She didn't ask me to stay completely still while she did what she wanted. I hope she realizes that because I can't stop myself from touching her after the way she *interrupted* me to ask. Like she couldn't wait another second to get the words out and my lips on hers.

Her legs fall open when I reach for her, making space for me between them. She pulls me even closer, letting my arms find a home around her waist as she pushes her hands into my hair, her thighs around my hips. I look deep into her eyes, wishing, hoping, *praying* she doesn't push me away.

Now, *or* when this kiss is over.

When she doesn't look away or act like she's not exactly where she wants to be, I close my mouth over hers, tasting her for the first time in so damn long. Her lips open under mine, and if that's not a crystal-clear invitation, I don't know what is.

Breathing her in, exploring her mouth, feeling her hands on me, her legs around me, her body in my arms and pressed so tightly against mine, I feel like I'm exactly where I belong. I feel like something is clicking into place, a flip is being switched, and my whole life is righting itself again.

It's heaven and hell all the same time. Heaven, because she's my everything and this is what I want, her and me, tangled up in the best possible way. Hell, because I still don't know. Is this a final kiss goodbye, or a *welcome-the-fuck-back* kiss?

She pulls away much too soon, because I don't want to ever stop. I don't know when or *if* I'll get to do it again. Her eyes are still closed as she leans her forehead against mine, taking a deep breath. Her lips are pink and swollen from our very thorough make-out session, and I still only want to kiss her again.

For the rest of eternity.

Pushing me away, she slides down my body, dropping her feet onto the floor. After meeting my eyes, she reaches for my hand. "Can I show you around?"

You can show me anything, my heart screams. *As long as you hold my hand and talk to me with that sweet smile, you can lead me anywhere.*

I simply nod.

"Obviously, this is the kitchen, and that's the living room." Leading me down a small hallway, she pushes one of four doors open. "Here's the only bathroom. Over here is the basement where the washer and dryer are. I'm not looking forward to carrying the laundry up and down those rickety stairs, let me tell you."

I look them over quickly while refusing to let go of her hand. "That's probably not too bad to fix, I can help you with that."

She sends a knowing smirk my way, pulling me farther down the hall. It's a little house, but it's cute for just her. The door on the left is open and she calls it the spare room. All it holds is more unpacked boxes. The door on the right is closed, but she slowly pushes it open for me to see. "This is my room."

Her bed is against the wall, made and ready for her to jump in to go to sleep. Her dressers drawers are open, and it looks like she may have been unpacking in here when I showed up. After looking around at the scattered boxes, I get pulled back into the kitchen with her. "What do you think?"

"I like it. Do you have a backyard?"

"I do. It's kind of big. I'll have to pay a neighbor kid to mow it or something."

"Or something?" I ask, a smile tugging on my lips as I start to feel more and more confident.

"Yeah." She steps in close to me. "A neighbor kid for a few years. Then I'll probably nag my husband to do it instead of playing with the kids all the time."

"Is that right?" I mumble, almost physically unable to speak I'm so worried about screwing it up, right here, right now, when she's about to give me the answer I've been waiting for. "Does that mean I get another chance?"

Chewing on her lip, she looks up at the ceiling. "You're not seeing anyone else?"

"There's no one, G. Only you."

She flashes a brilliant smile at me when I call her G.

I'm good. *We're* good. I'm getting my second chance and there's no way I'm going to screw it up. Well, I'm sure I'll screw it up, but not as badly as before. I know what it's like trying to live without her. I'm not doing that ever again if there's any way I can help it.

"And you love me?"

"Genny... I love you more than anything in the world."

"I think... maybe..." She draws it out, taking as long as possible to give me the best news I've heard in months. "Maybe you should move in with me, and we'll see how it goes?"

"*What*?!"

I was not expecting *that* curve ball. She immediately starts pouting, unsure of herself, and I brush my hands across her face, wanting to touch her and reassure her at the same time. "How much did you drink tonight, G?"

"Only two."

"You realize moving in with you is a hell of a lot more than a second chance, right?"

"You keep swearing you won't screw it up. I'm not saying I'm gonna *marry* you! Well, not yet... That's a few months away at least... But we've wasted a lot of time over both of our stupidity, and I don't see why I can't give you a second chance while living with you at the same time."

"What did *you* do that was stupid?" I ask, ignoring the marriage comment completely.

"I didn't even try to explain, Walker. I was so mad at your for thinking I'd cheat on you or go back on my promise that I didn't fight for what we had. I didn't stand up for myself and make you realize what an ass you were being."

"Genny, what happened was entirely my fault. I didn't even give you a *chance* to explain."

"You *would* have if I had *tried*," she insists. "I love you, Walker. You love me. If you really trust me, there's no reason for us to not be together, and I'm tired of living without you."

I'm tired of living without her, too, but this is too much, too fast. I came over here hoping for a second chance, I never expected her to ask me to move in with her. "Can I sleep on it? I feel like this is kind of a huge step and I don't want you to regret this in a day or a week or a month."

She sighs out an annoyed groan. "Take however long you need. I'm pretty used to waiting on you by now."

Laughing at her nonchalant way of telling me I take way too long to let us pass all the important milestones in our relationship, I pull her hand up to my mouth and press a kiss to it. "I love you, G. Can I sleep on it here? With you?"

"I thought you'd never ask..." She drags me back to her room, flipping off light switches on the way.

Once in her room, though, I don't know what to do. I don't feel right watching her change, not after everything we've been through lately, not since as of ten minutes ago, I still wasn't sure I'd ever get to see her again after tonight. Walking back out to the hallway, I tell her I'm going to brush my teeth. I don't have a toothbrush, but I'll use hers. Considering how far down my throat her tongue was earlier, I think it'll be ok.

Genny takes the toothbrush from me when I'm done, brushing her own teeth in that tempting cami and her very short pajama shorts that I remember all too well. She hurries back into her room, obviously not at all uncomfortable with watching *me* undress.

"Are you gonna behave tonight?" I ask as I slide into her bed. She rolls her eyes, crawling under the covers and plastering herself against my body.

She's jumping back into this with no hesitation, trusting me so much more than I deserve after everything we've been through.

"Yes, I'll behave." Reaching over her shoulder, she turns off the bedside lamp before snuggling back into my chest. "I'm exhausted. It was a long day. If you don't start anything, nothing is happening."

"What happens if I start something?"

"Whatever you want to happen, Friend."

My heartbeat kicks into overdrive when she uses my nickname, reminding me of when we were good, when we were together, when we were happy. "So, if I tell you I wanna have sex with you..."

"I'll shout halle-*freaking*-lujah from the rooftops."

Chuckling at her very enthusiastic response, I hold her close, unable to believe this is really happening. I'm in her house, in her *bed*. She's in my arms again, *and* she asked me to move in with her. She's willing to have sex with me, tonight, right now. I'm touching her again. I can sleep with her and wake up with her and just plain *be with her.*

"What're you thinking so hard about?" she asks quietly, her lips brushing against my jawline.

"It's just hard to believe this is real. I keep waiting for you to tell me it's all a joke and you never want to see me again."

She rolls over so I can spoon her, pulling my arm tight around her waist and lacing her fingers through mine. "This is real, Walker. Get used to it. Cherish and trust it. Take good care of it. Take advantage of it."

Take *advantage* of it?

What a strange thing to say.

It's true though, I should take advantage of every second I have with her. Just because we're together and we love each other doesn't mean our time together is guaranteed. Pulling her a little closer, I kiss the back of her head, hearing her sigh contentedly in return.

She made the comment about always waiting on me... Maybe she's *tired* of waiting on me. Tired of waiting *for* me.

Squeezing her fingers, I decide maybe I don't want to wait anymore. "I love you, G."

Genny presses our hands to her mouth, kissing the back of my hand. "I love you, too, Friend."

It's the first time we've ever made that simple but intense exchange. It feels good. It feels right. It feels like it should be celebrated.

"Hey, come here," I ask quietly, feeling her roll again to face me. She throws a leg over mine, her arm sliding up my side to rest against my chest. "Have you unpacked our toy yet?"

"No." She presses a kiss to my lips, a clear invitation for more if I want it.

"Do you know where your condoms are?"

Her mouth tips into a smile against my skin, and her hand slips between us to stroke me through my boxers. "I happen to know there's a couple in my purse."

"You should go get your purse."

Throwing the covers off, she flips the bedside lamp back on before turning to me. "Are you sure? I don't wanna pressure you into anything."

"If you don't go get your purse, I'm gonna get it for you. That'll take a lot long longer since I have no idea where to even start looking."

Her teeth land on her bottom lip and she looks up at me from under her eyelashes. "Promise me lots of kissing?"

Since when is she nervous and *I'm* pushing for sex?

"When *isn't* there lots of kissing with us, G?"

"Promise me you won't regret this in the morning?"

Pulling her back into my arms, I start the kissing now. I'm a big fan of kissing Genny. I can't get off on it like she can, but I can and have done it all night long. *I'm* the one to pull away this time, but not for long. "As long as kissing you is involved, my sweet Genevieve, I promise I won't regret anything."

She moves to straddle me, and I worry she's gonna get this party started without me. She's just warming up though, devouring me with her mouth and her tongue until we're both breathless and beyond ready.

She pushes off me without a word, disappearing through her open doorway.

Tossing her purse onto the bed two minutes later, she starts pulling off her clothes before sliding back under the covers with me. "I have two. How do you feel about little to no foreplay, and fast and hard this first time? Then slower and sweeter with tons of foreplay once we've released the tension that's been between us almost since we met?"

"And tomorrow we buy a lot more?"

"I like the way you think, Friend." She smiles again, nipping at my bottom lip. Then she's searching through her purse and I reach to feel her, one hand grazing over her sensitive nipples while the other moves between her legs.

"Walker," she moans. "I'm never gonna find them if you keep distracting me."

"Just keep looking. I can't keep my hands off you." After sucking her peaked nipple into my mouth, I smile as she cries out, holding me to her with one hand.

"That's not your *hand*," she scolds me.

"I can't keep my *mouth* off you, either. Both hands in your purse, please."

Moving down her body, I lean her back into a semi-horizontal position. She's propped up on her pillows, so she can still search her purse, and either I'm a huge distraction, or she has way too much shit in there, because it's taking *forever*.

"Oh!" she whimpers as I settle my mouth between her legs and push my fingers inside her. "I... oh, yes!... I found... *Fuck*, Walker!"

"You found one?" I eventually ask, licking one last circle around her clit.

"Yes..." She hisses at the friction of my fingers still inside her. "Don't stop, please."

I get on my knees, my fingers still lazily pumping into her, so I can lean over to kiss that sweet, delicious mouth. As she licks her own wetness off my lips, her hips start moving of their own accord, rocking her closer to the point of no return.

"G, I wanna be inside you when you come."

I slow my fingers even more.

She moans, letting her head fall back against the pillows, the first waves of her orgasm already here. Stopping it in its tracks, I pull my fingers from her, grabbing the condom and ripping it open, sliding it on and settling between her legs.

My eyes raise to hers. "Tell me you want this, Genny."

"Lord, Walker! Haven't we waited long enough?"

I kiss her lips again, wanting that smart mouth on me in any way. She pushes one hand into my hair, deepening the kiss, even as she guides me to her entrance. Her tongue is hot in my mouth and her hands are gripping my short hair when I finally thrust into her for the first time. Moaning at how fucking good she feels, I break from her kiss and look into her eyes.

"I love you, G."

Her answering smile is wicked as she flexes her muscles around me, pushing another soft groan past my lips. "I love you too, Friend. Now shut up and give me a fireworks show."

Genny's Epilogue

November – Two Months Later

"What the hell is *that*?!" Reese hisses as I walk through her back door. Following me is Walker, with a box containing all the fun goodies we decided Zeke needed.

"Pickles replacement," Walker calmly tells her, before yelling for his nephew.

Reese mumbles under her breath, obviously not very happy that we got Zeke another pet. Pickles, the hamster, died last month. After a touching burial and a couple weeks in mourning, Zeke started asking for another pet.

Since starting her part time job, Reese decided there was no way they were getting another animal because she has too many other things to worry about. Money is now a very big worry for them, but they never complain.

Reese works every other weekend; the same weekends Steve is away for work. She wanted to work when he was home, but Walker and I nixed that idea fast. They need their time to grow and be a family. Plus, if Reese is working when Steve isn't home, they need a sitter. Which is where *we* come in.

The boys get dropped off at our place every Saturday morning they're parents are working. Reese picks them back up Sunday night when her shift is over. Walker and I put a bunk bed in the guest room, which for now, is called the boys room.

Walker did move in. Officially, he changed his address to mine a little over two weeks after I moved in to my little house. I think it was my first migraine there that finally convinced him. It started on a Sunday evening. He worried the entire time, constantly checking on me even though I told him I just needed to sleep it off. When he got there to check on me Monday afternoon, it was gone, but he acted like he hadn't seen me for weeks.

We talk about it sometimes, our time apart. The conversation we had on the trail. What helped make my decision to give him *a hell of a second chance*, as he calls it. He still doesn't believe that most of the flaws he listed are ones that I also have. He doesn't understand that I think he's perfect for me, just like he thinks I'm perfect for him. He messed up, big time, but so did I.

In the end, we learned from it. We changed from it. We grew from it.

Things aren't always perfect, he still puts way too much sugar in our coffee every time he makes it, but life with Walker is just like that coffee. Sweeter than I ever imagined it could be. It's fuller, richer, way more interesting. Every day holds something good, and I thank my lucky stars I had that one horrible day that brought him to me.

That one stressful day changed everything.

"Uncle Walk! Genny!" Zeke runs into the room, with Finn pumping his tiny little legs to keep up. Zeke has discovered that little brothers are a pain in the butt when they can follow you around everywhere. Sliding to a stop next to me, Zeke hangs on to my jeans, one hand clinging to my back pocket, his other fingers digging into the pocket on my hip. Walker eyes his nephew's hand on my ass and rolls his eyes.

We're still working on the jealousy thing. From both sides. Walker is a very attractive guy, and some girls don't know to not flirt with him while I'm standing right next to him. Chloe is still an issue every time we go to Kane's restaurant. Even when Walker throws his arm over my shoulders and kisses me in front of her.

Some girls will never learn.

I'm not one of them.

I've learned that Walker's heart belongs to me, just like mine belongs to him.

I still don't mind letting any girl who looks too closely at him know that she's barking up the wrong tree.

"Genny, what's in the box?" Zeke quietly asks, his voice full of barely contained excitement.

"You'll have to ask your Uncle Walk, Zeke."

His eyes fill his face and his mouth forms an "o" before he practically pushes me out of the way to get to Walker. Grabbing Finn, who was about to climb onto the table, I join Reese, leaning against the counter to watch the show.

"Zeke, buddy," Walker starts. "I kind of have a problem. I was at the store and I saw this really cool fish. It's blue and red and has these long flowy fins and tail. We all know I'm a sucker for pretty things..." Walker looks up, flashing me a smile. "So I just *had* to buy it. But when I took it home, Genny yelled at me. She said that we're not home often enough to have a pet."

Zeke looks at me with harsh disappointment, upset that I wouldn't let his uncle have a fish in our house. Which is bullshit, Walker can put a fish in our house. Walker can put whatever he wants in our house, because I don't have to take care of Walker or anything he touches.

Walker is very used to taking care of himself. I don't have to pick up after him or cook for him. I don't have to do his wash or ask him to take the garbage out or put the dishes in the dishwasher. He wasn't kidding when he said he was self-sufficient. I almost wish he wasn't as self-sufficient as he is, because at times, I don't feel needed.

That's usually when Callie calls me, asking me for a recipe, or why her laundry is suddenly pink, or crying because she doesn't have time to clean her apartment, and how the hell did I do it all for years?

And if Callie doesn't call me, Walker takes time to explain how he needs me. Sometimes he just *shows* me. He's very good at showing me. There's usually a fireworks show involved.

Walker gives the *best* fireworks shows.

"Since Genny is being so mean about this fish, I thought maybe you could take care of it for me. You would have to feed him *every single day*. And your mom will probably have to change the water for you sometimes, but other than that, he just needs a friend to talk to him. What do you think? Can you take care of this really pretty fish?"

"YES!" Zeke starts hopping up and down on his feet as his fist does its own little dance. "Can I see it? Did you bring it now?"

"I did. Where do you think we should put this fish bowl?"

Zeke runs from the room, looking for the perfect spot for his new friend to live. Walker grabs the bowl, chasing after him.

Glancing at Reese, I find a reluctant smile on her face. Since Walker moved in with me and we get the boys so often, I've started to get to know her a lot better. We like a lot of the same things. We want a lot of the same things out of life. She keeps telling me that Walker and I need to have some kids, so Zeke and Finn have some cousins to play with. I keep telling her one thing at a time. Although if I leave it up to Walker it will take us forever to even start trying.

Walker isn't exactly hasty when making decisions that progress our relationship.

I told Walker once that I couldn't believe we got together in the first place. It should have taken him months to ask me out. He reminded me about the first night I saw him. The night I watched him in a dark, hazy bar but went home with Chad instead. He admitted he'd thought about asking me out then. But he just watched me all night. Even when Chad approached me just before last call.

I'm glad he didn't hesitate to help me when I was sitting on the bench outside the pharmacy. He may not have asked me out, but whatever he said certainly made a good impression. I remember laughing, even though I was freaking out in my head, unable to see, in a weird place, with no one around that I knew, and no way to get ahold of anyone, or to get home.

Even then, Walker made me feel safe.

After coming back into the kitchen, Walker fills the bowl with a jug of water we brought with us, so it would be room temperature. He explains to Reese how to treat it, since town water will kill the fish. Plopping the bag with the betta fish into the almost filled bowl, he sneaks a kiss onto my lips before disappearing again.

Over Zeke's excited voice at seeing his pretty new fish, Reese asks about our plans for Thursday. "What time should we get there? And what should I bring? I can't show up empty handed."

"Get there any time after noon. We're gonna try to eat at two. If you want to bring a pie, that would be awesome. My request to have off Wednesday was denied, so I won't be able to bake any desserts."

"And you're sure you wanna have Thanksgiving at your place? I mean, our family *and* yours? There's gonna be a lot of people in that little house."

"I'm sure. I've never gotten to host Thanksgiving for more than just me and my siblings before. Our house is going to be filled with people, food, love, and happiness. Plus, Callie can't wait to see Zeke and Finn again."

Reese smiles, watching me with Finn. "I have a lot to be thankful for this year," she whispers. I know she's thinking about the adoption process she and Steve are going through with Zeke. And how I helped make that happen.

I think about Walker and Reese and these beautiful boys. About our little house, the future we're planning, and the present we're living. About the past and how Kane showed me how to work through my emotions in a healthy way. About the fact that I have a sister-in-law and my brother is successful and happy. About the fact that my sister is out there, on her own, working and living and being an amazing person.

I made new friends, I changed, I learned how to love, and how to forgive.

This year held nothing but surprises for me. But knowing where I'm ending up now, I wouldn't have it any other way.

"So, do I, Reese. So, do I."

Walker's Epilogue

January

Genny: Will you meet me downtown after work?

Wondering what my sweet girl is up to now, I reply that I will. She must've sent the text on her lunch break. I'm just getting out of work and instead of heading around town to our humble little abode, I turn into it. Checking my phone again as I sit at a red light, I find another text from her.

Genny: I'm parked in front of the courthouse.

I start looking for a parking spot as I drive down the main street. It's a crazy time of day, kids getting out of school, people getting out of work, stopping downtown for whatever they might need before going home for the night. It's the end of January. Christmas season is over, which means work is slowing down. I'm thankful for the change of pace, but I'm even more thankful for the time off I was granted next week.

Genny and I are both taking some time off together starting this Friday and lasting all through next week. We told everyone we plan on turning up the heat and spending the entire time naked, so they'd all better stay away. Not everyone believed us, but I swear to God if anyone shows up without an invitation, they're going to get an eyeful.

Of *me*. Not Genny. No one gets to see Genny naked except me.

There's an open spot a block down from the courthouse and I put on my turn signal to parallel park. I get out and lock up, zipping my jacket against the bitter cold.

As I'm passing by a gallery that sells local art, I stop long enough to look through the window and find one of Callie's paintings. Despite the outcome of our bet, she entered the contest, winning by a landslide. Practically all her painting that I was familiar with sold within the first month.

She says *this* painting is a spin-off of one of her favorite famous pieces, Starry Night. Hers is more realistic. It's more *emotional*, at least to me. She captured the darkness of night, but also the hope that the smallest source of light can bring. There's only one star in her dark sky, but it's enough.

It reminds me of how I hung onto the hope that Genny would give us a second chance, even after she broke down on her run away from me that day on the trail to Widow's Peak.

I check my phone again as I start up the sidewalk to my girl.

Genny: Come to me, Friend.

Gladly.

I'll still follow her anywhere.

Walking briskly up the street, I find her car parked on the corner, Genny standing on the sidewalk next to it. She's in her work uniform and with her black down jacket and black slacks, she looks like a dark angel. *My* dark angel, who's every bit as nice as Reese wanted for me, and every bit as *not* nice as I hoped I'd someday find. Flashing a happy smile in my direction, she meets me halfway with a kiss hot enough to make me not need this jacket.

"Hey, G. What's going on?"

"Do you have your wallet with you?"

"Yeah. You wanna get takeout or something?"

"Not exactly." She slips her hand in mine and we walk slowly up the sidewalk. "I've got some plans for our staycation. I want to tell you what they are and see how you feel about them."

"Plans other than being naked with me? I can tell you right now, I don't approve."

"Hmph." Her teeth graze her bottom lip as she side-eyes me. "Hear me out anyway?"

"Is this like Christmas and already a done deal? Or do I actually have some say in whatever this is?

Christmas morning, Genny told me she went off birth control. It's hard to believe that was only a few weeks ago. It's hard to believe she decided we were ready for kids without really consulting with me. Sure, we had talked about it. Many times. We even said we'd start trying this year. But Christmas morning, I was a little freaked out at her news. She explained that it took a few months for her body to regulate her hormones and something or other, so it still gave me a couple months to think about it before there was a possibility of us getting pregnant.

I haven't told her yet, but I'm definitely ok with the idea now. I really like the trying part. I tell her all the time that we need to practice, so when her hormones *are* regulated, we're experts, everything happens the way it should, and we get to be the winners.

I don't know who the competition is, but after all the practicing we've been doing, we're going to smoke them.

"It's not a done deal yet, but I'm hoping you'll keep an open mind and just go with your heart."

"Ok..." I sigh, having no idea what to expect from her today. "Lay it on me."

She's holding both my hands in hers and her eyes are searching mine, but there's no mistaking that they're clear and happy. She's excited about whatever she's going to suggest and that makes me a little excited. Genny being happy makes *me* happy.

"I thought maybe we could go in the courthouse and get a marriage license."

Narrowing my eyes, I try to fill in the blanks. "You want us to get a marriage license... And what? Get married on our staycation?"

"I want to marry you on *Friday*. Our staycation can be our honeymoon. I want to be a Kelley. I want to be your *wife*, Walker. I want you to be my *husband*."

Despite the shock her words cause, a grin plasters itself onto my face. There's so much to figure out, so much to plan. It's Tuesday. She wants to get married *Friday*? How is that enough time? I've listened to Zander and Heidi talk about wedding plans for almost a *year*. About how much everything costs and the time you need to get everything perfect. Genny is nothing like Heidi, but doesn't she want her wedding day, the day she marries me, to be perfect?

"Maybe we should wait so we can get everything just right. I don't want you to regret anything about our wedding day."

"Walker, the only thing I need on my wedding day is you at the end of the aisle agreeing to love me until the day you die. I don't need anything else. You're the love of my life. You're going to be the father of my children. I want you to be my *husband*, and I don't want to *wait* to start the life we've been planning together... We're only doing this if you want to, Walker. I *want* to marry you. But if you're not *ready* to marry me, we'll wait."

Why would I *not* want to be married to the woman of my dreams?

We've talked about getting married. We've talked about kids. We've talked about how many kids we can have in that tiny house before we have to move to a bigger one. We've talked about her going to college once we're done having kids and they're in school. We've talked about our future at least once every day since we got back together.

Our whole future is planned out if things work out the way we want.

But Genny is here, in front of me, right now, asking me to actually *do* it. To not just *talk* about it, but to make it *happen*. And why shouldn't she be? I made her wait for sex, and we both expected that. But she also had to wait for me to have *faith* in her. She waited for me to *trust* her and really *believe* in what we found together.

I was a fool before. I'm not making that mistake again.

"I'm ready, Genny. I wanna marry you."

"Yeah?" she asks, her smile full of hope and surprise at my eager answer. "Are you absolutely certain?"

"Genny, I'll marry you today, right now. How set on a bouquet were you?"

She chuckles softly. "There's a three-day waiting period after we get the license."

"Friday it is." Pulling her closer, I whisper against her skin, "You wanna be a Kelley, huh?"

Nodding, she rubs her nose against mine before that sweet mouth melts under my lips. My heartrate picks up, *racing* as it hits me that by the end of the week, Genny will be my *wife*.

Am I ready for that?

Am I ready to commit to her for the rest of my life?

Fuck yes.

Genny is everything I've ever wanted. She's perfect for me, and while I still don't think I'm perfect for her, she's helping me become a better man. She *wants* me, she *chose* me....

And I want and choose her. Every single day, I will choose *her*.

Genny is my future.

Genny is my *everything*.

I'm done making her wait.

The End.

Thank You for Reading!

This story is one of the first I wrote, and I feel like it's never quite perfect. Every time I read a few sentences or paragraphs, I find *something* I want to change. But there comes a time when the changes I make aren't adding anything to the story, so ready or not, it's time to put it out there for the world to see.

I hope you enjoyed Walker and Genny's journey, and how they learned about trust and love.

Sometimes trusting life and the plan it has for you is hard. You're used to living your days as you've always lived them. When something wonderful gets handed to you, just falling into your lap, unexpectedly, it can be hard to believe it's going to last. You didn't struggle for this gift, and you struggle for everything! This gift must be a joke, or something that will just teach you another of life's many lessons…

But sometimes, love just finds you, and the lesson you have to learn is not only accepting it, but trusting it, too.

Before you go…

While I currently have a select group of beta readers that give me awesome feedback, they have *lives*, and I can't count on them to just read for me nonstop! (The injustice of it, I know!) If you're interested in reading some of my books while they're still in progress, and providing feedback to help shape the finished product, please email me at bricashauthor@gmail.com.

Thank you to my beta readers! You helped me fix a couple problems that didn't jive with the character's personalities, and made things more believable. This story wouldn't be what it is without you, and I appreciate you taking time out of your busy lives to help me with this project, as well as being honest with me about what you thought needed changed completely or just tweaked.

Also, thank you to my wonderful husband, who puts up with so much from me while I'm writing, my incredibly smart editor, who helps me out of the goodness of her heart, my supportive friends and family, and Cole Gordon from fiverr.com, who not only designed the cover, but who was also incredibly helpful while I was traversing this journey of trying to publish my first book. This never would've happened without any of you. Thank you!

Made in the USA
Lexington, KY
20 November 2019